The Rabbi and the Nun

The Rabbi and the Nun

a novel by
Mordecai Schreiber

10/8/91

to Jim Moses
best wishes,
Mordecai Schreiber

Shengold Publishers, Inc.
New York

ISBN 0-88400-150-4
Library of Congress Catalog Card Number: 91-060448
Copyright © 1991 by Mordecai Schreiber

Published by Shengold Publishers, Inc.
18 West 45th Street, New York, NY 10036

Printed in the United States of America

Put me as a seal upon your heart
as a seal on your arm
for love is as strong as death—
Many waters cannot extinguish love
rivers cannot wash it away.
(Song of Songs)

When you enter the chamber of the
bridegroom, you may carry a shining
lamp in your hand and meet him with
joy. May he find in you nothing sordid,
nothing dishonorable, but a snow-white
soul and a clear and shining body. Thy
beauty is now all for the King's delight.
He is thy Lord and God.
(Final Profession)

Part One:

Quincy, Ohio, 1969

✧ 1 ✧

It was an ordinary day at Suburban Temple. As usual, Joshua Kaye went back to his study immediately after the weekly staff meeting, took out a yellow legal pad, and was about to jot down an outline for his Friday night sermon. This morning, however, he did not seem to come up with any new ideas. Lately, it seemed he had lost his impetus to deliver fiery sermons, patterned after those of his superior, the great Alvin Blumenfeld. He was not quite sure why, nor did he mention it to anyone, but for several weeks now he had been pushing himself to sit down at his desk and organize his thoughts, as if it were a chore forced upon him, rather than his chosen vocation.

He could, of course, pull out an old sermon, revise it, change some names and dates, and make it relevant to the current situation. But somehow it did not seem right. It was a trap one could easily fall into, only to find out that getting out of it was not all that easy.

He tried to busy himself with some administrative work, dictating letters, answering phone messages, updating files. But he was barely able to concentrate on any of those tasks. Before five o'clock he went out of his study and started to pace the long corridor leading to the sanctuary. He found himself inside the huge empty sanctuary and sat down in the back row. He watched the last rays of the afternoon sun set fire to the inscription above the ark:

I HAVE SET THE LORD BEFORE ME ALWAYS

The gold letters carved in the white marble above the tall, electrically-operated bronze doors guarding the Torah scrolls blazed in the darkened hall with a blinding light. The junior rabbi nearly gasped. For a moment he thought he had heard a voice emanating from the ark beneath the inscription. It was only his imagination. No voice had come out of the ark. The burst of sunlight began to fade. He kept watching, pondering the message flashed at him during that brief instant of light, and got up to leave. Halfway down the aisle he stopped, straining to see the barely visible letters.

"Set the Lord. . ." For the first time those familiar words, which he had always taken for granted, had taken on a new meaning. "Set the Lord. . ." Did he, really? Did anyone at Suburban Temple set the Lord before him?

As he stood there, puzzled by the question, he was suddenly seized by an inexplicable, overpowering fear. "Set the Lord. . ." It was not a statement of fact. It was an order directed at him personally with a force that made him recoil and grasp the back of the seat behind him. "Set the Lord. . ." For three years he had been conducting services to the Lord in this decorous sanctuary, welcoming the congregation to the house of the Lord, blessing them in the name of the Lord. . . But did he ever set the Lord before him?

He lingered for a moment, waiting for an answer to come, but none came. He could hear the custodian locking some doors outside in the hall. It was time to go home.

At the dinner table that evening with his wife, Felicia, and their one-year-old son, Kaye couldn't stop thinking of that flash of light, as if it were a message waiting to be deciphered.

"What're you dreaming about, dear?" his wife inquired as she eased the baby into the highchair.

"Oh, nothing."

"You've hardly touched your dinner."

"Yes, I know. I'm having trouble coming up with an idea for my sermon."

Felicia looked at him questioningly.

"How come?"

He thought about the flash of light in the sanctuary. "Set the Lord. . ." Would Felicia understand if he told her about the fear that had gripped him while standing alone in the darkened sanctuary? He was not quite sure he understood it himself. He said,

"Oh, I don't know. I guess you can run out of ideas once in a while. I'll look up some things in the temple library tomorrow morning. I'm sure I'll come up with something."

When he walked into the temple lobby the next morning Kaye was assailed by a strange cold feeling he had never felt before. As he crossed the shiny, newly waxed parquet floor, it felt like walking into the headquarters of a large corporation instead of a house of worship. He walked past the sanctuary door and stopped in the middle of the lobby, drawing a long breath. He now remembered he was going to stop at the temple library to look for some references for his sermon.

He saw Roz Pins, the temple Sisterhood president, standing next to the circulation desk, surveying her surroundings. Roz always struck Kaye as a grand duchess holding court. Everything about Roz spelled elegance, propriety, impeccable taste. She did most of clothes shopping in New York, from where she often brought *le dernier cri* in fashion. She had a passion for hats, and was rarely seen with the same hat twice. This morning she wore a white sporty outfit and a scarf tied around her neck.

"Rabbi!" the Sisterhood president beamed at him, "I'm glad to see you. I have a very special friend with me I'd like you to meet."

Roz turned to a young woman who stood on tiptoes at the far corner of the library, straining to reach a book on a high shelf. Kaye went over and offered to help. The book she was reaching for was titled *The Jew in American Fiction*. He took it down and handed it to her and she thanked him. Roz smiled approvingly.

"Sister Eve, I'd like you to meet Rabbi Kaye."

The young woman gave him a hesitant look and lowered her eyes. He was not quite sure what to say. Sister Eve? A nun? What was she doing with Roz Pins in the library of Suburban Temple? She wore a plain blue short sleeve dress and flat shoes. Around her neck she had a chain with a small silver medallion.

"How do you do?" he was not sure whether it was appropriate to shake a nun's hand.

"Sister and I are taking American lit at St. John's," Roz explained. "I did tell you I went back to school for my Master's, didn't I?"

"Oh, yes, you did," Kaye confirmed. He did not recall Roz ever telling him about it.

"What do you say, Sister?" Roz said with a wink, "Isn't our rabbi handsome?"

The young nun was visibly embarrassed. She attempted a smile and started to fidget with the book she was holding against herself.

"I told Eve we had a fine library here at the temple and she decided to stop by on her way home and look up some references for her thesis. She's considering writing it on the Jew in American fiction."

"Oh, really?" Kaye turned to the nun. "Well, there are certainly some good ones—Morris Bober, Moses Herzog, Alex Portnoy."

"Not Portnoy," Roz protested.

"Roz and I have a running argument about Philip Roth," Kaye explained.

"Well, let's not get into this now," Roz said, waving her hand as if to say, this is where the discussion ends.

"Good luck on your thesis," he turned to the nun.

"Thank you," she said in a shy voice, speaking barely above a whisper. "I'll need it."

Back in his study Kaye wondered why would a nun choose to write a paper about American Jewish novelists. He heard a knock on the door. It was Roz Pins.

"Sorry to bother you, rabbi," the Sisterhood president apologized, "I know you are very busy. But Sister Eve just gave me a wonderful idea I thought you'd like to hear about."

He knew Roz did not come to ask for his opinion, but rather to tell him about something she had in mind to do. No one around the temple ever challenged Roz's ideas, not even the senior rabbi. Nee Strauss, Roz was the sole heiress to the fortune of the Strauss family, one of the richest Jewish families in America. Her great-grandfather, Tobias Strauss, was the founder of Quincy's Suburban Temple, the largest and most prestigious synagogue in the Midwest. Married to Joe Pins, a corporate lawyer recently elected president of the temple, the Pins were known as Mr. and Mrs. Temple, with the emphasis on Mrs. When he first came to Suburban Temple, Kaye had no doubts in his mind as to who the boss at that place was. Why, the great Alvin Blumenfeld, of course, who else? After serving as Blumenfeld's assistant for a few months he found out differently. Blumenfeld, the man who two years ago became a household word in America as the rabbi who was assaulted by the Klan in Alabama, the man who was on a first name basis with the President of the United States, stood in fear and trembling before this little lady whose word was law around this temple. While to the outside world it always seemed the temple was led by its senior rabbi, whose decisions reflected a consensus of the members, and while the board of trustees prided itself on running a truly democratic institution, it was Roz Pins and a few other wealthy trustees who made what they called "the hard decisions."

Kaye pointed at the vinyl sofa. "Won't you sit down?"

She thanked him and sat on the edge of the sofa, smoothing down her tight dress and pulling her legs together.

"Sister Eve just gave me a marvelous idea for our next Sukkot guest speaker," Roz let the young rabbi in on her news. The Sukkot guest speaker was Roz's brainchild. In recent years attendance at

Sukkot services—following closely on the heels of the High Holy Days—had dropped to zero. Roz, who at the time was the Sisterhood's program chairperson, came up with the idea of sponsoring an outside speaker from other faiths. The first year it was a blind priest who packed the place. He was followed by a missionary who had just been released from jail in Red China. Last year it was a black minister who had worked closely with the late Dr. King. It was a sure fire idea, as each year it filled the sanctuary with worshippers.

"It's about time we had a woman speaker," said Roz. "Eve suggested we invite Sister Theophelia McPherson of the College of the Sacred Heart in Mt. Vernon, New York. Dr. McPherson is the leading Catholic woman theologian in the United States, and I understand she's a marvelous speaker."

Kaye tried to picture a nun standing on the bimah, addressing a gathering of Jews on a Jewish holy day. "Set the Lord. . ." Whose Lord will they be setting before them as they listened to a nun speak on the festival of Sukkot?

"Well?" Roz inquired eagerly.

"I don't think we should," said Kaye.

"Invite a woman speaker?"

"Invite a nun."

"Why not?"

"Because Sukkot is a Jewish holiday. The right time for an interfaith service is a secular holiday like Thanksgiving, not Sukkot."

"But we have been doing it now for three years, and each time we practically fill the sanctuary."

"Yes, I know. But what does it prove? Obviously, our members are not interested in coming to services on Sukkot. We cannot pretend we're actually celebrating the festival of Sukkot by bringing a nun as our guest speaker."

Roz hesitated. She was unaccustomed to having the rabbi disagree with her ideas. What could have possibly prompted Blumenfeld's assistant to veto her project? She stood up and said in a strained voice.

"Very well. I'll have to think about it."

He saw the Sisterhood president to the door, wondering whether he had overstepped his bounds. His secretary, Ruth Levy, handed him his daily stack of mail with a dozen pink telephone message slips on top. He realized he had enough letters to dictate and phone calls to make to keep himself busy for the rest of the day. It now occurred to him that during his three years at Suburban Temple he had gotten to know less than one hundred out of the two thousand member families. Most of the members came once a year on the High Holy Days—the only time the place was filled to capacity—and lapsed back into anonymity during the rest of the year, so many names on the membership list and neatly arranged mailing plates in the addressograph. The letters he wrote and the phone calls he made, no matter how warm and personalized, were directed at total strangers.

He made his phone calls and worked on his letter dictation without breaking for lunch. At ten to five the phone rang. It was the temple president, Joe Pins.

"Joshua, I understand you and Roz are having a disagreement."

Joe was his usual friendly, collected lawyerly self.

"You must be referring to the Sukkot guest speaker."

"That's correct. You know, Joshua, I can see your point. I myself am not too crazy about a nun guest speaker. But what's the alternative? An empty sanctuary?"

"Two wrongs don't make a right."

"Well, I think you're being a little bit too harsh," the temple president replied. "I'm not sure this is quite the right way to put it. A guest speaker from another faith may not compensate for the fact that Jews choose not to come to temple on their own holidays, but it certainly helps us create a better understanding with our Christian neighbors, which I'm sure you are not against."

He knew there was no point in pursuing this discussion any further. Joe was letting him know in a nice way he had overstepped his bounds, since this was not his decision to make in the first place. The Sisterhood president did not come to him to ask for his permission, but rather to inform him of her auxiliary's plans.

"No, of course not," said Kaye. "I just gave Roz my own personal opinion. It's certainly her decision to make as Sisterhood president."

He felt like slamming the phone as he hung up. Joe had certainly let him know who was the boss. Leaning back in his leather-cushioned swivel chair, he recalled the day he first walked into this study, almost three years ago, newly ordained. He felt as if he were standing on top of the world. Everything inside this study spelled conviction, solidity, a visible token of a higher power. The massive mahogany desk. The black leather swivel-chair. The vinyl sofa. The floor-to-ceiling bookcases. The heavy golden drapes. And, most important, the diploma on the wall proclaiming JOSHUA KAYE, RABBI.

Rabbi? What did that mean? A teacher, a leader, a prophetic voice? Or did it mean a rubber-stamp to some rich trustees who told the rabbi what to do and where to get off?

When he first came to serve as junior assistant to the great Alvin Blumenfeld he couldn't image questioning the meaning of his title. When Blumenfeld, the rising leader of American Jewry, heir to Stephen Wise and Abba Hillel Silver, proclaimed from this pulpit that the purpose of Liberal Judaism was to perfect the world in the image of the kingship of God, he heard himself say "amen." Blumenfeld had the courage of his convictions. He was one of the first rabbis who went down South in the early sixties to help Dr. Martin Luther King fight for what Blumenfeld called "a just and humane society." Some of the lay leaders of the congregation objected to the senior rabbi spending more time on saving the world than ministering to his own congregation, but Blumenfeld had enough followers on the board who helped him silence his critics.

In those days Joshua Kaye used to think, If God is not here at Suburban Temple, where else could God be?

All this now seemed light years away. In three years things had changed beyond recognition. A year ago King was assassinated. Blacks were now fighting their own battles. Jews had turned to their own affairs. America was knee-deep in Vietnam. What had become of the dream of a just and humane society? Who was perfecting the world in the image of the kingship of God?

He sat there for a long time waiting for an answer, but none came. If God is not here, he thought, then what is the point of my serving as rabbi of this congregation and presuming to speak in the name of God?

"I've been doing a lot of thinking today," Kaye told his wife when he got home that evening. He got up and started pacing the room. Running his fingers through his short trimmed dark beard, he stopped and turned back.

"The board will be voting on my contract next week. I'm told Joe Pins has proposed a three year contract with a substantial raise."

Felicia lit herself an after dinner cigarette.

"You don't anticipate any problems, do you?"

"No, not really. But I've been wondering whether it's time. . ."

He was interrupted by their one-year-old son who started whimpering in the other room. Felicia went into the baby's room to find out what it was. Kaye watched his wife flit across the room in her flowing robe, light yet sure-footed, her supple breasts heaving, and thought of her words to him the other night, "It's time to start thinking about a little brother or sister for Danny." Felicia was eight years his junior. At twenty-two, she seemed to have their future all mapped out. Lately she started talking about selling their apartment and buying a house. She was active in the affairs of the temple, especially the Young Couples' Club, which she helped organize, helping put some new life into the moribund social activities of the temple's younger set. "Felicia is a real *rebbetzin*," the temple women told Kaye on more than one occasion. "You are lucky to have a wife like Felicia."

He heard Felicia calm the baby down in his crib. How would she react to his idea of leaving Suburban Temple? She grew up in this congregation. Her father, Dr. Zamenhoff, the eminent professor of Jewish Mysticism at the Quincy Rabbinical Seminary, was an honorary member of the board. No doubt, her fondest dream was to see her husband become one day the senior rabbi of this synagogue.

Kaye stretched down on the living room couch, dropping his shoes on the floor. Felicia came back and sat down next to him. He put his arms around her and pulled her toward himself. She lay next to him and rested her head on his shoulder. He ran his fingers up and down her back and heard her purr. He slipped his hand under her robe and cupped her breast in his hand, feeling her nipple harden. She slapped his hand and laughed. "Not now," she said, pushing his hand away and closing her gown. "Later."

She got up and started putting the dishes in the sink.

"You were saying," Felicia called out from the kitchen, "you've been doing a lot of thinking."

"Yes," he raised himself and sat in the corner of the couch, folding his legs. "I have. You know, there's something really wrong with Suburban Temple."

"Like what?"

"Like the attitude of the rich board members who think they own the temple. The other night at the board meeting they brought up this business about raising half a million dollars to build a museum for housing Sam Halpern's Judaica collection. Jack Geiger, the optometrist, spoke against it. He didn't see any point in spending half a million dollars on a museum when the money could be put into much better use, like a social action center or a youth camp. Before Jack was able to finish, this old millionaire, Lou Rosen, gets up and tells Jack he has no right to speak on the issue, since Lou and a few other wealthy trustees were putting up the bulk of the money and were only asking the congregation to contribute a token one hundred dollars per family. I couldn't believe my ears! You have no right to speak unless you are one of the big contributors!"

"You may be overreacting," Felicia told her husband. "You know Lou Rosen likes to shoot off his mouth. You can't take him too seriously "

"Yes, I know. But that was only half of it. The real letdown was Rabbi Blumenfeld. The old man had told me he was against the museum and was going to make his feelings known at the meeting. Instead, he just sat there all evening and didn't say a word."

"Did you ask him why?"

"I was going to, but it occurred to me that the whole thing with Lou Rosen had been carefully orchestrated by Joe Pins and the executive board. They must've told Blumenfeld to keep out of the discussion."

"That's hard to believe."

"Well, things don't seem to be the same at the temple. Last year, when Blumenfeld became president of the Conference of Presidents of Major Jewish Organizations, I was sure he was going to let those people know who was boss around here. Instead, he no longer seems willing to take a stand on any controversial issue. It's very frustrating to work for a rabbi who doesn't stand up for his principles."

During breakfast the next day Kaye told his wife it was time he started looking for his own congregation. After three years as junior associate at Suburban Temple he had learned all he needed to know about running a major synagogue. Besides, he wanted to look for a congregation that would be receptive to his own ideas and where he could start putting his own beliefs into practice.

"We can do it," Kaye told his wife as she lifted the baby out of the high chair and put him in his playpen. "The two of us working as a team can manage a good size congregation. It would give us the base from which to work on important Jewish and general issues."

Felicia sat down and took a sip of her coffee.

"I agree," she said. "You *should* start looking for your own congregation and become your own man. But you should talk to Blumenfeld first. See what he has to say."

He told his wife he would. He was greatly relieved. He had expected her to disagree with his decision. The women of the congregation were right. He was lucky to have a wife like Felicia.

Before he left for work Kaye embraced his wife and told her he considered himself a lucky man.

"I couldn't do it without you, love."

She stood up on her tiptoes and kissed him.

For over a hundred years *Anshe Chesed* Congregation occupied a red brick building in downtown Quincy. In the early sixties a new, three million dollar edifice was erected in West Hills—one of Quincy's affluent new suburbs, and the synagogue was renamed Suburban Temple. The parking lot alongside the building was so long it made one think of an airport runway. The main building housing the sanctuary looked like an Egyptian pyramid with its top cut off. Kaye's father-in-law called it the Ziggurat. He was down on the "Edifice complex" that gripped American Jews in the fifties and sixties, the years of Jewish prosperity and nouveau richeness. Kaye readily agreed. The monuments of Judaism are of the spirit, not of stone and brick, he expostulated in one of his sermons shortly after he came to Suburban Temple. The temple trustees present that night did not consider it one of his better sermons.

Blumenfeld's secretary, as usual, was on the phone. When she saw the junior assistant she put her hand over the mouthpiece and told Kaye his boss wanted to see him. He felt relieved. It would be easier to break the news to his boss as an aside, rather than lead right into it.

The senior rabbi was in his study going through his mail. Blumenfeld's study was an enormous wood-panelled room. The entire wall on the left was lined with book shelves and a huge glass cabinet full of antique Jewish ritual objects—silver candelabras, Torah crowns, breastplates and pointers, ornate etrog boxes and filigree spice boxes, medieval marriage contracts and Renaissance illuminated manuscripts, as well as ancient coins dating back to the Second Temple and the Bar Kokhba rebellion, and clay and bronze oil lamps Blumenfeld had started to bring back lately from his frequent trips to the Holy Land. Next to the bookcases was a long conference table with tall leather cushioned chairs, used for staff meetings. On the opposite side of the room, under tall draped windows, was a crushed velvet L-shaped sofa, big enough to accommodate a dozen people. In the far right corner of the study, next to a wall covered with diplomas, citations, awards and photographs of the rabbi of Suburban Temple in the company of the famous and the powerful, was Blumenfeld's horseshoe-shaped desk, at the corner of which stood a bronze replica of a statue of the prophet Isaiah snapping a sword in two, to be fashioned into a plowhsare.

"Morning," Kaye greeted his boss who was scrutinizing a letter.

Without looking up, Blumenfeld motioned to his assistant to sit down.

Kaye sat on the edge of the sofa next to the desk.

"I would like to take the month of August off and leave you in charge of holding down the fort," the senior rabbi said as he finished reading the letter. "You don't have any plans for August, do you?"

Kaye was surprised by the announcement. It was customary for the rabbis of Suburban Temple to take their vacation during June or July, since August was the beginning of the pre-High Holy Day season, when both rabbis became extremely busy.

"No, I don't," Kaye replied, "but won't it be too hard for you to get away in August?"

Blumenfeld thought for a moment, then stood up and started pacing the room. He walked over to the couch and sat down next to his assistant.

"I'm telling you this in strict confidence, Joshua. I'm seriously considering announcing my retirement next year, effective next June. I'm finding it increasingly difficult to wear two hats as both rabbi of this large congregation and president of a national Jewish organization."

Kaye waited for his boss to continue.

"I'll stay on as rabbi emeritus," Blumenfeld went on, "but I won't be actively involved in the running of this place. I'm purposely leaving you in charge right before the High Holy Days because I think it will be an excellent opportunity for you to show the board you can handle this job and should be considered for the succession. I realize, of course, you've just turned thirty, which would make you the youngest rabbi in America in charge of a congregation of over two thousand families. But I believe you have a good chance and you should pursue it."

When Kaye gave his wife the news later that afternoon her first reaction was a nervous, incredulous laugh.

"You can't be serious!"

"Well, that's exactly what he said. He wants to retire next year and he thinks I have a good chance to become his successor."

Felicia shouted and laughed and threw herself into his arms.

"Josh!" Can you really picture yourself as the senior rabbi of Suburban Temple?"

He settled into the living room couch and remained silent for a long time.

"I think I can do it," he finally said. "The question is, can I do it

on my own terms? Those rich trustees think they own the rabbi.
This is *their* temple. The rabbi works for *them*. So they are the ones
who call the shots."

After dinner they decided to go and see Felicia's father and ask
for his opinion. Dr. Zamenhoff listened intently to his son-in-law.
After a short reflection the professor said,

"Yes, Josh, everything you say is true. Unfortunately, the rich do
have this attitude. Blumenfeld has fought his battles in his day,
and he did win a few. His involvement in the civil rights movement
these last few years has taken a lot out of him. The man is tired.
Now he's involved in national and world Jewish affairs. He hasn't
got the time or the energy to fight them on an issue like the Halpern museum. You are young. If you take Blumenfeld's place, you'll
have a golden opportunity to turn this place around. But you can't
do it overnight. You will have to do it gradually and tread lightly,
especially in the beginning."

Back at the apartment that night, Felicia told her husband she
was convinced he could do it. It was the chance of a lifetime, and
they had to start laying the groundwork.

"What would you have me do?" he asked skeptically. "Blumenfeld
has not even made a formal announcement."

"You don't have to wait for a formal announcement," she said.
"We should start inviting over some members of the board and get
to know them better. I know you don't like politicking, but it's all
part of the game."

"But do I want to play the game?"

"You said you wanted to be the rabbi of a major congregation,"
she reminded him. "This way you would have a base from which to
work on important Jewish and general issues."

He told his wife he was no longer sure a rabbi of a rich congregation like Suburban Temple was free to act on his own convictions.

On Sunday, when he came home from teaching Sunday school,
Kaye found his wife leafing through the *Quincy Times*. Some
department stores were having a pre-season sale of men's clothes.
It was a good opportunity for him to update his wardrobe.

"You have to project a more rabbinical image," Felicia observed.

"What's wrong with my image?" Kaye answered gruffly. "I'm not
campaigning for anything. If Suburban Temple wants me they
would have to take me the way I am."

She told him he was being stubborn. What was he trying to
prove, anyway? The trustees had just agreed on a substantial raise
for the junior rabbi for next year. He had to admit they were being

very generous. But they did expect something in return. What was the point of antagonizing them?

They argued for two days about his "rabbinical image," when he finally gave in and agreed to have himself fitted at Hathaway's with a new pin-stripe summer suit, French cuff shirts and a Pierre Cardin tie. On the way home Felicia made a remark about their old Chevy convertible. Rabbi Blumenfeld drove a new black Buick which looked "dignified" without being ostentatious. It was time they started looking into trading their ten-year-old car.

This time he decided to put his foot down.

"You know, Felicia, you have really become obsessed with this whole succession business."

"You don't have to get upset," she tried to mollify him. "I'm not suggesting we run out and buy a new car. But you should ask yourself what kind of a car do people expect the rabbi of Suburban Temple to drive."

"My idea of a rabbi is not someone who always worries about what people expect of him," Kaye retorted.

"You know everything, don't you?" she snapped back. She turned her face to the side window of the car and did not say a word until they got home.

They made up that night and spent the next three days trying to reconcile their differences. Felicia attributed her husband's behavior to the magnitude of the challenge facing him. It was her task to help him come to his senses and overcome his misgivings. She told him he owed it to himself and to his family to go after the job, try it for a year or two, and then see how he felt about it. He could always change his mind later on. Kaye disagreed. He would not allow himself to be seduced by the high salary and by the glamour of the position. Once he did, he might start compromising himself the way Blumenfeld did. He was not quite ready to give up his principles.

One night Kaye came home late from temple. Felicia reminded him he had said he would be home early. Some friends had called and asked if they wanted to go out to the movies. She had called the temple around seven and was told he had left. She wanted to know where he went.

"You could at least have called to let me know you were going to be late."

He told his wife he had an unexpected visit from a former classmate who had his own congregation in a small town in Massachusetts. He had come to town to talk to the dean of the rabbinical school about coming back to work on his PhD. He had become disillusioned with the pulpit, and was considering going into teaching. They went out for a drink and became so absorbed in conversation that by the time he checked his watch it was almost ten o'clock. It seemed that their respective problems with the pulpit were identical, except for the fact that, unlike Suburban Temple with its clique of wealthy trustees, this small congregation in Massachusetts only had one rich family which owned half the town and considered the rabbi its hired hand.

"So what conclusion did you reach?"

"I'm seriously considering taking a year off from the pulpit. I need to find out if I want to continue in the rabbinate or do something else."

"What about me, what about us?" she pointed at the baby. "You have a family, you know. What are we supposed to do for a whole year while you are making up your mind?"

"We'll manage."

Felicia looked at her husband as if he had lost his mind.

"You're being offered something on a silver platter and you're throwing it away!"

"I've got to do it!" he insisted.

"Goodbye!" she blurted out and stalked out of the room. He followed her into the bedroom.

"What is that supposed to mean?"

"It's supposed to mean that you don't give a damn about your own family," she shouted, shaking with anger. "It's supposed to mean that I am sick and tired of living with someone who doesn't know what the hell he wants. For God's sakes, when will you grow up?"

It seemed all they did that summer was fight. Their son would be crying in his room while they fought in the master bedroom. One night, as they lay awake, Kaye suggested a trial separation. Felicia objected. If the marriage was hopeless, the best thing to do was to get a divorce. Their son was still young enough to call someone else Dad, someone, Felicia added, who would not only think of himself and his own needs, but also of his family.

They had reached an impasse. They had both stated their case and there was nothing more to add. For a while an uneasy truce prevailed, but they knew it was only a temporary lull. Some kind of a solution had to be reached.

One night as they sat down to dinner, Felicia told her husband she had some good news.

"Guess what," she said excitedly, "I spoke today to Milt Rubin. You know the Rubin brothers own the largest Buick dealership in Quincy. Milt checked with his brother. They have this beautiful new dark blue Buick they're willing to sell us for fifty dollars above cost."

"There's nothing wrong with the Chevy," he told his wife.

"Except for the fact that it's ten years old, it needs a paint job, and it's certainly not the kind of a car one would expect the rabbi of Suburban Temple to drive. Besides, you're getting this car very cheap, and you know the Rubin brothers carry a lot of weight on the board and it won't hurt to have them on our side."

"You better call Milt and tell him to forget it."

Felicia lost her cool. "Why the hell don't you call him yourself?"

"Because!" Kaye exploded, "you had no business talking to him without discussing it with me first!"

He brought his fist down on the table, making the dinner plates rattle. The baby in his highchair started to cry. Felicia picked him up and rocked him in her arms.

"Stop running my life," he told his wife after the baby quieted down.

"Sure, Josh," she lashed back at him, "throw away your future, see if I care."

After a long round of recrimination Kaye got up and put on his jacket.

"Where're you going?" Felicia asked, alarmed.

"I think you should give my idea of a trial separation some thought," he said, drawing a long breath. "I'm going away and I'll be back tomorrow night. This should give both of us a chance to think things over."

Felicia was livid with anger. Her face blanched inside the circle of light cast by the kitchen lamp. She started to cry, then stopped and blew her nose.

"If you leave now you'll never see me or the baby again," she said, suppressing her anger. "I've tried very hard to do what's best for you, for us. I don't see any point in a trial separation. I'm willing to try to work things out. If you're not willing, then—leave!"

About to walk out, he stood there, hearing her out, and as soon as she finished he walked out without saying a word. He spent the night at a motel, and when he came back the next day Felicia and the baby were gone. There was a note scrawled on the kitchen pad that read:

> I went back to my parents.
> Congratulations—you won.
> You can now take all the time
> you need to think things over.

He could scarcely blame his wife for not wanting to go back to her parents for a trial separation. Ever since she was a little girl, Felicia dreamed of leaving home. Her father, the celebrated professor, was too wrapped up in his teaching and his scholarly pursuits to pay much attention to his daughter. Felicia's mother doted on her husband who, Kaye soon realized, was taking up all her time and energy, which made Felicia feel left out of her parents' affection. His mother-in-law, Kaye further realized, felt threatened by Felicia's keen mind and quick wit and was constantly tangled in futile arguments with her daughter. It was really a harsh thing to do to Felicia, asking her to go back to her parents. But there was no other way. They were not quite ready to give up their marriage. They both needed some time away from each other to try to work things out.

He heard the phone ring. A thought crossed his mind: It was Felicia, calling him to insist he make up his mind one way or the other. He went into the kitchen and answered the phone.

"Hello, Josh? This is Sol."

The voice sounded familiar. Presently he realized it was his father-in-law. He had never called the professor by his first name, nor was he able to bring himself to call him Dad. Since calling him Dr. Zamenhoff sounded too officious, he avoided calling him anything at all.

"Oh, hello."

"How've you been?"

"Fine, fine. How's Felicia and the baby?"

"The baby is wonderful. Felicia is doing as well as can be expected. Hmm, Josh, I was wondering if you and I could get together for a little *shmoos*."

One of the hardest things about being separated from Felicia was going to be being separated from her father, his teacher and mentor.

"Sure, any time."

There was a moment of uneasy silence on the other end.

"Felicia and I need some time away from each other," Kaye explained. "There're certain things we need to figure out."

"I understand," the voice on the wire said. "These things are bound to happen, especially in the early years of marriage."

They agreed to get together at the school during Zamenhoff's office hours.

Kaye got up and started pacing the apartment. Three short years after his ordination he was at the peak of his career. If he played his cards right he was almost certain to succeed Blumenfeld. "You have to *do* like a rabbi," Blumenfeld had once told him, shortly after he became Blumenfeld's assistant. "What do I mean by that? A rabbi is basically an actor. The better you play the part the more effective a rabbi you become. You cannot impress the congregation with your learning and erudition, since the level of their Jewish education is that of a thirteen year old. In a way, our function is that of the biblical priests, the descendants of Aaron, if I may offer an analogy. We have to minister to the needs of these people. We would like to be prophets, bring them the great biblical message. But in order to be prophets we first have to be priests." Blumenfeld paused and gave his assistant a fraternal wink. "You've got what it takes, m'boy. Learn how to play the part. You will go far if you do."

So this is what I spent all those years studying for, Kaye thought. Play rabbi to some rich Jews at this ziggurat they call temple. This is what the prophetic message of Liberal Judaism comes down to—acting the part. And to think that it took me three years to find out I was a phony!

He felt exhausted. He got up and staggered across the hall to the bedroom. He could not bear to look into the baby's room and walked straight into the master bedroom. As he turned on the light he saw the framed picture of Felicia coming home from the hospital with their newly born son in her arms. He had taken that picture a year ago as Felicia walked in the door, bringing their son home. The young mother's eyes were bright with the joy and pride of maternity. Suddenly he realized what Felicia must have felt when she picked up the baby now, a year later, and went back to her parents. Her hurt, anger, shame, humiliation cut through him like a knife. He buried his face in his hands and cried like a child.

✧ 2 ✧

Things always got hectic at the temple around the High Holy
Days. Rosh Hashana was early that year, and with Blumenfeld
away right before the holy days, Kaye had his hands full and did
not have much time to think about his own personal problems. He
did not get around to seeing his father-in-law until the day before
Sukkot. They talked about his marriage, but they did not get too
far with it. He told the professor he and Felicia did not see eye to
eye on too many things. He had many questions about his career,
about the direction he seemed to be headed it, about his boss,
Blumenfeld, and about Suburban Temple. Felicia and he, Kaye
went on to say, always seemed to be at opposite ends when he tried
to discuss those things with her. Dr. Zamenhoff listened patiently
and said little. They agreed to meet again in a week or two.

On the morning of Sukkot, the autumn harvest festival, Kaye
woke up to a cloudy sky and a cold drizzle. They were going to have
a nun guest speaker at services that morning. Roz Pins had told
him it was a sure-fire idea, guaranteed to fill the place with wor-
shipers. For what purpose? he thought as he got dressed. If they
are not interested in their own holidays, why bother bringing them
to shul?

When the junior rabbi arrived at the temple that morning the
place was humming with Catholic nuns. He had never seen so
many nuns before. Where did they all come from? They couldn't all
be local. They must have come from as far north as Columbus, or
across the river from Kentucky, or ever from farther away.

As he worked his way through the crowd dispensing his clerical
greetings, he was struck by the great variety of religious attire he
found himself surrounded with. Here and there he saw the familiar
long black habit that only revealed a white rimmed circle of face.
Interspersed in the crowd were also white habits that looked less
austere and somewhat modified, substituting a veil for the starched
headdress. As he progressed through the crowd the nuns' dresses,

skirts and veils seemed to progress in an evolutionary order. Some revealed ankles, arms, necks and hair (did the ones who wore head-dresses shave their head?) Others wore skirts—gray, white and different shades of blue—reaching just below the knee, and a small veil pinned on the back of their heads. Finally he saw two nuns who wore no veil at all. They wore plain light blue dresses not quite reaching to their knees, and flat shoes. The only religious article they wore was a silver medallion hanging from a chain around their necks. He stopped and looked at the two. There was something familiar about them. He now remembered: They wore the same outfit the nun Roz had introduced him to at the temple library was wearing. What was her name?

"Morning, rabbi," he heard a familiar voice ring out behind him. It was Roz Pins. She was her usual elegant self. She wore a black silk suit with a white scarf around here neck, and a tight fitting black hat.

"*Gut yontiff,*" Kaye replied, wondering what *gut yontiff* had to do with a gathering of nuns.

"*Gut yontiff,*" Roz echoed back with a faint blush. The two nuns in the light blue dresses had turned to look at the tall dark bearded young man in the gray suit who had just been addressed as "rabbi." The gist of the repartee between him and the Sisterhood president must have been lost on them.

"Quite a gathering," Roz offered, beaming.

"Yes, quite," Kaye agreed, wondering whether it sounded like he meant it.

Roz consulted her diamond studded watch. Her face shifted from glee to concern.

"Rabbi Blumenfeld is not here yet. I hope he gets here in time for the service." Translated, it meant, "Aren't you rabbis accountable for each other? Can't you see to it that the senior rabbi gets here in time to play host to our guests?"

No, Kaye thought, I'm afraid I cannot. I take orders from the senior rabbi, I don't give them. Sporting a smile, he said,

"I'm sure he'll be here any minute."

The two nuns in the light blue dresses were still standing there, looking at them. He greeted them and tried to think of something clever to say, but couldn't think of anything. There was a moment of awkward silence. They kept smiling pleasantly, waiting for him to proceed. He wanted to ask them what had brought so many of them to a Jewish place of worship on a Jewish holiday. What did they expect to find there? No, he had better stick to amenities. Get on with

the service and get it over with. His own fellow Jews were now
recovering from what to most of them was their once-a-year visit to
the synagogue. So they needed Catholic nuns to give the festival of
Sukkot a new lease on life.

Roz peeked again at her watch. It was almost time to start.
Through the glass doors Kaye saw Rabbi Blumenfeld's black Buick
turn into the reserved parking space across from the main
entrance. The senior rabbi emerged from his car and walked in in a
huff. He waved to Roz and kept walking precipitously towards a
side corridor leading to his office. Kaye excused himself and followed his superior. Blumenfeld's brisk pace belied his age. He was a
short, stocky man, more pudgy than solid, yet skillful in making
himself appear the dashing athletic type, which he was not. His red
hair, now thinning, his beetle eyebrows over wise, steady blue eyes,
his strong chiseled nose, stiff upper lip and somewhat protruding,
sensuous lower one, were all used to his best advantage both on the
speaker's stand and in tete-a-tetes.

Old Alvin sure knows how to play the part to the hilt, Kaye observed as he followed the older man to his study. They quickly
removed their jackets and put on their white robes and stoles. The
congregation was waiting for them quietly in the pews as the
strains of the organ ushered in the rabbis and their bimah guests,
including the guest speaker. The congregation consisted mainly of
the Sisterhood ladies, mostly in their late fifties or older (the
younger women were either playing tennis, carpooling their
children, or doing the rounds of the shopping malls). Their Christian counterparts were mostly those groups of nuns Kaye had met
in the lobby. They sat interspersed throughout the congregation,
distinguishable by their various ecclesiastic garb, accompanied by
Catholic lay women. My grandfather would turn in his grave if he
saw this, Kaye reflected as he occupied his tall crushed velvet seat
on the bimah.

After a brief service, done mostly in English, the senior rabbi
rose and introduced the guest speaker, Dr. Theophelia McPherson,
a Maryknoll nun, professor of theology, who had just returned from
a two year mission to Latin America. Surely the good Sister would
like to share her experience south of the border with the congregation, the rabbi suggested, as he turned to the speaker with a welcome wave of his hand.

Sister Theophelia, broad, toothy smile, lean, erect torso, and
resolute gestures, reminded Kaye of the Kennedy women. She
spoke briefly about the places she had visited and the work she had

done in Peru, Ecuador and Venezuela, and then asked the congregation's indulgence and changed the subject. She wanted to say a few words about her favorite Jewish philosopher, Martin Buber. Kaye could tell the minds of the Sisterhood ladies began to drift, one by one, as the speaker was getting deeper into her subject. Roz Pins was making a brave effort attempting to follow the expose on I-thou and I-It. Before long, the only ones who were listening were the nuns in the congregation and the two rabbis on the bimah.

As soon as the service ended the rabbis and their bimah guests marched back to the social hall where they formed a reception line and began to greet the congregation. The rabbis smiled and shook hands, making small talk. Some nuns shook their hand and joined in the amenities, while others were more reserved, only allowing themselves a small bow and a hint of a smile, and only shook the hand of the guest speaker. The reception over, everyone was invited by the Sisterhood hostesses to a buffet brunch of tuna fish, egg salad, juice and coffee. Kaye excused himself and went back to his study to change back into civilian clothes. He closed the door behind him and heaved a sigh of relief. He had his fill of nuns for one day. He was going to stay in his study till they left. He was not about to return to the social hall and play social director. Let Rabbi Blumenfeld do it. He seemed to relish the role and was able to play it with aplomb. This reception was his show. Let him have all the honor to himself.

Kaye leaned back in his swivel chair and lifted his head, locking his hands behind his nape, and thought about the service. What was the point of organized religion? What was the point of all those nuns with all their paraphernalia, all those different habits, the medallions, the crucifixes, all the different orders, and, least comprehensible of all, the vows? Clearly, it was a show. Better yet, it was two shows vying with each other. The show of Suburban Temple on the one hand, with its two thousand seat sanctuary, its well trained usher corps, its professional choir, and its renowned rabbi. And this other, much greater show, perhaps the greatest show on earth, the Roman Catholic Church.

Wasn't his own show enough, he needed this other one too? Rabbi Blumenfeld was no dummy. He recognized this whole affair for what it was—a show. He chose to play along with it. Felicia was no dummy either. She also realized what it was all about. But she had been seduced by the glamour, the prestige of being the wife of the junior rabbi of this great institution. Blumenfeld was the one

who had let him down. He had expected better from him. Felicia
did not surprise him. He disagreed with her, but he could see why
she would enjoy the social status that went with the position. But
what about her father, Professor Zamenhoff? More than anyone
else, Zamenhoff had helped him reach the decision of pursuing a
pulpit career and secured for him the position at Suburban Temple.
Didn't Zamenhoff, the leading scholar of Liberal Judaism in
America realize what it was all about? And if he did, shouldn't he
have said something to his son-in-law? Look here, Josh. The rabbinate is a farce. You may be better off pursuing an academic
career, or going into business, or doing anything, but stay away
from the pulpit. It is certainly no place for anyone who's got his senses about him. Then again, Zamenhoff earned his living teaching
future rabbis.

There, on the wall facing his desk, was Solomon Zamenhoff's
signature on the bottom of the framed rabbinical diploma, surrounded by the signatures of all the other members of the faculty,
headed by that of the chancellor of the seminary, Dr. William
Lowey, the world renowned biblical archeologist. As he kept staring at his diploma, as if puzzled by its message, it all came back
to him with startling vividness. The night before his ordination.
Waking up at four o'clock in the morning in a cold sweat. Tomorrow morning he will be walking up to the bimah and become
rabbi in Israel. No longer Mr. Kaye. No longer plain Josh. That
awesome title will be appended to his name forever. Was he ready
for it? There was still time to back out. Then, the next morning,
he woke up as cheerful as a bird in springtime, ready as can be. It
was a beautiful ceremony. Everyone was in high spirits. Dr.
Lowey looked deeply into Kaye's eyes as he laid his hands on his
shoulders and whispered some words in his ears concluding with,
"Are you ready?" Yes, he was ready. He vigorously shook the
chancellor's hand after receiving his diploma, a rolled and rib-
boned scroll of parchment. It was all so clear and natural. It
couldn't be any other way. And here he was three years later, staring at the framed diploma, wondering whether a piece of parchment, words whispered by a biblical archeologist, the signatures
of a group of Judaic scholars, turned one from an ordinary Jew
into a rabbi. Did Hillel have a diploma? Did Isaiah, did the Baal
Shem Tov?

He heard a knock on the door. He was almost certain it was Roz.
She came to pull him out of his hideout and put him back where he
belonged. He put on a smile and, clearing his throat, went to open

the door. No, it was not Roz. It was a young woman in a pale blue dress who looked vaguely familiar.

She stood in the hallway as if afraid she might be scolded for knocking on the door, reminding him of a frightened pupil who had just been sent to the principal's office. He now remembered she was the young nun Roz had introduced him to at the temple library before the High Holy Days. Sister Eve, was it? She made him feel uneasy. Should he ask her to come in? What could she possibly want with him?

"Please come in," he finally offered.

She took a few hesitant steps and remained standing in the middle of the room, staring at the floor.

"Won't you sit down" he pointed at the sofa.

She sat on the edge of the vinyl sofa with her hands in her lap and looked straight ahead at the lower shelves of the bookcase across the room. He went around the desk and sat in his chair, facing her. The strangeness he had felt earlier in the morning when he walked into the lobby and found himself surrounded by all those nuns came back as he watched this one nun sitting across the desk from him in the privacy of his study. He recalled her discomfiture when Roz Pins had made the remark to her in the library about his good looks. Now she made him feel uncomfortable with her excessive humility and self-effacement. It almost bordered on sanctimonious arrogance. She was a young woman, probably in her early twenties or even younger, yet she seemed to strive to appear older. She wore no makeup. Her short hair was a dull wax color. She was pale, so pale her skin seemed translucent. Her high cheeckbones and broad forehead had a solemn, meditative air about them. Her eyes were almost without lashes or eyebrows. There were bags under her eyes, making him wonder whether she was in the habit of crying.

The sky outside had grown darker. The drizzle had turned into rain that came down in sheets, lashing against the study windows. They both looked at the window and said at the same time,

"Nasty weather."

He chuckled. She showed a faint hint of a smile.

"Must be a jinx," Kaye said, trying to keep the conversation going.

"Something like that," she said, "I'm not sure." She spoke in a soft voice, almost is a whisper.

He said he was not an expert on superstitions.

She nodded, non-committal.

"Where're you from?"

"Lourdes, over at Cliffwood."

"Oh, yes, I know where it is. I went to school around the corner from Cliffwood. In fact, the rabbinical school is right across the ravine from the convent."

"I'm new at Lourdes," she said, "It's my first year."

"What about all the others? They couldn't all be local."

"Oh, no. We are having a national conference of women religious in Quincy this week. Sister Theophelia spoke at the opening session yesterday and made quite an impression, so many of the sisters decided to come here today and hear her speak again."

"I see."

He waited for her to proceed.

"Well," she cleared her throat, getting down to the reason for her stopping in. "Mrs. Pins had mentioned she and I were taking this course in American Literature over at St. John's? I've decided to do a paper on the Jew in Contemporary American Fiction. I was wondering if I could ask you a few questions."

"Go right ahead."

"I'm trying to decide which character in the work of contemporary American Jewish writers is the most authentically Jewish."

Kaye chuckled. "*Authentically* Jewish? Well, I recently gave a sermon on the *in*authenticity of the American Jew as reflected in contemporary fiction."

"Roz Pins told me about it."

"Did she really? She totally disagrees with my view about Alex Portnoy."

"She says you overrated the book."

"Well, Portnoy in my opinion is the most authentic portrayal of the inauthenticity of the American Jew."

"I'm not sure I follow."

"I don't want to bore you with my sermon. In a nutshell, I took three characters—Morris Bober, Moses Herzog and Alex Portnoy, and I asked the congregation to think of them as three generations of American Jews. Bober is the immigrant who comes to America, attracted by the myth of gold in the streets. He is no great *talmid chochem*, rather an ordinary Jew who sheds his Jewishness in pursuit of the American Dream which he never attains. Herzog is the first generation American Jew. He has made it, as the expression goes. He is a great intellectual, an authority on Western Civilization. His Jewishness is basically a childhood memory he recalls with nostalgia as he keeps drifting away from it. Portnoy represents the present generation of young American Jews, who, as Jews, are confused, disoriented and disaffected. They are seduced by American Gentile hedonism and frustrated by their own Jewishness which seems to get in their way of becoming true-blue Americans, whatever that means. I realize not too many people in the congregation agree with my analysis. Portnoy challenges their own idealized self-image, and besides, they are afraid of what the Gentiles may think of them."

He stopped to catch his breath. "Well, I don't know if I've been of any help to you. But I do hope I've given you some food for thought."

He could not understand for the life of him what had prompted him to deliver himself of such a discourse when all he wanted to do was get this unexpected conference over with and take off.

The nun, however, did not seem to mind. She sat there in rapt attention, hanging on his every word. It suddenly occurred to him there was something more personal than a college paper that had prompted her to come see him. What was it? Was she so interested in Jews? Why did she look so intense? What was she holding back from him?

"Yes, you have," she said reflectively, "But I must admit Portnoy is not one of my favorite characters, and I certainly hope he is not the most representative American Jewish fictional character. My American lit professor considers him a caricature, an exaggeration. But what is clear to me from what you say is that my question raises other questions which I'll have to deal with first."

"I'd like to see your paper when you're finished," said Kaye. In spite of himself, he found himself intrigued by this strange young woman, whom, begrudgingly, he had to accept as his colleague.

"I'll be glad to show it to you," she said gratefully, "Oh, dear, I have taken too much of your time. I do appreciate your being so open and honest with me in discussing this subject."

She got up to leave. He walked her to the door and showed her the back way to the social hall. She thanked him again and, after a brief hesitation, turned back and, offering her hand, she said,

"*Gut yontiff*, rabbi."

Later that afternoon, alone in his apartment, Kaye found himself thinking about that young nun. He was not quite sure what to make of her. That whole Sukkot service, attended by all those different orders of nuns, was a charade. And yet there was something about that one young, shy, reflective, intense nun that lingered on in his mind and made him hope he would hear from her again.

He felt relieved being alone in the apartment. He wanted to be left alone, not see anyone. He took the phone off the hook. No calls tonight. He was unavailable. Incommunicado. He scoured the refrigerator for whatever leftovers he could find and ate absentmindedly, watching the evening news, washing the food down with a can of Miller High Life. The news rambled on, but he had stopped watching. He got up, took out another can of beer and went out on the balcony. He settled into a wicker chair, propping his feet on the round slate table, and watched the city in the gathering dusk.

He felt a dull pain in his side, the same pain he had been getting for over a month. He made a mental note to call Dr. Perkins first thing in the morning. Health always comes first, he recalled his father's favorite admonition. He hadn't seen his father in over a year, and suddenly he felt an overwhelming desire to see the old man, hear his voice, kid around with him, get into an argument, reach an impasse, and go out for a game of handball. He could almost hear the old man's heavy gait, pacing the balcony in the dark. Grave, purposeful, yet boisterously playful and self-deprecating. He was startled by the palpability of his father's presence, and he strained his eyes in the dark to make sure it was only his imagination.

What would his father's reaction be if he told him about that Sukkot morning service? He would probably let out a short, visceral blast of laughter, shrug his shoulders, and, throwing back his head, he would stare at his son with that familiar look, as if to say, I told you so.

Kaye's thoughts wandered back to that evening in Los Angeles ten years ago, shortly after his parents were divorced. He had gone out for a game of handball with his father, and they had dinner afterwards at that Mexican restaurant, when his father announced he was going to fulfil his life-long dream and settle in Israel.

"You want to help the Jewish people?" his father said rhetorically, "There's only one way to do it— Israel. Religion? We Jews today only have one true religion—Zionism. A rabbi? Liberal, Orthodox, it makes no different. It's all an anachronism. It all ended in the gas chambers and the ovens of Auschwitz, where Jews, about to die, saw God die. . ."

The old man paused and wiped his eyes.

"Sorry," he said, "I didn't mean to get emotional. But I must be honest with you, Josh. Here in America Jews are no longer really Jewish. We Jews have left Europe and came to America not because we were looking for religious freedom but because we were looking for Mammon. Yes, it's true, America's been good to us. It has rewarded our drive and intelligence. It has let us become successful businessmen, doctors, lawyers, and the like. But it has also exacted a price for all of this. We had to learn how to look, act, think like white Christian Americans. We had to invent new Jewish denominations which became a Jewish imitation of Christian denominations. It's only a question of time now before Jewish life in America disappears altogether."

Kaye smiled as he recalled his answer to his father. He was in his junior year in college at the time, and had just made up his mind to go to rabbinical school in Quincy and pursue the teachings of Liberal Judaism.

"Yes, Dad, Jewish life in America does have some very serious problems. But I'm not sure I agree with you that God died in Auschwitz. The 'Death of God' idea is both pagan and Christian, but certainly not Jewish. In Judaism God was not born, and therefore cannot die. The problem, as our Hillel rabbi on campus, Joe Wasserman, has put it, is that God has ceased to be a living force in the life of most Jews today. Joe told me about the Quincy seminary. At that school each student is free to pursue his own ideas and beliefs within the broad philosophical spectrum of Liberal Judaism, yet all the students and the professors are bound by a common purpose, which is a total commitment to Jewish survival and the renewal of Judaism as a prophetic faith."

Yes, Dad, Kaye thought, you did tell me so. After you left for Israel I thought a great deal about your statement that God had died at Auschwitz. That religion was no longer relevant. That Jewish life in America was doomed. My visit to Quincy confirmed my disagreement with your views. A year later I enrolled at the seminary. Remember the letters we wrote to each other at the time? The first year was very difficult for both of us. Mom remarried shortly after the divorce, and apparently got what she wanted—a husband who knew how to pamper her and cater to her many whims. You were lonely, and so was I. By the end of the second year things began to fall into place. I met Felicia and the Zamenhoffs took me under their wings. You had gotten your government grant and started working on the desalination project in Elat, to which you took—forgive my eschatological allusion—with messianic fervor. It seems the ensuing years were years of great promise for both of us. You were going to solve Israel's water problems, while I was going to become a great rabbi and spread the blessings of liberal Judaism among my fellow Jews. And then came the offer from Suburban Temple. Newly ordained, I was heading right for the top.

That was three years ago. And here I am now. Sitting on this dark balcony overlooking my city of promise and fulfillment, separated from Felicia, as I begin to realize Suburban Temple was a mistake, and, if God exists, He is certainly not here at Suburban Temple, and, yes, I know, you told me so.

✧ 3 ✧

In the morning Kaye received a phone call from his boss. Rabbi Blumenfeld wanted to see his assistant right away on some urgent matter. Kaye did not ask what it was. He got dressed quickly and stopped on the way at a fast food place for a cup of coffee and showed up at Blumenfeld's office half an hour after he received the call.

The older man peered at his assistant over his reading glasses and motioned at the chair next to his desk. Kaye walked across the study and sat down in that chair.

"You look a little rundown," Blumenfeld said, taking a closer look at his younger colleague. "Feel okay?"

"Feel fine."

"How's Felicia?"

"She's well. Her mother isn't feeling so well, so she is staying with her for a few days."

Did Zamenhoff tell Blumenfeld about the separation? Was that the reason he was called in?

"I do appreciate your filling in for me right before the Holy Days," said Blumenfeld. "I know I've laid a heavy burden on you. If you'd like to take a week off around Thanksgiving please feel free to do so."

He thanked his boss.

Blumenfeld put down the letter he was holding and removed his glasses.

"Joshua, I got a call at six o'clock this morning from the Pins. Their daughter, Sue, informed them last night she was going to the West Coast to live on a commune. She's leaving this afternoon. Roz, needless to day, is beside herself. Joe is ready to disown her. I offered to meet with Sue but she refused to see me. Roz says Sue likes you. She would like you to come to the house and try to talk to her."

"I doubt whether I can do any good," said Kaye. "I'm sure you remember all I had to go through last year, when Sue dropped out of Ohio State and Roz and Joe were trying to get her off drugs and away from her hippie friends. I spent countless hours getting all those papers ready for her to go to Israel and work for a year on a kibbutz, and at the last moment she suddenly takes off and goes back to her friends in Columbus and we are right back where we started. You don't really expect me to get her to change her mind this time, do you?"

"No, not really."

"Then why go through this again?"

"I suppose because it's our job," Blumenfeld gravely expostulated. "You know what Roz and Joe have been through with this kid. For three or four years they have had an army of doctors and psychologists working with her. She had put them through hell. When all else failed they came to us. And that's the whole point, my dear boy. When all else fails they come to the rabbi and they ask the rabbi to perform a miracle. That's right. 'Rabbi, you are a man of God. You He will listen to. How can He say no to you?' Rubbish! We are no miracle workers. The most we can do is be sympathetic, hold their hand and lend them our ear. And this is exactly what you did for Joe and Roz a year ago when you tried to get Sue to go to Israel and work on a kibbutz. You did a commendable job, helping them through that difficult time, going out of your way for them, showing them you really cared. Knowing Joe and Roz as I do, I can assure you they are most grateful to you."

"Yes, I guess you are right," Kaye said slowly, reflectively. "I did get quite involved with this thing. And, yes, I suppose in some small way I did help Joe and Roz get through that crisis. But I must confess to you, this whole experience with Sue has really gotten to me. Even now, a year later, I'm still trying to figure out why would such a beautiful super-intelligent kid who's got everything going for her, turn her back on all of us, on this entire society. Sue is not a typical mixed-up spoiled rich kid. She is trying to tell us something, and I'm not sure I know what it is. Rabbi, where have we failed Sue and her entire generation of sad, unhappy, confused kids?"

Blumenfeld's face clouded. Whenever challenged in a discussion, the senior rabbi would lift his chin in a gesture of defiance and, with a twinkle in his eye, would offer a rebuttal that invariably put his opponent on the defensive. This time too he threw up his chin, yet, instead of replying, he stood up and started to pace the room. It was odd seeing the celebrated orator at loss for words. After a moment's hesitation he made some innocuous remark about institutions not being perfect, the synagogue being no exception. The youth of today was rebelling against all institutions. But they will come around. It was only a question of time.

"Very well," said Kaye, "I'll call Roz."

He went into his own study across the hall and dialed the Pins' home number. Roz answered the phone.

"Roz, it's Josh."

"Rabbi? Oh, rabbi, I'm so glad you called. I called your house last night but your phone was busy and I couldn't reach you."

"Rabbi Blumenfeld told me about Sue," said Kaye.

He heard Roz sigh.

"Rabbi, could you come over and talk to her? I can't speak too loud. Sue's in the other room. I would like you to talk to her. She'd made up her mind. She's going to California to live on a commune. You know Sue. She won't listen to me. I hate to bother you, but Sue is being picked up by a friend in about an hour. She is all packed up and ready to go. I'm on my way to temple. I'm leaving in a few minutes but Sue will be here till ten. I would appreciate it if you had a word with her, for whatever it's worth. What have we got to lose? Yes, Sue, honey. I'll be off the phone in a minute. It's Rabbi Josh. He wants to stop here on his way to temple to say goodbye to you. All right, rabbi, Sue would love to see you."

Roz's voice dropped to a whisper. "Rabbi, please, I wish you could do something! I'm heartsick over this child. I don't know what to do anymore."

He promised he would do whatever he could.

What could he do? it was preposterous of him to even suggest to Sue not to try out that commune. What could he offer her in its place? Suburban Temple? West Hills? American Jewish utopia?

A few years ago Sue had put up in her room the clipping with the now famous newspaper picture of Rabbi Blumenfeld, taken after the rabbi of Suburban Temple was assaulted in Alabama by members of the Klan. One eye puffed shut. Blood running down the side of his face and on his white shirt. She had since taken it down, arguing that the rabbi, while giving the impression he was fighting for justice, did not really care about people. That he was a pawn of the rich, her own parents in particular, and did not practice what he preached.

"Sue is too smart for her own good," Kaye recalled Joe telling him as he drove up the Pins' circular driveway and parked in front of the main entrance. There were no cars on the premises. Joe was at work and Roz was out. Was Sue still home?

He rang the bell. He waited and rang again. He heard a voice calling out inside the house.

"Just a moment, I'll be right there."

The door flung open and there stood Sue, all flushed up and eager.

"Oh, I'm sorry. I thought you were someone else. I'm waiting for someone to pick me up and drive me to the airport. Please come in."

She had changed since he last saw her. Her short clipped hair had grown into soft, furry auburn curls. She asked him to follow her into the living room. She looked at him with her big blue eyes.

"I'm sorry I'm in such a rush. I'm being picked up in a few minutes."

She plopped into a huge satin armchair and propped her sandalled feet on the armrest. He sat down on the edge of the sofa next to her.

"How've you been, Sue?"

"Great. Never felt better in my entire life."

"You look good."

"Thanks. How've you been, rabbi?

"You can call me Josh."

She nodded, looking straight into his eyes, and giggled. A moment later her expression changed. She looked down and knit her brow.

"Josh, I'd like to apologize for putting you through all that trouble with that deal about going to live on a kibbutz for a year, and then dropping out of sight. I hope you understand."

He smiled at her. Yes, he understood. Never mind the trouble he had been through. His only concern was her welfare. It didn't matter whether or not she spent a year on a kibbutz. That was the means, not the end.

"Your parents, Sue, were terribly upset when you suddenly disappeared without saying a word. The thought of you going back to drugs was killing them."

"I didn't," she said. "I'm finished with that whole drug scene. Honest. I'm clean like a newly born child. I'm getting away from all the evils of civilization. I'm going to live in a place out in Southern California where there is no electricity, no plumbing, no cars, really God's country, where people say what they think and do what they feel. I'm starting a new life, going back centuries in time. Isn't that what people who started the kibbutz did? They went out into the wilderness and started a new life, a new kind of community."

"You make it sound very inviting, Sue. I'm almost tempted to join you."

She looked at him with eyes wide open with surprise.

"You're not serious."

"Why not?"

She giggled, then burst into a loud ringing laughter. She laughed so hard that before he knew it he was laughing along with her. They kept laughing until both of them ran out of breath. They looked at each other. He now realized he was holding Sue's hand. He squeezed her hand, and she squeezed back. Her eyes looked into his, tender and expectant. Her lips parted, the lips of a young girl barely turned woman. His heart pounded. He hadn't felt that way since the time he started to date Felicia, which now seemed ages ago. No, he couldn't kiss her. Not the way she wanted him to. He was still her rabbi. He let go of her hand.

"You know, Sue, it's the first time I ever heard you laugh. I mean, really laugh."

She looked at him with eyes full of tenderness and bit her lip.

"Yeah, I haven't laughed like this in ages."

"I wonder what it is that made you laugh so hard."

"Well. . ." She laughed again. "No, seriously, I had to laugh, because, my mother had called you and asked you to come over and see if you could talk me out of going to live on that commune. And here you are, telling me you might want to go there yourself. You know, for a moment you had me believe you really meant it."

"What makes you think I didn't?"

"Well," she turned serious again, "you have a wife and child. You are the assistant-rabbi of the biggest temple in the Midwest."

"So?"

"So."

"Sue, what kind of a commune is it?"

"Bahai."

"You mean the Bahai religion?"

"Yup."

"You didn't. . ."

"Yes, I did. I don't believe in any organized or institutional religion. Bahai is none of this."

"But why? Why Bahai?"

"Because I love people."

"What has this got to do with it?"

"Are you familiar with the Bahai religion?"

"Somewhat."

"Well, the Bahai maintain that all the major religions of the world are valid. That all people are spiritual brothers and sisters. They make no distinction between, say, Jews, Christians and Moslems. They believe in love, harmony, beauty. This is exactly what I believe in."

"In other words, you accept every belief of every religion in the world."

"I accept everything that is good and beautiful in any religion. Don't you?"

"I guess I do."

"But you believe Judaism is better than other religions."

"For me it is."

"You wouldn't officiate at my wedding if I married a non-Jew, would you?"

"No, I wouldn't. I believe Jews should marry Jews or we may disappear altogether in a few years."

"So what if we disappear? Haven't Jews suffered enough already for no other reason except their Jewishness?"

"There is a purpose for the suffering."

"Like what?"

"To perfect the world in the image of the kingship of God."

"This sounds to me more like the purpose of the Bahai religion than Judaism. Millions of people believe in Jesus. The Bahai do not necessarily believe that Jesus is the son of God. But they accept him as a great prophet. Now Jews are afraid to even talk about Jesus."

"I'm not afraid to talk about Jesus."

"Well, most Jews are. Like my parents, for instance."

He was wondering if there was any point in pursuing that discussion.

"There is one thing I don't understand, Sue. Why can't you be a Jew and still love all people and respect all religions?"

She gave him a slow look, as if unsure whether she should reply.

"I don't mean to hurt your feelings," she finally said. "But in what way does Suburban Temple promote love for all people?"

"It doesn't."

"Then. . . why are you working as a rabbi of that temple?"

"Because I'd like to change it."

She laughed.

"Why don't you start by talking to my Dad's friend, Hal Braverman? You know Hal. He is one of the big shots on the temple board."

"Why Hal?"

"Because Hal is also on the board of Armor & Gambit, and because Armor & Gambit makes napalm."

"Armor & Gambit makes laundry detergent and toothpaste."

"I know. But on the side they make napalm for burning women and children in Vietnam."

"Are you sure?"

"Ask Hal."

He made no reply. Hal was a close friend of Joe Pins. The two of them were often seen together. It was rumored lately that Hal, a wealthy lawyer and former chairman of the Democratic party in the state of Ohio, might be running in the next elections for the U.S. Senate. Sue might have overheard her father and Hal discuss Hal's connection to Armor & Gambit."

She put her hand on his shoulder.

"Well, Josh, would you like to come with me? You can be a Jew and a Bahai all at the same time."

"No, thanks," he said, "being a Jew is enough."

He got up to leave. Sue jumped up and followed him to the door. She opened the door for him and walked him to his car.

"I like convertibles," she said, patting the black canvas top.

With sudden compulsion she threw her arms around his neck and kissed him on his lips. He felt a strange stir. His cheeks were burning.

"*Shalom, rabi,*" she said in Hebrew, "*ani ohevet otcha.*"

He was surprised to hear her speak fluent Hebrew. before he had a chance to respond she turned around and ran back toward the house. Her small buttocks did a dance as she ran. She waved to him without looking back.

As he drove off he felt a tug in his heart. Poor Sue. First it was drugs, free-wheeling friends. Found half-dead in the gutter, sick with hepatitis. Drugs again. Now it's this Bahai thing. Love the whole world. Save the whole world. Instant salvation. Shortcuts to heaven. Anything goes. . .

Yes, but why couldn't he win her back? Why didn't he have anything to offer her? She saw through him, as she saw through Blumenfeld and her own parents and their rich and powerful friends. Change Suburban Temple. . . Don't waste your breath, rabbi. No one is going to change that illustrious institution.

✧ **4** ✧

The next day Kaye told his boss about his meeting with Sue. Blumenfeld listened dutifully. Kaye could tell that as far as the senior rabbi was concerned, it was a closed case.

"Did you know that Armor & Gambit was making napalm?"

"No, I didn't," said Blumenfeld, raising an eyebrow.

"Hal Braverman is on the board of Armor & Gambit."

"Yes, I know."

"I feel as a rabbi of this congregation I have a moral responsibility to speak out on this issue."

"You should feel free to speak your conscience," said Blumenfeld. "But let me first give Hal a call to check it out."

Later that afternoon Kaye's secretary buzzed the junior rabbi in his study.

"Hal Braverman is here to see you," Ruth Levy said.

"Tell him to come in."

Kaye got up and rushed to the door to greet the eminent trustee. Harold Braverman, dressed impeccably in a tailored gray flannel suit, red striped shirt, and a pearl-studded deep blue tie, beamed at the junior rabbi through his thick tortoiseshell glasses, offering a strong, deft handshake, and apologized for dropping in without prior notice. Like Joe Pins, Braverman was one of the most prominent lawyers in town. Unlike Joe, who came into wealth through his wife, Braverman was a self-made man. At fifty he had made all the money he had cared to make, and was looking for new horizons. He became active in political campaigns, and for the past two years had been serving as the chairman of the Democratic party in the state. By now he had become totally absorbed in his political work, and was hardly ever seen at the temple.

Kaye invited Braverman to sit down, and sat at the other end of the couch. Braverman was a tall, athletic, distinguished looking man. He had fine wavy gray hair. His expression was scholarly, always examining everything around him, always weighing his words, always listening intently. Kaye felt a certain strangeness in his presence. What made this man tick? How did he *really* feel about his Jewishness, which he did not appear particularly comfortable with? How did he feel about people? He was considered a great liberal, a civil rights activist. Yet he was part of the plutocracy. Could one make millions without taking advantage and stepping on other people? Rumor had it Hal, who was never active in temple affairs before, had bought his seat on the board by giving a one hundred thousand dollar donation for the construction of the new building.

"So," Hal Braverman started rubbing his hands and sporting an amiable smile, "have you recovered from the great onslaught of the High Holy Days?"

"Just about."

"I never quite understood how you rabbis do it. Especially on Yom Kippur. You go for twenty-four hours without any food or drink, praying non-stop, giving sermons. It must be quite an ordeal."

Kaye nodded, smiling in consent.

"How's Felicia? She is quite a girl, you know. You're a lucky man."

Kaye thanked Braverman. The man is politicking, he noted.

"Joshua, I know you're busy and I don't want to take too much of your time. The reason why I came to see you is this. I got a call today from Rabbi Blumenfeld. He says you plan to speak out on Armor & Gambit's contract with the Department of Defense."

"I was told Armor & Gambit manufactures napalm."

"This unfortunately is true."

"As a Jew, I consider it immoral."

Braverman flinched, then drew a deep breath.

"I've no business telling a rabbi what to say from the pulpit. I myself am not happy with this whole thing. I wish we could bring this whole mess in Vietnam to an end. Hopefully we will, soon. But, believe me, Joshua, there's nothing to be gained at this point by attacking Armor & Gambit. I really can't go further into it at this time, but, trust me. You'll soon find out I'm right."

"I'm sorry," said Kaye, "I can't promise you I won't speak out on this issue. Not unless I have a compelling reason not to."

Braverman stood up.

"Very well. Why don't you think about it for a day or two and give me a call."

"I hope you understand my position," Kaye said as he saw the trustee to the door.

"Quite all right," said Braverman, slapping the junior rabbi on his shoulder. "I'm sure you'll make the right decision."

He remained seated in his chair long after Braverman had left. Blumenfeld had let me down again, Kaye thought, shaking his head. Why didn't he share with me his conversation with Braverman? He knew Braverman would come to see me after he, Blumenfeld, had informed him about my intention to speak out on the napalm issue. Was he afraid to confront me with it, and, instead, chose to walk away from the problem and let the heat be turned on me?

He was about to pick up the receiver and call Felicia to let her know what happened, when he realized Felicia and he were separated. Damn! Who else could he talk to? Dr. Zamenhoff? How could he turn to his father-in-law for help when he had just informed him he wanted to be left alone? Ruth Levy? As a temple employee she was not allowed to intervene in temple politics. Blumenfeld? Blumenfeld would be the most natural person to talk to, but Blumenfeld had made it clear by his own actions he wanted to be left out of this.

He had no one to turn to.

He couldn't dismiss the Braverman affair from his mind for the rest of the afternoon, and it continued to prey on his mind when he went to bed that night. After he retired for the night, his phone rang. It was Joe Pins.

"Rabbi? Sorry to call you so late. You have a minute?"

"Sure."

"Hal Braverman called me this evening. He's quite upset about this whole business with Armor & Gambit. He really wishes you would hold off on making any comments about it from the pulpit. Believe me, Josh, it's best to leave this whole matter alone at this time."

Kaye struggled to keep calm and not raise his voice.

"It's the principle of the matter," he said in a thick voice.

There was a pause on the other end of the line.

"I respect you for your principles," Joe finally said. He spoke slowly, weighing his words. "A rabbi without principles is not a rabbi. But there has to be some give-and-take when you work with people, especially in a situation as sensitive as this one. I know it's late and I don't want to keep you on the phone. But I'd like to tell you something I never told you before. Josh, you have a great deal to offer. I have known Rabbi Blumenfeld since his early years in the pulpit. 'Silver tongue Alvin' we always used to call him. But I can honestly say that when he started out he never gave a sermon nearly half as good as the one you just gave on Rosh Hashana. What I'm getting at is this: I personally believe that you are the right man for us when Rabbi Blumenfeld retires. I'd like to see you become the next rabbi of Suburban Temple."

"I'm honored," said Kaye. He made sure he sounded deeply appreciative. He knew this man had just bestowed upon him what to him was one of the highest honors in the world. How could he possibly tell him he was not altogether sure he wanted to become the senior rabbi of Suburban Temple? He said,

"I'm supposed to get back to Hal. I'll probably be talking to him tomorrow."

He lay awake in bed late into the small hours of the night. The choice presented to him by Joe was clear: either drop the subject of Armor & Gambit or forget about his chances to stay on and become the spiritual leader of Suburban Temple. Joe respected him for his principles. He realized a rabbi without principles was no rabbi. He also made it clear what he meant by principles, without actually coming out and saying it in so many words. Why, sure, it was admirable of him to have principles, as long as he, Joe, had the last say as to when and how those principles were applied.

Perhaps it was all for the good. Why not write a letter to the board of trustees explaining the reasons why he had to speak out on this issue, and offer his resignation if the board did not uphold his decision? In a way, he would be putting the board between the rock and the hard place. How could the board go on record ordering a rabbi not to speak out on a moral issue? By upholding his position, then, the onus would be shifted from him to the board, and Braverman would have to go along. Hal might be sore, but in time he would get over it. What's more, there was an excellent opportunity to present the board with a test case. Rabbinic principles were derived from a higher authority than that of lay leaders. People like Joe and Hal might not want to recognize that fact, but he, Kaye, might force them to.

But did he really wish to fight that battle? And even if he won the battle, could he ever hope to win the war?

He remembered Sue's laughter when he told her he wanted to

change Suburban Temple. Nonsense. No one was going to make those people over. What they wanted out of a temple and what he believed a temple ought to be were two different things, poles apart. The temple, at best, was tangential to their lives. Joe and Roz, granted, had a strong bond to the temple. Not because of religious feelings but rather because it was through the temple as a social institution, founded by Roz's family, that the Pins asserted themselves as leaders in the community. Hal Braverman, on the other hand, and many others like him, saw the temple as a vehicle for personal advancement, social, economical, or political. Religion was part of the American way, so in order to keep up with the Gentiles a Jew who sought status had to belong to a synagogue. Out of two thousand member families, were there ten people at Suburban who belonged to the temple simply because of the love of God, Torah and Israel?

Then again, wasn't it his mission in life, as a rabbi, to educate those people? If he, the rabbi, quit, who was left?

To educate Jews, to teach them the love of Torah, this is what his life was all about. The temple, however, might not be the right place for this. Suburban Temple was a political institution. The synagogue had become an institution dedicated to material, rather than spiritual pursuits. Wasn't it the material and social status that attracted him to his present position in the first place? It took him three years to find out what price one had to pay for the status and the prestige. Now that he found out, what was he going to do about it?

To become prophets, Blumenfeld had proclaimed, we first have to be priests, ministering to the needs of these people. Hal Braverman needs to hide the fact that Armor & Gambit makes napalm. If I go along with him, what moral claims can I have the next time I want to speak out on an issue?

When he walked into his study in the morning Kaye found a message from Joe Pins, inviting him to lunch. Joe was more affable than the usual when they met at the restaurant, all smiles and solicitation. As soon as the waitress took their orders Joe informed Kaye he had given some serious thought to what he had told him last night about succeeding Blumenfeld. He, Joe, wanted the young rabbi to know he fully endorsed the idea of Kaye's candidacy as the next spiritual leader of Suburban Temple. Roz and he had decided to take the assistant-rabbi under their wings, so to speak, and make sure he played his cards right during the next four years,

after which time Blumenfeld would be ready to announce his retirement and the board would have to decide on a successor.

Kaye could tell what was coming.

Joe drew a deep breath.

Kaye nodded sympathetically.

Here Joe asked Kaye to keep in strictest confidence what he was
about to tell him.

There had been rumors circulating lately about Hal Braverman's
interest in the office of junior U.S. Senator from the state of Ohio.
The rumors were true. Hal had begun to enlist support within the
party, including Joe's. Joe believed Hal would make an outstanding
senator, as a liberal, as a man respected by both big business and
labor. Also as a staunch supporter of the State of Israel. It was
going to be a tough battle. To begin with, Hal had to beat Chuck
Kallahan, former governor of the state, a highly popular man.
Secondly, Ohio was traditionally a Republican state. And third,
Ohio had a relatively small Jewish population, which gave Hal's
ethnic background no edge over his opponent. Which brings us to
the question of Armor & Gambit. It would be a great embarrassment to Hal Braverman to have his own rabbi denounce the company he was associated with right before the elections.

Here Joe put a warm palm on the back of Kaye's hand. "This,
m'boy, is where *you* come into the picture. It's your big chance. Give
it some serious thought. You get my meaning, don't you?" Joe added
with a wink, signalling the waitress to bring the check.

Out in the street Joe gave the young rabbi a strong handshake,
wished him good luck, and walked briskly back toward his
downtown office.

It was a bright warm day, almost Indian summer. The streets
were crowded with shoppers, office workers, conventioners, street-
walkers, a varied swarm of humanity. Kaye drifted through the
crowd, his hands tucked in his pockets, trying to sort out his
thoughts. In spite of his disagreement with Joe, one thing he had to
admit—Joe was acting in good faith. Joe and Roz were convinced
they were his friends and had his best interest in mind. Looking at
it from their perspective, it was all very clear—Kaye now had a
golden opportunity to win Hal Braverman over to his side. It was
his turn now to be political. His future at Suburban to all intents
and purposes, would be secure.

No, thanks, Kaye thought. I did not become a rabbi in order to be
a politician, and I do not intend to be one now.

He heard someone call his name. When he turned around he saw a young woman in a blue dress. She looked at him with a shy smile.

"Remember me?"

"Oh, yes, of course."

She offered him her hand.

"Eve," she said.

"Josh," he smiled, "nice seeing you again."

"Likewise."

"How's your paper on Jewish novelists coming along?"

"I'm almost finished. I'm on my way to the public library to look up some references."

"Oh, I'm going in the same direction. You mind if I join you?"

He was actually heading in the opposite direction.

"Please do."

He felt awkward walking with a nun in downtown Quincy, almost a pickup. Thank God she was wearing an ordinary dress, not a habit.

"I was thinking about your comments on those American Jewish fictional characters," the nun was saying. "You were saying that American Jews weren't too Jewish, that they had gotten away from living according to the teachings of Judaism. It got me thinking about American Catholics, at least the sophisticated, urban variety I come in contact with. I suspect you could say most of them are not too Christian either. Perhaps the problem is not Judaism per se, but religion in general."

Kaye gave the nun a long look.

"What would you say the purpose of organized religion is?"

"To transform the individual," she replied without hesitation.

"Why, then, does it seem to fail to do it?"

She looked back at him. Again, as happened when she came to see him in his study on the morning of Sukkot, he could tell she was holding back something. She spoke in a soft voice, almost in a whisper, cool and detached, showing no emotion. When she made the remark about Catholics not being too Christian she was echoing what he had been saying all along about Jews. There was, however, one subtle difference—whenever he spoke about it (as he must have when he made his comment to her about American Jewish novelists the other day at his office), his voice would betray his emotions, no matter how hard he tried to control it. Several times Felicia had told him not to become so carried away with his feelings. "You don't hear yourself," she would say, "you sound angry. You can make the same point without raising your voice." He would disagree. When you feel strongly about something there is nothing wrong with letting your emotions show. If he, the rabbi, did not feel strongly about Judaism, who will? Now, listening to this nun make her comment about Catholics, he remembered Felicia's observation. This Sister Eve must feel just as strongly about Catholics not being too Christian as I do about Jews not being too Jewish. Yet she says it so casually, so matter of fact, as if it were part of God's plan which she, as God's servant, must accept without questioning. And yet, there was more to her comment than met the eye. This young woman was trained to speak softly, acceptingly, practice humility, charity, forgiveness. She only looked at him for a second, then cast down her eyes. She was so pale he could see blue veins on her forehead and neck. Her neck was long and slender, like a flower stem. The sun reflected in her face and through her sparse, closely cropped light hair, making her blink, and as she turned her face away from the sun her profile reminded him of a Renaissance painting of a young woman at prayer.

He felt a strange stirring. This young woman was unlike anyone he had ever met before. She was a total stranger, remote, unreachable, incomprehensible. She was the embodiment of something he had felt all his life, the personification of that otherness he had always known yet never came face to face with as he did now, so palpably, so directly. And yet she was totally familiar, almost an extension of himself, a restatement of his own person. It now occurred to him she was aware of his thoughts. They kept walking for a while without saying a word, slowly progressing through the crowd, stopping for the traffic light to change, crossing the street, passing from light into shadow and back into light again. Weaving through the crowd his shoulder lightly touched hers, and he noticed how she looked away in embarrassment. Across the street, the movie theater marquee announced,

MIDNIGHT COWBOY
starring
Jon Voigt and Dustin Hoffman

Above the marquee was a giant color poster showing a husky young man in a cowboy hat reaching down to a statuesque blonde in a flowing negligee lying at his feet in a compromising position.

"Powerful movie," Kaye remarked. "A good commentary on our contemporary society."

To his surprise she said she saw the movie a few days ago and agreed with his observation.

"It hits a sensitive spot of our American temper," she said, "our weird fascination with sex. As if sex is the answer to everything."

"Isn't it?" he said teasingly.

She gave him a grave look.

"Only kidding."

He saw her blush. She seemed to regret having made a comment about sex.

"I'm curious," he said, changing the subject, "What had prompted you to pick Jewish novelists as a subject for your paper?"

"I'm interested in Judaism," she said. "I feel I can understand my own religion better by studying the culture of the people who originated my religion. I also feel an affinity with the Jewish people. It's difficult to explain. Perhaps if I showed you my paper you will understand what I mean."

They had reached the steps leading up to the main entrance of the public library.

"Please do," he said, "I'd love to see it."

He drove back to the temple and told Blumenfeld's secretary he had to talk to his boss. As expected, Blumenfeld was not in, but he might try to reach him at home. He called Blumenfeld's house. When the senior rabbi got on the line he told him he had to see him on some urgent matter. Could he stop over for a few minutes? Come right over, his boss said.

Blumenfeld greeted him at the door and showed him into his private study. Playing the gracious host, the senior man offered his assistant a drink, which Kaye refused.

"What's up, Josh?"

"This business with Braverman," Kaye said.

"Oh, yes," Blumenfeld motioned to his younger colleague to sit down. "Hal called me this morning. He wants me to talk you out of speaking out on the Armor & Gambit issue. I told him I have never stopped any of my associates from speaking their minds from the pulpit. Freedom of the pulpit is one of the sacred tenets of Liberal Judaism, which I have always upheld. Hal lost his temper and gave me a real dressing-down. The nerve of that man! I told him I was not a child and I refused to be spoken to in that manner."

"I'm sorry," said Kaye. "You think I'm doing the wrong thing in taking this stand?"

Haunched in his leather-lined armchair, Blumenfeld knit his brow and his jowl worked.

"This matter is quite involved," he muttered, "quite involved." He looked up at his assistant over his half-lenses. "It's a real dilemma, unlike anything I have ever encountered in my long years in the pulpit. I would've liked to speak out on this issue myself, but I don't wish to harm Harold Braverman's chances of being elected to the U.S. Senate. I know this is one hell of a moral conflict. Really a no-win situation."

"Yes, it is," Kaye agreed.

As he drove home he mulled over his conversation with his boss. He could just hear Hal Braverman saying, This Joshua Kaye, who the hell he thinks he is? Does he think he is holier than the Pope? It is all right for the great Alvin Blumenfeld to keep quiet on this issue, but not for him? Wait, I will fix his wagon. We shall see how tough he is at contract time! He could also hear Roz and Joe saying to each other, It's too bad, he had the chance of a lifetime to make it straight to the top and he blew it. Well, at least he was spared having to listen to his wife. He could just imagine what her reaction would be.

✧ 5 ✧

The abdominal pain he had been getting for over a month recurred that night and again in the morning. Kaye called Dr. Perkins' office and was told to come in at 1:00 p.m.

Bill Perkins was an expert on rabbis. While attending medical school at Quincy U., Bill lived in the dormitory of the rabbinical school down the street where, in return for his services as medic-in-residence, he received free room and board. Kaye first met his future physician in the steam room of the Jewish Community Center. Bill was telling some rabbi jokes to a group of avid listeners, and when he finished he turned to Kaye and greeted him, waiting for Kaye to introduce himself. When Kaye revealed his title Dr. Perkins apologized profusely for any disrespectful references to the men of the cloth he might have made inadvertently. When Kaye mentioned the incident later on to his father-in-law, Dr. Zamenhoff laughed and told Kaye all about old Bill, who happened to be the Zamenhoffs' family physician.

Bill was the son of a Southern Baptist minister. While living at the rabbinical school he adopted many Jewish mannerisms and became known as an expert on Yiddishisms and Jewish humor. Zamenhoff showed his son-in-law a book Bill had written and published at his own expense, titled *Humor in the Bible*. Bill's thesis was that both Jews and Christians were guilty of taking the Bible too seriously when, in reality, the Good Book was rather humorous. Thus, Noah was a drunk, Abraham gave God a hard time arguing with him, Jacob was a trickster, Moses was a stutterer. The real trouble, Bill went on to say, started with the New Testament. The Old Jewish Testament was at least open and honest about the faults and foibles of its characters, while the Christian one went out of its way to make its characters look like marble statues devoid of human failings. Bill, Zamenhoff summed up his assessment of Dr. Perkins, albeit a rather offbeat character given to hyperbole and bravado, was nonetheless a big hearted man and a thoroughly dedicated physician who thought nothing of making a house call in the middle of the night and to whom rich and poor, the high and the lowly were all equals.

Kaye could hear Bill's booming voice through the office door. No doubt he was lecturing some patient about failing to take care of himself. Presently an old man came out of the office looking like a schoolboy who had just been reprimanded by his principal. The nurse came in and told Kaye to go into the examination room and strip from the waist down. She left him perched on the examination table in a rather unrabbinic posture, and, assuring him Dr. Perkins would be with him in a minute, walked out.

Dr. Perkins did not open the door but rather flung it wide open. His conical bald head, barrel chest, and mischievous, smile-wrinkled crystal blue eyes made Kaye think of the T.V. commercial of Mr. Clean. The doctor held out two hairy arms in a gesture of welcome and bared his smoke stained teeth.

"Joshua Kaye! I'm truly honored!"

Kaye wondered whether the Zamenhoffs' family doctor knew about the separation.

"Well, Josh," Dr. Perkins blurted out, then suddenly lowered his voice, looking Kaye straight in the eye. You know I'm mad at you."

"I swear I'm innocent," Kaye said.

"Shame on you, rabbi! You know you're not supposed to swear."

"Sorry."

"Listen, I haven't seen you at the health club at least since last Pesach. Anything wrong?"

"Everything's fine."

"Then why are you here?"

"Oh, yes. This thing started a few days ago. I keep getting these abdominal pains. I also felt dizzy a few times. It feels like my system is off."

Dr. Perkins ordered his patient down on his back and began to examine him, pressing his flesh with deft fingers which belied the man's bearlike appearance.

"Where does it hurt?"

"Right here," Kaye pointed beneath his navel.

"I see. Okay. I'll order the tests. Upper and lower G.I. You'll have to go down to Good Sam tomorrow morning without fail."

"Whatever you say, doc."

"Good. Now put on your pants and give my best to the Zamenhoffs and that old gizzard, your boss, what's his name? In the meantime take it easy, don't overtax yourself. I'll let you know about the results in a couple of days."

He spent the next morning in the X-ray department of Good Samaritan Hospital, swallowing barium cocktails and stretching himself on the cold metal surface of the X-ray table, naked except for a short hospital gown, having his insides photographed. Two days later he was summoned to Dr. Perkins' office.

"Well, boychik," Bill Perkins roared, "what would you like to hear first, the good news or the bad news?"

"The good news."

"Okay. The good news is, you're going to live. The bad news, you have what appears to be a mild form of regional ileitis."

"Meaning?"

"You're a typical rabbi," the older man sighed and shook his head, "always asking questions." He leaned back in his swivel chair and puffed on his cigarette, studiously dropping the ash in the waste basket.

Cut out the theatrics and get to the point, Kaye thought.

"In simple medical terms, ileitis is an inflammation of the small intestine. What causes it, medical science is yet to find out. For lack of a better answer, it is caused by some germ or virus which is yet to be isolated. So much for the medical jargon, which, as you can see, tells us very little. And now for Dr. Perkins' theory, based upon twenty-five years of experience of working specifically with rabbis, dozens of them. Now, you will be surprised to learn how many rabbis suffer from one form or another of intestinal disorders. Are rabbis generically exposed to the same germ? Of course not. What are rabbis exposed to? Congregations, of course. What do congregations do to rabbis? To use the old Jewish expression, eat out their *kishkes*. That's right. They put you guys under such stress, they force you to internalize so much, they make you play the nice guy, always smiling, always ready to please, when all the while you eat out your insides, and, sooner or later, your insides begin to strike back. Now, what is the cure for ileitis? I'm going to put you on a bland diet, and I'm going to prescribe some sulpha tablets. But most important, I would like you to start learning how to relax. You better listen to old Bill. You must take a solemn vow not to let those bastards get to you from here on out. This time you may have gotten off cheap, only a mild case of regional ileitis. In a few weeks you may forget you ever had it. But if you let them get to you it will get worse, much worse.

Easier said than done, Kaye reflected.

"How 're things at home?" the doctor asked.

"Felicia and I are having some difficulties."

"You don't want to talk about it?"

"I don't want to take too much of your time."

"Don't worry about my time. Go ahead."

"Felicia and I are going through a difficult period. I suppose in the early years of marriage this is bound to happen."

"I see."

"Felicia is staying with her parents till we work things out."

"So what do you plan to do"

"I'm not sure."

"Have you spoken to Dr. Zamenhoff?"

"We've met once. We're going to meet again next week."

Dr. Perkins wrote out the prescription, then stood up and stretched. Kaye got up and waited for further instructions.

"Here," the doctor handed him the prescription. Thinking for a moment, he said,

"Josh, I'm talking to you like I'm talking to my own son. Felicia is a tough cooky. You need a tough cooky to look after you. You're not such an easy person to live with, you know. You're a dreamer. You don't always have your feet on the ground. And now you've started to hurt yourself physically. I believe your kind of ailment is basically self-inflicted. If you want to get better you must take a hard look at yourself and see to it that you stop hurting yourself, if you don't mind my saying so."

No, he didn't mind the advice. He was not sure, though, he was prepared to accept everything Old Bill had propounded. Granted, he had let things get to him. Suburban Temple might not be the right place for him. Yes, he was a dreamer. He was not willing to accept things the way they were. No, thanks, he was not about to change. What he had to learn was how to continue to stand up for what he believed without making himself sick in the process. Yes, Felicia was a tough cooky all right. But Felicia and he were obviously having some very serious disagreements. He was not about to compromise himself because she wanted him to. Or because Blumenfeld wanted him to. Or Joe Pins. Or Hal Braverman. Or anyone.

Going through his mail at his temple study that afternoon Kaye found a letter written in a neat yet firm handwriting on light blue stationery. Attached to the letter was a typewritten college paper titled "The Jew As an American Fictional Hero," by Sister Eve Gruner, HHM. The letter read:

Dear Rabbi,

It was good seeing you downtown the other day. Once again I would like to thank you for sharing so much of your time with me on Sukkot morning. It is not often that someone you meet for the first time is willing to be so open and share so much with you. This is especially true when it comes to nun, who for some reason or another seems to put people on their guard, almost as if she were a creature from another world, which of course she isn't. It is also true about the few contacts I have had with Jewish laymen and rabbis. You are the first rabbi I have met so far who has not felt constrained to make me feel as though we were on opposite sides of the fence. I'd like to thank you for being a person and letting me be one.

What I really wanted to say is that it is always a welcome revelation to realize that others have similar insights, similar reactions. And though I feel stupid when I consider all I have to learn and understand, and somewhat backward when I sense the limited experience of my life, I'm encouraged when someone else lets me see a little into their own depth and expands the vision for you... I believe there is a unity more real than all the religious distinctions we make. That is why I want to know Judaism more thoroughly and why I feel there is such a need to share our experience of God...

I've taken the liberty of enclosing my paper on the American Jewish Fictional Hero. I may expand it later on into my master thesis. As you can see, I have devoted most of my discussion to Bernard Malamud's masterpiece, *The Assistant*. I'm sure it will come to you as a surprise that I consider Frank Alpine, the Italian drifter, who on the last page of the book converts to Judaism, the major Jewish hero (or antihero?) of the book, rather than Morris Bober, the old Jewish grocer. Bober *happens* to be a Jew. He is the proverbial Jewish *schlemazel* (or is it *schlumiel*?), an old fashioned Jewish victim in the old East European tradition. Frank Alpine, on the other hand, chooses to become a Jew not because of religious dogma but because he feels he had become part of the Jewish fate and because he is in love with Bober's daughter. There is a biblical dimension here. Frank reminds me of Jacob, also a drifter, a man who is forced to live by his wits. Jacob works for Laban because he wants to marry Laban's daughter, Rachel. Similarly, Frank works for Bober because he is in love with Bober's daughter, Helen. Jacob becomes Israel, the Jewish patriarch, after he wrestles with the angle of God, and Frank becomes a Jew after his long struggle with himself and with the harsh reality around him.

So much for my biblical expertise. I guess my own understanding of what a Jew is—and this is what I believe Malamud was trying to say in his story—is that being a Jew is more than just being a member of a certain religious or ethnic group. Frank Alpine—a drifter, a stranger, a man alienated from himself and from others, a man desperate for love, family, community—represents the Jewish condition which is, ultimately, the human condition carried to its extreme.

Sorry for such a long-winded letter. I have a light load at St. John's this semester—only one course—and an idle hand writes long letters. I trust all is well at Suburban Temple, and I hope we will have a chance to see each other again. Take care,

Shalom,
Eve

He sat there for a long time watching the trees in the parking lot outside shed their few remaining brown leaves. The leaves swirled on the ground like tiny cyclones and got caught in the picket fence which had already been put up against the winter snowdrifts. He thought about his chance encounter with that shy nun the other day after his lunch with Joe Pins. No, it couldn't be. And yet, why not? Back in his study on Sukkot morning he already had that feeling, yet he quickly dismissed it as an absurd fantasy. When he walked her to the library after that chance encounter it came back, more vivid than before. Again he had suppressed it. And now this letter. No, it was not an ordinary letter. It was not Frank Alpine she was talking about. She was talking about herself, and she was talking about him, the disaffected rabbi. She was talking about the two of them. But what was she saying? What was she driving at?

She wanted to know Judaism more thoroughly. But why? What honorable intentions could a Catholic nun have toward Jews? He thought of all those Catholic nuns he had seen at the Sukkot Interfaith service. What an absurd spectacle that was! All those different habits, the medallions, the crucifixes. All those different orders, half of them a throwback to the Middle Ages, and the other half—like Eve's—a lame effort to catch up to the twentieth century by changing outward appearances. She complained about people, especially Jews, not being at ease in her presence. How could they? How could a Jew begin to make sense out of marrying off a healthy young woman to the Son of God? Jews had enough trouble with the idea of God having a son in the first place. But this at least could be dismissed as an abstract belief which one could accept or reject. This here, however, was no abstraction. This was a flesh and blood young woman who was going to spend the rest of her life believing and expecting others to believe she was married to God, set apart from the rest of mankind in a way that contradicted the natural law and defied human understanding.

This young woman, this Sister Eve, was reaching out to him in a way which puzzled and mystified him. What was it about him that attracted her? Was it the rabbi, the Jew, or was it the man? Was it really her own experience of God, as she put it, that she wanted to share with him, or was it something else?

There was a knock on the door. He heard Rabbi Blumenfeld's voice, asking whether he could come in. He got up and opened the door and let the senior rabbi into his study.

Blumenfeld plopped into the vinyl sofa and motioned to his younger colleague to sit down.

"I spoke to Hal Braverman," Blumenfeld came right to the point. "I told him I couldn't censor another rabbi's sermon, not even my own assistant. He told me I had to make an exception this once. We went back and forth for a few days. He wouldn't take no for an answer. So at this point I can only tell you we are at an impasse."

"Hal must be quite upset."

"Quite. Hal, as you know, is a very strong-headed fellow. He has researched this whole question quite thoroughly. He even looked up Talmudic statements on the morality of war and tried to prove to me that there is a time when a rabbi is not supposed to speak out on this issue.

Kaye chuckled. "I didn't know Hal was a Talmudic scholar."

"He is not. But he happens to be one of the most powerful Jews in America. If he is elected to the United States Senate he will become even more powerful. The Pins, as you know, are deeply involved in his campaign, as are several other influential members of our board of trustees. This is a hell of a time to get on Hal's wrong side."

"You won't be personally affected by this, would you?" Kaye inquired.

"No, I won't. I have a lifetime contract. Hal may get back at me by withdrawing his contribution to our new museum, which may force us to cancel our plans. But he can't touch me."

"Well, I don't have a lifetime contract," Kaye said, "and I'm beginning to put two and two together."

The older rabbi knit his brow. From the way his lower lip jutted Kaye could tell the two of them were thinking alike.

"I don't know what to say, Josh. But it certainly wouldn't hurt to take a look at your options."

"I was going to anyway." Kaye said.

The senior man was taken by surprise.

"Oh?"

"I haven't had a chance to discuss it with you. But I've been thinking about it, oh, for several months. It is precisely the kind of attitude of people like Harold Braverman that has made me wonder whether I'm the right man for this job. This institution is a far cry from what they'd taught me about rabbis and synagogues in rabbinical school. I suppose an institution like Suburban Temple is necessary. Mostly in a political sense. It gives Jews in America political clout. It also provides leadership for Jewish philanthropy, which is perhaps the main function of American Jewry vis-a-vis world Jewry, particularly Israel. Who knows. Perhaps organized religion to a certain extent has to be political. But the kind of Judaism I was taught in rabbinical school and have come to believe

in does not sacrifice the soul of the individual person for political
ends. Here at Suburban Temple we do a fine job reaching people's
pockets, but do we reach their souls? Look at Roz and Joe's
daughter, Sue. She has turned her back on us. She went to live on a
Bahai commune somewhere on the West Coast. After all we have
tried to teach her here in our Hebrew school she turns to another
faith."

Kaye paused, realizing he was becoming emotional. Lowering his
voice, he said,

"The purpose of religion, as a Catholic nun I met recently has
put it to me, is the transformation of the individual. How have we
succeeded in transforming our people's lives?"

Rabbi Blumenfeld studied his assistant for a moment.

"Your question, obviously, is rhetorical."

"Yes and no. I'd love to be proven wrong."

"Well," Blumenfeld cleared his throat, "I'm not going to try to
prove you wrong. In fact, I was smiling before because as I was listening to you you reminded me of myself when I was your age. As
you very well know, I have fought my own battles. I haven't been
exactly what you might call a yesman. I'm not pretending to be
some kind of a hero or martyr, but, after all, we both come from the
same school. Have the years made me wiser? I don't really know.
But the years have taught me this: some problems don't go away.
They only get older. Everything you have said about Suburban
Temple is unfortunately true. And, certainly, Suburban is not atypi-
cal, only in some ways it is more so because it is richer and bigger
than most. This is how religious institutions are today, and this is
what the rabbinate is like. Yes, I know. Our school has taught us to
follow in the footsteps of the prophets. To tell our flock what an officer in the Israeli army tells his men, *acharay*, follow me! Our
people, sadly enough, are not too anxious to follow. Hal Braverman
doesn't want to follow, he wants to lead, not only as a senator from
the state of Ohio, but also as an expert on Judaism, which of course
he is not. Our youth today rejects the institutions of their elders.
They believe in some brave new world which does not exist, except
perhaps in drug induced hallucinations, false promises by gurus
and faith healers, and the deafening noise of rock music. So where
do we, their so-called spiritual leaders, fit into the picture? It's not
very clear, not clear at all. We do the best we can, I suppose, and we
pray a little. But when all is said and done, we have to say to ourselves, yes, I want to be a rabbi, whatever that means, or, no, this is
not for me, I'm opting out."

"Which is precisely what I'm trying to decide," Kaye confirmed.

He was greatly relieved after the senior rabbi had walked out of his study. He had finally brought himself to tell Blumenfeld how he felt about Suburban Temple and the rabbinate. In a way he was glad things had turned out the way they did with Braverman. This way it became very clear where everyone stood, and there was no longer any need to play games. These people did not want a rabbi. They wanted a master of ceremonies. They did not want Judaism to make any demands on them. They wanted it to suit itself to their own purposes, whatever those purposes might be. Every rabbi, these rich Jews seemed to think, had his price. Well, let him find out here was one rabbi they couldn't buy.

Later that evening when he went home after teaching a post Bar Mitzvah class there were some snow flurries in the air, and the forecast called for an inch of snow by morning, the first snowfall of the year. When he woke up in the morning, however, and looked outside he found out there was no snow. Instead, it was a mild, sun flooded day, with hardly a cloud in the sky. He felt expansive, ready to take on the world. Blumenfeld had suggested he look at his options. He might do just that. Taking his coffee out on the balcony, he looked at the city down below and for the first time it occurred to him he would soon be putting Quincy behind him. By next June, if not sooner, he would be moving on. Where to? It didn't matter. Wherever his calling would take him. What was his calling? He was yet to find out.

He dictated some letters to his secretary in the morning. Before noon he decided to go to the JCC for a swim. For the first time in two weeks he put down the convertible top. He was savoring the gold and blue autumn day as he drove down West Boulevard and swung into Brenton Woods. At the main intersection before turning right on Clinton Road he saw a small sign with an arrow, *To St. John's College*. Wasn't that Sister Eve's school? The school was right there over the hill behind the woods. Why not go over and see if she was there?

He was surprised by his urge to go and see that nun. Didn't he have anything better to do? He hadn't been to the health club in months. He had finally brought himself to go, and now this nun? What in the world for?

Overruling his own objections, he turned left and followed the sign to St. John's. It was a small campus, and in no time he found the English department. He asked for the class in Contemporary American Lit, and was directed to a classroom down the hall. The class was still in session. He waited in the hallway when he remembered Roz Pins was in the same class. He was not about to be seen there by Roz. He walked into an empty classroom and sat in the corner, discreetly out of view. Moments later the class was dismissed. He could see the backs of the students as they passed by. He saw Roz leaving in her usual quick gait. The students were gone, but no Sister Eve. He walked out into the hall and back to the American Lit classroom. The teacher was still there, talking to a student. When the teacher, a tall broad shouldered middle aged man, moved to one side, he saw the student was Sister Eve.

He waited outside the door. She was thanking her professor for his help. The professor gave a small bow and turned to leave. She collected her books and followed him outside. As she passed by he tapped her on her arm. Surprised, she turned around, and when she recognized him she smiled knowingly, as if she had been expecting him.

"Oh, hello."

"Hello there."

She was wearing a white blouse, short blue skirt, and a long bulky blue sweater. Her only religious sign was a small silver medallion. Her face was flushed. She was visibly happy to see him. She pressed her books against her chest as the two of them stood there, smiling embarrassedly at each other, not sure what to say.

Overcoming his embarrassment, he said,

"Well, I happened to pass by and I decided to stop and see you. I hope you don't mind."

No, she didn't mind at all. She was glad he did.

"I read your paper. I thought it was very good."

She thanked him for his kindness.

For the first time he could tell she was not being formal with him. She had let her guards down. This nun mask had all but come off. She was a person. Eve. An American Lit student. A young woman in her early twenties. An avid reader with a questioning mind who was asking questions similar to his. She was glad to see him because she had been waiting for a long time for someone like him to come along. A like-minded person. A kindred spirit. Someone who felt the way she did about the things she cared about. There was no need to say it. All those feelings were transmitted without words, in one brief moment, standing in that hallway, seeing that smile in her eyes and feeling his breath quicken, making it hard for the words to come out.

"What are you doing for lunch? he finally came out with it.

She had no special plans.

"Is the cafeteria here acceptable?"

She laughed. Yes, quite.

He laughed, putting his arm around her waist and leaning his head against hers. Her body received his touch passively, without responding. Touching her he could tell she was wearing a hard girdle under her short skirt. He recalled reading somewhere about those chastity belts women in Medieval Europe were made to wear when their husbands were away. Well, underneath it all she was a nun after all.

"You're funny," she said, laughing again.

"I feel funny," he said, "a rabbi and a nun. We sure make a fine pair."

The air outside was cool, but as they crossed the campus they were greeted by warm sunshine.

"Beautiful day," they both said at the same time.

"Jinx," she laughed.

He spat three times on the grass.

"Against the evil eye," he explained.

"You don't. . ."

"No, of course not. Just being facetious."

She suggested getting some sandwiches and going outside for a little picnic. He thought it was a splendid idea. After he paid the cashier he found an empty cardboard box on the cafeteria counter and fashioned it into a picnic basket. He followed his picnic-partner outside, across the parking lot and down the football field to where the woods started. As he followed her he remembered how unattractive he thought she was when he first met her on Sukkot morning in his office. She sure had fooled him, standing there with downcast eyes, pale and sickly looking in her plain blue dress, talking in a whisper. Was it the same person? As he followed her across the field she moved gracefully, like a gazelle, he thought, light and swift and radiant. Eve. The first woman. The helpmate. The temptress. The beloved. The cursed. A nun! Yes, that's right, a nun of all things! How ludicrous! How absurd!

God help me, he thought, I'm falling in love with a nun.

They had reached a small clearing out on the edge of the woods. She took off her long sweater and laid it down on the ground and sat down on it. He sat next to her on the ground and took the food and the drinks out of the box.

They ate in silence. Looking at her from the corner of his eye he could tell she was deep in thought.

"You look sad," he said, "anything wrong?"

Her chest rose and fell.

"What's the matter?"

She looked at him. There were tears in her eyes.

"Nothing," she said, smiling through her tears. "Really I'm fine."

She looked down, smoothing her skirt over her knees, then raised her eyes and looked up at the blue patch of sky above the trees.

He moved back and sat up.

"I hope I'm not causing you any trouble."

"Oh, no. I'm so glad you came. I'm sure you have more important things to do right now. I really feel silly having talked you into coming out here and spending all this time with me."

He drew closer and looked into her eyes.

"I'm the one who feels silly," he said. "You know, I keep thinking to myself, I've never before in my life spoken two words to a nun. I should be feeling very awkward right now, and, in a way, I do. But, there's something about you which makes me feel very close to you, and I'm not sure what it is. We're different. But there's something which attracts me to you, and, I suspect, there's something which attracts you to me. So you write me this letter and I come out here to see you and here we are on this beautiful day having this lovely picnic and we sit here afraid to tell each other what's really on our minds. Am I right?"

She agreed, nodding in consent.

"Well?"

"It's about my friends," she said, looking down. She paused, as though finding it difficult to go on. "The other sisters." She looked at him and he could see the pain in her eyes. "And it's about my struggle with my own beliefs. I don't know, I guess it is mainly my own fault. I must be expecting too much out of life, out of people. I take things too seriously when I should be more accepting and forgiving."

"What about the other sisters?"

"No one thing in particular. I guess it's all that pettiness, the lack of sensitivity, and especially the lack of a sense of purpose, which has been getting to me. I've been very disillusioned for a long time. Lately I've become very depressed and I have even considered suicide on one or two occasions. I've wanted to be a nun since I was a little girl. Maybe this is part of the problem. I've always idolized priests and nuns. They were steady guests in our house when I was little, and I always looked up to them and thought they were perfect, or pretty near perfect. Of course when I got older I realized they had faults like everyone else, but subconsciously I continued to idolize them. When I entered the order I must have made a total emotional commitment. Of course I was very young and naive. For over a year now I've been feeling very isolated, very much alone, not part of the religious community of sisters. This is what started me reading about Judaism. I felt a spiritual kinship with Jews because I saw them as being alone in a hostile world, and I found myself identifying with their plight and their constant questioning, of themselves, of the world, and, ultimately, of God."

"Have you considered leaving the order?"

"Yes, many times."

"Are you going to?"

"I'm not sure."

"I'm seriously considering leaving the pulpit," Kaye said. "I'm no longer sure organized religion is where God is."

She looked down and remained silent. The blue patch about the trees had turned gray and it grew cold. They gathered the remains of the picnic and got up to leave.

"When will I see you again?" Kaye asked.

"You can call me at the convent," Sister Eve said, "If I'm not in you can leave a message and I will get back to you as soon as I can."

✧ 6 ✧

Dr. Zamenhoff shook his son-in-law's hand. The handshake was friendly yet tense.

"Sit down, Josh, sit down. Make yourself comfortable. You and I haven't had a good chat in a long time. You look thin. Have you lost weight?"

"Probably. Haven't had too much home cooking lately."

"That's right, that's right."

"How is Felicia?"

"She is doing okay, considering."

"The baby?"

"The baby is wonderful. A real boy. Full of mischief. I bet you miss him."

"Yes, I do."

The professor looked haggard. It's no picnic having Felicia and the baby at home, Kaye thought.

"I know certain things are bothering you," Dr. Zamenhoff said, clearing his throat. He was a small, bald, fair skinned man in his mid-sixties. He had a prominent nose, thin, sensitive lips, and small, eager, good natured eyes. Kaye could tell he was straining to appear calm. As a scholar and teacher, Dr. Zamenhoff was strong willed, argumentative, authoritarian. As husband and father, however, he was self-effacing, meek, indecisive. His mental energies, it seemed, were totally spent on his rigorous intellectual pursuits. When it came to domestic affairs, he was at the mercy of the formidable Mrs. Z., who was proud of her status as wife of the eminent professor and enjoyed babying her husband. Prominent in stature, jovial, and a chain-smoker, Kaye's mother-in-law reveled in her favorite role of hostess, known for her Friday night and holiday dinners, always attended by students, faculty, friends, and an occasional Jewish celebrity passing through town. Her nemesis, however, was Felicia. Felicia seemed to bear a grudge against her mother, which Kaye attempted to analyze many times, finally arriving at the conclusion that Felicia felt her mother's real child was her husband, while she, Felicia, was left out of her parents' affection. She was awed by her father, and had repressed her resentment against him. Her mother she resented openly, and the relation between mother and daughter was continuous warfare with an occasional ceasefire during which the adversaries would prepare for the next round. Kaye could imagine what it must have been like at the Zamenhoffs' household since the day his estranged wife went back to stay with her parents.

His father-in-law paused, weighing his words.

"I'm talking to you as a friend, Josh, not as Felicia's father. You and Felicia will have to work out your differences. I don't want to prejudge, but, personally, I feel you are very well suited for each other. Again, you two will have to come to a decision. But regardless of what you decide to do, I would like you to always consider me your friend."

"I appreciate it."

"I would like you to know you will continue to be my son-in-law, my grandson's father, no matter what happens."

Kaye nodded. They both remained silent.

"How about a little schnapps?"

Kaye did not know his father-in-law kept liquor in his office.

"Sure."

The professor produced two small glasses from a cabinet behind his desk and a bottle of J&B.

"*L'chaim*, Josh, to your health."

"*L'chaim*."

Closing his eyes, Dr. Zamenhoff downed his drink, then smacked his lips and sighed contentedly, blood quickening in his cheeks.

"How are things at Suburban Temple?"

"I had a long talk with Blumenfeld the other day," said Kaye. "I told him in essence I thought the rabbinate was a sham, and I was seriously considering leaving the pulpit."

"I see."

"Someone, of course, has to do it. Someone has to give sermons and try to teach Torah. The fact is, no one today really listens to sermons, and hardly anyone is interested in studying Torah. Someone else may find this situation acceptable. Not I."

"I don't blame you," the professor said, scratching the stubble on his chin. "What you are saying is unfortunately true. Here and there, there are small groups of Jews who try to study Torah and live Judaism. Perhaps they are the *she'erit ha'pleita*, the saving remnant, who knows. But I can see how an institution like Suburban Temple can hammer the soul out of an idealistic young rabbi like yourself. You may recall, Josh, shortly before your ordination I had suggested to you to go on with your studies and work on a PhD. You said at the time you had been going to school for too long, and now the time had come for you to go out into the world and find out what the real world was like. Well, now you have found out. I'm sure the experience you have gained is invaluable. You have learned something about the world and about yourself as well. You may very well be able to make a much greater contribution by pursuing scholarship and teaching rather than work in the pulpit."

Solomon Zamenhoff gave his son-in-law a long, searching look. He leaned forward across his desk as if about to share his ultimate secret.

"Listen. American Jewry is in critical condition, right? Okay. Now, you, Joshua Kaye, are truly concerned about the future of Judaism, right? What has saved Judaism during the last two thousand years? Learning, scholarship, *talmud torah*! I say to you, if American Jewry in the next ten, twenty years can produce a few top notch Judaic scholars, a Rabbi Akiva, a Rashi, a Maimonides, we will have won the battle. In my book you are a serious candidate for this exclusive club!"

"Thank you," Kaye said, "I hope you are not overestimating me. Well, you may be right. Perhaps I ought to look into furthering my studies. I will give your suggestion some serious thought. Yes, I did want to go out into the world three years ago. Now it seems I have found more questions than answers. Are the answers here, in this institution of higher learning, or are the answers out there in the world? This is what I need to find out before I make any decisions."

After he left Zamenhoff's office Kaye felt light-headed and somewhat wobbly from the drink. He buttoned up his wintercoat and thrust his hands in his pockets and started to roam the snow covered grounds of the rabbinical seminary. The seminary campus perched on the crest of a hill. The front side overlooked Brenton Road and the edge of the sprawling campus of Quincy U. The back side bordered on an abrupt drop in the hillside which ended in a deep ravine running out of sight several hundred feet below in the general direction of the Ohio River. The other side of the ravine was a vast, barren cluster of hills which formed an uneven skyline. Nestling in those hills against the skyline was the old, austere, red brick building of the Sisters of the Holy Humility of Mary, the Lourdes Convent. While attending rabbinical school, Kaye now recalled, he and his friends used to take walks down the hill and along the ravine. On one such walk they ran into a group of nuns from the convent up the hill. The nuns, all young, were laughing and frolicking. When they saw the rabbinical students they all fell silent and stood off to one side while Kaye and his friends passed by. Looking back he realized that ravine was more than a physical space separating the two institutions. It was a state of mind. Over there, behind the hills, was Cliffwood, an old working class Catholic neighborhood. He had driven through Cliffwood once or twice, taking a shortcut on his way back to school from downtown Quincy. The most imposing buildings in Cliffwood were the Catholic church, the parochial school, and the convent. It was the other Quincy, of Polish and Irish and Italian Americans, the other America.

The Cliffwood convent was Eve's home. Her convent was separated from his rabbinical seminary by a ravine and by an ideological chasm. And yet at that moment, milling about the grounds of the seminary, he felt closer to her than to any other person in the world. Not Eve the Catholic nun. Rather Eve who, like himself, had come to realize her religion did not have the answers. Her institutions had let her down. Eve who felt isolated, alone, drifting, as he did. Go back to school and work on a PhD? Become a scholar like his father-in-law? He was not sure he agreed with Zamenhoff's thesis. Granted, scholarship was of paramount importance. It was the lifeblood of Judaism. He loved and revered the study of Torah, and he held people like his father-in-law in high esteem. But what good was Torah if it did not reach the masses of Jews out in the world, if Jews did not live Torah? Learning without deed was like a tree which gave forth beautiful flowers without producing any fruit. The teachings of Zamenhoff and his colleagues failed to touch and transform the lives of Jews. This rabbinical seminary where for five years Kaye had pored over the pages of Torah, Talmud and Kabalah, over the teachings of Jewish scholars and sages and poets, now, three years later, seemed so completely removed from reality. And over there, across the ravine in that austere looking convent, a young Catholic nun had found out that her own faith had failed to transform her life and did not bear the fruit she had dreamed of and hoped for.

Kaye felt a shiver run through his bones. All those years of study. All those high hopes and aspirations now come to naught. A gray sky hung overhead, gray and alien, as if he had never seen it before. He trudged slowly across the snow, leaving the seminary grounds. He got into his car and started the engine and turned on the heat. Despite the heat, the shiver came back, making his teeth chatter. His stomach tightened and convulsed. Where did he go form here? Get in touch with Felicia? Let her know he was seriously considering leaving Suburban Temple and would like to know whether she wished to give the marriage a second chance? Felicia would probably think he was crazy to give up his position at Suburban Temple. No, Felicia was not ready to deal with all of this. She was too wrapped up in their present life which, unbeknownst to her, was now coming to an end. Felicia was too much a part of those seven years of his life in Quincy, of the seminary and Suburban Temple and all those big dreams and high hopes which he now knew were coming to an end.

Part Two

Sister Eve

✧ 7 ✧

Several times that week he was about to pick up the phone and call the convent but decided against it. What was he going to say? Hello, this is Rabbi Kaye. May I speak to Sister Eve? His voice would have betrayed his true intentions. He had a great need to talk to her. There was so much between them that was left unsaid the other day at the clearing on the edge of the woods. She had started to confide in him, and he was anxious to tell her more about himself, about the letter of resignation he was about to write, and especially about his separation from Felicia.

He finally decided to write her a note to find out where and when he could see her. As he started to write many questions came to his mind and soon the note grew into a lengthy epistle. He started out by saying he hoped she considered him her friend. He had a very special feeling for her. He felt he could talk to her more freely and openly than he could to any of his close friends. Yet, on the other hand, the more he thought about it the more he realized how little he understood her, her life, her beliefs, whatever it was that made her tick. Frankly, as a Jew, he failed to understand how an attractive young woman could be removed from the world, cloistered in a place like Lourdes Convent, and be considered married to God's son. He hoped she was not offended by his questions. The only reason he allowed himself to raise them was because he felt special closeness to her and wished to understand her and know her better. Of course she did not have to answer any of those questions if she found them inappropriate. From talking to her the other day he could see she had her own doubts and misgivings. That made two of them. And that made him feel even closer to her and more anxious to see her again.

After he mailed the letter he started having some qualms about what he had written. Was he being too forward with her? Would she take offense at what he had written?

Later that week as he walked into his study at Suburban Temple to make arrangements for cancelling adult education classes for that evening because of an imminent snow storm, he found a letter in an envelope marked Lourdes Convent. He tore it open and read it through standing behind his desk. She wrote:

Dear Josh:

The feelings are mutual. I'm taking the liberty of addressing you by your first name because I too feel we have a very special kind of relationship. And, at the same time, I too am having conflicts over the relationship, and the fact that I told you things about myself which I haven't told anyone else. I don't know what prompted me to do it. I certainly didn't wish to burden you with my personal problems. You started to say you were considering leaving the pulpit. I would like to know more about it. Is the decision final?

I'm writing in a hurry because I'm on my way to a religious retreat and I'm being picked up in about an hour. It's a beautiful place about two hours ride from here in the hills of Kentucky, and I'm looking forward to it. I'll be back Monday night and I'll call you as soon as I get back to see when we can get together. You raised questions in your letter which are too difficult to discuss in a letter, especially when one is in a rush. I can certainly understand your perplexity. Why would someone like me choose to give up the things of the world for the monastic life? One certainly would not be inclined to do such a thing unless one believed that the reward was worth the sacrifice. As for being married to Christ, this I must confess I'm having great difficulties with. How am I supposed to come to terms with the idea of being married to a man who lived and died two thousand years ago? And if we call this man God, how can I be so presumptuous as to believe I'm actually married to God? What does this make me? A divinity? And yet I chose this life and have accepted those beliefs. I'll let you figure it out.

Take care, hope to see you soon,
Eve

When he left the temple that afternoon the snow had begun to pile up on the roads. He had to shift into low gear and make his way slowly through the hazardous traffic, hardly able to see through the iced and fogged up windshield. When he finally got home he was worn out. He felt listless, out of sorts. During the ten o'clock news he fell asleep. He woke up a five o'clock in the morning

with a strange sensation in his bowels. Half asleep, he staggered in
the dark and groped his way to the toilet. Presently he realized he
was losing blood. The hemorrhaging recurred several times during
the early morning hours. He called up Dr. Perkins' office. The nurse
told him to stay on the line. Dr. Perkins was with a patient and she
was going to see if she could get him to the phone. As he stood there
holding the receiver he felt wobbly, and he sat down to steady himself. His mind drifted as he waited, when, in a haze, he heard the
doctor's booming voice. He told Perkins about the bleeding and
asked him what he thought it was. His physician responded with
his usual "there's nothing to worry about," and ordered a blood test.
He told Kaye to call Dr. Cass, the gastroenterologist, for an ap-
pointment. Kaye could tell Bill was holding back something. What
was it? What did this sudden bleeding signify?

He was too weak to drive to the doctor's office. He called City
Taxi Service and ordered a cab. He then called his secretary to let
her know he was not coming in. Ruth insisted he let her drive him
to the doctor's office. She picked him up and drove him to Dr. Cass's
office and waited until he was called in for his tests. The nurse took
a blood sample and prepared him for a proctoscopy, strapping him
down to a reclining table. Dr. Cass, a short bouncy round-faced
man, came in and peered at him through thick glasses and
proceeded to explain what a proctoscopy entailed. He was going to
examine his insides and put him through some discomfort. He
wanted Rabbi Kaye to let him know when it started to get too uncomfortable so he could stop. Kaye nodded, steeling himself.

As soon as the examination was over, Kaye was told to see Dr.
Cass in the adjoining office. The doctor was seated behind his desk
jotting down his report. He stopped writing and looked up at his
patient. The proctoscopy did not reveal the cause of the bleeding,
which might have originated further up in the small intestine. He
was sorry he could not be more specific. All he knew at this point
was that Kaye had lost too much blood and had become anemic. He
was arranging to have him admitted into Good Samaritan Hospital.

He had never been hospitalized before. Later that afternoon
when Ruth came back to drive him over to the hospital he did not
let her in on his feelings, keeping a calm exterior. A vivid, overpowering feeling came over him: he was seeing the outside world
for the last time. It had started snowing again, a light, soft, pow-
dery snow, coming down slowly, glistening like millions of tiny
diamonds. Ruth's face glowed with a silvery, otherwordly light as
she drove silently, intently. His insides throbbed and his vision

blurred. A total, cosmic calm descended upon him. So be it. He was about to leave this world. It may all be for the good. Was he having visions of another life, another place, a place without conflicts and pain, of perfect harmony and peace? Yes, he was ready. He had no regrets. And then he was seized by an overwhelming desire: to see Eve. See her one more time. Tell her he knew there was a better world and he was going to meet her there. Of that he was certain.

Ruth had to help him out of the car. A black orderly came over pushing a wheelchair. He helped him into the chair and wheeled him into the lobby. At the admission office a plastic ID bracelet was attached to his wrist, and he was taken up to his room. There were two nurses in the room. One was straightening his bed while the other helped him put on his hospital gown and took his valuables and put them in a basket for safe keeping. Eve, he heard himself pray, where are you? I need you. I need to see you, hear your voice, touch your hand. He was eased into bed by the nurse who bid him good night and left the room, turning off the light.

As he turned over on his side he suddenly felt a weakness come over him. His heart began to pound, and everything was sliding into darkness. About to pass out, he gripped the chord next to his bed and squeezed the emergency button. Next thing he knew he was starting to wake up. A needle was stuck in his left arm. He was being given a blood transfusion.

His mind began to clear up. He had been revived. He was weak, but he was still alive. For the first time since he was brought into the room he became aware of his surroundings. There was another patient in the room, sleeping in the other bed to his right, his face turned to the wall. The door to his left was open to the hallway outside. In the hallway light he could see the edge of the counter of the nurses' station. Next to the counter on the adjoining wall hung a large wooden crucifix, suffused with light. "How am I supposed to come to terms with the idea of being married to a man who lived and died two thousand years ago?" He heard Eve say. The question kept running through his mind like a litany, over and over again, echoing back and forth between him and the wooden statue outside. "I'll let you figure it out," Eve was saying, "let you figure it out, figure it out, figure it out. . ."

A bride of Christ. . . *Iesus Christus Rex Judaei*. King of the Jews. The Roman mockery become Christian affirmation. The pagan world accepting the Jewish king whom the Jews reject. Eve, looking for her betrothed. A bride of Christ coming to him, Rabbi

Joshua Kaye, to look for her beloved. Was she coming to him to find Christ or to find him, Joshua Kaye, a man, a lover?

"... And yet I chose this life and I have accepted those beliefs." It was not that simple. She did accept those beliefs, and yet she had her doubts about calling this man God and being considered married to him.

How incongruous, he thought. A Jew who lived two thousand years ago, hanging on his wooden cross in the hallway of Good Samaritan Hospital in Quincy, Ohio, looking down at me in his moment of agony, looking watchfully and waiting—for what?

His mind began to drift into sleep. He had a dream. He saw the crucified man descend from the cross. He was small and frail, wrapped in a blue and white prayer shawl, bound in black straps of phylacteries, his black hair dishevelled and his earlocks flowing. His sad Jewish eyes burned like black coals and he was smiling at him like an old friend whom he hadn't seen in years.

"*Yehoshua*," he heard a voice addressing him in Hebrew, in a strange accent which he had never heard before. Why are you afraid?"

"I'm not afraid," he said, "only confused."

"Yes, you are confused. Do you hate me?"

"No, I don't hate you."

"But you don't love me, do you?"

"I can't. Too many Jews have been tortured and killed in your name over the ages."

"Do you blame me for it?"

"No, I don't blame you. It was certainly not your intention for this to happen."

"No, it wasn't. Nor was it my intention to be deified. As you know, in my day it was our custom in Eretz Yisrael to refer to God as Our Heavenly Father. I always spoke of God as my father. Later on those who founded a new religion in my name took it to mean I was God's one and only begotten son."

"Are you?"

"All people are God's sons and daughters."

"Do you approve of the religion which was founded in your name?"

"It was not my intention to start a new religion. My intention was to spread the religion of my fathers, of my fathers' God, and of God's messengers, the prophets. I was born, I lived and I died a Jew. Had I not been deified my teachings would not have given rise to a new religion. Judaism would have become the universal religion."

"But it didn't, as it turned out. Rather your teachings, instead of bringing a messianic age, instead of creating a world of peace, love and brotherhood, have given us two thousand years of war and bloodshed, in which your fellow Jews have been the main victims."

"Not so. I did not teach war and bloodshed. Those who made war and shed blood in my name took my name in vain. They were descendants of the ancient Barbarian tribes of Asia and Europe who outwardly accepted my teachings but never really practiced them. No, I'm not about to defend the religion which was founded in my name. But I will say this: everything is ultimately in the hands of God. I too was nothing but an instrument of God's will. Yes, I did hope my death would bring about a world of peace and love and brotherhood, a true kingdom of heaven on earth, but it did not. Did I die in vain? Nearly two thousand years after my death the world has shown it had never really learned how to live by my teachings. Recently in Europe I was crucified again six million times. I was sure the end had come. I was prepared to say Kaddish for my people and for the world. But, as you see, *Yehoshua*, Israel still lives. And as long as Israel lives, I can still hope I did not die in vain."

When he woke up in the morning he looked out the door at the cause of his dream. In the cold morning light the crucifix outside was another inanimate object, part of the hallway decor. To those who called this man God it was a sacred object. But by calling him God they had done away with his humanness and had perverted his teachings. No, the statue out there in the hall had nothing to do with his own correligionist who lived and died shortly before the destruction of Jerusalem and the long exile. Thou shalt not make unto thee any graven image, or any likeness of anything that is in the heavens above or in the earth beneath . . .

The total calm which came over him yesterday on the way to the hospital now came back. Last night he was revived with a blood transfusion. Now he was being fed intravenously. A clear bottle had replaced the dark one at the top of the rack, and the same needle stuck in his arm was now passing sugared water into his bloodstream. He recalled Dr. Perkins' admonition. Yes, Perkins was right. He had put himself under constant stress. Whatever his disease was, it was at least in part self-inflicted. All this was behind him now. In a way it was all for the good. He welcomed his condition. Learn to accept, that was the secret of life. Make your move and then accept the outcome no matter what happens. If this was the end of the line, so be it. He did what he believed was right. He did not sell out, the way Blumenfeld had. Rabbi did not mean compromiser. It meant seeker. If the pulpit did not permit a rabbi to seek the truth he would seek it elsewhere. His search had started years ago, perhaps the day he was born. It has brought him here to Quincy, to this seat of Jewish learning in the heart of America. It brought him to the great institutions of American Liberal Judaism. The search did not end here. Quincy did not have the answers. If and when he got back on his feet he would resume the search, wherever it may take him.

His room was on the top floor of the hospital. His roommate, an old, rotund, gray haired man with a long Polish name, was asleep. Outside it was a bright November day without a cloud in the sky. Life went on outside as it did every day, as it will continue to go on whether he was part of it or not. With his free hand he lifted the phone, propped it on his bed and dialed his office number. He told Ruth not to let anyone except for colleagues know he was in the hospital. He had to go out of town because of an emergency. He preferred to be left alone, at least until the cause of his bleeding was determined.

For the next three days he was undergoing tests which dragged on for many hours. His secretary, who enjoyed the role of confident and accomplice, came to see him for a little while every afternoon after work. She tried to fill him in on what was going on at the temple, but he asked her not to bother with it. He was not interested in the Las Vegas night, the quarrel over the funding of the new museum, or the Sisterhood Soiree. Certainly not on an empty stomach and while running the gauntlet of the hospital tests. Ruth Levy complied, giving him her sad, despondent smile. She was visibly worried about him. He did not have the heart to tell her he had already made up his mind about submitting the letter of resignation.

On the third day a second biopsy was taken of the lining of his small intestine, and later that evening Dr. Cass came into his room with the diagnosis. It was nothing fatal. Kaye's intestinal condition had been aggravated and the wound started hemorrhaging. With proper diet, a steady dose of sulpha, and a few weeks of rest his conditional could be put under control and he could resume his normal activities. Cass, who seemed happy to be the bearer of good news, bid him good night and left.

It took a long time for the realization to sink in: the uncertainty, thank God, was over. Life was not over yet. He reached for the copy of Gideonite Bible in his night table drawer and opened it to the Psalms of thanksgiving.

The next evening he had an unexpected visit.

He had turned off the reading light and was about to retire for the night when he heard someone call his name. At first he thought it was the night nurse coming in to dispense her sleeping pills. He was about to tell her he didn't want any when he realized the woman at the door was not a nurse. She wore a long navy blue winter coat and a woolen cap and was holding some books in her arms. Her face was a dark silhouette as she stood in the doorway with the hall light behind her. It was long past visiting hours. Nearly everyone on the floor was asleep. There was a hush outside, except for an occasional moan from the room across the hall.

"Josh?"

He recognized the voice.

"Eve!"

His blood quickened. She stood there like an answer to a prayer. A miracle! Holding her books in one hand she removed her cap with the other. He switched on the reading light. Her face was flushed. She laid down her books and cap on the chair next to his bed and looked down at him. Next thing he knew he was holding her hands as she stood there next to his bed, her hands responding to his touch, and he could tell she wanted to embrace him, throw herself into his arms, but was holding back. His hands reluctantly let go of hers. His heart ached as her lips parted and closed. She looked at him with a shy smile.

"I called your office this afternoon. Your secretary told me you were in the hospital. I had a makeup test this evening, so I came over as soon as I was done."

"I missed you, Eve."

She looked away in embarrassment.

"I'm sorry. I can't help the way I feel."

She raised her eyes and looked at him as if searching for words. There was pain in her eyes.

"Yes, I know, it doesn't make sense. A rabbi missing a nun. Look," he pointed at the crucifix outside, "you see who is watching over me?"

She looked displeased. "This is a community hospital," she said. "They should respect everyone's beliefs. There is a chapel down on the first floor for those who need it."

He was surprised by her vehemence. He looked at her and

smiled. "You look uncomfortable," he said, "why don't you take off your coat and stay for a while?"

"It's late," she said, "I'm not supposed to be here."

"There is a guest lounge down the hall. Why don't we go there and catch up on things?"

As she walked out he eased himself out of bed and got into his slippers and strapped on his long red house robe and followed her into the lounge. She had taken off her coat and stood in the middle of the lounge in her V-neck mohair sweater and woolen skirt. There was a certain longing about her as she stood there, her hands crossed over her chest, and looked through the dark window at the distant lights outside. He recalled touching her that day at St. John's college and feeling the hard girdle under her skirt. Was that what attracted him to her? The total contradiction between her femininity and her vocation? Was she making a statement about womanhood, about life? Did one have to renounce life in order to grasp it? Was that the spiritual element which was missing in his own life?

She looked at his robe in surprise.

"What's the matter?" he looked down and checked himself.

She burst into high, resonant laughter.

"You look funny in this red robe and this scraggly beard."

He shrugged his shoulders and grinned back at her. "Who do I look like? Let's see, Elijah? John the Baptist?"

"Not quite. You look more like a convict."

"I've felt like one since I came here. But I'm afraid I'm going to live."

They sat down at opposite ends of the sofa in the corner of the room.

"Eve, I feel like I've known you all my life when, in fact, I hardly know you. When you walked into my room a few minutes ago it was like seeing an old friend again. No, 'friend' is not the right word. It was more than a friend. What exactly it is I'm not sure. I have never felt anything like it before."

She lowered her eyes and blushed.

"Am I embarrassing you?"

"I'm sorry."

He felt her hand touch his. When he looked up she was gazing into his eyes. With sudden compulsion he kissed her on her lips. She recoiled and looked away and he could see the blood vanish from her face. He was startled by what he had done. A shiver ran through his spine. He was waiting to be struck by lightning.

He gasped her name, his heart pounding. "Eve, are you all right?"

She nodded slowly, then turned back and looked at him with a faint smile.

"Yes, I'm fine."

He took her hand in his and caressed it.

"Eve, I love you."

"I love you, Josh."

He pulled her against himself and held her in his arms. He heart beat violently against his chest. What am I getting myself into? he wondered. better yet, what am I getting this young nun into? What can come out of this except sorrow and grief?

There were footsteps outside in the hall. She pulled back and sat up and straightened her hair. They sat next to each other for a long time without saying a word.

"What are you thinking?" he finally said.

"I'm confused," she said. I'm having all sorts of confused feelings."

"Like what?"

"Like the way I feel about you. When I came here tonight to see you I didn't realize I felt about you quite the way I did."

"Are you sorry you came?"

"No, I'm not."

"Do you feel any guilt, remorse, fear?"

"No, I don't, which is why I'm confused. I know I shouldn't be doing these things, and yet I don't feel we are doing anything wrong."

"But you *are* breaking your vows?"

"Yes, I am."

"I don't share your beliefs," he said slowly, reflectively. "We Jews do not believe in celibacy. But I can understand why one would want to choose between, shall we say, the life of the flesh and the life of the spirit. Perhaps it is not possible to have both. Perhaps in order to become spiritual we have to make a certain sacrifice. I'm not a monk. I'm a rabbi who is separated from his wife and alienated from his congregation. You came into my life at a moment of great doubt, and while my first reaction to you was one of scorn and rejection, I could feel right away you were making a certain statement. Not anything you said or did, only being who you are. Our beliefs differ, and yet I feel you have the kind of a relationship to God which is missing in my own life and which I would like to have."

She listened intently and after he finished she shook her head.

"I don't know that I do," she said, looking at him questioningly. "I once thought I did, but that was a long time ago, when I first took my vows. When I met you at your office in Suburban Temple on that rainy Sukkot morning I was going through a great inner crisis. I came close to taking my own life. I was no longer able to pray. I became cynical and disillusioned. Everything around me seemed hypocritical, a charade. Everything I always held sacred had lost its meaning. I felt totally isolated, drifting, I couldn't trust anyone, I had no one to turn to. Then I met you. The moment I met you I knew I was not alone. I almost saw myself reflected in you. You were going through the same struggle I was going through. Yes, I knew you were attracted to me, and I also knew it was more than physical attraction. You know something, Josh? I know this would sound strange to you, but you helped me find Christ."

"In what way?"

"It's hard to explain. When I went on that prayer retreat last week each time I closed my eyes to pray to Christ I saw you. You were right there next to me, and you made me feel steadfast and confident. I know you don't share my beliefs, so I hope you don't mind my telling you these things."

"I feel a little jealous," he said.

"Of whom?"

"Of Christ. I have this strange notion that if he walked into the room right this minute and took you by the hand you would walk out of here without even looking back."

"It's ironic, isn't it?" she said, "you helped me find Christ and now it seems that my belief in Christ comes between us and separates us."

"As a Jew I cannot accept the divinity of another human being."

"I cannot argue with it," she said. "I'm not sure I understand it either. When we Catholics fail to understand something in our theology we call it a mystery. I have to accept it on faith."

As she got up to leave he helped her put on her coat and walked her to the elevator. Before she stepped into the elevator she kissed him on his cheek and said she would be back to see him in a day or two. He stood next to the elevator long after she disappeared behind the sliding doors and after the light above the doors running through the floor numbers' panel indicated that she had reached the lobby and had walked out.

✧ 8 ✧

Dr. Perkins popped in in the morning and without further ado told Kaye he could expect to be going home by the end of the week. Perkins mentioned he had been invited to the Zamenhoffs for Thanksgiving dinner and told Kaye he hoped to see him there. Without waiting for an answer he waved goodbye and ran off to see his next patient.

Kaye did not look forward to Thanksgiving. He was glad to be getting out of the hospital, but the thought of Thanksgiving depressed him. Thanksgiving since he first arrived in Quincy had come to mean a dinner at the Zamenhoffs. He had to hand it to his mother-in-law: she knew how to put on a feast. She went all out on festive occasions, religious or secular. In fact, she went overboard. There was always enough food left over for days. This was particularly true on Thanksgiving. In the middle of a long table covered with a white linen tablecloth, a cornucopia-shaped straw basket greeted the guests with an outpouring of fruit and nuts. There were always other main courses besides the traditional turkey—roast beef, brisket, cornish hens, and more. The wine flowed freely and there were several toasts of champagne. Then, after everyone had stuffed him or herself at the constant exhortations of the hostess, came the parve desserts, the jello molds and the apple strudel and the fruits and nuts. After dinner, as the guests retired to the living room, Dr. Zamenhoff would wheel in a serving cart with a connoisseur's collection of after-dinner liqueurs.

They could kill you with kindness, Kaye smiled to himself as he recalled the Zamenhoff Thanksgiving.

He hadn't seen Felicia now in nearly three months. Before he went into the hospital he was going to call her up and discuss their future. Then came the attack and for two weeks now he had been out of touch with the world. A sense of remorse came over him. Whatever he felt toward her, it was unfair and even cruel of him not to have gotten in touch with her all this time, especially since he did promise her father he was going to call her and try to come to an understanding one way or another. He made up his mind to call his estranged wife that evening and find out how she was doing and let her know he had been hospitalized and was about to be discharged.

She beat him to it. Later that afternoon she walked unannounced into his room and stood at the foot of his bed and said hello. He put down the book he was reading and looked at the small young woman who he realized was his wife, Felicia. She had cut her hair short and had lost weight. Her green eyes seemed larger and her lips tighter. She stood there and looked at him with a detached expression. She was waiting for him to say something. Her cold stare made him feel uneasy.

"I was going to call you this evening."

She didn't seem to believe him.

"Why don't you sit down?"

"I don't want to take too much of your precious time."

"There is no need to be sarcastic. Why don't you sit down so we can talk?"

She took off her black fur-trimmed coat and sat down at a discreet distance.

"How is the baby?"

"He's fine." She sounded as if she wanted to say, "you could really care less."

"How do *you* feel?" she narrowed her eyes and stretched out her neck to get a closer look at him, as if trying to remember how he used to look before the separation.

"Much better, thank you. I should be out of here by the end of the week."

"What are you doing for Thanksgiving?"

"I don't have any plans."

"Daddy says you are welcome to join us for Thanksgiving dinner. Don't get all shook up! It won't change anything between us. You can come like any other guest."

"Let me think about it."

"Talking about change, have you given any thought to what you may want to do?"

"About what?"

"About us!"

She was seething with anger. Her chest heaved and he could tell she was making a great effort to control herself.

"Please Calm yourself down." he said.

She turned her head away and looked out the door. From the way her shoulders rose and fell he could tell she was crying.

"Felicia. . ." he started in a softer tone.

She looked at him with eyes filled with tears. Whenever she cried she cried angrily, a hard, bitter cry.

"Get a hold of yourself," he said. "Let's not start this thing all over again."

Suddenly she calmed down. She blew her nose and wiped her tears and seemed in perfect control of herself. She was right. He had let this uncertainty drag on for too long. She had a right to know where he stood.

He felt a stirring for her. He now realized he had been suppressing his feelings for her for months. He had been fighting that hold which she had over him, but he was not able to shake it off. He longed to hold her against himself and feel her body melt in his arms and taste that irresistible sweet joy of reconciliation he felt each time they made up after a long fight.

No, he was not about to be drawn back into that familiar cycle.

"I want to ask you one question, Josh."

"Go ahead."

"Do you still love me?"

"Yes, I do."

"Then what seems to be the problem?"

"Things have changed between us."

"Is there another woman?"

He thought of Sister Eve. Yes, Felicia, there is this nun I have become very friendly with. "No," he said, "Not really."

"Then what is it?"

"It's mainly me, I suppose. I have changed since we first got married and since I became the associate-rabbi of Suburban Temple. I have done a great deal of thinking about it since you left. I know you think that becoming the associate-rabbi to the great Alvin Blumenfeld was the greatest thing that ever happened to me. I know many people feel that way. Well, that's exactly how I felt at first. But I found out I was wrong. I didn't spend all those years of study to become a rubber stamp for Roz and Joe Pins and Hal Braverman and some other rich Jews who pay a handsome salary and look upon a rabbi as a hired hand. I guess this is where you and I part ways, Felicia. You don't seem to have any trouble with it. I do."

"I know about this problem with Braverman," Felicia said as she took out a cigarette and lit it, blowing the smoke away from his bed. "I talked to Rabbi Blumenfeld the other day. I didn't tell him about us. I only called to say hello and make up an excuse for not having shown up at temple since the High Holy Days. He told me about the talk you had, and that you had questions about staying on at Suburban. He felt that your insisting on speaking out on the Armor and Gambit issue had brought it to a head. I know how strongly you feel about the freedom of the pulpit, but I'm not so sure this was not an exceptional case. After all, you have to look at the greater picture, which is Hal's running for the Senate and what it means to Jews. But okay, I don't want to argue about it. I'm not saying that you must stay at Suburban no matter what. I'm not interested in Suburban. I want to know about us, you and me."

"I know," he said, "so do I. I don't like this state of uncertainty any more than you do." He paused, thinking of a way to get it across to her without getting into an argument he was not ready yet to make any decisions. He could feel her tension. How could he make her understand her impatience was one of the big problems in their relationship? She was always pressing him about one thing or another. Couldn't she at least wait until he was out of the hospital and back on his feet?

"Well, then?"

"You are right. The question is no longer Suburban Temple. I've made up my mind. I'm handing in my letter of resignation as soon as I get out of here. When I first found out that Hal Braverman did not want me to speak out on this issue I decided to give the board an ultimatum—either they back me up on this issue or I resign. Well, I have since realized I was wasting my time. Either way I was going to lose. So I decided to let them know I was resigning and I would speak out on this issue after I get out. The question right now is what will I do with myself after I leave the temple."

"You may want to look for your own congregation."

"I'm not sure."

"What, then?"

"I would like to find God first."

She looked at him as if he had lost his mind.

"Meaning?"

No, she wouldn't understand. What was the use of prolonging this discussion?

"I need to get away for awhile. I may go out west to visit my mother. I'm not ready to accept the status quo."

"You let me know when you are ready," she said as she got up to leave. "Take your time. But don't be surprised to find out when you decide you are ready I won't be there."

Eve came to see him that evening, bringing in with her some of the rain from the outside on her clear plastic raincoat and on a stray tuft of hair hanging down over her forehead. He was pacing the hall outside his room when he saw her come out the elevator and head straight for his room. He held out his hands to her as she came closer, and was surprised by her perfunctory handshake. He looked at her questioningly, and for the first time he noticed a distraught, troubled look in her eyes. He asked her if she was feeling all right. Yes, she felt fine. But there was something she wanted to discuss with him. He helped her take off her raincoat and invited her to the guest lounge down the hall. There were several patients and visitors in the lounge. She looked back at him: was there some place where they could be alone? He said they could try the lounge on another floor, but since it was visiting hours all the lounges might be occupied. Eve suggested the chapel on the first floor. Why, sure. What could be a better place for a rabbi and a nun to meet?

The chapel, as expected, was empty. He liked the simple decor. Plain wooden pews. A small confessional in the corner. A simple low alter, and an unimposing crucifix behind it. A few indirect lights here and there, and a muted brown carpet on the floor, muffling their footsteps.

They walked down the side aisle and sat in the back pew. Eve had calmed down and seemed more at ease. She is on home ground, Kaye observed.

"It's about you and me," she started and stopped, hesitating.

It had to come sooner or later.

"Well, I know I have been fooling myself. Last night after I saw you I walked back to the convent and it suddenly hit me: I was trying to eat my cake and have it. I can't have it both ways, Josh. If I'm going to keep my vows I'll have to stop seeing you. And, besides, even if I were to leave the order, we would still be miles apart in our beliefs. I'm not that kind of person. I can't just let myself go. I have to know what bearing my present actions will have on the future."

She sounded almost as if she had been rehearsing her lines. It was her mind speaking, not her heart. It now occurred to him that in pursuing her vocation she must have spent years disciplining herself to deny her feelings, particularly those of the flesh. She was doing it now, and yet he could hear her struggling inside her mind.

They sat close to each other, their knees almost touching, and he could see the tautness in her arms and in her cheeks as she hesitated, formulating her thoughts, her body leaning toward him, longing for him. She meant what she said. Of that he was sure. She was a nun, and her vocation came before all else in her life. And, to her, he was, first and foremost, a rabbi. That dual reality had set them apart, yet, in a mysterious way, it brought them close together. Her vocation impelled her to reach beyond the familiar rituals she had been taught to follow. It prompted her to regard him as more than the religious functionary the title "rabbi" had made him out to be. The simple fact was, they were attracted to each other as man and woman. But it went much further than that. Their seeking out each other and their sitting in that chapel at that moment made him feel something which was unlike anything he had known until now. The moment they got together he could feel it and he knew she felt it as well. There was something between them, a presence, a bond, a mystical coming together. And now, sitting in this dimly lit chapel, at opposite ends from her sacred objects, the feeling, the presence, became more palpable, more real than ever before. They sat silently for a long time, her hands, long, tapered, soft yet firm fingers nestling in her lap, her eyes cast down, motionless. She was so close yet so remote. He knew her so well and yet hardly knew her at all. A terrible loneliness came over him. A pain gripped his heart, his very soul, as if his soul had suddenly turned into ice.

"So we have to stop seeing each other."

She covered her face with her hands and he could see she was crying.

"Eve!"

She cried bitterly.

"Eve!" he took her in his arms and pressed her head against himself and stroked her short cropped hair, feeling the wetness of her tears on his neck and chest. She cried for a long time, as if washing away years of pain and loneliness and broken dreams. As she cried she pushed closer against him and clung to him as if afraid he might let go of her and leave. He kissed her eyes, drying her tears. She opened her eyes and looked at him and he could see doubt, fear, consternation running through her mind.

"It's all right, he said. "Don't be afraid of your feelings. There is nothing shameful about the way you feel."

"God help me, Josh," she said, crying and laughing at the same time. "I love you. I can't help myself."

He took her hands and put them against his chest.

"Kiss me, Eve."

"Here?"

"Yes, here."

She closed her eyes and waited. He kissed her on her lips, a long tender kiss which, for a moment of eternity, sent his soul soaring as if about to depart from this world.

"I love you, Eve. I don't want to let you go."

She drew back and smiled at him, letting him stroke her hand, and shook her head.

"We've got a big problem, don't we?"

"Yes, we do."

"I'm torn, Josh. I know I have to make a choice, and I don't know what to do. Only last week I went on that retreat and I renewed my pledge to Christ. And look at me now. I had sworn to forgo the things of this world and live only in and for God. But I failed. I'm being a hypocrite. And to make it worse, I feel no remorse, no regret, nothing, nothing at all. I feel suspended between my love for you and my love for him. It's strange, as I think about it, I'm not even sure I can tell you two apart. . . Oh, God, I'm so confused! I don't know what to believe any more. Don't you see, this whole thing is crazy. It doesn't make any sense."

He had let go of her hand.

"No, it doesn't," he said. "It *is* crazy. And yet I feel there is something providential about the fact that we have found each other. There is a great deal that is wrong with the world and with religion, all organized religion, yours and mine, it makes not difference which. You and I are not willing to accept this state of affairs, and so we need to do something about it. I'm not quite sure what we can do, but I feel that together we can figure it out. I'm looking beyond our personal relationship. I'm thinking about what the two of us, working together, may be able to accomplish. Let's not give it up. Let's explore it together."

"What exactly do you propose we do?" She asked skeptically.

"I don't know. First I have to get out of this hospital."

"And then?"

"I'm going to hand in my letter of resignation as soon as I get back to work."

"You sound like your mind is made up."

"Yes, it is."

"And then what?"

"I'll come to visit you at the convent."

"By all means do," she laughed.

✧ 9 ✧

The night before his discharge from the hospital she came back to see him. The moment he saw her he knew she had had a change of heart. He showed her to the lounge and once inside he was about to put his arms around her when she drew back, holding her hand against him, signalling him to stop.

"Let's talk," she said, pointing to a small round table and two chairs in the corner.

They sat across from each other. She was calm and poised. There was quiet determination in her eyes.

"I thought about what you said the other night, Josh. you know, about organized religion and about people like us wanting to do something about it. I agree with you. We do have to do something, and, yes, I am not sure what. And this is what I'm really getting at. Our uncertainty. It's easy to talk about changing the world. But how do you go about doing it? I know there is a whole lot wrong with my own religion. I've turned to Judaism, hoping your people had the answer. But it seems that neither one of us has it. Am I right?"

He smiled at her and nodded.

"Yes, you are right. We don't have the answer. Right now all we have is each other."

"This is precisely the point, Josh," she cried, then looked around and lowered her voice. "Having each other is not good enough. Not when it comes to the two of us. I'm not really ready to leave the convent. I'm certainly not ready to come to your doorstep and say, here, take me, I'm yours! And, you know something? You are not ready for it either. So what do we do? Sneak around and meet in parks and in dark corners until someone finds out about us? Can you really picture us doing such a thing?"

No, he couldn't. It was pure madness.

"I agree," he said. "Yes, you are right. But I need you, Eve. I'm trying to understand what is happening to us. I'm trying to see it from both our perspectives. Perhaps this whole thing is some kind of a temptation we have to overcome. Perhaps our relationship is different. I'm willing to accept that. I need your friendship more than anything else in the world. There is no one I can talk to the way I can talk to you. Why can't we just be friends?"

"I would very much like to," she said. "I know our feelings for each other go deeper than that. There must be one part of me which craves what every normal healthy young woman craves—the love of a man. And I certainly understand your physical feelings for me. You haven't told me anything about your marriage, except that you are separated from your wife. Your initial attraction to me might have been intellectual, but obviously you have another, more basic need than, shall we say, an intellectual friendship. How serious were you when you said you wanted to come and see me at the convent? Well, I think perhaps you ought to find out more about my way of life. Perhaps you will begin to see me in a different light. Let's not try to define our relationship. Let's wait and see what happens."

He nodded, forcing a smile.

"Okay," he said, "you are right. I guess I'm a dreamer. You certainly help me come back to reality. Who said, *amor omnia vincit*? I guess that's not always true."

"Oh, Josh," she said vehemently, shaking her head. "You know how I feel about you. I do hope you understand."

"Yes," he smiled, "I understand."

By doctor's orders he stayed home for a week before going back to work. During that week he did a great deal of thinking about Eve. They had agreed to remain friends, and yet it was clear there was something between them which went much deeper than friendship. There was a certain harmony between them which encompassed all the disparate parts of their lives. When he forgot for a moment that she was a bride of Christ and that he was a rabbi, there were only Eve and Josh, the two of them, in the guest lounge at the hospital and downstairs at the chapel, letting themselves go, finding each other. And yet Eve was right. They wanted everything, but they couldn't have it all. They had to choose, draw the line. His first attraction to her was not physical. It was her faith that attracted him to her, the faith he was looking for. Paradoxically, bound as she was by such strict rules and by an ecclesiastic hierarchy which controlled every aspect of her life, she appeared nonetheless free in her faith, unbound by any human authority. There was nothing passive about her monastic life. It was *her* choice, a choice she struggled with, doubting, questioning. He sensed it for the first time when they met on that Sukkot morning. Imperceptibly at first, she was offering him the faith-model he had been looking for.

But this was only the half of it. The spirit was made flesh. The night she came to see him at the hospital they found out their attraction was more than ethereal. How does one draw the line between the spirit and the flesh? Are the two separate and contradictory, or are they two sides of the same coin?

There was no clear line between the spirit and the flesh. Human love and the love of God flow naturally to and from each other. But this was not the case here. Sometimes the flesh must yield to the spirit. This was the first lesson she taught him in his spiritual quest. If one was truly searching for God, one had to make certain physical sacrifices. Eve had made hers. It was his turn now.

He sat down and wrote her a long letter. He was letting her know he was giving the temple notice of his resignation, effective January thirty-first. He felt at once excited and apprehensive. It was the excitement of freedom mixed with the fear of the unknown. He was severing all ties and setting himself adrift. He realized it was the only way to find out—excuse the expression—what his "calling" was. He was giving up the security of his home and his career, the friendships Felicia and he had made in three years, many cherished relationships, not the least of which was the one with his father-in-law, the professor of Jewish Mysticism. He realized as soon as the news of his separation and resignation got out there would be much eyebrow raising and head shaking, and for a few days it would be the talk of the town. Why would anyone in his right mind do such a thing, people would be saying. Well, it was no longer a matter of choice. Some inner force was pushing him to do it. As for Suburban Temple, they would have no difficulty finding some social climbing rabbi who would be happy to step into his position and become a rubber stamp to the whims of the rich trustees. Yes, he did feel apprehensive. There was no guarantee he was going to find what he was looking for. But if he didn't try now he might never have another chance. He wanted her to know she had given him the inspiration to reach the decision. As a nun, she too had severed all ties with the world, giving up her personal happiness and fulfillment for a higher goal. There was much he could learn from her. He wanted to find out more about her life, her vocation, the source of her relationship with God. He realized that Christ was central to her life, but he believed there was a common ground which transcended her belief in Christ, and it was on that common ground that he hoped to meet her.

The first day he showed up for work after his recovery Kaye had stopped behind his secretary's desk and greeted her with a loud boisterous good morning. Ruth Levy was startled by his greeting, and when she turned to look at him her jaw dropped and her tinted glasses nearly fell off. He stood there and looked at her with a broad smile. The befuddled secretary kept staring at him, at loss for words, almost as if she were not sure whether it was her boss, Rabbi Kaye, she was looking at, or some stranger who had just happened to walk in.

He was at first surprised by her reaction, when it occurred to him he had just broken some of the cardinal rules of Suburban Temple. During the month or so he was away he had let his hair and beard grow long. His hair curled over his ears and neck, and his beard had filled out, scraggly and unruly. When he first grew a beard almost a year ago, some of the members of the board of trustees had objected to it. It did not fit their image of a modern, "man-about-town" rabbi. Kaye suspected they had some latent fears about his beard. For one thing, it must have reminded them of Orthodox rabbis and legalistic Judaism which they dreaded and rejected. For another thing, beards in the late Sixties had become a symbol of youth rebellion and "anti-Establishment" attitudes. It took some savvy on Roz Pins' part to allay the fears of those elder statesmen of the congregation. After all, Roz proclaimed in her mildly admonishing, matriarchal tone, we do want Rabbi Josh to appeal to the youth of the congregation, and what better way than by looking like one of them? The beard was not exactly the hippie variety, but rather a short, neat, well groomed affair. The youth were not fooled by it, and the old timers learned to accept it as "distinguished looking," "becoming," and a few other well reasoned adjectives, and soon the teapot storm was forgotten.

Now, a year later, the beard no longer conformed to acceptable standards. Kaye could tell Ruth was worried lest a member of the congregation happened to walk in and see him. What Ruth did not know was he no longer felt bound by the rules of the place. As he looked around him he felt as though the temple had taken on a different character and purpose during his absence. When he first came here he was led to believe this was a house of God of which he was about to become a spiritual leader. He was going to apply some of the great lessons of Judaism he had learned during five years of rabbinical school to the large membership of the temple. Well, he found out it worked quite the other way around. They had tried to apply a few lessons to him. Why, they were the ones who had the power and the glory. Theirs was the richest and most prestigious congregation in the entire Midwest. Surely by learning *their* secret of success and by walking in *their* ways he would find his own fulfillment as a rabbi. No, thanks. They could have their temple. He no longer cared to have any part of it.

Ruth's astounded stare shifted from Kaye's long hair and beard to his clothes. He was clearly violating Suburban Temple's dress code. The proper attire for a man of the cloth was either a business suit or coat and tie. Instead, he came in this morning wearing an old plaid sport jacket, black turtleneck sweater, old corduroy pants, and boots. The expression on Ruth's face told him some explanation on his part was in order.

"You look great, Ruth. Not having me around for a month must have agreed with you."

"But. . . what in the world. . ."

"Yes, yes, I know. You are not used to seeing me like this. Ah, well, don't concern yourself. I may still be on duty, but I no longer feel duty-bound, if you get my meaning."

No, she didn't get his meaning.

"Here," he took a folded piece of paper out of his inside coat pocket. "I have a letter I would like you to type."

She slowly unfolded the letter and read the first paragraph, then looked up at him and her lips tightened.

"Please Ruth, let's not have a scene. I've had enough of that lately. No tears, please. Come, let's go into my study."

They sat down on the vinyl sofa in his study.

"It was a hard decision, believe me. But now that I made up my mind I feel good about it. In fact, I haven't felt so good since I graduated from the seminary."

"You look very cheerful."

He took her hands and clutched them in his.

"You are about the only person around here I'm going to miss. It's ironic, isn't it? Over two thousand families, and after three years I look back and I realize I have hardly touched any of their lives or been touched by them. It only comes to show you. No, my leaving is no great loss, whichever way you look at it."

When he walked into his confirmation class that afternoon the students at first looked at him incredulously, as if he were pulling some kind of a trick. He perched on his desk and crossed his arms

and looked at them with a benign smile. Their expressions gradually changed from wariness to amusement. Some girls in the back of
the room began to whisper in their neighbor's ear and giggled. One
boy stood up and cleared his throat.

"Yes, Jimmy."

"Er, rabbi, you look very different today."

"How do I look?"

"Well, sort of like a hippie."

"Thank you, Jimmy. Thanks for the compliment."

The boy sat down to a chorus of laughter from his peers. He appeared unsure whether the rabbi was being serious or sarcastic.

Kaye asked the class to open their Bibles to the Second Book of
Kings, chapter one, and proceeded to read the story of Elijah, the
man of God, a hairy man who wore a leather belt and wandered in
the mountains and in the desert, who was not afraid to chastise the
King of Israel, who spoke his mind and got into trouble because of
it. The biblical prophets, kaye explained, were the original hippies.
Society today was once again in need of prophets. Whether those
people in America today who grew their hair long and spoke out
against injustice and discrimination and war were prophets he
could not say. The prophets of old were always ahead of their time,
and their teachings were not recognized and appreciated until
much later, usually when the destruction and exile they predicted
had already taken place.

After he finished talking he realized that, for the first time perhaps, he had those teenagers' undivided attention. He was not sure
they related to what he had said, but given his appearance and the
conviction with which he spoke they must have sensed he believed
in what he said and made an effort to listen.

The next morning the president of the congregation, Joe Pins,
stopped at Kaye's study and gave him his usual friendly greeting.
Kaye could tell the corporate lawyer was straining to sound casual
and unruffled by the associate rabbi's appearance.

"How are you doing, Josh? All recovered from that ileitis
episode?"

"Doing fine, thanks."

"Alvin showed me your letter of resignation. I respect your
decision, of course, but I can't say I'm not sorry to see you go. Our
agreement calls for a two month notice. So I suppose you will be
leaving by the end of January."

"If it's agreeable."

"Yes, yes, of course." Joe paused and looked down at his shoes, then looked up and pushed his chair closer and propped his arms on the rabbi's desk.

"Look, Josh, I'm speaking to you now as a friend, not as the president of the temple. Someone called me last night and said his son told him you told your confirmation class you have become a hippie. Is that true?"

Kaye laughed, "No, of course not. One of the kids made a remark I looked like a hippie, so I explained to the class a hippie is not necessarily a bad person."

Joe looked at the rabbi's beard and hair and at his casual clothes and nodded. Kaye could tell Joe was thinking about his own daughter, Sue. Not enough he had the dubious distinction of having a hippie daughter, now he had a rabbi who looked like one.

"How is Sue?"

Joe did not appear elated by the question.

"I guess she is all right."

As the president walked out of his study Kaye realized his career as a rabbi of Suburban Temple had officially come to an end. He leaned back in his black leather swivel chair and heaved a sign of relief. It now occurred to him for three years he had been teaching, preaching, counselling, getting involved in one cause after another, and, in the end, nothing seemed to add up. It was almost as if someone else was calling the shots, some invisible power was at work, guiding the lives of the people whose spiritual welfare had been entrusted to him. What was that power? Money? Politics? The System? The American way? What did religion have to do with all of this? Was religion anything more than a tool in the hands of that invisible power? And where did that power emanate from? Was there some clique at the top which used institutions like Suburban Temple for its own ends? Is this where people like Joe Pins and Hal Braverman took their cues from, and, in turn, made rabbis like Alvin Blumenfeld and Joshua Kaye take theirs as well?

Good old Sue! She understood it all too well. At an age when other kids still believed in the tooth fairy and Superman she was turning her back on all this rich man religion. How was she doing out there in that Bahai commune? Did she find the peace, love and joy she was looking for?

He was wondering about Sue when Ruth brought in the morning mail with a letter from Eve on top of the stack. The letter, written on self-designed convent stationery, read:

Dear Josh:

Thank you for your kind words. I'm not quite sure how to

react to your decision to sever all ties and go out into the world. I feel humbled when you say I have given you the inspiration to reach your decision. I haven't taken any risks. Quite to the contrary, I have chosen a sheltered and secure life in which few risks are taken and most decisions are made for you.

You say you want to find out more about my life. Well, I'm not sure it is all that exciting. We are getting ready for Christmas around here. There is an eager mood in the house with everyone relaxed and themselves for a change. I have a lot to do but it's nice not to have any scheduled responsibilities like going to school or teaching hanging over my head. . . Would be nice though if you could come and visit and meet some of the people I live with. Atmosphere-wise it is like another world, simpler and poorer than out there where you live, but real, in a deep way, to me. — If you wouldn't feel uncomfortable or out of it in any way, you are more than welcome to come to midnight mass on Christmas Eve. It's a joyous ceremony here, with breakfast afterwards. However, the time is a little ridiculous and maybe not worth the trouble of going out of your way. I'll let you decide.

Hope to see you soon, Shalom,
Eve

He put down the letter and looked at the gray winter sky outside. I should have know, he muttered to himself, shaking his head. Where did I come off getting myself involved with a nun in the first place? Now she is trying to gracefully get out of the whole thing. She is not sure how to react to my decision, and she is not sure I would find her life all that exciting. She is apparently not so sure there is anything between us that is worth pursuing any more, but she cannot bring herself to come out and say it. So what does she do? She invites Rabbi Kaye to midnight mass on Christmas Eve, as she would invite any poor soul who needs a place to go on the most joyous night of the Christian year. Sister so and so, I would like you to meet my friend, Rabbi Kaye. Rabbi Kaye, this is Sister so and so. How do you do? How good of you to spend Christmas Eve with us here at the convent!

That first time she came to see him at his study on Sukkot morning, he recalled thinking how her excessive humility and self-effacement seemed to border on sanctimonious arrogance. Now she was putting on that false humility act again. She hasn't "taken any risk." Rather she chose "a sheltered and secure life. . ." How naive of him to have entertained the notion all this time this young woman was different from all the rest of them. Despite her qualms and questioning and disaffection she was one of them, and when all was said and done she was Sister Eve, a Catholic nun, who was taught to put a distance between herself and others, especially men. To her, the only way to salvation was through the one and only true Church and the one and only true Savior.

Later at night in the solitude of his apartment he took out the letter and read it over again. Had he overreacted to it? She did want to see him. It was only natural for her to invite him to her Christmas celebration. Why was he reacting so negatively to her invitation? It was his idea to visit her at the convent in the first place. It could very well be that she was afraid he might be disappointed by what he saw, and thought it would be best if he came out on a special occasion like Christmas Eve.

The first thing he realized as he was about to call the convent the next day was he did not have the telephone number. He looked up "Lourdes Convent" in the telephone book, not quite expecting to find it, as if it were some kind of a secret society or an otherworldly place. Yet there it was, like any other local institution. He dialed the number and waited. The phone kept ringing, when, about to give up, he heard a low voice come on the line, sounding like an older woman (the mother superior?) Lourdes, may I help you? Yes, please. He wanted to speak to Sister Eve. Just a moment please. He waited for a long time, when someone finally picked up the receiver.

"Hello."

"Sister Eve?"

"Yes, oh, hi!"

"Hello, Eve."

"Josh! What a pleasant surprise! How do you feel?"

"Much better, thanks."

"That's good."

"I hope I'm not interrupting anything."

"No, not at all. Are you back to work?"

"Afraid so."

"How are things at the temple?"

"Business as usual. How are *you* doing?"

"Okay."

"Getting ready for Christmas?"

"Yes, sort of. We don't make such a big to-do over Christmas around here."

"I see. I got your invitation for Christmas Eve. I'm not sure I'll be able to come."

"That's okay. It was only a thought."

"But I would like to see you."

There was silence on the other end.

"I thought I might drop in some time this week."

"Here, at Lourdes?"

"If it's all right."

"Sure. Any time this week is fine."

He arranged to go over and see her that afternoon. After he hung up he felt relieved. He was afraid she might be offended by his turning down her invitation to the Christmas celebration, but it didn't seem to matter. Convent or no convent, the only thing that mattered was the two of them. She had been waiting for his call. Like any woman waiting to hear the voice of the man she loved, all their conflicts and misgivings notwithstanding.

It was a gray December day, cold and damp. Old gray clumps of snow nestled on frozen grass patches along the street. He started the car and turned on the heater and charged out of the underground garage into the afternoon traffic. He drove through familiar streets, passing Good Samaritan Hospital and the rabbinic seminary. At the first traffic light past the seminary he turned right into Cliffwood. He was now in foreign territory. An old poor Catholic neighborhood, mostly Polish, Irish and Italian. It was only a few minutes' walk from the rabbinic seminary, where he had spent five years, but he had never set foot inside that neighborhood. He was now on Eve's homeground. He parked the car at the curb outside the convent and got out into the cold dampness of early afternoon. He looked around himself. So this is where Eve had chosen to live. Narrow streets of row houses branching off Cliffwood Avenue, the main thoroughfare. The neighborhood clustering around the tall steepled stone church at the high point of the hillside, the long two-story parochial school building next to it, and the large brick building of the convent at the opposite end. He was struck by the total contrast between West Hills and Cliffwood. Instead of the manicured lawns of his own affluent suburbs here the weeds sprung out of cracks in the pavements and prowled around the houses, as if threatening to swallow up the neighborhood and make it revert to its primordial state. Some windows in a corner building were boarded up, while others had yellowing plastic sheets replacing broken panes. The stores along Cliffwood Avenue were old gaping dark holes: a pawnshop, a thrift shop, a corner grocery.

It now occurred to him that besides the vows of chastity and obedience, Eve had also taken the vow of poverty. Was poverty a Christian virtue? Blessed are the poor, for theirs is the kingdom of heaven. . . Was God more readily found among the poor than among the rich? At one time Jews also lived in poor neighborhoods like this one and worked in sweat shops and dreamed of the *goldene medineh*. They learned quickly how to play by the rules of the American game, the rules of free enterprise and higher education, and they have moved out of those neighborhoods. They now lived in the gilded ghettos of the suburbs, and they had erected monuments to their success, pyramids and ziggurats, as Dr. Zamenhoff had put it, multi-million dollar temples and synagogues which he, Rabbi Kaye, was now escaping.

Lourdes Convent was an old stately red brick building which had seen better times. The brick was no longer red but rather a sooty brown. The flagstone steps leading up to the main entrance were in an advanced stage of disrepair. Worn with age, they were scarred with cracks and had begun to disintegrate. Long planks had been placed over the steps, riveted together, the first phase of repair work which for some reason had been abandoned. As he walked up the steps he felt a strange chill. He was so completely out of place in this neighborhood. He stopped on the landing before the door and waited. He was about to enter the *sanctum sanctorum* of this neighborhood, violate the sanctity of its vestal shrine. What gave him the right to do it? He studied the ponderous wooden doors, overlaid with coats of black varnish, as if looking for a clue. Should he walk in? Turn around and leave? He took a deep breath and tried the door. To his surprise, the door was open. He walked in and found himself in a dark vestibule, scant light seeping in through a small skylight in the high ceiling. When his eyes got used to the dark he saw another door with a peephole and a white button to the right of it. He pushed the button and waited. Presently he heard a voice behind the door asking who he was. He identified himself by name, omitting his title. The door opened and he found himself facing an old nun. She peered at him through steel rimmed glasses. Her skin was yellow wrinkled parchment, and she wore the old traditional habit. Sister Eve? Sure, this way, please. She hardly looked at him as she spoke, turning around and motioning him to follow her. Did Eve also wear this habit inside the convent? The thought of it nearly paralyzed him with fear. He could not bear the thought of seeing Eve dressed like this.

He followed the old nun down a long dark corridor to an empty hall. He was told to wait while Eve was being paged on the house phone. There were wooden chairs in the corner. He sat down and waited. What was he getting himself into? Was it really he, Rabbi Joshua Kaye, sitting inside a convent waiting for a nun?

"Joshua!"

He turned around and looked in the direction of the voice. A young woman came nearly running toward him. She wore an open neck sleeveless blouse, short loose skirt and open sandals. Eve! Thank God she was not wearing a habit.

He got up to greet her. She gave him a hug and drew back, squeezing his hands in hers. His blood quickened. His lips longed for hers. He was about to kiss her when she said,

"You really look good. Are you all better?"

He nodded and smiled.

She let go of his hands.

"I'm so glad you came," she said, her eyes glowing. "What's the matter? You look surprised."

"Oh, nothing. It's just that I guess I expected you to wear a habit."

"Oh, really?" She sat down and he sat in the chair next to her. "Why is that?"

"This other sister who let me in was wearing the old black traditional habit."

"Mother Thomas?" She chuckled. "Well, she belongs to the old guard. Vatican Two totally missed her, as it did most of her contemporaries. Thank God we have a choice in our order. All of us young rebels have given up the habit almost two years ago."

She crossed her legs, cupping her knee with both hands, and gave him a sidelong smile. His heart pounded. He was aching with desire for her. He wanted to squeeze her and cover her with kisses. Did she expect him to do it? She appeared so carefree, sensuous, in fact, downright seductive. Was it because she felt completely at ease inside the convent? Had she been longing for him all this time, her decision notwithstanding?

She seemed to have read his thoughts. She uncrossed her legs and laid her hands in her lap and looked down.

"Are you disappointed?" she asked.

"With what?"

"My not wearing a traditional habit."

"On the contrary. Why would anyone want to wear medieval clothes in this day and age? In fact, I think you look more at home here in your casual clothes than Mother Thomas does in that stiff habit."

"I'll take it as a compliment," she laughed. "Come," she said, taking him by the hand, "I'll show you around."

Her excitement had made him forget his qualms about coming to this place. It was he who was encumbered by all sorts of inhibitions and misconceptions regarding convents and nuns. Movies and books had sure created a distorted picture of these places. Penguin-like women moving about slowly, secretively, never speaking above a whisper, if at all. Well, this obviously was not Eve's world.

"Where are all the other sisters?" he asked.

"Most of them teach at the school down the street. Others are working at the shelter for unwed teenage mothers around the corner. Some are downstairs in the kitchen."

They walked into what Eve called a reading room. It was a multi-purpose room which seemed to have been furnished by parishioners who showed their devotion to the convent by donating discarded couches, armchairs, bookcases, coffee tables, and old radios and phonographs. A magazine rack stood against the wall. *Commonweal. America. Nun's Life.* In the corner of the room he was surprised to see a set of drums and a guitar on a small wooden stage.

"Is this what you expected the inside of a convent to look like?"

"Not quite," he said. "I thought all you women ever did was pray."

"Not quite." she laughed.

"Who plays the drums and the guitar?"

"We do," she said proudly. "We love singing and making music."

"Not bad, not bad."

He looked out the window at the drab neighborhood outside.

"So I take it you like it here. And yet you have seriously considered leaving the order."

She made no reply. When he looked back at her he could see she was fighting back her tears.

"What's the matter?"

"Oh, nothing," she forced a smile and bit her lip, shaking her head.

"You don't want to talk about it?"

"It's hard for me to talk about it," she said. She walked over to the window and looked out at the neighborhood outside. "Look," she pointed at the school building down the street, "this school, where

I've been teaching now for the past two years may be closed next year."

"Why?"

"Money. The bishop claims he doesn't have enough money to run schools in poor neighborhoods."

"Is there anything you and the other sisters can do about it?"

"I spoke to some of them," she turned and looked at him, "I didn't get anywhere. You know what the problem is? Those sisters who have strong convictions and are outspoken are, for the most part, quitting the order. The others, who are meek and acquiescent, are staying. They don't want to make any waves. At this rate the Church, instead of moving forward, can only go back."

"I'm sure the Church has its faults," Kaye said. "But at least the Church is here, where the poor are. It has people like you, who have taken a vow of poverty, who dedicate their life to the poor. You have given up your personal well-being in order to live and work here. This, too, is the Church, is it not?"

She gave him a stern look.

"Please, Josh, don't make me out to be some kind of a saint."

"I'm not," he said. "I'm only stating facts. Look at me. What have I done for the past three years? I've lived in the lap of luxury in my three million dollar synagogue. My people have been fortunate. They have come up in the world and they have left the ghettos and the inner city. The fact remains, the Church, with all its faults, is still here, where the poor are. Perhaps it is not doing such a great job, but at least it takes responsibility for them and carries the burden. What burden do I carry?"

She leaned back, pressing her back against the windowsill, and crossed her arms. He moved next to her and looked into her eyes.

"In order to find God we first have to give up something. Is that right?"

She smiled at him, nodding slightly.

"I'm learning," he said. "I'm glad I came here."

"So you are going out into the world to look for your burden."

"Yes. This is exactly what I'm about to do."

✧ 10 ✧

His departure from Suburban Temple came sooner than he had expected. It was a cold, bright Friday morning in early December when Rabbi Kaye found himself preparing his farewell address to be delivered that evening before the congregation.

He still had another month to go on his contract, but by mutual agreement his term was shortened. By now word of his resignation as well as his separation from Felicia had gotten out, and the rumor mills of Quincy's Jewry were busy circulating and interpreting the news. The gist of the rumors was Rabbi Kaye had become a hippie, as evidenced by his long hair and beard and his shabby clothes. This sudden transformation took everyone by surprise. Why would anyone in his right mind throw away a brilliant career, a prestigious marriage, an assured future, and follow a path leading nowhere?

Ruth Levy kept the junior rabbi abreast of the rumors, which he found amusing. The temple president called him one week after the meeting during which Joe Pins officially accepted Kaye's resignation, and told him he was having a problem—his phone did not stop ringing for a moment. Nearly every member of the board of trustees called to complain about the junior rabbi's appearance. The lay leaders of the congregation felt Rabbi Kaye had become a source of embarrassment to the temple in the eyes of the community, and they would prefer to make his resignation effective immediately. Kaye made a remark about the trustees' lack of understanding of Liberal Judaism's basic principle of personal freedom, but did not object to their demand. It was agreed the following Friday would be Rabbi Kaye's last service, and, clearing his throat, Joe added he hoped he and Kaye would part as friends.

The temple bulletin that week invited the congregation to services to bid Rabbi Kaye farewell and extend him good wishes for his future.

Kaye did not expect an overwhelming turnout. Once the initial excitement died out, the good people of Suburban Temple would turn to their own personal affairs and would forget the whole thing. better yet, by labelling him a "hippie" they had drawn the line and had lumped him together with the rest of the misguided radical youth who, though seen, should not be heard. As far as they were concerned, he had already made his statement, which they, esconsed in their palatial suburban homes and surrounded with all the blessings of the good life, had no interest in hearing.

It was just as well. He did not want his departure to turn into a special event. It was customary at Suburban Temple, whenever an assistant rabbi was about to leave, invariably in order to take his own pulpit, for the senior rabbi and the president to make farewell speeches during the service, and for the Sisterhood to entertain the congregation after services with a special Oneg, a festive reception during which the congregants wished the departing rabbi success and happiness in his future career. Kaye had called Rabbi Blumenfeld and Joe Pins and asked them to dispense with the speeches, to which they agreed. He then called Roz Pins, the Sisterhood president, and asked her not to bother having a special Oneg. Roz was reluctant to part with tradition, and asked him to reconsider. She also wanted to know if it would not be too much to ask that he wear a suit and tie this once, in deference to the dress code of the congregation. He agreed to the suit and tie, but informed Madame President he did not plan to stay around for the reception.

When he woke up on Friday morning the first thing that occurred to him was it was time to move out of his fashionable apartment. Ever since the day Felicia took the baby and went back to her parents he had felt like a stranger in his own home. At first he tried to rationalize it was more his apartment than hers. It was his family, after all, not hers, that had put up the money for this new condominium. But the money was not the issue. She was the one who had picked the apartment, furnished it, taken pride in it. She had fashioned the apartment, as it were, in her own image. It belonged to her more than it belonged to him. If she wanted to move back in she was welcome to it. He could make do with a one bedroom rented flat in one of the older parts of town. He had had enough of suburban living. Leaving Suburban Temple meant leaving Suburbia. besides, he was not going to stay much longer in Quincy. He was going to do some travelling, see what was going on out there in the big world, and decide what to do with the rest of his life.

It was the usual crowd at services that evening. A fraction of the large membership, mostly older people. Joe Pins was the board host for the service. He found Joe pacing the hall outside Rabbi Blumenfeld's study. Blumenfeld, as usual, was late, and Joe was nervously peeking at his watch and muttering under his breath about irresponsible rabbis. He was about to make some excuse for the senior rabbi when he realized it was no longer necessary for him to do it. He was through with this charade of keeping up appearances and humoring the members of the board. From now on Blumenfeld will have to account for his own actions.

The small crowd was sitting in the front rows of the vast sanctuary. The strains of the organ were setting the mood for the Sabbath, playing a classical Sabbath hymn set to a dignified Germanic tune, sung for over a hundred years at Suburban Temple:

> Come, O Sabbath day, and bring
> Peace and healing on thy wing,
> And to every troubled breast
> Speak of the divine behest:
> Thou shalt rest, thou shalt rest!

As the last notes of the organ faded, two members of the choir in blue robes came out of the choir loft and led the congregation in singing the blessing for the Sabbath candles. It was now Rabbi Blumenfeld's turn. The senior rabbi rose and walked slowly to his pulpit, pushing back the flowing sleeves of his black robe. He cleared his throat and looked back at his younger colleague who was sitting at the other end of the bimah next to the opposite pulpit, and nodded. Kaye acknowledged the nod.

"My dear ones," Blumenfeld turned to the congregation, "tonight, as you know, is Rabbi Kaye's last service as associate rabbi of Suburban Temple, and I know you all join me in wishing him *mazal* and *hatzlacha*, good luck and success, in his future endeavors. I promised Rabbi Kaye I would be brief, and, indeed, it is more fitting that you hear from him tonight, rather than from me. Speaking as a senior colleague, I'm sorry to see him leave. We have worked closely together for three years, and in many ways it has been a most rewarding association for me."

Kaye looked at the congregation. He saw Roz Pins, sitting erect in the first row, looking straight at the speaker, nodding her head in approval. In the back of the crowd he saw his secretary, Ruth Levy, sitting with her husband. He could tell Ruth was straining to appear calm, as she kept fidgeting with her prayer book. The rest of the congregation just seemed to be there, as it had been for years and would continue to be for a long time after he left.

"Life, my friends," Blumenfled went on, "has always been unpredictable, and life today is certainly far from predictable. We live in a time of great change, and we rabbis are not immune or impervious to change. My colleague and friend Rabbi Kaye is an idealistic young man and a deeply committed Jew who, after three years in the pulpit, has decided it was time for him to move on and find out how he could make his best contribution to his people and to all people. I respect his decision and I trust we will keep in touch and share many joyous occasions in the future. God bless you."

The service continued with responsive readings in English and choir singing in Hebrew, and after the soloist sang the blessing over the wine it was Rabbi Kaye's turn to speak.

He walked up to the lectern and put on his rimless glasses.

"You will forgive me," he started, "I did not prepare a formal sermon for tonight. Tonight I would like to speak from the heart. There is a saying in Hebrew, 'Words which come out of the heart go into others' hearts.'

"Tonight, with your indulgence, I would like to speak a little about myself.

"I came to Quincy seven years ago. Quincy has been good to me. It has given me everything I have. It gave me a degree, a title, a family, a prestigious position. I know people have been saying, Rabbi Kaye has everything going for him, why is he giving it all up?

"It is very difficult to explain. Perhaps when someone has everything going for him or her, one begins to realize that certain things are wrong. This is what I began to realize a few months ago. I found out one day I wanted to pray, I wanted to talk to God, but no one was listening. I said to God, *Ayekhah*, where are you, but God did not answer. I came into this sanctuary one afternoon when no one was around and I sat down for about an hour over there in the back row, and I waited to hear some message, some indication of what it was God wanted me to do. But I heard nothing. It was then I began to doubt my own calling and my own role as a rabbi.

"What is a rabbi? I went to rabbinical school for five years and then one day the chancellor of the seminary put his hands on my shoulders and proclaimed me a rabbi in Israel. Then I came here to Suburban Temple and for three years I have been conducting services and giving sermons and everyone seemed quite pleased with my performance. Then one day I asked myself: What was I really accomplishing? Whose life was I touching? Whom was I helping? Did I really make any difference in anyone's life?

"My answer to myself, I'm sorry to say, was negative. Forgive me for rambling. I'm used to writing down my thoughts in an organized fashion. But what I am telling you now is, so to speak, off the record. It is not part of my official sermonizing. It is, if you will, a *cri de coeur*.

"What was finally getting to me were the young people of the congregation. The youth, I realized, was no longer finding this institution and yours truly relevant to their lives. Why? Think about it, why would young people who have everything, who lack nothing, who go to the best schools, turn their backs on their parents' heritage and say to us, we don't want your temple, we don't want your religion, we have no use for Judaism any more. We are not interested in opening this prayer book and talking to God. We are not even interested in discussing whether God is living or dead. As far as we are concerned, God, that is, God as presented to us by you, is boring.

"Boring. Irrelevant. These are the words they use. And so they stop caring. They turn elsewhere for their causes and for their spiritual fulfillment.

"For a while I agreed with those who argued that these young people were spoiled. They had everything, and so they became bored and started to bite the hand that was feeding them. Give them time. They will come around. In the end they will realize they are not acting wisely.

"Only they are not coming around. Some of they are marrying out of their faith, and they are leaving us. Others no longer join synagogues and Jewish institutions. Some are turning to Eastern religions and to cults. But why?

"I have been asking myself these questions, and I believe I have found the answer. Our young people, you see, have finally come to realize that the words of our prayers have become just that—words. We pray, 'It has been told you, O man, what is good, and what the Lord requires of you, only to do justly, and love mercy, and walk humbly with your God.' But is this what we, American Jews, have done? Quite to the contrary. We have waxed rich, and we flaunt our wealth in places like this edifice. We have turned the house of God into a political institution, a symbol of power. We have let ourselves be ruled by money. We have turned our backs on the poor and the needy, and we continue to lower out heads in pious prayer and say, O God, help us to perfect the world in the image of the divine.

"Our own grandparents and great-grandparents were, for the most part, much less affluent than we. In fact, most of them were quite poor. But they were rich in spirit. When they prayed the words had meaning. When they spoke to God they really spoke to Him. They cried out to Him. They thanked Him from the bottom of their hearts for life's blessings, which may have been few, but which they considered plentiful. What has happened to that spirit? Why have we inherited so little of it?

"Is it because we came to America not in search of spiritual fulfillment, or even religious freedom, as some Christian groups did, but rather in order to improve our economic condition? Is America our new Egypt, our new flesh pot? Our new spiritual bondage?

"I came to Quincy seven years ago, drawn by the Quincy Rabbinical Seminary and by the dream of Liberal Judaism, the answer to the spiritual needs of the modern Jew. I still believe in the promise of Liberal Judaism, for I believe that Jews are free to make choices and decisions through the historical perspective of the Jewish dialectic. But what I have found out during the last three years is that few choices are made, few decisions are reached, by Jews who call themselves liberal."

He paused and surveyed the congregation. He was not reaching them. Chastising them was pointless. They could not relate to what he was saying. They sincerely believed they were good parents, devoted Jews, upright citizens. Why, they gave their children everything money could buy. They contributed generously to the temple, gave to the UJA, supported civic causes. They were busy business executives, lawyers, doctors, accountants. They did not have the luxury Rabbi Kaye had of sitting around and wondering whether or not God was listening. They did not have time to keep up with all the strange ideas young people seemed to be getting into their heads these days. Clearly, this young rabbi had become a radical, and his views could not be taken too seriously by level-headed people.

Kaye's voice became softer:

"And so, my friends, I've made my choice. I have chosen to give up the comfort of home and office, the Jewish utopia of suburbia, and go out into the real world, where someone who calls himself a rabbi may well be needed. My good people, don't you see? You can replace me within twenty-four hours. You can put someone else in my place who would go through the motions I have been going through, and no one would know the difference. But for me this is no longer good enough. I would like to see Judaism come alive once again. I would like to help make it real, relevant! So tonight I would like to thank you with the biblical words, 'I am unworthy of all the kindness you have shown me.' You have been kind and generous, for which I'm grateful. but now I must be on my way, and, hopefully, as Rabbi Blumenfeld has said, we shall keep in touch, and some day with God's help our paths will cross again, *amen, ken yehi ratzon.*"

After the service ended he joined Rabbi Blumenfeld and Joe Pins at the reception line. The same handshakes as always. The same "I enjoyed your sermon" and "that was a good message," as if his words had nothing to do with them, as if he had spoken about someone else. What would it take to shake those people out of their complacency? he wondered. He joined Blumenfeld in the blessing over the bread, and as soon as the crowd began to help itself to coffee and tea and pastries he unobtrusively slipped out into the cold night.

✧ **11** ✧

Eve gave him a questioning look. They sat across from each other at a downtown restaurant on early Sunday afternoon. She wore the same blue mohair sweater she had on when she first came to see him at the hospital. She kept rearranging the laundered napkin in front of her, as if trying to arrange her thoughts, or, better yet, her feelings. When he called her the night before and told her he needed to talk to her, she hesitated at first. She had to attend to some chores on Sunday and was not sure she could get away. He had asked her to try and later that evening she called back and said it was okay.

"What did they say after you gave your sermon?" she asked, smoothing her napkin.

"I left as soon as the service was over. What would have been the point of sticking around and listening to their inane comments? 'Oh rabbi, that was a beautiful sermon!' 'Jack and I are so sorry to see you leave!' Well, anyway, I'm glad I'm no longer part of that rabbi-congregation game they play."

A young waitress came by and waited for their orders. They ordered egg salad sandwiches and coffee. The waitress scribbled a hieroglyph on her pad and left.

"I may not be staying at Lourdes much longer," Eve said. "I heard a rumor yesterday there are no more funds to run the school and they may close it down in June."

"What would you do?"

"Our community may be assigned to some new school in the suburbs."

"I see."

"It's ironic, isn't it? We take the vow of poverty and then we're told to turn our backs on the poor and minister to the rich."

"Yes, it is ironic," Kaye agreed. "Well, what are you going to do about it? Just go along?"

"I'm afraid so. What choice do I have?"

"Can you ask to be assigned to another school like Cliffwood?"

"I could. But who's to say in another year or two that school would not meet with the same fate?"

"I guess it all boils down to money and politics," Kaye said. He leaned over and looked into her eyes. "Listen," he lowered his voice, as if about to share a secret, "let's be honest. We both see through all this sham of organized religion. It's a business, that's all it is. What was it about religion that attracted us in the first place? We don't need the titles and the symbols and all those intricate rituals to believe in God, do we? Do religious institutions make one more spiritual, more just, more caring? Or are they in effect another form of political and economical power? Are religious organizations in today's world the force for good they are purported to be? And if they are not, shouldn't we look for some other way to do the things we believe in?"

"Like what?"

"Like strike out on our own."

"I suppose I could quit the order," Eve said and gave him a slow, searching look. "What would I do then? Become a social worker? A political activist? Yes, I agree. Religious institutions are not doing what they are supposed to do. Does that mean we do away with them? No, I'm not hung up on titles or symbols or rituals. Most of them, in fact, embarrass me. But people seem to need these things. It's hard for them to grasp abstract ideas and act on their own. They need structure. They look to their religion to hold them together."

She stopped. He waited for her to go on.

"Perhaps I'm a coward," she said, dropping her eyes. "I'm afraid to strike out on my own. I need the Church to give me the support system without which I would be lost."

"I understand," Kaye said. He leaned toward her and looked around to make sure no one was listening. "But don't you see? Your Church and my Synagogue are both spiritually dead! I saw you at that convent. I saw how lonely you were. Detached from everything. What is it about you Catholics that makes you so damn obedient, so accepting? How did you ever get to be that way? Is this really what Christ has taught you? Was Jesus of Nazareth an obedient, unquestioning conformist? If he were, would he have preached those new radical ideas totally at odds with the Jewish beliefs of his time?"

He sat up on the edge of his chair.

"Tell me," he said, "what support system did Jesus have?"

"His heavenly father, I suppose."

"And that's not good enough for you?"

She laughed. "I guess not. My faith is not as strong as his."

"I think it is," he said gravely. "In fact, I'm sure it is. You know something? I can feel it in my bones: you and I can start something which may change the world."

"Like what?"

"Many people in the world today—Jews and Gentiles—have turned their backs on religion. It's not the teachings of religion per se they're rejecting, but rather religious institutions. They see through the sham of those institutions which are supposed to promote peace and social justice but instead are promoting themselves. They know that there's a unity more real than all the religious distinctions we make, as you yourself once told me. They realize that unless all of us find a way to work together to eliminate the ills of the world, those ills will be the end of us all."

He leaned forward and grasped her hands.

"Eve! For once we need to put aside our religious distinctions and look at the common good, not just our own good. We need to find a way to mobilize those people across ideological lines and start to put the teachings of our religious traditions into practice, to perfect the world according to God's plan, to begin to establish the kingdom of heaven here on earth."

He drew a deep breath.

"We may be running out of time. If we don't do it now we may never have another chance. Religion—yours and mine, it makes no difference which—is in a greater crisis today that ever before in history. More than once in the past one hundred years God has been pronounced dead. I'm not ready to accept the diagnosis. God, the God of the universe, transcends death. But man's relationship to God can die. Last summer I walked into the sanctuary of Suburban Temple one afternoon, and suddenly I experienced the death of my relationship to God. I later realized it was within my power not to let it die, and so I did something about it, and here I am now. I agree with Voltaire's remark that if God did not exist we would have to invent him. If humanity's relationship to God dies then all is lost. It is within our powers to prevent that from happening. My religion teaches me that we have a choice, we have free will. We can restore the knowledge of God to the world, and make it fill the earth as the waters cover the sea."

She smiled at him radiantly. "You sound like Isaiah," she said. "The vision of the end of days. But what has this got to do with the two of us?"

"You and I could start working on it. I know it's a superhuman task. But someone has to start. It may as well be you and I."

"You are a dreamer, Josh," Eve said and looked whimsically into his eyes. "Why don't you eat your sandwich before it gets stale? I think what you really need is a little vacation. After that illness and this whole experience with the temple you have got your mind all charged up. You need to put things back in perspective."

Out in the street it was a clear, windy December afternoon. The sun slanted against the windows of the tall office buildings casting long shadows across Liberty Square. As they came out of the restaurant he offered her his arm. She hesitated at first and then wrapped her arm around his and cuddled against him. They walked down the street quietly and headed for the parking lot around the corner. Downtown was deserted except for a solitary wino tottering on the edge of the sidewalk, waiting for a car to stop at the light to go over and ask for a handout.

"We may be fooling ourselves," Kaye said, pointing at the tattered, befogged drunk. "Maybe it is ourselves we are trying to save, not the world."

Driving Eve back to the convent he turned off the road and parked the car on a lookout ramp overlooking the city. The Ohio River down below had caught on fire as the sun began to set over the distant hills of Kentucky. Eve unbuttoned her winter coat, took off her gloves, and straightened her hair. A golden haze blurred her face as she sat erect in her seat, smoothing her gloves over her lap.

He put his hand over hers. Her hand did not respond to his touch. He withdrew his hand.

"Why are you so quiet?" he inquired.

"I was thinking. You never told me anything about your wife. Except for the fact that you are separated."

"What would you like to know?"

"Anything. What's her name?"

"Felicia."

"Felicia," she echoed back as if trying to imagine what a person named Felicia might look like. "It means happy. How did Solomon put it? 'Be happy with the woman you love.' I guess it didn't quite work out that way, did it?"

"No, it didn't."

"Do you still love her?"

He did not expect such question. What was she driving at? It now occurred to him he should have told Eve about his indecision regarding his marriage. He had been suppressing his feelings for Felicia, had put them on ice, so to speak, deferring a decision.

"Yes, I guess I still do."

"Is there a chance you might get back together?"

The way she asked the question made it sound like she hoped they did. Catholics did not believe in divorce. One had to do everything within one's powers to salvage a marriage. But what made her bring up his marriage all of a sudden? When he thought about it later on he realized it was perfectly natural for her to bring it up. He further realized he had kept his relationship with Eve separate from all his other personal relationships, as if the two of them existed in a world apart where no one else was admitted. Now that she brought Felicia into this private world she had shattered the illusion of exclusiveness.

"I'm sorry, what did you say?"

"I asked whether there was a chance you might get back together?"

"I know Felicia would like to."

"What about you?"

"What about me. . ." he looked down at the wheel. "Yes, I suppose I do want to have a wife and a family, like most people. Isn't that what life is really about? I remember Kafka's hero saying at one point: To have a wife and children and be a useful member of the community, isn't that what it's all about? Kafka's hero does not seem to be able to pull it off. He is too busy looking for the master of the castle. Or is it the judge presiding at the trial? I forget which.

I may be a little like that character, caught up in this metaphysical search, which may exclude such normal aspects of life as marriage. Your Church may have the right idea. Your priests and nuns are not allowed to marry. You are married to God, which is perhaps the way it ought to. . ."

"Forgive me for saying this," she interrupted. "But it seems to me you are evading the question. I'm not so sure you are like Kafka's hero. And as for celibacy, I can see both pros and cons. But that's besides the point. We are not talking now about our religious institutions. We are discussing you, Joshua Kaye, and your wife, Felicia."

God bless her, she would not let him off the hook.

"Fair enough."

"Josh, do me a favor. Talk to her. Make sure you are not doing anything you may regret later on."

He was surprised by her vehemence. She did not even know Felicia. Why was she getting so emotional about it?

"I don't mean to poke into your personal affairs," she said in apology. "It's really hard for me to talk about these things because of the way I feel about you. You told me when you called me last night you needed to talk to me." She stopped and closed her eyes and took a deep breath. "I can imagine how you must have felt when you walked out of the temple and then walked into your empty apartment. Oh, Josh, I wish I could give you what you need. Yes, I know what you are thinking: Where did I ever come off getting myself involved with a nun? I hope you didn't think I was overstepping my bounds when I suggested you see Felicia and talk things over with her."

He shook his head and smiled at her.

"No Eve, I didn't. You are right. I appreciate your candidness. I really do. Yes, I will talk to her. I'll call her tonight."

✧ **12** ✧

When he called his estranged wife that evening he was afraid she would start an argument over the phone. For one thing, he thought she would insist they sell the apartment and divide the money, with the main share going to her because she had the baby. To his surprise she said nothing of the kind. She spoke calmly, without recrimination. He told her he was ready to get together and discuss the future. When would it be a good time for her? She said she could see him in the morning around ten o'clock. Did she want to come over to the apartment? She readily agreed.

The doorbell rang at five past ten. When he opened the door he saw Felicia standing outside, holding their one year old son in her arms.

He was surprised to see her smiling at him.

"Please come in," he said, steadying his voice.

She walked into the living room and looked around.

"Mmm, you have kept the place pretty neat."

"I've tried."

She put the boy down. "Danny, say hello to your Daddy."

The boy took a few hesitant steps and headed for the glass top table in the middle of the living room. He had just learned how to walk. His silky hair had grown in abundant curls over his ears and neck.

"He doesn't remember me," Kaye said. He bent down and picked up the boy and tried to hold him against himself. The child stared at him with wide blue eyes and started to pout, turning to his mother.

"It's your beard," Felicia said. "He is not used to it."

"Why don't you take him to his room?" he said. "He'd probably like to see it again."

She took the child to his room. He looked around intently and then seemed to recognize a picture on the wall opposite his crib, a wide sombreroed Mexican boy riding a burro. He started babbling and reaching out for it. Felicia put him down. He turned to the toy chest in the corner of the room and started to pull things out.

"He is happy to be back in his room," Kaye said. "You can leave him here for a while. Why don't we sit down in the living room?"

Felicia settled into the corner of the living room couch and crossed her legs. He expected her to take out a cigarette, but she didn't. He told her he had made some coffee. He went into the kitchen and poured two cups and brought the coffee into the living room.

Taking a sip, she asked him whether he had fully recovered from his ileitis.

"It's a chronic condition," he said. "I'm afraid I'll have to learn how to live with it."

What was she up to? By all right she should be boiling with anger. Instead, she appeared calm and friendly, as if nothing had happened between them.

"You look like you lost weight," he said.

"I have."

"You look good."

She thanked him. They remained silent for a long time, each waiting for the other to proceed.

"Well, I'm finished with Suburban Temple," he finally said. "I gave my farewell sermon last Friday."

"Suburban Temple had a lot to do with our separation," she said. "You weren't happy there. I think you were overwhelmed by the bigness of that place and by the big-time politics. You were also disappointed in your idol and mentor, Alvin Blumenfeld. This had colored your attitude toward me. You kind of lumped me together with that whole crowd, as if I were part of some kind of plot against you. Actually, Josh, I just wanted you to be happy there. I believed, as did other people there, that you were the right person to succeed Rabbi Blumenfeld when it was time for him to retire. That didn't make me your enemy, did it? But okay. Now this whole thing is over. Where do we go from here?"

"You want me back?"

"Do you want *me* back?"

"Why do you always answer a question with a question?"

"Because I'm Jewish."

He laughed.

"Yes," she said, "I want you back provided we can get it together, like they say. You have to be doing something you believe in and feel comfortable with. Otherwise I'm afraid we'll be right back

where we started. I know Daddy suggested that you look into getting your PhD and go into teaching, but you weren't too interested."

"I'm interested in the real thing. I don't think books have the
answers."

"Are you going to look for your own congregation?"

"I don't think that is the real thing."

"What then, is?"

"This is what I need to find out."

"Being a rabbi, helping people, is not the real thing?"

"Helping people is. It's the rabbi part I'm having trouble with. I
just wrote a letter to the *Quincy Times* to denounce Armor & Gambit for making napalm. I deliberately left out my title when I signed
it. You see, the title 'rabbi' no longer holds much meaning for me. I
no longer feel comfortable with it. It carries with it a whole host of
connotations which I no longer wish to be associated with. Institu-
tionally, organized religion no longer has the answers for people.
Something new is needed. Something which is not subservient to
money and self-interest and politics. Something truly humane,
loving and caring. I know I'm being vague, and I know I don't have
anything concrete to offer. I also know it's always easier to tear
down than it is to build up. But I can no longer go along with
preserving this system and being part of it. It's self-defeating. I
must go out and find a way to do something about it."

"And where does that leave me? How do *I* fit into your scheme of
things?"

"Are you willing to go along with me? I don't have much to offer.
I'm not even sure I'll be making enough money to pay the bills at
the end of the month. I don't know where I may be going. I'm sure
there will be hardships, heartaches, doubts, misgivings, scorn, even
despair. I can't help it. Like you say, I have to do something I
believe in. So, you still want me back?"

She looked at him in disbelief and shook her head. Fighting back
her tears she said,

"No, Josh, I can't say I do. Do you really know what you want? I
can't believe what I'm hearing! I thought once you left Suburban
Temple you would start putting things back in perspective. Now
you don't make any sense at all!"

"Calm yourself down," he said, "You don't have to get yourself all
worked up."

She blew her nose and looked at him with flashing green eyes.
She then heaved a sigh and settled back in her seat.

"I'm sorry," she said, "I'd promised myself before I came here I

was not going to make a scene. Okay. I guess I really don't understand this whole thing about not wanting to be a rabbi and being
turned off by the whole thing. I wish I could help you, Josh. I wish I
were smarter and could figure this whole thing out. I've discussed
it with Daddy. He feels you are too idealistic. You don't quite have
your two feet on the ground, to use his own words. He thinks you
will come around. He wants me to give you a chance to come
around. He says I should wait. Well, I don't have to tell you what
it's been like. I don't want you to feel sorry for me. I certainly don't
want you to give up whatever it is you believe in. That won't do
either one of us any good. You go ahead and find whatever it is you
are looking for. Then we'll see. If it still looks like we are ready and
willing to get back together, we will. I'm not angry at you, Josh.
Honest. I was too young to get married in the first place, and you
had too many unsettled questions. We should have waited. Things
would have probably turned out much better that way. But it
doesn't really matter. It's done. Let's wait and see what happens."

By the middle of the week he had moved into a small flat on the
lower West Side. Felicia had agreed to move back into the apartment, and the transfer was worked out amicably, without a hitch.

The day after he moved in he called Eve. He told her he had seen
his wife and they had talked things over. They did not see eye to
eye, and decided they were not ready to get back together. Felicia's
attitude toward him, however, had changed. The old anger and
resentment were gone. She appeared to be concerned about his welfare. She seemed to feel that he had lost his way and needed someone to look after him, and she wished there was more she could do
for him. He told Eve Felicia had agreed to move back into the
apartment, since he was willing to make do with a small inexpensive flat on the lower West Side. He was happy she did. It was only
fair, especially because of the baby. He felt greatly relieved. Felicia
had a degree in library science and was looking for a part time job.
She was the independent type, self-reliant and assertive, and she
would do better pursuing her own career than playing the part of
the *rebbetzin*, the wife of the junior rabbi at Suburban Temple. It
was all working out for the best as far as he was concerned.

Eve listened sympathetically. You can't push it, she said. You
have to wait and see how things turn out.

He asked her if he was still invited to midnight mass on
Christmas Eve. Yes, of course. She'd love for him to come.

The flat he had rented was a furnished upstairs apartment in an old two family house. He rented it for only one month. He did not expect to stay in Quincy much longer. In a month or two at the latest he would be on his way. Quincy was not the place to start something new. Here everything was too staid, too resistant to change, too set in its ways. Soon he would be moving on. Where to he was not yet sure. He would soon find out.

The old West Side where he took up quarters bordered on the downtown business district and abutted on the Ohio River. Jewish life in Quincy started on the West Side over a hundred years ago. All the synagogues on the West Side had long been sold and converted into churches. Poor blacks from the South had moved into one section of the West Side, down by the river, and poor whites from the hills of Kentucky had been moving in closer to the business district. The Jews were long gone. Here and there there were some pockets of old residents of German or Irish descent whose forebears had settled here before the Jews. They refused to leave their ancestral home or were too old to move. Kaye's landlady, old Mrs. Paddock, was one of those residents. She was the sole survivor of a Quincy family which traced its ancestry back to the Revolutionary War. She lived alone on the ground floor and sublet the upstairs. The rent was minimal. The old lady, it appeared, was interested in having a male tenant in the house for safety reasons rather than for profit.

I have wiped the slate clean, Kaye reflected. I'm now ready to get in touch with my soul.

Yes, Felicia might be right. He might have lost his way in the world. But he was much happier now than he ever was before, when he had everything going for him. He had left all his expensive clothes in the apartment with Felicia—the business suits, the tuxedo he used for officiating at weddings and for attending gala dinners, the French cuff shirts, the Pierre Cardin ties, the expensive shoes. He only took along some casual clothes, two cartons of books, and toilet articles. He had divested himself of all the material possessions he had acquired during his brief rabbinical career. He no longer had to worry whether one of the members of the temple saw him walking down the street in an open shirt or a pair of jeans. He no longer had to impress anyone, say the right things, laugh at dumb jokes, smile sweetly at boring matrons. He was his own man now.

Shortly after settling in his new surroundings he law awake one night and thought about Eve. The two of them had to get away from Quincy. She was not happy there any more than he was. They

had to go to a new place and make a new start. Where exactly it did
not matter. Between the two of them they could organize Jews and
Christians to form a new coalition of people dedicated to peace and
social justice. They could talk to other clergy—ministers, priests,
rabbis, nuns—who shared their views. There had to be quite a few
of those, although many of them needed a push from someone in
order to come forward and be counted. The youth of America was
looking for direction and guidance. Who was going to provide it?
Where was all the turmoil and struggle of the waning sixties leading to? Was it all going to go to waste? Was America going to revert
back to its old ways, as the good people of Suburban Temple wanted
it to, now that they had made their spiritual leader, Rabbi Alvin
Blumenfeld, give up the struggle, and tried to make him, Joshua
Kaye, do the same?

The more he thought about persuading Eve to go away with him
the more he realized his motive was not altogether altruistic. He
missed her. He missed being with her. She was on his mind all the
time. Now that he had attained his freedom, there was a great void
in his life which needed to be filled. Could she fill that void? First
she would have to stop being who she was—a nun, a Catholic.
Could she do such a thing? Did he want her to?

Clearly, the sensible thing for him to do was to go his own way
and let her be who she was. It was the only fair thing to do. This
liaison between them had gone far enough. Eve was right. They
were attracted to each other in a way which made it impossible for
them to draw the line, no matter how hard they tried. Why couldn't
he come to terms with it? Why couldn't he learn to accept that
which was beyond his powers to change?

The question, then, was where to go and what to do. He had
many grandiose ideas, but there was no clear indication where to
start. One thing had become clear to him: he could not do it all
alone. He had to find a community of like-minded people with
whom he could start putting his ideas into practice. Once he
decided where he was going he would begin to look for such people
and start such a community. That would be the beginning. From
that point on things would begin to happen on their own momen-
tum.

It was the week of Hanukkah. He had bought Hanukkah candles
and lit the menorah on his windowsill each night. The street outside was overhung and bedecked with red and green Christmas
decorations. And here he was, one Jew alone on the West Side,
celebrating the ancient Festival of Lights. Outside in the street

Christian America was busy with its Christmas shopping. It seemed that the most important ritual American Christians performed each year in anticipation of their holy event was shopping. He thought back on Hanukkah at Suburban Temple. Jewish parents trying to outdo their Christian neighbors by giving their children gifts on each of the eight nights of Hanukka. Little Stevie and Scotty and Susy should not be left out, God forbid.

The next morning he sat down and wrote Eve a letter about his thoughts on the matter. No doubt Hanukkah and Christmas were related. Both must have had their origins in a pagan winter festival, in which fire was worshipped because it helped man keep warm in the dead of winter and chased away the darkness. Later on both religions sought to spiritualize the pagan holiday by relating it to events in their own history. To Jews it became the holiday of Jewish survival in a pagan world. To Christians it became a celebration of the birth of the savior was to establish peace on earth and good will toward man.

Forgive me, Eve, he went on. But what has this holiday season got to do with peace and good will? What is the difference between Christmas in America today and the pagan winter festival of the pre-Christian era? The lights, the decorations, the self-indulgence, the buying orgies? Hanukkah, for that matter, has become for most Jews a sort of a Jewish Christmas, not a very convincing imitation, at that.

Here, on the West Side, he continued, poor people go into debt because of Christmas. There is something sad and ironic about their striving to keep up with the rest of society by spending all that money on trees and decorations and expensive gifts and food and liquor, and, he was sure, feeling guilty because they did not really have enough money to spend on Christmas as good Christians should. Is this how religion expects to bring about a better world?

She wrote him back to let him know she was in full agreement. Yes, Christmas did become a pagan holiday. It had become a source of embarrassment for people like herself. People who called themselves Christians were making a mockery of Christian ideals. She wished something could be done about it, but in this instance the will of the laity was stronger than the will of their spiritual leaders. Here at Lourdes, she pointed out, we try in our own small way to counter this show of paganism. When you come to the convent for midnight mass you will see what I mean.

✧ 13 ✧

Mrs. Paddock prayed for a white Christmas and a white Christmas it turned out to be.

When he left the house on Christmas Eve Kaye found himself knee-deep in snow. The West Side had suddenly changed from an old shabby neighborhood into a virginal fairyland. He stood outside in the snow and filled his lungs with pure crystalline air. The thought of going to a convent on Christmas Eve to celebrate the birth of the Christian Savior with some Catholic nuns gave him pause. He would have begged off at the last minute, were it not for the fact Eve wanted him so much to come. She had assured him it was a simple celebration in which everyone was being himself or herself, without any airs or pretense. He did not have to act in any particular way. He could just be himself and enjoy the holiday spirit. That is, of course, if he did not feel in any way uncomfortable, or "out of it."

The ten minute ride to the convent took over an hour. The snow ploughs had been at work on the steep road leading up from the West Side to Cliffwood, yet fresh snow kept falling and the snow tires were barely able to grip the road. After much skidding and swerving he finally reached the top of the hill and began the slow ascent into Cliffwood. He slid into a parking space in front of Lourdes Convent. In the snow the old convent looked like an enchanted castle. A narrow path had been cleared on the steps leading up to the massive oak doors. He climbed the steps and let himself into the building and walked down the long corridor to the waiting room where he had waited for Eve the first time he went to the convent. After waiting for a few minutes two young nuns came in and nodded at him. He asked for Eve.

"Is she expecting you?" one of the two asked. She did not look much older than twenty, perhaps even younger. She looked at him with eager brown eyes and her cheeks dimpled when she smiled.

"She invited me to midnight mass."

"I'm Anne," the young nun said. "This is Enid."

"Joshua Kaye."

"Oh, Rabbi Kaye! Glad you could come! Here, come this way."

"Did Eve tell you I was coming?" he asked Anne as he followed her down the hall.

She looked back at him, her brown eyes flashing in the dim light.

"She sure did! She speaks very highly of you. I'm glad we finally get to meet you."

As happened before, now too he was surprised to find out other people were aware of that little world inhabited by only Eve and himself. He was intrigued by this young nun. She was open and spontaneous. Her playfulness and her disarming smile had put him completely at ease.

"I'm sure she exaggerated," Kaye replied. "I hope I won't disappoint you."

The two sisters took him into the large room he remembered from his first visit, which they called the reading room. The room was now brightly lit and there were people standing around. In the corner he noticed a small, sparsely decorated Christmas tree.

"Evie, your company is here," Sister Anne called out.

Eve turned to look. She wore a long flowing plain white dress. When she saw him she waved at him and came over, walking quickly across the room. He recalled seeing her move across the field at St. John's College. Like a gazelle. Light and swift and radiant. It was the first time he realized he was falling in love with her. Seeing her now he knew he wanted her more than anything else in the world. No, he couldn't have her. It was a folly. Pure madness. By all right he should tell her he was too weak to resist his desire for her and then leave and not see her again. Go back to his own kind and let her live her own life. This whole thing was absurd. What was he doing inside a convent on Christmas Eve, in love with a nun?

He could feel her breath on his face. In a fog, he could tell she was giving him a welcome kiss.

"Did you have any trouble getting here?" he heard her say, his mind in a daze.

"Not too bad," he stuttered, his cheeks burning.

"What's the matter, are you okay?"

"Oh, yes, I'm fine."

Get a hold of yourself, a voice inside him ordered.

"Here," he handed her a gift wrapped bottle of wine. "I didn't know if it was appropriate, but I brought it anyway."

"Oh, it's fine," she laughed. "We will drink it tonight."

"You look beautiful in this dress," Kaye said, "You really look great in white."

He saw her blush.

"What's the matter? We are old friends, aren't we?"

"Yes, friends," she said, looking whimsically into his eyes. "Not lovers."

They kept looking into each other's eyes, and they both laughed.

"It somehow feels different tonight, doesn't it?" he said.

"Like what?"

"Like you and I. Like maybe I should rescue you from the master of this castle and carry you off to never never land."

"And where, may I ask, is this never never land?"

"Wherever the two of us happen to be together."

"Well, then, we are together right here, so there is no need to go anywhere, right?"

"Yes, Eve," he sighed, "You are right, as usual."

More people drifted into the room. He counted some twenty sisters. There was also a young man in the room, about sixteen years old, and a ruddy, white haired priest, telling a joke to a group of nuns in the corner.

"Who is he?" Kaye motioned at the priest.

"Father Woods," Eve said. "He will be celebrating mass tonight. Come, I'll introduce you to him."

Father Woods shook his hand warmly and asked him to call him Brandon. Eve and the other nuns turned away and left the two men to themselves. Brandon Woods, Kaye found out, was an Irishman who had spent many years in Latin America. Kaye mentioned he once lived in Mexico for a year, where his father was working on an irrigation project for the Mexican government. He made a remark about how he was struck by the abject poverty he saw in Mexico. Brandon looked at him with a pained expression. Poverty? Yes, granted, there was a great deal of poverty in Mexico, but it got worse as one kept moving on down the continent. Brandon had worked among the poor in Guatemala and Honduras, and later in Peru and Bolivia. He himself had come from a poor family in Belfast, but that was nothing compared to a country like Honduras, where most people's daily diet consisted of two or three tortillas and a cup of black bean soup, where one out of every three babies dies at birth, where the average life expectancy was under thirty-five. Brandon considered himself fortunate to have had the opportunity to share the lot of those people, who are among the most wretched members of the Church, yet he felt a deep sense of frustration when he had to leave, not having been able to do more for those people who, you could rest assured, will some day revolt, and when they do, a great deal of innocent blood will be shed.

Brandon paused and turned to Kaye with a smile, putting his hand on his shoulder.

"Well, tonight we won't talk about the woes of the world. Tonight we will rejoice and hope for a better world."

The nuns had now gathered in front of the small band stand at the other end of the room. They sat in a semi-circle before the stage. Sister Anne, the young nun who had greeted him when he arrived at the convent, got up on the stage, rolled back her sleeves and took a guitar out of an old case. She sat down on a wooden bench and started to tune the guitar. The other sisters waited in rapt attention. Father Woods invited Kaye to join the group. Kaye went over and sat next to Eve.

Sister Anne invited her colleagues to join in the singing. They started with familiar Christmas carols. Kaye could feel the intensity of their feelings as they sang. To them those songs were not ordinary holiday songs but rather hymns and prayers which touched their innermost being. They sang with fervor, with hasidic *kavanah*, as it were, some with their eyes shut, swaying to the time of the music, some glowing with joy, others looking on with deep yearning in their eyes. Father Woods joined in, singing in his deep resonant baritone, buoyed by the spirit of the caroling.

Sister Anne stopped. She seemed to be getting ready for her favorite number.

The song turned out to be Silent Night. The songleader started in a soft, plaintive voice. The others joined in. The leader's voice rose on the closing note:

> Sleep in heavenly pea-eece
> Slee-eep in heavenly peace. . .

As she repeated the song Kaye found himself singing along. He had known this song all his life, but had never before heard it sung with such feeling. He could see tears sparkle in some of the sisters' eyes.

Everyone remained silent long after the song ended. Sister Anne smiled at the group and took a deep breath.

"Well," she said with a sigh of relief, "that was good. Real good. Oh, by the way, we have a special guest with us tonight, Joshua Kaye. For those of you who don't know him, Josh has served until recently as the associate rabbi at Suburban Temple in West Hills."

They all turned and looked at him with welcoming smiles. He smiled back and nodded at them. They kept looking at him in apparent expectation, waiting to hear him say something befitting the occasion.

He stood up and cleared his throat.

"Well, I'm very happy to be here tonight and share this beautiful celebration with all of you. I'm reminded of Jacob's words when he stopped for the night at Beth El. 'Indeed there is God in this place.' Indeed, I can feel it tonight."

He paused. Many of them smiled in approval.

"Hear hear," Father Woods said with a twinkle in his eye.

He looked at Eve. He could tell she was pleased with what he said.

"Eve told me you play the guitar," Sister Anne turned to Kaye. "Here," she held forth her guitar, "it's your turn now."

He was about to decline when some of the sisters applauded, urging him to proceed.

What could he possibly play at a convent on Christmas Eve?

He went up on the stage and took the guitar and strapped it on.

"Well, let's see. I've never played a Christmas carol before."

"Do something Jewish," one of the nuns called out.

"Okay," he agreed, relieved. I'll do a hasidic round."

He ran his thumb over the strings and cleared his throat. "A hasidic round, by the way, is a form of prayer through song," Kaye explained. "Hasidic Jews, who outwardly appear austere and sombre actually believe that God can only be worshiped through joy. Music to them is the language of joy. It comes directly from the heart and has the power to reach the heavenly throne. A hasidic round uses few words and generates a great deal of feeling. Sometimes it has no words at all, only a repetitive sound, da da dai or ya ba ba bam. When they do use words they are usually taken from Scripture or from the liturgy. The song starts slowly, like a sigh or a murmur, and is repeated over and over again, each time a little louder, more buoyant, with growing fervor, until it finally reaches a climax of joyous ecstasy. I would like to teach you some of those rounds, and I hope everyone will join in."

He threw back his head and began to strum softly.

> *Od yishama b'harei Yehudah. . .*
> There will yet be heard
> In Judea's towns. . .

He felt the joyous rhythm of the song sweep over him.

> . . . and in the streets of Jerusalem

Some of the nuns began to clap to the time of the song.

> . . . the voice of gladness
> And the voice of joy,
> The voice of bridegrooms
> And the voice of brides. . .

He stood up and asked his listeners to repeat each line after him. He went over the song a few times until everyone had learned the words. The nuns were good students. They learned quickly. The spirit of the song buoyed and surged. What meaning did they find in Jeremiah's words? Was it his promise of national redemption for the Jews, or was it something more personal, something about the brides of Christ who some day will be united with their beloved in the heavenly Jerusalem?

As the song went on they were all singing and clapping.

> The voice of bridegroom
> And the voice of bride
> In Judea's towns
> And in Jerusalem's streets. . .

Swept by the song, he found himself standing in the middle of the room, surrounded by a circle of nuns, with Sister Anne leading the way, teaching them how to do the hasidic dance.

> *Kol sason v'kol simcha.* . .

They had real hasidic spirit, those nuns did! They were soon dancing around the room, their feet barely touching the ground, a small circle forming around him inside a larger circle as he kept dancing with them, dancing and singing, their faces glowing as they moved toward him as if about to embrace him, the whole room dancing with them. And suddenly everything begins to spin and blur around him and he starts to sink down, his knees folding, stretching out his arms to hold on to the dancers who now stop dancing and huddle around him looking at him with surprise and alarm in their eyes, reaching down to him as he starts to black out.

When he woke up he was lying on a narrow bed in a small dark room. A glimmer of light slanted across the room from a high window near the ceiling. At first he did not know where he was or what time it was. Was he back in the hospital? It certainly did not look like a hospital room. When his eyes got used to the dark he made out a wooden cross on the opposite wall. It all came back to him: He was in the convent. He had been dancing with the nuns and he had passed out. He had not yet fully recovered from his illness, and he must have overexerted himself. He consulted his watch. It was four o'clock in the morning. He had been lying here for hours.

He was about to get up when the door opened.

"Who is it?"

"It's me, Eve."

She closed the door behind her and came over and sat down on the bed next to him.

"How do you feel?"

"Much better, thanks."

"You sure gave all of us a scare."

"Sorry I did. I guess I got a little carried away."

"It wasn't your fault. We are the ones who got carried away."

"I hope I didn't spoil your Christmas Eve."

"Not at all. They all told me how much they enjoyed you. They were only sorry this thing happened to you. They could have gone on for hours."

"What about midnight mass?"

"Oh, that was a while ago. Father Woods gave a beautiful talk. I'm sorry you missed it. We just had breakfast, and now everyone is either hanging around or resting up."

He took her hand and stroked it.

"Merry Christmas, Eve."

She leaned down and kissed him on his lips.

He pulled her toward himself and held her in his arms. "I love you, Eve."

"Don't, Josh, please don't."

"Why not?"

"I'm afraid."

"There is nothing to be afraid of. There is only you and me. Nothing else matters."

She let him pull her toward himself. She lay on the bed next to him, motionless.

He lifted the covers and put them over the two of them.

"Look how well we fit together."

"Yes, we do."

"Do you love me?"

"Yes, Josh, I do."

He arched over her and kissed her eyes.

"My darling. . ."

"I love you, Josh."

She pulled him down and pressed him against herself. From the way she lay flat on her back, stiff and awkward, he could tell she had never made love before. He caressed her breast and her thigh, trying to arouse her desire. As he brushed her face with his lips he felt wetness under her eyes.

"You are crying," he said. "What's the matter?"

"I don't know," she sobbed. "I'm sorry."

He felt his desire ebb.

"I'm sorry, Josh," she clung to him. "Don't mind me. You go ahead. Don't stop."

He rolled back and lay next to her.

"No," he said, "I can't do it alone. It has to be both of us. I'm sorry, Eve. I was pushing it. We are obviously not ready for it."

They lay next to each other for a long time without saying a word.

"Someone may walk in," he finally said.

She turned and looked into his eyes. "Are you mad at me?"

He touched her face with his fingertips. "No, I'm not. I'm very glad I came. It was really beautiful. It was one of the most beautiful nights of my life. It's too bad we have to set limits on love, isn't it? Christians, Jews, all those man-made distinctions we must learn to live with. You and your vows, me and my 'thou shalt not this' and 'thou shalt not that.' There's got to be a better way. Perhaps some day we will find out."

He got home at the crack of dawn. He crawled into bed with his clothes on and slept until late afternoon. When he woke up it was dark outside—an overcast sky signalling an imminent storm. He had a hollow sensation inside him, as if his insides had been completely emptied out. At first he thought it was hunger. He had not eaten anything since yesterday. He dragged himself out of bed and staggered into the kitchen and looked for something to eat. No, it was not hunger. He had not appetite. He sat down at the kitchen table and propped his elbows on the bare formica top. The emptiness was not only inside but all around him. With a sudden throb he remembered saying goodbye to Eve as he was about to leave the convent shortly before daybreak. He recalled the expression in her eyes—sadness and longing—as they stood in the vestibule next to the heavy wooden doors. When he leaned to kiss her goodbye she offered him her cheek instead of her lips. He had asked her when would he see her again. Instead of answering she clung to him with sudden compulsion, like a child, her chest heaving against him, and when he walked out into the cold, as yet unborn day he felt this numbing emptiness which now came back.

What did that look in her eyes, what did her clinging to him signify?

She was not happy at that convent. She wanted to leave. She wanted him to show her the way. In her room last night she wanted him to make love to her. Perhaps he should have. Even if it would have meant pain and disappointment and would have made both of them feel shame and guilt. Perhaps it was necessary to go through all this in order to come to terms with their relationship, find a way to define it, call it by its right name. In spite of her vows, in spite of his commitments, in spite of their totally conflicting beliefs, they needed each other. There was no getting away from it.

He needed to talk to her. let her know it was no use fighting it. She had to leave the convent. They would work together for a common goal. She as a Catholic and he as a Jew. As for their own personal relationship, they would have to define it rather than deny it. It won't be easy. But there was no getting away from it. Somehow they would find a way to come to terms with it.

When he called the convent the next day he was told Eve was away. Where did she go? She was off from school for winter vacation, but she did not leave a word where she went. He left a message for her to call back.

He did not hear from her all week when, on New Year's Eve, he found a letter from her in his mailbox, postmarked Fairview, Kentucky. She wrote:

Dear Josh,

I'm sure you wonder where I have disappeared to. I'm alive and well and staying with an old friend here in Fairview, Kentucky. Alive, yes. Well, I'm not so sure. When you left on Christmas morning I became so depressed I did not eat all day and was not able to sleep all night. It was during the night that I decided to go away for a few days and get a hold of myself.

I'm slowly coming out of my depression. It took me three days to be able to start sorting out my feelings and work out my emotional conflicts. Let me try to explain, although I know it won't be easy.

After you left that morning I was overcome by a feeling of unworthiness. I had let you down, and I had let myself down. I was unworthy of you, and I was equally unworthy of my own vocation. I'd put myself in what was clearly a no-win situation. I wanted you to share my holiest night of the year, my celebration of faith, and at the same time I over-stepped my bounds because of the way I feel about you, which is unlike anything I have ever felt about anyone else. So I ran away. Like Jonah running away from God. But, again like Jonah, I know I cannot run away from God, or, if you will, from our relationship. I need to explain myself to you. I need you to understand.

Remember you said to me the first time you came to visit me at the convent, "In order to find God we first have to give up something?" You gave up your career. You decided to go into the world and strike out on your own. You wanted me to join you, look for the new way, but I was not ready for it. I wish I could, Josh, but I can't. You will be leaving town soon, and as for me, I no longer find Lourdes to be the right place for me. I'm going to ask to be transferred. Where exactly I'm not sure yet. I have come to realize I need to make a greater sacrifice than I have made until now if I'm going to fulfill my vocation.

What it really means is that we may not see each other for a long, long time. I wish this wasn't (weren't?) so. It's going to be very hard for me not to see you—we have shared so much these last few months. but maybe it's just as well. We need to put distance between us, give ourselves a chance to work out our conflicts. I will be thinking of you and pray-ing for you.

Love always,
Eve

A cold shiver ran through his bones. Served him right! What kind of a person was he, seducing a nun in a convent on Christmas Eve? He slowly folded the letter and tucked it in his shirt pocket and put on his old winter jacket and went outside for a long walk. He was numb with anger, pain, shame. Who was he angry at? Was he angry at her for letting him down, for running away, or was he angry at himself for succumbing to his weakness? The cold wind swept across the street. It ran through him, buffeting his ears and streaking his face with tears turning into icicles. The tears trickled down his cheeks and were caught in his beard where they lodged, frozen. His former secretary, Ruth Levy, had invited him to a small gathering of friends at her home to welcome the new secular year. He was not up to it. He decided to stay home instead. He was not up to greeting any new year.

Later, alone in his apartment, he sat in his small living room, motionless, for hours. Mrs. Paddock was generous with the heat—it was steaming hot in the room. Despite the heat, he could not rid himself of the chill in his bones. He had wrapped his heavy wool blanket around himself and sat in the large padded armchair in the corner of the living room, as if hibernating for the winter, out of touch with the world.

He did not notice when it turned dark. It was the last night of the year. The waning year flashed before his eyes. What has he made of his life? Is this where it all ends? In this old house on the old West Side? What rhyme or reason did he have for chasing after that nun? What demented dreams was he pursuing?

Felicia might be right after all. Yes, he had lost his way. He was all alone now, with no one to turn to and nowhere to go. He had reached the end of the line. What was Felicia doing for New Year's Eve? Was she celebrating the advent of a new year with her friends, or was she staying home, brooding, as he was doing right now? Even if she did go out she would probably have to put on a good show to pretend she was happy. Why did he keep her hanging? If he wanted to get back together, now was the time, this very minute, before the year rung out. If not, he should pick up the phone and tell her to forget about it, call it quits, give her a chance to make a new start, forget about him, find someone who could give her the things she needed. . . a husband, a father for Danny. . .

No, he was not ready to call her up. Felicia was no weakling. If she wanted to call it quits she would not hesitate to call *him*. She wanted him, that much was clear. She was waiting for him, willing to forgive and forget. What was stopping him from calling her? He was not ready for it. He was not ready to settle down and once again become part of the life he had just turned his back on. He missed her. He missed the baby. He missed his father-in-law. He hated himself for hurting them. But something inside him would not let him capitulate. Not yet, anyway.

Later that evening he aroused himself from his intermittent sleep on the living room armchair and dragged himself across the room and fell into bed, exhausted. When he woke up it was New Year's Day. Fresh snow had fallen during the night. As he looked outside he had a new feeling. It was a new secular year, inaugurating a new decade. The tumultuous Sixties were over. The affair between him and Eve was over. Eve did what she had to do. She had made her choice. She was not ready to strike out on her own. He did not blame her. She had to follow her own calling. As for him, he had to move on, find like-minded people who were not afraid to turn their back on all that was safe and familiar and make a new start.

Somewhere, somehow, a new world was dawning. A new age was about to begin. He was going to share in the making of it. Find out where it was happening and be there.

A new sense of excitement came over him. He was ready to move on, take on the world. He was done with Quincy. He no longer called it home. He called his mother in L.A. and told her about the separation. When she pressed him for more details he said he was coming to visit at the end of the month and would tell her all about it.

Part Three:

The New Way

✧ **14** ✧

He paid the rent for January and told Mrs. Paddock he was leaving sometime before the end of the month. He then called Felicia and told her he was going to L.A. to see his mother and try to get a handle on things.

The night before his departure Kaye called his father-in-law to say goodbye. Dr. Zamenhoff was unhappy about his going away. He was taking the separation personally, as if it were his own fault. He did not do enough to bring his daughter and son-in-law back together. Kaye did not have the heart to tell the professor he was leaving Quincy for good. He told him he needed some time away—a month, perhaps longer. He promised to keep in touch.

Felicia's father made one last attempt of trying to talk his son-in-law into staying. He told him it was the wrong time for him to go away, what with his wife and son needing him, and he needing them. Kaye stood fast. He had to do it. It was hard on him too. But there was no going back now.

He took a non-stop flight to L.A. He hadn't been back to the West Coast in five years. California was the place he left when he decided to become a rabbi. It was the scene of his youth, growing up, moving away. But there was another side to it he hadn't thought about since he left to go to rabbinical school, seven years ago, in the early sixties. It was a place where new ideas had the courage to be born and tried out. It was the place where he first met Rabbi Joe Wasserman at the Jewish Student Union in his junior year in college and learned about Liberal Judaism and its doctrine of personal freedom. It was the place where people like Sue Pins went out to look for social experimentation and spiritual answers.

But it was also the place where he had to confront his mother and try to make her understand what he had been through.

His mother came to the airport to pick him up. He had written her about his resignation from Suburban Temple without going into any details. He would tell her all about it when he saw her. As expected, the first question she asked him was how Felicia and the baby were doing. When the baby was born Kaye's mother was about to leave for Europe, and she stopped on the way in Quincy to see her new grandson. Now, a year later, could she grasp what change had taken place in her son's life since she last saw him?

He did not expect her to understand. They had drifted so far apart over the years. When his parents were going through their divorce nearly ten years ago he had found himself siding with his father. The old man and he had their differences as well. But at least with his father he could have an ideological discussion and then go out for a game of handball. His mother's only ideology, as he saw it, was the here and now. To her America was the ultimate good, and she certainly had made the most of it. She had sold the family's small house in a middle income suburb of L.A. and had moved into her second husband's mansion in Beverly Hills. Jack LeVine, her new husband, was a successful accountant whose clientele included some of Hollywood's top stars. He adored the former Mrs. Kaye, a tall, striking woman who held her own among the luminaries of the motion picture industry, and made her wish his command. Kaye had never warmed up to Jack, but he was happy for his mother. She sure knew how to go about getting what she wanted.

Mrs. LeVine picked up her son in her new silver Mercedes. Kaye felt awkward when he got into the posh car in his old faded jeans. His mother was an elegant woman, a good dresser. She and Roz Pins would certainly understand each other. She looked smart in her deep blue suit and polka dot silk blouse. He envied his mother. Life to her was so much more spontaneous, uncomplicated. She was not concerned about the ills of the world. She enjoyed life. She believed in the good life and scooped it up with both hands. Why couldn't he be more like her? Wouldn't he be much better off?

He was glad Jack was away on a business trip. It made it that much easier to start his visit with his mother, which had to be eased into gradually.

His mother had prepared a Mexican dinner, one of his favorites. After dinner she brought out a large bowl of fresh fruit.

"I have many reasons to be mad at you, Joshua," his mother said. "I may as well bring it up now so we can clear the air and make a new start."

"What is it, Mom?"

"You don't tell your mother anything. You treat me like a stranger."

"What do you mean?"

"You never told me you were sick and had to go to the hospital."

"I didn't want you to worry. It was nothing serious. Only a mild case of ileitis."

"And what about your problems with Felicia?"

"I told you I would let you know all about it when I got here."

"Felicia wrote me about it in confidence back in August."

"It's too hard to explain everything over the phone or in a letter. So I decided to wait till I saw you."

"You had to wait for six months to let your own mother know you were separated?"

"Well, we've kept it a secret from everyone until recently."

"I'm glad to know I'm everyone."

"I'm sorry. I've been having a very tough time going through all of this. You're right. I should've told you sooner."

"It's too bad you can't confide in your own mother," she said, shaking her head, looking hurt. "Perhaps if you did things would turn out different. Felicia wrote me a long letter about your job at Suburban Temple. You know you didn't get religion at home. Your father is a secular Zionist, and as for me, I guess I'm a non-observant Jew. The decision to become a rabbi was entirely yours. Now it seems to me you had a good thing going at that temple. You were one step away from becoming the senior rabbi. Why did you have to give it up?"

Without waiting for him to reply she went on:

"Now Felicia says you don't even want to look for another congregation. What is it you plan to do?"

"I don't know yet. I'll have to see."

"Josh," she leaned forward and put her hand on his. "I don't want you to get mad. I know you are not going to like what I'm about to say. But you know something? You are just like your father."

"In what way?"

"The moment he had things going for him he would get bored. He was always looking for a greater challenge. He never had his feet on the ground. Didn't seem to be able to leave well enough along. Why did he have to leave? Was I such a terrible wife? All I ever wanted was for him to be happy, learn how to relax, enjoy the fruits of his labor."

She stopped and suddenly her eyes brimmed with tears. She got up and went into the kitchen and came back dabbing a tissue at the corners of her eyes, composing herself. She sat down and smiled at him through her tears.

"I never said this to you, Josh, but it's time I did. I loved your father, I really did. And I still do. You really think this big beautiful mansion and all these things I've surrounded myself with really make me happy? Jack is a good man, Josh, I've no complaints. He is a wonderful husband. A hard working man. He doesn't drink. He doesn't play around. And, believe me, he's had plenty of opportunities. But you cannot erase twenty years of marriage. At least I can't. Your Dad and I went through a lot together. We had something very special going for us, which money can't buy. Well, I certainly hope he is happy over there in Israel, although I often wonder."

He got up and went around the table and put his arms around his mother. He pressed her head against him and stroked her hair.

"I'm sorry, Ma. Please forgive me. I guess I could've done more to try to keep you and Dad together, but I didn't. I'm really sorry."

"Don't blame yourself," she said and looked up at him tenderly. "It wasn't your fault. You were too young to understand." She drew back and pressed his hands in hers. "I guess I'm not the one to preach to you about making a go of your own marriage. Obviously, I didn't do so well with mine. But, on the other hand, you can learn from your parents' mistakes. I really think Felicia cares about you. And I also think you need someone like her to look after you. Josh, you are not going to change the world. Why don't you learn how to accept it the way it is and make the best of it?"

"Because I can't, Ma. Some people cannot accept things the way they are. I would probably be better off if I could, but I can't."

His mother shook her head and gave him a commiserating look. She knew there was no point in arguing with her son. Stubborn like his father. He will have to learn the hard way.

His mother was glad to have him back. For the first time in memory they were beginning to communicate as two adults and were actually enjoying each other's company. It took getting used to at first, as if the person he had known all his life was someone else. Soon he realized she was the same person all right. Rather it was his attitude toward her that had changed. He no longer felt angry at his mother for not being the person he once wanted her to be. She had chosen her own way of life, just as his father had chosen his, or, for that matter, he, their son, was now looking for his. His mother's life in Beverly Hills was not much different from the life he had just left behind in West Hills. The same smug newly-rich suburbs insulating themselves from the ills of the world. The same hedonistic attitudes which had turned a religious institution like Suburban Temple from a house of God into a place for worshipping money and power

And yet there was a fundamental difference between the people of Suburban Temple and people like his mother. The former had clothed their hedonism in pietistic self-righteousness. God was on their side, as was evidenced by the fact that theirs was one of the largest and most opulent synagogues in America. His mother, on the hand, did not make any false claims. She believed in the good life—here and now—and did not put any ideological labels on her belief. She had left labels to others—her former husband, for instance, or her son. She seemed to be saying, "This is who I am, for better or worse. I believe in 'live and let live.' I believe in having a good time and in letting others have as good a time as they can. Is there anything wrong with that?"

No, Mom, Kaye smiled from afar as he watched his mother sunning outside in her beautiful Japanese garden by the side of the kidney-shaped pool. No, Mom, there is nothing wrong with it. We are all different, you, me, Dad. And, I suppose, all three of us are the independent, single-minded type. We know what we want and we are not afraid to go after it.

He spent a week at his mother's not doing much of anything. yet it was one of the best weeks of his life. He was beginning to recover—physically and emotionally—from the stress and turmoil of recent months. He found himself transported seven years back, to the time when he was a student here in L.A., about to finish college. It was May or June of 1963. The Kennedy Era. High hopes and great dreams. America was on the move again, challenged by an eloquent idealistic young president to build a better world. This is where I came from, Kaye observed. A child of the dream. This is when I decided to apply to the Quincy Rabbinical Seminary, to become a disciple of the great Alvin J. Blumenfeld, the great rabbi and civil rights leader, and heed his call to go out and "perfect the world in the image of God's kingship."

That, Kaye concluded, was the moment of my spiritual birth.

It made sense back then to be a rabbi. Even after the President was assassinated. The dream, rather that die with him, was kept alive. So it seemed at the time. It was not until the end of the sixties that he found out otherwise.

And now he was back where he started seven years ago. Did he waste all those years? Was religion, as his father had put it, an anachronism?

No, religion was not an anachronism. Rather those who headed religious institutions and called themselves religious leaders had failed. They had become functionaries rather than leaders. Priests rather than prophets. They had forfeited their right to be the voice of conscience of the people they purported to lead.

One morning Kaye woke up before the crack of dawn and went out into the garden to watch the sunrise. He sat on the edge of a stone terrace out in the garden, overlooking a rolling green meadow lined in the distance with a column of tall straight cypress trees. The haze began to lift as the sun came out in the east. He had barely started to wake up. He felt a powerful presence in the newborn day. "Who renews every day continually the work of creation," he recited the words of the morning prayer.

There is a God! the thought flashed through his mind. So simple, so self-evident, and yet so powerful. He was shaken to his very core by the sudden illumination, "He told you, O man, what the Lord demands of you!" Yes, He did! He certainly did!

And suddenly through the haze he sees a figure running toward him with outstretched arms, light and swift and radiant, like a gazelle. His heart pounding, flooded with joy. Eve! Oh, Eve! It is you! You have come to see me!

He jumps up on his feet and starts to run toward her. Soon he realizes she is not coming any closer. She remains at the far end of the field, although she keeps running toward him.

He slows down and takes a few steps and stops, looking on in disbelief. Eve also slows down and stands there, looking at him, her eyes filled with infinite sadness. And then a light seems to shine behind her, moving closer to her, and she turns to look at the light and her arms rise and reach out for it. The light is now enfolding her, as if with human arms, lifting her off the ground, carrying her away into the rising sun.

When he woke up from his dream the sun had already come out. He rose and went back into the house and joined his mother for breakfast. All day he kept seeing the vision of Eve running toward him Where was she now? Did she stay at Lourdes or did she do what she said she was going to do, namely, seek a greater sacrifice in order to fulfil her vocation? What could that greater sacrifice be? He had heard of orders of nuns who were completely secluded from the world. Nuns who took extreme vows, who flagellated themselves, or even worse.

No, not Eve, it couldn't be. She was too concerned about people and about the real world to turn her back on it.

That evening he sat down and wrote Eve a long letter. He did not know whether that letter was going to reach her, but he wanted her to know she was always in his thoughts, and that there was something special between them that would always be there, for him, and hopefully, for her too. He had come to accept their parting of the ways, and he wished her all the happiness in the world in her chosen vocation. He wanted her to know he was ready to make a new beginning here on the West Coast where—he could feel it in his bones—he saw the opportunity to put new life into his Jewish faith. The dreams he once dreamed here, when he first decided to become a rabbi, have not died. He was going to make them a reality, and he was going to start soon.

✧ 15 ✧

By the end of the week Kaye went to see Joe Wasserman, his old mentor and campus rabbi.

Rabbi Joe had aged since he last saw him five years ago. He was now in his mid-fifties, no longer the youthful "older young man" of a few years ago. He was sitting in his office at the Campus Ministries wing of the Student Union, counselling a student. Kaye waited outside and watched Joe, who was completely absorbed in his counselling, through the open door. For a moment he thought he saw himself sitting in that chair, being counselled by Joe. What was it about Joe that had appealed to him so much in his student days? Why did this middle aged campus chaplain have such an impact on his life?

When he first met this man who was old enough to be his father he found him to be a kindred spirit, a person who was not afraid to question and challenge everyone and everything around him. Joe's questioning was not cynical or disaffected. It was anchored in a deep commitment and faith in the human spirit. Joe once said the reason why he had made the college campus his life's venue was because he felt that during their college years young people were in touch with their soul. He considered it his life's mission to help them keep in touch with their soul after they graduated and went out into the big world where they had to compromise themselves. Joe argued that most college professors did not teach students how to think and use their own judgment, but rather tried to impose their own ideas on them. I'm a religious person, Joe once told Kaye. A truly religious person is never bound by human authority, since religion, by definition, is the worship of God, not of man. No religion, Joe added, understands that better than Judaism. The Jew by nature is a rebel who always challenges established authority. American democracy might have borrowed its outward form from ancient Greece, but its spirit and morality were borrowed from ancient Israel and from the prophets of Israel.

Kaye had fully agreed with Joe. To him, in his junior year in college, Joe was the right person at the right time. In spite of his secular upbringing, Kaye had spiritual yearnings, and Joe was the man who helped him define those yearnings and pursue them. In addition, Joe and Kaye shared a love for good music, literature, art, philosophy, all of which Joe considered genuine expressions of what he called the "holy dimension" of the human soul. His old apartment on the edge of campus was a daily Mecca for students who came to browse through his thousands of books and classical music records. Students—and Kaye among them—loved to go out with Joe to a concert, an art show, a play or a movie. They would always stop afterwards for pizza and beer, and even if they had to study for a test that night, they would find themselves absorbed in a discussion late into the night, ranging far beyond the evening's experience, and would invariably deepen their appreciation of the human spirit.

Kaye saw the young student Joe was counselling—a Jewish shiksa with straight blond hair down to her rump and a peace emblem sewn on the seat of her pants—getting up to leave. He walked in and greeted his old mentor. Joe got up, a rotund, balding, swarthy man with quick movements, and peered at his visitor through the thick lenses of his black framed glasses, trying to decide who the person behind the beard and the long hair was.

"Joshua Kaye!" he finally burst out in his visceral voice. He gave Kaye the powerful handshake Kaye remembered so well. "My, my, how you've changed! If I saw you walking down the street I wouldn't recognize you!"

"How're things, Joe?"

"Hectic, hectic. I think I'm ready to retire. Not so easy to keep pace with today's college crowd."

I know what you mean."

"So tell me about yourself."

"I quit my job at Suburban Temple."

"You did? How come?"

"It's a long story. Have you had lunch?"

"As a matter of fact, no. Why don't we go over to that old joint, Corkie's, the one we used to frequent in the old days, and you'll tell me all about it."

They rode in Joe's rumbling old Pontiac and parked in the back of the restaurant. The hostess showed them to a booth in a quiet corner of the restaurant. They sat across from each other as Joe squeezed his rotundity into the narrow space between the seat and the table.

"So how's the rabbi?" Joe inquired, beaming at his former disciple.

"Never felt better."

"You enjoy being unemployed?"

"I enjoy being away from that mausoleum."

"How are Felicia and the baby?"

"We've separated."

"Oh!"

"A trial separation."

"I see."

There was an awkward moment of silence between them. Joe was the man who had counselled him to go to Quincy. He had co-officiated at his wedding and had taken personal pride when, upon ordination, Kaye was elected associate to Alvin Blumenfold.

"Felicia and the baby are fine," Kaye said. "That whole experience with Suburban Temple was bad news. For me, anyway. It turned me off completely. I doubt I will ever take another congregation.

"You're not the only one," Joe observed. "More and more young rabbis are quitting the pulpit."

"What's wrong with organized religion, Joe?"

"It's not organized religion per se. It's society as a whole. We are living in a time of great social upheaval. The old forms are breaking down."

"Yes, I agree."

"You can see it here on the West Coast perhaps better than anywhere else. Even the Catholic Church, the most powerful religious organization in the world, is coming apart here in L.A. One of the largest orders of nuns in town is about to break away from Rome. Some four hundred nuns are giving up papal authority in order to start their own community."

"I guess Quincy is behind the times," said Kaye.

"Well, it usually takes the Midwest ten to fifteen years to catch up with the Coast."

"What about Jewish life?"

"Well, you know how it is with Jews. We always find ourselves in the forefront of any upheaval—social, political, whatever. Hardly a week goes by without my finding out that one of the Jewish students I have been working with here on campus has joined some radical group or some new cult. I don't know how much you've

heard about those cults back in Ohio. Here on the Coast they've
been spreading like wild fire. Most of them are run by charlatans
who brainwash young people, make them abdicate their minds,
and, in fact, turn them into zombies. The other day I ran into a
young man who last year was one of my most active members here
at the Jewish Student Union. Would you believe a tall husky blond
Jewish boy with his head shaven, a tassel of hair left in the middle
of his scalp, wearing a long salmon color robe. . ."

"Hare Krishna."

"That's right. There he was, in the middle of the lobby of the L.A.
International Airport, soliciting donations while a group of his bud-
dies was doing some kind of rain dance. I swear I wouldn't have
believed it in a million years. Not Doug. He was the last person in
the world I would've expected to meet under such circumstances.
He was practically my right hand man last year. He was getting
other Jewish kids to come to services and sign up for Jewish
studies."

"Did you talk to him?"

"I tried. He was really spaced out, barely able to communicate. I
was able to find out where his home base was, a place they call ash-
ram, not far from campus. So I went to see him there. I just
couldn't believe what I saw. Man, was he into it! I took him aside
and I said to him, 'Hey Doug, what the fuck you think you are
doing?' He gave me that innocent saintly look as if he had never
heard that word before and told me I belonged there too, I had to
give it a try."

"Did you find out what made him do it?"

"No one thing in particular. It's some kind of malaise, a spiritual
vacuum these young people are suffering from. Doug, of course, is
an extreme case. More typically, what happens to young Jews today
is that they are going through what you might call a passive rebellion. They just tune out their Jewish heritage, Jewish values,
everything Jewish."

"Well, what do we, their so-called spiritual leaders, do about it?
Do we blame them or do we blame ourselves?"

Joe looked down at his dark heavy hands grown with curly black
hair up to his fingernails. He took off his glasses, blew on them,
and wiped them with his shirtsleeve.

"I'm just a tired old campus rabbi," Joe said. He spoke slowly in a
mock-rabbinic, pseudo-pontificating tone. "By the time I get those
kids they have already been fucked over by their parents and their
rabbi and Hebrew School teachers. The damage is done. The few
who were raised right or who grew up right in spite of the way they

were raised I do okay with. The others—the great majority—are beyond help. You can't start making them love Judaism here on campus, when they have already been turned off by everything Jewish. You have to start long before they get to college. The kids are right, Josh. The System has failed. We need a new system."

"Yes," Kaye echoed, "we need a new system."

Joe smiled. "Well, Joshua, how about you giving it a try?"

"I very well may," Kaye said, smiling back.

The next day he got a call from Joe, inviting him to go out on Saturday night to see a new play. It turned out to be a social protest play written by a new black playwright. After the play they stopped at Joe's place for a nightcap. When they were through discussing the play Joe started to talk about alternate Jewish lifestyles. "What we need is some kind of a Jewish commune," Joe remarked. "I understand they've started one up in Boston. A group of college students bought an old house and moved in. I forget what they call their group. I believe they refer to this new kind of lifestyle as *havurah*, or fellowship. They pool their resources. They study together. They pray. They experiment with new ways of making Judaism a vibrant, exciting religion. They also do community service projects. This may very well be what we need here in L.A."

"A Jewish commune," Kaye said reflectively, cradling his brandy glass in the palms of his hands. "A Jewish commune," he repeated to himself, slowly, testing the sound of the new concept. "A *havurah*." He looked at Joe and nodded. "Yes, a Jewish commune. I like it. I like it very much. I think we are on to something."

"It's a great idea," said Joe. I started working on it several times, but I had to stop. I just don't have the time."

"I'm willing to give it a try."

"Good! I was hoping you would."

"Where do I start?"

"The Jewish Community Federation of Los Angeles owns an old house near campus. I think I may be able to talk them into letting us use it, rent free."

"When can I see it?"

"Any time."

On the way out he slapped Joe on his shoulder.

"You know, Joe, I think we're on to something."

"Good to have you back, old buddy," Joe grinned, visibly excited, and gave Kaye a bearhug.

The next morning Kaye was surprised to find a letter in his

mother's mailbox written in familiar handwriting. He did not quite expect to hear from Eve, at least not for a while. He opened the letter with shaky hands, his pulse quickening. She wrote:

Dear Josh,

I didn't mean to let you slip out of my life. I apologize again for running away without saying goodbye. What can I say in my defense? I was too confused. I didn't know how to deal with my feelings. I kind of left things between us up in the air. So please forgive me.

I was really happy to hear from you last week. Your letter was forwarded to my retreat here in Pennsylvania two weeks late.

Thank you for your kind words. You too are always in my thoughts, and that something special between us will always be there for me as well. I need your friendship now more than ever before, although I know what I'm about to tell you may separate us even more, rather than bring us closer together. I'm about to make the most difficult decision of my life—I'm getting ready for my final vows. You may wonder what final vows (or final profession) are. I don't believe I have ever mentioned it to you before. But when I first started my vocation I only took temporary vows, which were renewable each year. The time has now come for me to make the decision about my permanent vows, which is why I'm here in this retreat house in Pennsylvania. It is hard for me to describe what it feels like to be faced with this decision. What it really means is that I renounce the world forever. I become dead to the world in more than just a figurative sense. I must admit to you I'm having many doubts and misgivings. But I'm also aware of the inevitability of what I'm about to do. I do want to serve, and I cannot think of any other way of doing it.

I know how you feel about organized religion. You have decided to quit your own religious organization and strike out on your own. you have asked me to join you and work with you on the new way. And here I am, asking you to give me your blessing for doing just the opposite.

Well, I guess I'm not prepared to give up what I've been taught to believe in. Who is to say I'm right? For better or for worse, I'm part of the Church, and I have to work from within. I do hope you understand and I do hope you realize how much I need your blessing and your support.

After I take my final vows I may be sent to Latin America

to help organize schools for the poor. I've already started to read books on life in that part of the world. I know it is going to be a hard life with many frustrations. I realize I'll be working against tremendous odds. But I firmly believe the ills of the world need to be met head-on where they fester the most. This to me is the true test of the validity of the Church and of my own vocation, if I understand correctly what Christ has taught us.

I do hope all is going well with you, and I'm glad to hear that you feel the West Coast is the right place for you to pursue a more meaningful Jewish experience. From what I hear and read about Catholic life in California, it seems to be quite a progressive place, open to change and new ideas, certainly more so than back here in the Midwest.

Do write again soon, and, again, *mea culpa*,

Love,
Eve

It took him a long time to absorb the contents of that letter. It had never dawned on him Eve was yet to take her final vows. As far as he was concerned, Eve was a nun, and that was that. Suddenly everything appeared in a new light. All this time she had been going through a trial period, and now at last her moment of truth had arrived. He thought of the two of them at the convent on Christmas Eve. Would things have turned out differently for her if they had made love that night? Would she then have decided not to take her final vows?

What strange fate had brought them together on that rainy Sukkot morning, when that shy sad-eyed nun who was looking to Judaism for an answer walked into his temple study? How strange the ways of fate were! She had come to him for answers, only to find more questions. As he got to know her better, he was finding out she was the one who had the answers for him, while, unwittingly, he was helping her reaffirm her faith in her own Savior. Then, when she came to see him at the hospital, the spirit suddenly turned into flesh, and it was no longer clear whether it was the love of God or the love of each other that drew them together.

That was more than they had bargained for. There was just as much pulling them together as there were things that separated them. Finally, they came to realize that neither one of their institutions had the answers. Yet, when all was said and done, despite all they had gone through together, despite all their shared experience, their affinity of mind and heart, the two of them had arrived at exactly the opposite conclusions.

She was going to commit the rest of her life to the Church. Despite all her doubts and misgivings, all the proofs to the contrary, she was putting her full unquestioning trust in the man in Rome, who was believed to have the keys to the Kingdom. He recalled Father Woods' words at the convent on Christmas Eve, how frustrated he felt when he came back from Latin America, not having been able to effect any significant change in the lives of the poor people he had worked with. What made her think she could do any better? Wasn't it a well known fact that the Church, as a political organization, was ruled by the rich landowners who refused to allow any change in that part of the world?

And yet, despite his skepticism, he could not help admiring her courage and determination. She was not looking for an easy life as a teacher in some middle class suburb. Nor was she seeking to quit the order as so many nuns nowadays were doing. She was willing to give up the comfort and security of her own culture and go to a strange country to work for total strangers for no tangible reward. She certainly had the courage of her convictions, preparing herself for a life of service and total self-sacrifice.

He wrote her back letting her know he admired and respected her decision. There were many ways to God, and he firmly believed each person had to follow his or her own way. She certainly had his blessing and his support in making her decision to take her final vows, and he certainly admired her courage and determination in going to Latin America to work with the poor. The only thing he had to question was the practical value of such a mission. True, the masses of those poor underdeveloped countries did need to be educated in order to improve their lot. But the work done by the Church was only a drop in the ocean. A much greater change was needed. She might find herself dissipating her energies without seeing any real results, beating her head against a stone wall. He was only expressing his own opinion. She certainly had to decide for herself. Obviously, they were now looking at things from a different perspective, she from within the institution and he from the outside. Yes, he agreed. Who is to say which one of them was right? They had to follow their own individual conscience and hope for the best.

✧ 16 ✧

The group of young Jews who gathered that Friday night at the old musty unfurnished house on the periphery of the L.A. campus had one thing in common: they all regarded their Jewish heritage central to their lives, yet they all felt—as one of them had put it—"turned off by the organized Jewish community." They all had been anxiously awaiting the opportunity to form a new group, unencumbered by organizational structures, in order to pursue what they called a "genuine spiritual experience" and put Jewish and universal values into practice.

Ironically, the house used as the home of the new group had to be secured from the main body of the organized community—the Jewish Federation of Los Angeles. As soon as the discussion on the formation of the groups started, a young woman with long dark hair and sad dark eyes named Naomi questioned the use of a house owned by the Establishment. Rabbi Joe assured her there were no strings attached. The group was free to pursue its own ideas and was only accountable to Joe, who had been given *carte blanche* by the Federation to use the house as he saw fit.

"The trick," Joe said in his paternal, reassuring voice, "is to take the resources of the Establishment and put them to good use."

The group, about twenty men and women mostly in their late twenties, sat on mats around the empty bare-walled living room under the naked light bulb, their eyes glowing and eager as Joe introduced Joshua Kaye as co-organizer and facilitator of the group.

All eyes were now riveted on Kaye. He could feel their eagerness and anticipation. Here at last was the group of like-minded people he had been looking for. He felt at once elated and apprehensive. This was the turning point. These young people were open and receptive. They shared his concerns and hopes. And yet, was it really going to work? He had given up his high paying job and his career for what was at best a questionable pursuit. He had traded the magnificent sanctuary of Suburban Temple for this ramshackle old house which would probably take months of hard work to bring up to some livable condition. How serious were those young people about this undertaking? Were they equal to the task? The organized Jewish community, no doubt, would soon come to look upon them as radicals, and they would be facing adversity and would have to decide whether they were willing to make a sacrifice in order to adhere to their convictions. Their resources were meagre. They would have to make do with little in order to achieve their common goal. Well, at least they were willing to try. All one could do right now was hope and pray.

"I've been listening carefully to everything that was said here tonight," Kaye started. "I fully agree. I guess until recently I was part of that Establishment you people have been talking about. I worked within the System, but I found out the System was no longer doing what we all hoped it would do."

He looked around the room.

"Well, this place does not look like much. But I'm sure we are not going to let it discourage us. Great things have often had humble beginnings. I know we are on to something that will change our lives and hopefully will enable us to make a real contribution. The place to begin, of course, is right here in this old house, and the key to our success is that we do it all ourselves. The trouble with the synagogue today is that to most Jews it no longer feels like a spiritual home. It doesn't provide a sense of community, of an extended family. This is exactly what we can create in this house, with whatever little means we have."

That weekend the group spent hours cleaning up and painting the house, which they named HOUSE OF PEACE. The work brought the members of the group closer together, and a bond of friendship was formed. As the place began to take shape the enthusiasm of the group grew. They were investing themselves in this old house and turning it into a place unlike any other place they had ever known before. They kept referring to it as "the house," and suddenly that simple word took on a whole new meaning, as if they had reinvented it. By the end of the week they all decided to spend the entire Sabbath, or Shabbat (they began to use more and more Hebrew words), in the house, from sundown on Friday to sundown on Saturday.

When the group gathered at the HOUSE OF PEACE late Friday afternoon, all dressed in white shirts and clean jeans and leather sandals, the spirit of Shabbat filled the house. Kaye was deeply moved as they all greeted one another with "Shabbat Shalom." he could tell what everyone was thinking at that moment. They had performed a miracle. In one single week they did something they had never dared dream could happen. They had recreated themselves as Jews. They had transformed themselves into a real community. And now they had come together to celebrate the traditional day of rest and get back in touch with their souls.

They had invited Rabbi Joe as their guest of honor, and Joe came a little late, apologizing for holding up the dinner. He had to see a student who had some trouble with the draft board. As soon as Joe arrived they all sat down for Shabbat dinner. No one spoke as they looked at the long table covered with a white tablecloth, a small braided hallah next to each person, freshly baked in their own kitchen, a goblet of wine next to each hallah, especially created by the potter of the group, and tall home-made Shabbat candles in the center of the table, next to a large bouquet of flowers. Joe raised his cup and held it up and invited everyone to join him. He stood up and asked the group to rise.

"Before we sing the *kiddush*, the blessing over the wine, let's pause for a moment of silent meditation. Let's give thanks to the Almightly for having sustained us and preserved us and given us this glorious occasion."

His eyes shut, Kaye thought of Felicia, his estranged wife. He wanted her to share the joy of that moment. To see for herself how Judaism could be made real. What would her reaction be if he called her long-distance and told her about it? Could she understand it without seeing it for herself?

Joe chanted the *kiddush* and everyone drank the wine.

Next they all joined hands around the table and sang, swaying to the time of the Sabbath tune,

> Shabbat shalom Shabbat shalom
> Bim bam, bim bim bim bam
> Shabbat Shabbat Shabbat shalom

They sat down to eat in high spirits. As they ate they discussed the experience of the week.

"This is the best Shabbat I've ever experienced," someone said. It was the dark haired young woman named Naomi. "This is what I've always thought Shabbat ought to be. I want to thank Joe and Josh for helping us do this."

"Hear hear!" someone called out, and they all raised their cups. "*L'chaim, l'chaim!*"

After dinner they discussed their goals and their plans for the group late into the night. many questions were raised. Should they seek more members or keep the group small? Should they open the House to the community or first concentrate on educating themselves? What should be their Jewish and general priorities?

After midnight Kaye suggested they retire for the night, since they could not possibly solve all those questions in one sitting. They had made a good beginning, and they had to allow time for things to grow and evolve.

Early the next morning everyone was up. They gathered in the unfurnished parlor for the morning prayers. Most of them were unfamiliar with the prayers, but they were all eager to learn. After the prayers they sat on mats around the room as Joe passed out copies of the Torah for the Shabbat study session prepared by Joshua Kaye.

Kaye asked the group to look at the first chapter of the Book of Genesis.

"In the beginning God created the heavens and the earth."

Bereshit, in the beginning. . . The first word in the Bible should have been *Adonai*, the Lord, which begins with Aleph, the first letter of the Hebrew alphabet. The first word, however, is *Bereshit*, beginning, which starts with the second letter, Bet.

What is the reason for that?

God wanted to show us that we are always given the opportunity to make a new beginning. One should never lose faith, never say it is too late, or it is too hard, there is no point in my starting now, I've missed my chance. God renews every day the work of creation. Man is given a chance every day to make a new start.

Right here in this house a new start was made. A group of young Jews took one week out of their lives and created a place where they could rediscover their faith.

God created the heavens and the earth. . . notice that the first thing God created was the heavens. And yet the next verse immediately states, "And the earth had been in total chaos and darkness over the face of the deep." Doesn't it follow that the earth had already existed?

Here again we are being taught a lesson. Our world begins here on earth, and we remain part of this earth throughout our mortal days. But our real source, the place we always aspire to, is the heavens.

How do we reach the heavens?

God had given us a taste of heaven. This taste is the Sabbath. The day of peace, harmony, perfect rest and inner joy. When God created the first human couple, he put them in a place which was neither heaven nor earth, yet both, called the Garden of Eden. In that place time as we know it did not exist. There were no seasons, no growth and decay, no day and night. It was a perpetual Sabbath, and everything was in perfect harmony. But man was not ready for this perfect state of existence. And man and his wife defied God's command not to taste of the fruit of the tree of knowledge of good and evil, and they were banished from the garden, and thus human existence as we know it began. But man is not altogether without the knowledge of heaven. Once a week, on the Sabbath, we can taste heaven, and someday, we believe, we will establish God's rule among ourselves here on earth and will attain the state originally experienced by man.

The Torah session was followed by communal lunch, singing and discussion. Each member of the group spoke about the experience of growing up disliking Hebrew school, which was rigid, dull and uninspiring; being turned off by the hypocrisy of the adult generation, which had built expensive synagogues one rarely set foot in; going to college with the idea of becoming part of the big world out there, and getting away from the parochial confines of one's background; and then beginning to feel a certain inner void and restlessness and looking for some spiritual answers.

Our parents should see us now, someone said, they would think we have lost our minds.

They all laughed.

Later is the afternoon they took a walk in the city park and watched the treetops catch fire in the setting sun.

They returned to the house and sat around in the gathering dusk and sang along with Kaye who had taken out his guitar and taught them a new Shabbat song he had recently learned from a roving Jewish troubadour:

> *Mizmor shir l'yom ha'shabbat. . .*
> The whole world is waiting
> To sing a song of Shabbos

Joe brought out a braided candle, a wine cup and a spice box, and they stood around the dark room with their arms joined, their faces glowing around the *havdalah* flame, and sang about Elijah the Prophet who will soon come to redeem the world.

That night, back at his mother's house, Kaye wrote Eve about the Shabbat experience. He finally found what he was looking for. He has done the right thing, leaving Quincy and going to the West Coast. Unlike the people at Suburban Temple, people here were open and willing to try something new. Something was happening here to people, Jews, Catholics and others. Religion was being transformed. People were going back to their roots and rediscovering their spiritual patrimony. Soon what was happening here would spread to the rest of the country and the rest of the world.

A week later he received a letter from Eve. She wrote:

Dear Josh,

Your letter arrived this morning as I was about to answer the previous one. First I want to thank you for helping me make the decision to take my final vows. You are very kind. I couldn't have done it without your support and understanding.

I read with great interest about your wonderful experience with that new community you call *havurah*. It sounds very promising. I hope it will revitalize Judaism and society as a whole.

You are lucky to have escaped the Quincy winter. We had a snow storm yesterday and everything came to a halt. You must be sitting right now by the side of the pool laughing at us poor Midwesterners. Ah, well, wait until I get to Guatemala, the land of eternal spring. The laugh will be on you.

Oh yes, I forgot to tell you. I was tentatively assigned to work at the Maryknoll Center in Guatemala City. I'm told Guatemala is one of the most beautiful countries in Latin America, but also one of the poorest and most backward. It has one of the highest illiteracy rates in the world. Of the country's four million people, three million are Mayan Indians whose standard of living is one of the lowest in the world. It is going to be a great challenge going there and working on organizing new schools for those people.

You say you are not sure of the value of the work the Church is doing in Latin America. Well, it seems to me that while the hierarchy of the Church is yet to catch up with the times, there are many priests and nuns over there who are becoming more militant and are looking to change things, which gives me hope. If I'm lucky perhaps I'll get to go by way of California and Mexico, rent a car or hitch a ride down the Pan American Highway. In that case I'll get to see you. Wouldn't that be grand?

Well, let's not get our hopes too high. I still have a lot to do before I leave Lourdes. I'll keep you posted on my progress.

Love,
Eve

✧ **17** ✧

Joe had arranged for Kaye to teach at the Jewish studies department. "You're a born teacher," he told Kaye. "You should've gone into academic work."

Kaye disagreed. he didn't have the patience and discipline of the scholar. He hated routine. He was looking to make a difference out in the real world. This is why he found the *havurah* to be the perfect vehicle for implementing his ideas.

He did, however, enjoy teaching those classes at the university. He seemed to attract students who were interested in new ideas, who were looking for a new way to experience Judaism, and after a month of teaching he had gotten several of his students involved in the *havurah*.

The group had grown by now to about thirty members. When the group was first organized, it included one married couple and one about to be engaged. By now there were seven new couples in the group, and two had started to discuss marriage plans. Someone suggested to change the name of the group from HOUSE OF PEACE to HOUSE OF PEACE, LOVE AND MARRIAGE.

"If nothing else comes out of the *havurah*," Joe told Kaye, "at least we will have done our duty in helping perpetuate the Jewish people."

In mid-March Kaye's mother joined her husband on a business trip to Europe. Kaye was now alone in the big house. He felt too secluded in that house, and was considering moving into the HOUSE OF PEACE.

One evening, after he finished teaching one of his evening classes, Kaye was approached by one of the students who had stayed after the rest of the class had left. She was tall and attractive and appeared to be in her late twenties. When she had first signed up for the class she had told him she was working on her master's degree in social work, and wanted to take a course in Jewish philosophy because she had had very little Jewish education and wanted to know more about her own heritage. Kaye suggested she sit in on one or two sessions before she made up her mind. At first

he thought she would quit after she found out the class was too advanced for her. She would sit in the back row, all by herself, cross
her long legs, light a cigarette, and look at him intently as she kept
shaking her long brown hair away from her face. She did not par-
ticipate in class discussions, and seemed to be taking few notes,
and the way she kept staring made him wonder whether she was
paying attention or had her mind on something else. To his
surprise, she decided to stay with the course. He did not question
her decision, but couldn't quite understand what prompted her to
attend that particular course.

He gathered his books and waited for her to proceed. She smiled
apologetically.

"I was wondering if you had a few minutes. Well, nothing really
urgent. It can wait."

"Something in regard to the course?"

"No, actually. . ."

"I'll tell you what," Kaye said, "I'm going out to get a bite to eat.
Would you like to join me?"

She looked at once uncertain and eager.

"Sure. Be glad to."

He walked her out of the building.

"This way, Miss Freund," he pointed at the parking lot.

"Lisa," she said.

"Josh," he replied.

The evening was warm and balmy. Lisa's long hair glistened in
the dark. He felt the urge to run his hand over her hair.

He opened the car door for her and then let himself in and sat
next to her. He felt a stirring he had not felt for a long time. She
wore a musky perfume which he found intoxicating. She had large
eyes which seemed liquid in the dark. She sat up erect, her body
beautifully sculpted, strong yet generous, self-reliant yet expectant.

They drove down Wilshire Boulevard and stopped at a light.

"I know a good fish restaurant not far from here," said Kaye.
"Quite reasonable."

"Sounds good," she said.

They asked for a booth in a quiet corner of the restaurant.

"Someone told me you are a rabbi," Lisa said after they sat down.

"Non-practicing," said Kaye.

She looked at the menu.

"You mind if I order shrimp?"

"Not at all. Go right ahead. As long as you don't mind if I order
the broiled fish."

She laughed, a shy, solicitous laugh.

They decided to share a bottle of Chablis.

Kaye offered a toast to Lisa's health and happiness. She reciprocated.

"I was wondering," said Kaye, "do you really find that Jewish Philosophy class interesting?"

She hesitated.

"Well, I find your way of teaching it interesting. I like the way you relate to the students. You really put them at ease."

"Thank you," said Kaye. "In other words, you are more interested in the teacher than in the subject matter."

He saw her blush.

"Sorry. Only teasing."

"Well," she said, taking a deep breath, "actually, I wanted to talk to you about myself. When I first sat in on your class it became clear to me that course was too advanced for me. But there was something about you which made me feel I might be able to talk to you about myself in a way I haven't been able to talk to anyone else."

She paused.

"You mind if I smoke?"

"Go right ahead."

He waited for her to light her cigarette. She blew the smoke away from the table.

"I'm not really sure where to start. There is really no great mystery about my life. No deep dark secret. I guess I'm a pretty ordinary person. I'm twenty-nine. I'll be thirty next month. I have worked as a hospital social worker for five years, and last year I started taking courses in the evening for my master's degree in social work. I have many friends. I go to parties. I date occasionally. In my work I'm with people all day. But lately I've been feeling increasingly lonely. I'm not quite sure what it is."

Kaye recalled going out with Eve on that picnic out in the woods at St. John's College, when she first told him about her conflicts and her loneliness. Why was it that each time he was experiencing loneliness he would meet some other lonely soul who would seek to make contact with him? Did Lisa Freund sense his own loneliness and was attracted to it the way Eve was?

In a way she reminded him of Eve. She had similar motions, slow, meditative. She chose her words carefully, and her voice had a familiar music. When he closed his eyes he could almost hear Eve speak.

"You don't feel lonely right now, do you?" he said.

"No," she laughed, "not right this minute."

"You're a very attractive woman," said Kaye.

She lowered her eyes and blushed.

"You remind me of a good friend of mine."

She looked at him questioningly.

"A Catholic nun."

"Oh!"

"That particular nun happens to be very attractive."

"I see."

She took a sip of her wine.

"What does she do, your friend, the nun?"

"She teaches in a Catholic school back in Ohio, where I've recently come from. She is about to be transferred to Latin America.

"That's very interesting."

"Yes, she is a very interesting person. Anyway, let's get back to you. You were telling me about feeling lonely. This is not a feeling I'm not familiar with. I've been feeling lonely lately myself. I'm originally from L.A., and I've only been back a short time. I was an associate-rabbi of a large congregation in Ohio. I was married for a couple of years when I separated, and I quit my job and came here. I've been doing some teaching and recently I've helped organize a *havurah*, a small community of Jewish students near campus. You may want to come out and visit us some time."

"I would very much like to," she said.

After they finished dinner he drove Lisa home. She lived not far from campus, in an old apartment building, on the top floor.

"Would you like to come in for a cup of coffee?"

"If it's not too much trouble."

"Not at all."

After she turned on the light she apologized for the mess in the apartment. She had had a busy week and did not have a chance to straighten out the place. The mess, he realized after she went into the other room to change, was a permanent feature of those living quarters. Layers of dust on the furnishings. Grimy floor, covered with old rugs and what appeared to be a meditation mat. A broken guitar hanging on the wall. Empty bottles everywhere. Ashtrays full of yellowing butts.

There is more to her life than she had let me in on, Kaye thought.

She came back barefoot, wearing blue jeans and an Indian cotton shirt without a bra. Her nipples stood against her shirt like two dark purple flowers.

She shook her hair away from her face and smiled.

"Is coffee okay, or would you like some wine? I have some very good Portuguese wine."

She is seducing me, Kaye observed.

His mind began to race. How did he feel about her? He hardly knew her. he was attracted to her, but what would happen after they made love? How much of a commitment was he willing to make?

"Sure," he said, "let's try that wine."

She put on some soft music.

We are two lonely souls, Kaye reflected, suddenly feeling sorry for Lisa and for himself. There is something deeply sad about physical love. Two human bodies reaching out for each other, trying to overcome loneliness and sadness and fear—mostly fear—by commingling their juices and their intimacies for a brief moment of oblivion.

They clinked glasses.

"To both of us," Lisa toasted.

"To both of us."

Well, professor, a voice inside of him nudged, go ahead and do your thing. . .

"Dance?" he offered.

"Sure."

He put his arms around her, and she clung to him, her face buried in the crook of his neck. Her undulating body was eager yet awkward in his arms. She was the passive type, waiting for him to take the lead.

They kept filling their glasses and dancing, sharing more and more of their intimacy in the warm, quiet night. Presently they began to undress each other and staggered into bed, nearly etherized with wine and fatigue.

He held her in his arms and kissed her and then rolled on his side and pretended to be fast asleep. She pushed against him, her flank pressing against his buttocks. He blinked in the dark, wondering what time it was. She nuzzled against him, cold nosed against his nape, and as he turned his head she pushed herself closer against him and began to run her fingers through his beard. Rolling over, he gathered her in his arms, weaving his thighs in hers. The heat of her underthighs aroused his desire. He stroked her hair and her large, undulating hips, summoning his desire. She responded eagerly, almost too eagerly, anxious to please him. She moaned as he pushed against her, and as he looked into her eyes he suddenly saw Eve's face with that look he remembered the time she lay in her bed at the convent next to him on Christmas Eve, telling him not to mind her but go ahead and do it. He pressed harder, but his desire, instead of rekindling, began to ebb.

"Too much wine," he muttered in her ear. "We'll have to try again later."

When he woke up before daybreak Eve's presence came back. Poor Lisa! How would she feel if he told her he was attracted to her as a surrogate to that Catholic nun? She stirred next to him and her naked arm reached out to him. He took her in his arms and held her close, stroking her long hair and kneading her compliant thighs and surging inside her in a burst of aching joy as he melted into her flesh.

Over coffee she told him about her broken engagement. She had been engaged to this Mexican doctor whom she had met at the hospital where she worked as a psychiatric social worker. She dated him for about a year when they decided to get married. She went with him to Mexico City to meet his family. She didn't hit if off with his family, particularly with his mother, who was a devout Catholic and wanted good Catholic grandchildren. When they returned to L.A. the doctor began to insist she convert to Catholicism. He began to argue that as long as she remained a Jew she was doomed to suffer eternal damnation. He insisted he wanted to save her soul, and told her he would leave her if she did not convert. She was devastated. She did not know what to do. She could not defend her own religion since she knew so little about it. Yet she felt she would be a total hypocrite if she converted to Catholicism, since she had little feeling for her own religion, let alone for a religion as austere and overpowering as Catholicism. Her relationship with her Mexican fiance began to deteriorate. He began to mistreat her, deride her, call her a stupid Jew, and one night he let himself into her apartment dead drunk and beat her up. She told him she would report him to the police and he begged her not to do it, since they might deport him to Mexico. She agreed not to report him, provided he agreed to break off the engagement and keep out of her life.

Lisa looked down and sighed. "It took me several months to get over it. I lost interest in everything. I felt like a total failure."

It was then she decided to go back to school for her master's degree and in addition take some courses in Judaism to become more knowledgeable about her own religion.

"You are the first person I've told all this to," she smiled at him, visibly happy. "I'm really glad I have met you."

"So am I," said Kaye, squeezing her hand, wondering whether the feeling conveyed through the touch went deeper than commiseration.

When he went into Joe's office before noon, the campus chaplain informed Kaye someone was in to see him.

"You'll never guess who it is," said Joe.

"Felicia?"

"Close. Felicia's father, Dr. Zamenhoff."

"What is he doing in L.A.?"

"He came here last night to give a lecture at some regional convention, so he stopped in this morning to see you."

Was professor Zamenhoff the bearer of a personal message from his daughter? Had Felicia reached a decision?

The professor was hidden behind a spread copy of the *Los Angeles Times*, burrowing in a corner of the big couch in the middle of the lobby of the Student Union. Kaye walked over and felt like saying something warm and personal like, "Hello, Dad," but could not bring himself to do it. He placed himself behind the newspaper and looked over it at his father-in-law who was absorbed in the paper. The professor looked up and jumped up on his feet.

"Joshua!" he gave his son-in-law a big embrace, then leaned back and examined him from head to toe. "You look good. How is everything?"

"Not bad. I've been doing some teaching here at the university."

"Good, good. I hope you've been giving my idea of going for your PhD some serious consideration. You would make a fine teacher. How's your Mom?"

"She is fine. She just left for Europe on some business trip."

"Yes, I tried to call the house. There was no answer."

The professor looked well groomed in his new seersucker suit and yellow silk shirt, but his face was gaunt and pale.

"How've you been?"

"Not too well," the professor sighed. "I had a mild heart attack last month. The doctor told me to slow down and watch myself. Well, my wife's been watching me like a hawk, God bless her."

"How long are you staying?"

"I have to catch a 2:30 plane."

"Then you have to leave for the airport in about an hour."

"Let's see—it's past twelve. You're right. I wasn't watching the time."

"Can I drive you to the airport?"

"I'd be delighted."

Suddenly Kaye realized how much he had missed his father-in-law. He was one of the special people in his life, one of the few he truly admired. He thought of his own son whom he hadn't seen now in two months. He was denied the joy of seeing the boy grow up, learn how to talk, develop his own little personality.

"When will we see you in Quincy?" his father-in-law asked as they drove to the airport.

"I'm not sure," said Kaye. "Perhaps in June, when school is over."

The professor filled him in on his son and on Felicia. Both were doing well. Felicia was now working part time as a librarian at the rabbinical school, and was planning to go to Florida for Passover to spend the holiday with her aunt.

Kaye embraced his father-in-law and kissed him on the cheek as they stopped to say goodbye at the entrance to the mobile tunnel leading into the aircraft. The professor tried to appear cheerful, but his eyes betrayed him feelings. Driving back from the airport Kaye felt tightness in his chest and wished he could cry.

✧ 18 ✧

On Friday night he took Lisa to the HOUSE OF PEACE and introduced her to the group by her Hebrew name, Leah. She acted shy and reserved. Back at her apartment later that evening he observed she had hardly said a word all evening. She told him she liked the group, but she knew so little about her religion she was afraid to sound ignorant, or make a *faux pas*. He assured her she did not have to worry. Most members of the group knew little about their religion and were learning about it just as she was.

"That makes me feel better," she said, relieved.

"Besides," said Kaye, "we are trying to unlearn many things we've been taught to believe in, and rediscover the true essence of Judaism. We all share a common conviction, namely, that Judaism has the power to redeem the world. That it *can* bring the messiah. Not the Judaism of the big synagogues and the big organizations, to be sure, but the Judaism of Abraham and Moses and Isaiah and Rabbi Akiva and the Baal Shem Tov. All those great leaders and sages had the remedy for the ills of society, but unfortunately the people they led only followed them up to a point. The biblical prophets told the Jews they were destined by God to be a 'light unto the nations,' to teach the world how to live by God's law of justice and loving kindness. But the Jews were not able to live up to their mission, and consequently lost their land and went into exile for two thousand years.

"But the fact is," Kaye thrust his finger into the air to make his point, as Lisa-Leah stretched on the couch and cradled her face in her hands as she listened, "we Jews have survived as a unique and separate people, and we cannot escape the mission or forget the assignment God has given us. Here in America we have grown fat and lazy. We have allowed big money to deaden our moral sense. We mouth pieties in our fancy synagogues but we let the rich get richer and the poor get poorer, we see America fight wars around the world designed to oppress the masses of humanity and make us richer, and not only do we look the other way, some of us even make millions as war profiteers.

"This is why we need to organize ourselves into groups like this *havurah*, which are not subordinated to big business and big religion. As Jews, our task is to teach the rest of society how to turn this country around and start to change the world."

"How are you going to go about doing it?"

"The *havurah* is now getting ready to celebrate Passover, the feast of freedom. We are going to invite non-Jewish guests to the Seder celebration, mainly clergymen who are involved in the current strike of the United Farm Workers. I want our group and our guests to find out that Judaism, as enacted in the saga of the exodus from Egypt, is a religion which advocates the liberation not only of the Jewish people but of the entire world. If we all join forces we can win this fight for the poor Chicano farm workers, and we can go from there to win the fight for human rights everywhere. I'm sure this *havurah* Seder is going to be quite a memorable occasion. Would you like to help us with it?"

"Only if you first scratch my back," said Lisa-Leah, giving him a sidelong smile, and threw her long hair over her head and down on her chest.

He moved in with Lisa that weekend. His belongings were few, and he was able to complete the move on Saturday night in two trips from his mother's house to Lisa's apartment. They decided to split the rent and all other house expenses. He was not entirely sure he was doing the right thing, moving in with her. He had only known her for a short time. He liked her. She was kind, affectionate, a good companion. She fit in with his new lifestyle, the *havurah*, college life, the new way. But she was obviously the type that needed someone strong and stable to lean on. Was he that someone? Could he give her all she needed? Could he take the place of that Mexican doctor who had let her down?

On Sunday they went out on a picnic in a pine grove overlooking the ocean. It was a glorious April day. The air was clear and pine scented, a wonderful respite from the L.A. smog. Lisa in her wide brimmed straw hat, loose braless white blouse and flowing wraparound cotton print skirt was a goddess of spring. She had brought cheeses, fruit and wine, hard rolls, egg salad and herring spread. She took out a red checkered picnic cloth and spread it on the grass and placed everything on it.

Life can be beautiful, Kaye observed. He thought of his mother, travelling in Europe. "Josh, you are not going to change the world," he recalled his mother telling him when he first came back to L.A. "Why don't you learn how to accept it the way it is and make the best of it?"

"Because I can't, Ma," he recalled telling his mother, "some people cannot accept things the way they are."

Looking at Lisa arrange the food, a scenario flashed through his mind: He had gone back to school for his PhD. He was now a full professor at the university. He had a beautiful home in the suburbs. He was coming home from work. Lisa was standing on the porch in the backyard grilling steaks. They were happily married. They had three all-American looking children, a big shaggy dog, a new station wagon, a Coupe de Ville, and so on.

Lisa seemed to have read his thoughts.

"Josh, what about us, you and me?"

"What about us?"

"How do you feel about me?"

"I'm very fond of you."

"It's funny, when you think about it. We've made love, but you haven't said you love me."

"Yes, I guess you are right."

"Where do you see our relationship going?"

"We are good friends. Well, actually, we are lovers."

"Is that all?"

"That is where it's at right now."

"What about marriage?"

"Well, we haven't gotten that far. I would first have to get a divorce."

"Are you planning to?"

"I haven't been pursuing it actively, but I guess I'll have to get going on it."

Why did she have to spoil an otherwise perfect day? They had a good thing going, a good arrangement, why did she have to push things?

Back at Lisa's apartment that evening he watched the ten o'clock news. The usual roundup of strife and conflict around the world. After the commercial break the camera shifted from the rice paddies of Southeast Asia to the lettuce farms of Southern California. Mexican farm workers, squat and dark, headed by their union leader, Ramon Perez, marching with banners, shouting, "*Huelga! Venganza, señores. Para su respecto y dignidad! Huelga, compañeros!*" Perez, a short, broad shouldered man with jet black hair, deep sad eyes and prominent Aztec nose, was seen marching arm in arm with his aides and sympathizers, including two nuns in short dresses and small veils and a tall sandy haired priest with a bandaged nose. The camera panned the scene and focused on the hecklers who stood alongside the road, husky teamsters kept in line by state troopers. "You sexy broad," a teamster yelled at a nun who passed by, "you ought to be ashamed of yourself."

The marchers started singing "We Shall Overcome," while the Teamsters retaliated by turning up the loudspeaker on a nearby truck, drowning their voices by playing "Bye Bye Blackbird" full blast.

The priest with the bandaged nose, Kaye found out from Joe the next day, was Father Chuck McCartney, a Jesuit, who worked with Ramon Perez on organizing farm workers. A teamster had smashed his nose a week earlier while he was sitting in a restaurant having a cup of coffee.

Kaye called Father McCartney and arranged to meet him. He told the priest about the *havurah's* willingness to help with the strike, and invited him and his associates to the Seder. McCartney readily accepted.

"I always wanted to attend a Seder," said the priest, "so I'll be delighted to come. I also appreciate your offer to help. We need all the help we can get."

He went on to tell Kaye about the migrant farm workers. They kept moving around picking grapes, lettuce and other crops in season, for an annual income of less than half the national poverty level. They were mostly Chicanos who were open to exploitation by the California growers. Since they were always on the move, their children hardly ever learned how to read and write, and could never better themselves. They had no health insurance, social security or old-age pension. They lived in shacks provided by the growers and paid inflated prices in grower-owned food stores. Their work was back-breaking—stooping and bending in the blinding sun, men, women and little children.

"Ironically," said the priest, "their work is vital to the American farm system, but they are not treated like human beings."

Kaye promised he would report to his group what Father Mc-
Cartney had told him.

The day before Passover, a splendid spring day full of promise of
new life and redemption, Kaye received an air mail letter covered
with foreign stamps. The return address read, *Maryknoll Center,
Guatemala City, Guatemala, Central America.* He had been
wondering lately what had happened to the author of the letter,
hoping to hear from her before she left for Central America, perhaps even get to see her if she happened to go by way of L.A., as
she had indicated she might. Did she stop in L.A. without getting in
touch with him, for fear she might succumb to temptation? Did her
vows prohibit her from seeing him again? She wrote:

Dear Josh,

Sorry I took so long to write. I'm all confused about the se-
quence of events of the last few weeks, so let me take one
thing at a time.

A week before I left for Guatemala I found out two sisters
down in Kentucky were driving to Mexico City via L.A. I
was going to hitch a ride with them and then take a bus
from Mexico City to Guatemala. At the last minute their trip
was cancelled and instead I had to take a Delta flight to
Miami and make a connection from there to Guatemala.
This was bad enough, because—I'm ashamed to admit—I
had never flown before, and I was really scared. Wait! You
haven't heard the best part of the adventures of the flying
nun! In Miami I boarded as old Guatemalan Airlines World
War Two plane which didn't look like it was going to take
off. Well, it took off, but as soon as the Florida coastline disappeared one of the twin engines of the plane caught fire.
You get the picture? There I am, my eyes shut tight, deep in
prayer as the plane is soaring in the air, when I hear the
captain's voice over the loudspeaker, telling us not to panic,
and I open my eyes and suddenly I'm flying on a chariot of
fire, like Elijah going up to heaven. Believe it or not, I became very calm. I was making my confessional prayer as the
plane started going down, and the next thing I knew we
were back on the ground in Miami.

To make a harrowing story short, they put us on a Pan
Am jumbo jet a couple of hours later, and that same day I
landed at La Aurora Airport in Guatemala City.

I've been here now for a little over a month. Guatemala is
a tropical country, very hot and humid down on the coast,

yet cool, spring-like weather all year round here in the mountains. Hence the appellation "The Land of Eternal Spring." It's truly beautiful country. Lush vegetation. Rich dark soil. Active volcanoes! How a country so blessed by God can have such wide-spread abject poverty is beyond me.

I've been going through an orientation here at the Maryknoll Center—a beautiful campus-like place, and next week I'm scheduled to start working with the local people. The population here is mainly Mayan Indians and Ladinos— a mixture of Indian and Spanish stock. These humble, taciturn people who rarely stand taller than five feet, make the poor back home in the States look rich by comparison. To buy a ten dollar transistor radio, made in Taiwan, they have to save for two or three years. How can they ever hope to get ahead? Well, we sure have our work here cut out for us.

Speaking of work, what are you up to these days? One of the sisters here just came back from California. She visited the Mexican farm workers in Southern California and she says their living conditions are horrendous. Several members of her order, lead by Father Chuck McCartney, have started working with the head of the Farm Workers Union, Ramon Perez, on organizing a strike. She told me Father Chuck was sitting in a restaurant one day when a Teamster, whose union opposes the strike, came over to his table, broke his nose with one blow, and walked off. How is that for Christian love?

Well, I better stop here. It's past midnight, and I'm really exhausted. Do write. I'm anxious to hear from you, especially now, being so far away from home. Take good care of yourself.

Love,
Eve

The next evening the *havurah* gathered at the HOUSE OF PEACE for the Seder. Father McCartney came early and brought along two coworkers—a nun who worked on organizing a health insurance plan for the farm workers, and a middle aged American Mexican who worked as Ramon Perez's personal secretary. Several other guests came later, including three clergymen—a Methodist, an Episcopalian and a Unitarian.

The preparations for the Seder had kept the group busy for over a month. The whole house was shining. There was new varnish on the staircase banisters. Polished light fixtures. The place was so clean one could practically eat off the floor. Bouquets of flowers were placed in homemade, painted clay vases. The walls were decorated with pictures and posters with words from the Haggadah. Kaye's favorite one read: "In every generation one should consider oneself as though he or she *personally* came out of Egypt."

Nehemia and Shulamit, the resident married couple, had supervised the operation. Shulamit had taken charge of the kitchen, the purchasing of Passover food, the cooking and baking, the grating of horseradish, the chopping of nuts and apples for the *haroset*. They had baked their own matzot and made their own wine. Nehemia had overseen the house cleaning and painting and the repair work. Joe and Kaye had been busy every night teaching the songs and prayers of the Haggadah and preparing special prayers and readings to complement the traditional ritual.

When they all sat down to the Seder table, resplendent with a fresh laundered white tablecloth, home-made candles and a profusion of flowers from their own garden, there was a moment of silent awe and wonder. It was unlike any other Seder they had ever attended before. Someone started to sing, "Behold how good and how pleasant it is for brothers and sisters to dwell together in unity," and everyone joined in the singing. One young woman began to read from the Song of Songs: "For lo, the winter is past, the rain is over and gone, the flowers appear on the earth, the time of the singing of birds is come, and the voice of the turtle dove is heard in our land."

Joe stood up and raised the matzah and spoke the ancient words, inviting all the wayfarers and the needy to join the Seder table and partake of the food.

"My brothers and sisters," Joe said, closing his eyes as if about to intone another prayer, "we can all feel how tonight's Seder is different from all the other Seder nights we have known in the past. In the past we were passive participants in the Seder. We celebrated an ancient tradition, something which happened to our forefathers. Tonight we're celebrating our own freedom. Tonight we've come together as a loving, caring community of free men and women who are not content to passively accept the world as it is, but who have begun to challenge the world around us, as our ancestors in Egypt challenged theirs, *l'taken olam b'malhut shadai*, to perfect the world in the image of God's kingship."

After the fourth cup of wine the door was opened to let in Elijah the prophet, who would usher the coming of the messianic age. Kaye stood up and asked for attention.

"Friends, we have now opened the door to let in Elijah the

prophet. We even have a special cup of wine waiting for him. I've often wondered what all of this means. What it really means, as I found out tonight, is that there is a little bit of Elijah in all of us. Elijah, we are told, will some day bring the messiah. Tonight, in preparing and celebrating this Seder, we have begun to do just that.

"Joe has told us earlier that we have begun to challenge the world around us. I agree. Last Monday night those of us who watched the late news saw the ugly incident that took place during the protest march of the Farm Workers Union. We need not go into details. Suffice it to say that these Mexican farm workers are treated like dirt, not like honest hard working people. In what way is their treatment any different from the way our forefathers were treated in Egypt?

"We talk about Elijah bringing the messiah. If we agree that Elijah is in all of us, and therefore we are the ones who will bring the messiah, what does that really mean?

"It means that we have a responsibility not only to ourselves but to those around us, especially the poor and the oppressed. We cannot be truly free until they are free.

"How can we help them? Aren't we too few in number to take upon ourselves the problems of the world?

"My answer to this is, the problems of the world are vast, but not insoluble. We may be few, but we are not alone. There are other groups like ours here in California and around the country, Jews, Catholics, Protestants and others. We can and should find a way to work together to change the world. As the popular song says, 'One hand can't build a world of peace; two hands can't build a world of peace; but if two and two and fifty make a million, we'll see that world come 'round.'"

Everyone was visibly moved by the speech. They raised their cups of wine as Joe began to sing:

> *Ani maamin. . .*
> I believe with perfect faith
> In the coming of the messiah.
> No matter how long it may take
> Still, I believe.

✧ 19 ✧

Chuck McCartney, Kaye found out, was a man with a mission. He was a kindred spirit. Like Kaye, he was highly critical of organized religion, yet believed that religion did have the power to change the world provided religious leaders were not afraid to put their personal safety and well-being on the line and fight for their beliefs.

"Christ is out there in the fields of Southern California," he told Kaye when they met to discuss joint action, "not in the churches of Beverly Hills and Orange County."

Pointing at his broken nose, he cautioned Kaye about the physical violence his group would have to face if they went down there to help organize the farm workers. Perez and his people were up against great odds. Only last week a Mexican was dragged out of his car by the Teamsters and stabbed several times with an icepick before his assailants realized he was not Perez.

"We are digging in for a long, protracted battle," the tall priest told Kaye. "I am sure we will win in the end, but how long it is going to take is anyone's guess."

Kaye assured him the *havurah* members were not going to be intimidated by physical violence.

They decided to invite the other clergymen who had attended the Seder to a planning meeting. Since Chuck had to go back to Coachella to meet with Perez, Kaye offered to make the calls. Everyone he called agreed to attend. At the meeting it was resolved to form an interfaith group called the *California Clergy Coalition*, and begin joint action on behalf of the United Farm Workers union.

The night after the meeting Kaye got a phone call from Chuck. The NBC Nightly News wanted to interview the members of the *California Clergy Coalition* in conjunction with the farm workers' strike.

"This will draw national attention to the cause," Chuck rejoiced. "It will put the Coalition on the map, and we'll be able to get other clergy around the country involved."

Father McCartney, Rabbi Kaye and Father Blake, the Episcopal priest, were chosen to represent the Coalition at the interview. Blake showed up at the studio wearing his ecclesiastic collar. Chuck wore an open Mexican shirt over his jeans. Kaye wore a blue shirt and an embroidered Yemenite yarmulka.

"We've interviewed representatives of the Teamsters' union and the growers," the TV interviewer told the three guests as they sat down before the camera to do the taping. "If it's okay with you, we will show segments of this interview and of the one we did with them. Basically, what they said was that your people are a group of radicals who are working without the official approval of your own religious organizations, that you're unfamiliar with the intricate problems of grower-Teamster-farm worker relations, and that the workers stand to lose more than they would gain because of your meddling in their affairs."

Small bullet-shaped mikes on a black sling were hung around their necks, and the camera crew trained the equipment on the three clergymen and their interviewer.

McCartney thanked NBC for inviting the Coalition to the program as the camera zeroed in on him. The bandage on his nose had been replaced by a band-aid.

"I'm Father Chuck McCartney. These are my colleagues, Father Blake and Rabbi Kaye. We're no radicals. We're clergymen in good standing. Our decision to help the farm workers organize was reached through our own personal conscience, not through our religious organizations. We don't claim to be experts on labor relations, but we certainly recognize human misery when we see it. We cannot sit down to our dinner table and thank God for the bounty of the land when we know that the lettuce and the grapes on our table were picked by fellow human beings who go to bed hungry, unable to dream dreams of a better future for their children. This land yields enough to support all of us. There's no reason on earth why some of us should prevent others from being fairly compensated for their labor."

"Our religious beliefs may differ," Kaye added, "but when it comes to fair labor practices and to the basic dignity of our fellow human beings we're all united in our belief."

As Chuck had predicted, the interview attracted a great deal of attention. It was prominently featured in the press, both local and national. Kaye started to receive letters and calls from colleagues, friends and relatives he had not heard from in a long time. Suddenly he had become a national celebrity of sorts. His former boss, Rabbi Blumenfeld, wrote him a warm letter, congratulating him on his courageous stand, pointing out that he, Blumenfeld, as President of the Conference of Presidents of Major Jewish Organizations, had gone on record in support of Ramon Perez's struggle to organize the farm workers. Blumenfeld went on to say he would be honored to recommend Kaye to the Sisterhood board as the next Sukkot guest speaker.

Least expected of all was a phone call he received one night after he turned off the light and was about to fall asleep.

"Hi, remember me?"

The voice sounded vaguely familiar, but he couldn't place it.

"I'm not sure."

"Sue Pins."

"Sue! Where're you calling from?"

"Right here in L.A.

"What are you doing in L.A.?"

"I've been living here for about a month."

"What about that Bahai commune?"

"It's a long story. I saw you on television. I didn't know you have moved back to L.A. I just called to say hello."

"I'd love to see you, Sue. You have some time tomorrow?"

"Sure."

"How about lunch?"

"Okay. Where?"

"The cafeteria on campus?"

"About twelve?"

"Twelve's fine."

She showed up at the cafeteria at half past twelve. He was sitting at a table by himself engrossed in Tailhard de Chardin's *The Phenomenon of Man*, pondering the concept of the noosphere, when he looked up and saw her standing behind the table, waiting to catch his attention. He nearly gasped when he saw her. She looked forlorn and emaciated in her threadbare denim outfit, as though she had not taken a bath in a month and had not had a decent meal in memory. Her beautiful blue eyes, set back in their pale translucent orbits, had a sickly cast, and barely seemed to focus, as if looking through him, away from him, at some other, distant reality.

He got up and embraced her, wondering whether she was back on drugs. He took her to the cafeteria counter and handed her a plastic tray and a set of tableware. She picked the avocado salad, a hard roll and a glass of milk. He took egg salad on a seeded bun and coffee.

After she started eating her taut expression softened and she seemed to become more aware of her surroundings.

"So I see you've given up on Suburban Temple," she said.

"Yes, I have."

"I knew you would. You didn't fit in with those moguls who think they own the world."

"No, I guess I didn't."

She gulped down her milk and wiped her mouth.

"Last time I saw you, Sue, you asked me to join you on that Bahai commune. I guess it didn't work out too well."

"No, it didn't. But I'm not sorry I did it. It was a good learning experience for me. I learned an awful lot about human nature. It helped me grow and mature."

"Do you still consider yourself a Bahai?"

"No, I don't. It's a noble idea, trying to unify all religions and all that, but it doesn't work."

"So you left the commune."

"About a month ago. When I first arrived there I thought I'd discovered utopia. It was one of the most beautiful places on earth, a small valley hidden in the mountains near San Diego. Beautiful vegetation around a blue lake, a bird sanctuary, tropical flowers, really paradise. The man who organized the commune was a young looking middle aged dark skinned Iranian or Indian, I'm not sure which, with a radiant smile and a flowing white beard, named Abbas. He appeared to be the gentlest, wisest, most carefree person I'd ever met. He'd worked at the Bahai headquarters in Wilmette, Illinois, but had broken away from the world organization and started his own brand of Bahaism. Some widow of a San Diego oil millionaire gave him that beautiful piece of land to start the commune. When I arrived I found some one hundred young people from all over the United States and even from as far away as Japan, Chile, and Israel. We were all put to work on building our own living quarters, according to Abbas's own blueprint, and we began to grow our own food. It was hard work. We worked from four in the morning till noon. But we didn't mind. We were building the ideal community. We were going to show the way to all mankind to unite and become one.

"It took two months to complete our wood and glass community house. Those were probably the happiest two months of my life. In the evening we would hold long open-ended discussions about our common goals. Abbas encouraged us to be totally open and honest about our thoughts and feelings, not hold back anything. We became one large intimate family. We began to discuss the social structure of our community and we soon agreed that monogamy was not necessarily the only socially desirable form of cohabitation. People were free to choose the way they wanted to live together.

The community was the extended family, looking after all its members, enabling each member to fulfil his or her own needs, as long as they did not conflict with someone else's needs. Within that larger family, one could form relations and terminate relations if things didn't work out. We called it contracts. Those contracts were entered upon for one year, and had to be renewed at the end of each year.

"One of the basic principles we'd all agreed on was what we called positive thinking, which meant that no one would make any critical, judgmental or negative comments about anyone else. If a problem arose, if someone had negative feelings about anything or anyone else, we would bring it before a general meeting once a week and discuss it openly and come to a decision how to resolve it. For positive reinforcement, each night after dinner we would spend an hour sharing all the good feelings of the day, about ourselves, our work, one another, nature, whatever.

"All went well for the first two months. After we finished building the community house and got settled in the new place, we had our first major disagreement. Some of us began to argue it was time to make our existence known to the outside world, reach out to other people, become involved in social issues, invite others to come and visit the commune and encourage people to start similar groups. Others spoke against the idea. It was too early to reach out. By doing so we might lose our unique character, become exposed to outside influences and finally lose sight of our goals and disintegrate."

"Which group did you side with?"

"The first."

"What about Abbas?"

"That was the whole point. Up until then Abbas never used to choose sides or exercise his authority in any of the discussions. This time he spoke up and sided with the second group, which really surprised me, especially since the members of that group were the timid souls, the ones who were afraid to take chances, who wanted to hide from the world. Abbas's intervention was really the turning point. From that day on the discussions were no longer open and democratic. Abbas pretended to remain noncommittal in his views, only making suggestions, but in reality his views were thinly disguised directives which everyone had to follow. In essence, he began to preach a new gospel of exclusiveness and superiority. None of the major religions, he went on to say, ever did follow the teachings of their founders and prophets. The Jews didn't follow Moses' ethical monotheism. The Christians didn't follow Christ's teachings of love and charity. The Muslims didn't follow Mohammad's rules of moderation and ethical behavior. And so on. The only ones who attempted to follow those rules were the Bahai, but even they have failed, and that only left him, Abbas, and the commune.

"So much for theory," Sue concluded derisively, her blue eyes flashing. "What was happening in reality was just the opposite. People were beginning to form a caste system. Those who were close to the leader became the privileged ones. They were given the easier tasks and were exempt from doing menial work. The others, like myself, had our workload doubled. It became clear to me we were no longer building a utopia, but have become another closed, intolerant sect like so many other. People were beginning to abdicate their individuality and became blind followers."

"So you quit?"

"One night I quietly packed my belongings and slipped out without saying goodbye. I walked through the hills for several miles and found the highway, and I hitchhiked back to L.A., where I found an old friend from Ohio State."

"But you say you're not sorry you did it."

"No, I'm not. I learned everything I needed to know about human nature, particularly group behavior, from that experience. Most people, I found out, are not leaders but followers. What we call democracy does not really exist. There's no such thing as the rule of the people. A country like the United States promotes the illusion of government by the people. Now you know as well as I who really runs this country. The fact is, people are not ready to govern themselves. Not even a hundred or so intelligent young people in that commune who really had the right idea when they first got started. Once they faced a difficult issue they stopped thinking for themselves. They let one person take over and become the undisputed authority, the guru, the rebbe."

"Then what is the solution?"

"Well, I watched your interview on TV the other night. What you guys are doing is certainly not the solution. Think about it. What are you really doing? You're fighting the Teamsters Union in order to establish the Farm Workers Union. When the first unions were organized in America the workers who were getting organized were oppressed the same way the farm workers are today. But look what had happened to unions like the Teamsters. They've become corrupt, violent, discriminatory. They are no better than Big Business. You're wasting your time, Josh, trying to work within the System. It will never work, because the System, by its very nature, can't work. Democracy is an illusion. At least democracy as we know it, under Capitalism. People are not ready for a just and humane society. They need to go through a transition period, during which the wealth will be redistributed among the people, the concept of private ownership will be abolished, and instead of exploiting others, people will begin to learn how to become unselfish and work together for the common good."

"In other words, Marxism?"

"Yes, pure Marxism, not the kind practiced in the Soviet Union, which is Marxism in name only, but the kind taught by Chairman Mao."

"So you've become a Maoist?"

Sue Pins, heiress to the Strauss fortune, puckered her mouth and gave her former rabbi a long look. She looked around and said,

"Can you keep a secret?"

"Sure."

"Shortly after I came back to L.A. I was approached by a Maoist group, an underground organization which works with other groups around the world to bring about a world revolution. I'm not supposed to say a word about it to a living soul. If they find out my life won't be worth much. I'm considering joining that group. I've given it a great deal of thought during the last couple of weeks. The more I think about it the more I realize those people are right. The world needs a radical change. None of those groups and sects I've been involved with is going to bring about that kind of change. Moses and Jesus and Buddha had some great ideas, but those ideas didn't bring about a world of peace and justice."

"And what makes you think Maoism will?"

"It works in China, and it can work in the rest of the world."

"That remains to be seen," said Kaye.

Before she left, he told her not to hesitate to get in touch with him if she ever needed anything.

The Farm Workers' strike was taking up all his free time. Logistically, it was hard to reach those migrant workers scattered over the vast fields and remote towns of Southern California.

"I don't see you anymore," Lisa complained one evening when he came back from a week-long trip that rook him as far as the Mexican border.

He was tired and tense. One had to be constantly on the lookout for those Teamster thugs, who had lately become more violent and were particularly down on clergymen.

"I'm sorry," said Kaye, "but I've made a commitment to those people and I have to live up to it."

"What about your commitment to me, to our relationship?"

He made no reply. Lisa did not share his goals and concerns. She didn't really take to the *havurah*, and although she didn't come out and say it, he could tell she felt he should not have become so involved in the Farm Workers' strike. He had no difficulty reading her mind: she wanted the two of them to get married, settle down, become a materially secure middle class couple. "Grow old with me, the best is yet to come."

Clearly, he had to choose. He couldn't have it both ways. He had chosen to give up material comfort and security in order to live up to his beliefs, and he was not about to make any compromises or accommodations. What Lisa wanted he had left behind in Quincy. It wasn't what he wanted. He had to come out and let her know how he felt. But then, as the good social worker she was, she would undoubtedly analyze his actions, his motives, conscious and latent, and would come to the conclusion that he was "going through a phase" and had to outgrow it. She would be patient, understanding, supportive. She would play the role of the martyr, the one who is willing to be "dumped on," take a beating in order to help him "work out his conflicts," acquire a better sense of reality, get his feet on the ground, and become a happy productive member of society.

No, it had to be a clean break. He had to let her know he was not ready to settle down. He could not offer her the things she needed, and he did not wish to mislead her. The two of them wanted something altogether different out of life, and there was no way of working it out. She was a young, attractive woman, and she had a great deal going for her. Having just turned thirty, it was time for her to form a lasting relationship, have a family, build a future. He did not wish to stand in her way of attaining those goals. He only wanted her to find the happiness she deserved, and part as good friends.

"You look unhappy," she said, standing next to him as he sat at the kitchen table. She stood behind him and put her arms around his neck. "I'm sorry, honey, I know you've had a rough week. I didn't mean to yell at you." She unbuttoned his shirt and ran her fingers through his chest. No, he didn't have the heart or the energy right now to confront her with his true feelings. It would have to wait.

"Come," she said, "lie down and I'll give you a rubdown. You need to relax a little. Your body is all tensed up and stiff."

She took off his shirt and ordered him down on his belly. She took a small bottle of rubbing alcohol and poured the liquid heat on his back and neck. Her strong fingers began to squeeze and knead his nape, making his body crawl with a sweet relaxing pain. Next she began to apply rhythmic chops to his shoulders and back.

"Feel better?"

"Much much better."

"You're not mad at me?"

"Of course not."

"Then kiss me."

He turned over and drew her down against him. It may be the last time we make love, he thought. He stroked her gently, as if afraid he might hurt her, wishing he were elsewhere, far away, not going through these motions of being less than honest with his feelings, leading her on, playing a part he did not wish to play.

Waking up late the next morning, he received a phone call from Joe. His older colleague asked him to come over immediately to his office at school.

He took a quick shower, got dressed and rushed over to see Joe. He was surprised to find a gray haired man sitting in the chaplain's office, wearing an expensive business suit and shiny black shoes.

"Rabbi Kaye, I'd like you to meet Howard Friedman. Howard is a member of the board of governors of the university and vice-president of the Jewish Community Federation of Greater Los Angeles."

Kaye shook the vice-president's hand.

"Rabbi Kaye," the gray haired gentleman started.

"Please call me Josh."

"Sure, and you can call me Howard. Well, then, Josh, I understand you work with that group at the HOUSE OF PEACE. I believe you call it *havurah*."

"Yes, we do."

"A very fine group of people. We're very happy to be able to sponsor you."

"I don't understand," said Kaye, "I thought we were self-sufficient. We do everything ourselves and we pay for everything with our own money."

"Yes, yes, of course, but the house you are using belongs to a foundation which is administered by the Federation and of which I happen to be the chairman. We have decided, for a good Jewish cause, we'd let you use it rent free."

"We certainly appreciate it, I'm sure."

"Well, Josh, let me come to the point. I received a call today from the regional office of the Teamsters Union. They say they have found out your group is involved in organizing the Farm Workers strike. Now, personally, I'm not saying you're right or wrong. I'm only concerned about one thing: the Teamsters are considering making a very large contribution to the Federation, and we sure would hate to lose the money because of some student activists. So what I'm asking you to do is talk to your people and tell them to hold off on getting involved in this strike."

"And what if they refuse to hold off?"

"Then they'll have to give up the house."

"I'll tell them," said Kaye, suppressing his anger. "They'll have to decide for themselves. Personally, I couldn't in good conscience go along with it. If a place called HOUSE OF PEACE has to kowtow to a gangster organization, then I for one would have to disassociate myself from it."

Joe looked on in dismay.

"That son of a bitch," Kaye snarled after the Federation officer walked out. "Who the hell he thinks he is? It's precisely because of the likes of him that I quit my job at Suburban Temple."

"Yes, I know," Joe said, heavy-hearted. "You are right. If he had any self-respect he would've never come up with such an ultimatum. But, unfortunately this is the nature of the beast. Money is the bottom line. It pays my salary. It pays for that house. It pays for everything. Go try to do something about it. You really can't. In the end the Howard Friedmans are always the ones who call the shots."

Kaye looked at his mentor, the man who had first taught him about Liberal Judaism and personal freedom and all the things he so fervently believed in. Joe looked old and haggard.

"I'm sorry," Joe said, as if reading his thoughts. "I'm just a tired old campus chaplain, and I am not ready to take on the world. There's nothing stopping you from helping Chuck McCartney with the strike. But obviously it cannot be an official project of the *havurah*. They need that house. There're certainly other causes they can get involved in."

"Yes, I guess you're right," said Kaye, drawing a deep breath. "I guess the kids at Kent State learned the hard way they couldn't fight the System. But Joe, I'm not ready to give up. Not yet, anyway. If, in the final analysis, the HOUSE OF PEACE is ruled by the same powers which rule Suburban Temple, then it's not for me. If religion is ruled by money then it'll never accomplish what it sets out to do. Joe, you're the one who inspired me to become a rabbi. I know this is not what you had in mind. You know I love you and I respect you. So please don't ask me to go along with it."

They embraced each other and remained silent for a long time.

He had a hard time falling asleep that night. It was a full moon night. Lisa was breathing quietly next to him, fast asleep. He had not told her about his meeting with Howard Friedman. He had to work it out for himself. Again, as had happened before, he was all alone, listening to that still small voice, waiting for a clue. Lisa's hair was spread on the pillow. Her naked shoulder gleamed against the moon. As he looked at the sleeping form he was shaken by a powerful thought. He had to see Eve. He had to discuss this idea with her. It was a simple yet bold plan, perhaps unattainable, but certainly worth trying. It might be just the kind of thing he had been reaching for during their long discussions before he left Quincy. He had to go away and find out.

It was the end of May. School would be over in a week. Now was the time to do it.

In the morning he told Lisa he was going away for the summer.

"Where to?"

"Latin America."

"For the whole summer?"

"I'm not sure."

"What about us?"

"I'm not ready to settle down. I need to get away. I hope you won't take it personally. I think you're terrific, I really do. I know you're going to make someone very happy, and I really envy that person. I wish I were him. But there's something inside me which makes me very restless and won't let me settle down and give you all the things I know you want and need. You've really been very good to me, Lis, you're an angel."

Tears rolled down her face. She shook her hair away from her face and wiped her cheeks with the back of her hands. Getting a hold of herself, she smiled through her tears.

"I knew it would happen," she said. "I've known it all along. Your mind, Josh, and perhaps your heart, too, were elsewhere, not here. I was hoping somehow things could work out, but it was wishful thinking. I'm not mad at you. I know you have to do whatever it is you feel compelled to do."

"I want to remain your friend, Lis."

She put her hand on his.

"Good luck, Josh."

"Run it by me again," Joe said, squinting at him through his thick lenses. "That Jewish Peace Corps, or whatever you call it."

They sat at an outdoor restaurant, overlooking the ocean.

"To our eternal friendship," said Kaye, raising his cup of wine.

"To Dr. Schweitzer."

"You think I'm crazy, don't you, Joe?"

"Yes, of course you're crazy. You're crazy all right. But aren't we all? Especially people like us, who chose to become rabbis?"

Kaye laughed. "Yes, especially people like us."

Joe poured himself another glass of wine.

"Excuse me," he said, covering his mouth as he burped. "You know, I'd go with you if I were twenty years younger. I'm getting tired of L.A. and I could certainly use a change of scenery. I would go with you, although I'm not sure I understand what you're driving at."

"The *havurah* is fine, Joe, but it's not enough. You saw what happened when we had to deal with that Howard Friedman. We Jews in this great land are controlled by the Establishment. We can only go so far but no farther. I guess as long as the *havurah* minds its own business there won't be any problem. But you know something? The time for Jews to be afraid to stick out their necks is over. There're many young Jews in this country who want to be challenged, to be given a purpose. This is why I'd like to look into this idea of a Jewish Peace Corps. We Jews have the brain power, in economics, medicine, technology, etc. and we can make a major contribution to solve the major problems of the world, not out of self-interest, but out of a genuine conviction that it's our moral mission, our *raison d'etre*, if you will."

"But why Guatemala?"

"Because Guatemala is one of the most backward countries in the world, and because I have a good friend there, a Catholic nun, with whom I used to discuss those things back in Quincy. I know she can be very helpful. I've visited the Peace Corps office here in L.A. and gotten the information about their operation in Central America. I want to see them in action over there and get some ideas. Like you say, I may be crazy, but I've got to give it a try."

"The *havurah* may want to give you a farewell party," said Joe.

"I'd rather not. Please tell them I'm going to Central America for a couple of months to learn about the Peace Corps. They should expect me back for the High Holy Days."

"Take good care of yourself," Joe said before they parted. They embraced each other. "Here," Joe handed Kaye a dark olive pocket-size prayer book. Kaye hesitated. "Take it," Joe said. "Something for you to remember me by."

Part Four:

Guatemala

✧ 20 ✧

Eve was right. As soon as he got off the plane and walked across the airfield toward the terminal building, Kaye came under the spell of the strange primeval beauty of that tropical country tucked away in the high mountains of Central American, called Guatemala.

Down on the coast, he was told, it was over 100 degrees. But here in the mountains it was mild spring weather, unvaried throughout the year. A huge blue sky hung overhead, dotted with snow white clouds one could almost touch. A profusion of flowers everywhere. Bougainvillea, oleander, roses. Against the horizon at the far end of the airport he saw some of the volcanoes Eve had written him about, towering massive black cratered cones threatening their surroundings. Guatemala City stretched across a long plateau in the middle of those mountains. It was easy to see why civilizations had flourished here since time immemorial.

He had not written her about his coming. He did not wish to explain himself, go into a lengthy discussion about his plans. He was not sure whether he would only stay for a few days or for a longer period of time. He was doing this whole thing on an impulse, for better or for worse. He hardly knew what to expect. Guatemala may or may not be the place to test his idea, although it seemed to be as good a place as any to find out if it could work. Nor did he wish to intrude on her life. She had chosen her own way. She was married, so to speak, to the Church, and in spite of their personal feelings for each other, he could not walk freely into her life and make demands on their friendship, as he had found out once before.

After he cleared through customs he turned to a policeman at the terminal's main exit to find out how to get to the American Embassy. He had written the Peace Corps coordinator at the U.S. Embassy in Guatemala City about his arrival. He wanted to do a field study on the agency with a view to organizing a similar operation among young Jewish graduate students and professionals. He would appreciate any help that the agency could offer.

Someone tapped his on his shoulder.

"Rabbi Kaye? *Bienvenido*. I'm Jorge Aguilar. You've written me at the Embassy about your interest in the Peace Corps."

The man was about his age or slightly older. His balding, egg-shaped head, thick glasses and shy look gave him a scholarly appearance and made him look older than his age. He wore a navy blue blazer, neatly creased gray slacks and a red striped tie.

"I'd be glad to take you to your hotel," Aguilar pointed at his car outside.

Kaye thanked the embassy official. "I hope I'm not inconveniencing you."

"Not at all."

They drove down a wide tree lined *avenida* and turned into narrow city streets. On almost every corner Kaye saw small dark brown soldiers wearing oversized helmets and keeping their fingers on the trigger of their U.S. made M-16 assault rifles.

"Why so many soldiers?" Kaye asked.

"Since the beginning of May the leftist guerrillas've stepped up their activities. There're rumors of an invasion of a large guerrilla force from Cuba, by way of Honduras."

"How true are the rumors?"

"It's hard to say. I've been hearing this kind of rumors since I first came here two years ago. The local guerilla bands, though, have been very active lately both here in the city and in the countryside. Only this week two local businessmen were kidnapped for ransom, and some of our military advisers were shot at and luckily escaped unharmed."

On a closer look Kaye noticed the soldiers wore bullet-proof vests.

"I'm surprised the papers in the States haven't written about it."

"Guatemala is not all that important to the rest of the world," Aguilar shrugged. "Just another banana republic where political assassinations and guerrilla activities are a way of life."

The official parked his car in front of the U.S. Embassy in the heart of downtown. He pointed at a stone and stucco Spanish colonial house across the street. Above the entrance the sign read CLUB AMERICANO.

"May I invite you for a drink?"

"I hope I'm not taking too much of your time."

Aguilar assured his guest he was in no rush.

"Besides," he added, "it's not every day I play host to a rabbi."

The inside of the club reminded Kaye of a scene out of *Casablanca*. Slow spinning ceiling fans. A piano in the far corner under a skylight. Few guests at scattered tables dining in the dim light. Instead of Humphrey Bogart and Ingrid Bergman, a man who looked like a travelling American businessman was chatting in undertones at a corner table with a willowy blond woman in a low cut, bare shouldered dress.

"Forgive my ignorance," the embassy official said. "Should I address you by your title?"

"It's hardly necessary," said Kaye, "Josh is fine."

"Call me George, or Jorge, either way is okay."

Over margaritas, Kaye found out Jorge Aguilar once considered going into the priesthood. He grew up in Puerto Rico, in a well-to-do upper class family. When he started high school his father was assigned to the U.S. Mission to the United Nations, and the family moved to New York. In San Juan he had lived a sheltered life, and it was not until he came to New York that he found out how poor and backward most of his people were. He became friendly with a young priest in his parish on the West Side of New York, and had long discussions with him on the subject of what was the best way to improve living conditions in Latin America. The priest told him that the Church was the most powerful ideological body in that part of the world, and could bring about a social and economic change if led by people who were not afraid to stand up to the rich landowners and the higher-ups in the Church itself.

Young Jorge decided to become a priest and go back to Latin America to work on improving the lot of his people. As it turned out, he finally came to the realization he was not strong enough to accept the rigors of the monastic life, and decided instead to study political science and international law. When President Kennedy launched the Peace Corps, he signed up immediately. He was sent for two years to the Dominican Republic, where he helped organize a legal aid system for the poor. He then went back to the States to complete his studies for his law degree, and started working for the State Department. Two years ago he was assigned to the U.S. Embassy in Guatemala as coordinator of the local Peace Corps operation.

Kaye asked how effective the Peace Corps work in Guatemala was.

Aguilar thought for a moment.

"To be very honest, the Peace Corps in objective terms has very little impact on living conditions in this country. It's mainly a good will gesture on the part of our government and our people toward the people of Guatemala. We are few in number and our resources are extremely limited. The change has to come from within the society, especially from the ruling class of Guatemala, that handful of families who practically own the entire country. Time, I feel, is running out. We may be fighting a losing battle, since the world, especially what has become known as the Third World, of which Guatemala is part, is becoming more and more militant, and we can probably expect more and more political violence in the future."

Kaye said he would like to volunteer his services to the Corps.

Aguilar looked surprised. "I thought you came to observe. I didn't realize you actually wanted to work for us."

"I feel I can best learn by doing. And it sounds to me like you guys can use all the help you can get."

"True. But this is not the way it is usually done. First you have to go through a training period, study Spanish, learn about Latin American societies, be able to deal with what we in the foreign service refer to as the culture shock."

"I spent a year as a teenage in Mexico, where my Dad worked on an irrigation project for the Mexican Government. I've also worked recently with Chicano farm workers in Southern California. My Spanish is adequate, and as for the culture shock, I don't think we have to worry about it."

"Fair enough," Aguilar smiled. "Let me think about it. I'll see what I can do."

Along with their drinks they were served typical Guatemalan dishes. Black bean dip, corn tortillas and *chile relleno*. As it grew dark outside, Aguilar offered to take his guest to his hotel.

Out in the street Kaye was greeted by a cool quiet evening. There were few people in the streets, and a few store lights were on.

They drove through a silent downtown when they saw a group of soldiers standing in the middle of the street. One of the soldiers ordered them to stop. The rest of the unit surrounded the car, their guns at the ready.

What am I getting myself into? Kaye wondered.

The commander asked Aguilar for identification. Aguilar flashed his diplomatic ID card. The soldier studied the ID for a moment and waved them on.

"What's wrong?" Kaye asked.

"Oh, nothing, only a routine check. You'll get used to it."

He took him to an old house with a sign above the entrance, PENSION LOS ALAMOS.

"Well, I hope you like it. It's clean and inexpensive."

"By the way," said Kaye, "I've an old friend here in Guatemala City I'd like to look up."

"An American?"

"Yes, a Sister Eve Gruner."

"A nun?"

"Do you know her?"

"I may. What does she do?"

"She works at the Maryknoll Center."

"How long has she been there?"

"About two months."

"Tall, skinny, short hair, wears regular clothes?"

"That sounds right."

"Oh yes, Sister Eve, from Ohio. I met her a couple of weeks ago. Quite an interesting person. Very idealistic. She asked me many questions about the Peace Corps."

"Is the Maryknoll Center far from here?"

"About a half an hour by bus."

He lay awake in his small *pension* room thinking about Eve. Did he do the right thing coming here? What would her reaction be when she saw him? Was she free to come and go as she pleased? Would he get to see her, spend time with her, discuss his plans?

He was beginning to feel the fatigue of the trip. He fell asleep and then kept waking throughout the night. He was having dreams in which Eve was the main protagonist. In one dream they were driving through the Guatemalan mountains. Suddenly they were caught in the middle of a shootout between Guatemalan soldiers and guerrillas. They swerved off the road and rolled down into the gaping ravine below. The ravine was actually in Quincy, and on one side he saw his rabbinical school and on the other Eve's old convent. When the car hit the bottom of the ravine he crawled out and went around to the other side of the car to help Eve out. He saw her face looking at him through the car window with a madonna-like expression of infinite compassion, when the car suddenly burst into flames and Eve's face disappeared.

When he woke up it was almost noon. He got dressed, puzzling over the dream, and went out for some breakfast. The streets of the capital city were much livelier in the daytime than at night. The soldiers he had seen when he first arrived were still there, guarding street corners, banks, public buildings, consulates, and foreign companies. They looked less ominous in the colorful crowds and traffic that choked the narrow streets. One street was closed to traffic and was lined on both sides with fruit and vegetable stands and with many *tiendas* stocked with a large assortment of local crafts and used merchandise, household items, hardware, tools, cheap transistor radios and what appeared to be Catholic religious objects, candles and icons and little statues of the Savior and the saints, which did not have the tall fair haired blue eyed Nordic look of their counterparts in the States, but rather the squat brown color high cheekbone appearance of the local populace. For the first time he saw the local Mayan Indians who apparently came from the towns and villages in the mountains to sell their produce at the city market. They wore their typical costumes, no doubt unchanged in centuries or even millenia, women in hand woven red and blue and yellow striated shawls and long wide skirts, some nursing their babies, and men in straw hats and embroidered shirts and wide striped pants, either wearing sandals or barefoot.

He thought of the Chicanos back home in California. Despite their poverty, they at least had started to fight for their social and economic rights. These Guatemalan Indians were left behind by history, back in some pre-historic state. They did not even seem to have thoughts of changing their lot. What made it even more ironic, Kaye thought, was the fact that before the white man conquered Guatemala, these poor illiterate Mayans were a proud race which had produced one of the most advanced civilizations in the world. He recalled reading how during Europe's Dark Ages they practiced an astronomy so precise that their ancient calendar was as accurate as the one employed today. They plotted the course of the celestial bodies, and, to the awe of the populace, their priests predicted both solar and lunar eclipses. They originated a complex system of writing and pioneered mathematical concepts. When Europe finally discovered them, they succumbed to the superior weapons of the Spanish Conquistadors, followed by the zealous priests and friars who came to civilize the red skinned heathens and convert them to the True Faith. As a result, their erstwhile glorious temples and citadels became ruins lost in the coastal jungles and covered by the sands of time. Their descendants were now growing corn and black beans and provided cheap labor for the coffee and cotton and banana growers.

These, then, were the people Sister Eve had set out to help. And here is where he, Rabbi Kaye, was going to try out his idea of a Jewish Peace Corps, a world wide network of Jewish volunteers who would contribute two or three years of professional service to raise the economic, educational, and health level of the world's most underprivileged people.

From the sublime to the ridiculous there is only one small step, Kaye observed as he rode the bus to the Maryknoll Center. We will soon find out in which direction I am heading.

The Maryknoll Center, located in a new residential section on the foothills north of the city, turned out to be a beautiful little campus, more like a New England prep school than a Guatemalan religious center. He walked in through the shrub grown gate between neatly kept flowerbeds up a path leading to a stucco ivy covered building with pink shutters. A nun in a modified brown habit came out with two young girls in green plaid school uniforms. It suddenly struck him the place was the exact antithesis of Eve's convent back home in the Cliffwood suburb of Quincy. Instead of the palpable poverty of Cliffwood, this place seemed to be an exclusive rich girls' school. Did he come to the wrong place?

He asked the nun in the brown habit if she knew a Sister Eve Gruner. Yes, of course. She just saw her in the garden in the back of the school building.

He walked around the building down a gravel path and looked around. He saw a beautiful white marble water fountain surrounded by beds of roses. He walked around to the other side of the fountain. On a stone bench he saw a young woman in a plain blue dress sitting opposite a girl in a green plaid uniform, reading from an open book spread on her lap. He plucked a rose from one of the bushes and went over and held it out to the teacher, who looked up in surprise.

"Sister Eve, I presume."

"Josh!"

Forgetting herself, she flew into his arms, trembling with excitement.

"Oh, Josh!" She drew back and squeezed his hands in hers. "Is it for real, or am I dreaming?"

"It's for real."

She turned to her student and told her to go back to her class. The little girl bowed and left.

"Let's sit down," he pointed at the bench. "Let me look at you. You look like you have lost weight."

"I had some stomach virus. I'm okay now."

He took her hand and stroked it. They smiled at each other. She looked entranced, as if unable to believe it was him.

"So," he edged up to her, "I've finally caught up with you."

"Josh," she said, laughing and shaking her head in disbelief, "I didn't expect to ever see you here, in Guatemala, of all places. I was hoping to take a trip to L.A. in September and see you there. I've just started looking into it."

"Stranger things have happened."

"How did you get here?"

"I offered my services to the Peace Corps."

"You did?"

"I have this idea about starting a Jewish Peace Corps."

"You're kidding!"

"No, I'm not. I'm dead serious."

"Jewish Peace Corps," she said reflectively, trying to decide whether it sounded right.

"Beautiful place you have here," he waved his head at the school building.

"Yes, it is," she said and shook her head. "It's beautiful all right. Who would have believed I came to Guatemala to teach at a rich girls' school."

"I don't understand. What ever happened to your Mayan Indians?"

"Nothing happened. They are still there and they still need me. I have put in several requests to be sent out to one of the villages, but they keep turning me down. It's not very hard to put two and two together. I'm finding out that the Church here in Guatemala, even more so than in the States, is having a problem working effectively with the poor. When I was first told about the need for teachers, they did have this plan to open new schools in Indian villages. But by the time I got here they put it on the back burner, so to speak. It seems that they ran into some difficulties with the government. This priest had explained it to me that the government was not anxious to educate the Indians since there were no jobs for educated skilled workers. Last I've heard, they want to scale down the program and only start with a few model schools. In the meantime I teach English here at the Maryknoll Center."

She paused and looked at him with a radiant smile. He took hold of her hands.

"I missed you, Eve."

She looked down, knitting her brow.

"Did you miss me?"

Her chest heaved.

"Well?"

"Yes," she said, "I did."

There was pain in her eyes.

"I want to kiss you, Eve."

"No, Josh, don't."

The nun in the modified brown habit materialized behind the marble fountain. He let go of Eve's hands.

"Eve, it's time for class."

Eve stood up.

"Marj, I'd like you to meet a good friend of mine from the States, Joshua Kaye. Josh is going to do some work for the Peace Corps."

The nun shook his hand. "Very pleased to meet you."

He arranged to see Eve over the weekend, when she was off from teaching. In the afternoon he went to the Embassy to see Jorge Aguilar and find out if there was any chance of his being placed with the Corps. Aguilar was glad to see him.

"You're in luck, my friend. One of our men at the village of Santa Teresa was taken to the hospital last night with some kind of kidney trouble, and it looks like we may have to send him back home to the States. We have one other young man working there, but he cannot do it all by himself. I'd be happy to arrange for you to go there."

"When do I start?"

"You can start tomorrow."

Later that evening he got a call from Eve. He did not have a phone in his room and had to go downstairs to the lobby to take the call. She wanted to know how he was doing, whether he had everything he needed. From the sound of her voice he could tell she was lonely. He also got the impression she felt badly she could not be with him, help him get settled, spend more time with him and listen to his plans, catch up with him on his experience in California and tell him more about her own world. Suddenly he felt the peculiar irony of the situation. Here they were, in a strange country, not having seen each other for months, Eve confined to her monastic quarters and he alone in this city, where he did not know a soul. He ached for her. A wild thought ran through his mind: he would go out there to the Maryknoll Center and arrange for her to sneak out and meet him secretly in the adjacent woods. He would give anything to be with her right now.

"Everything's okay, except for one thing."

"What's that?" she asked.

"I wish you were here."

"So do I."

"I'm leaving tomorrow for that village I've just been assigned to by the Peace Corps."

"Which village?"

"Santa Teresa de Avila."

"Oh, Josh!"

"You know the place?"

"It's only a few minutes by car from the Maryknoll Center, right up the mountain from here. I was there only a month ago. Josh, I'm so happy! Here I was afraid they would send you to some remote outpost and we would never get to see each other."

"So when do I get to see you?"

"I'm off Sunday afternoon. I'll come to see you at the village."

Her words sounded like magic. Things were falling into place. He was too excited to go back to his room. He tucked his hands in his windbreaker pockets and went outside and roamed the dark deserted downtown streets. He felt ready to take on the world. Rabbi Kaye and Sister Eve, here in the mountains of Guatemala, about to launch something that will change the world. Religion had the power to do it. Judaism and Christianity, at odds for centuries in a world of mutual distrust and conflict and hatred, where the privileged few have always oppressed the wretched masses. All it would take was one rabbi and one nun to change all of this. Working together for the common goal, the two faiths could begin to turn the world around. *Ani ma'amin*, I believe with perfect faith. The road ahead may be long and difficult, there will be many obstacles along the way, but they won't be insurmountable. "Behold, I have put before you today life and good and death and evil. . . for what I command you today is not beyond your power. . . it is not in the heavens. . . it is not beyond the sea. . . it is very close to you, in your mouth and in your heart, that you may do it."

His peace Corps partner came to pick him up at noon. He was a young man in his early twenties who spoke with a Texas drawl. He gave Kaye a strong handshake.

"Josh? Howdy. I'm Tom. Jorge told me all about you. I understand you are a rabbi."

Tom Sealy was extremely friendly. He had a quick, broad smile. He was a native of Galveston, Texas, and a graduate of the University of Texas School of Agriculture.

"It will be good to have a clergyman working on our project," Tom told Kaye as he started his jeep. "Has Jorge told you about the project?"

"Not exactly."

"It's basically a savings plan. I'm trying to teach the villagers how to save their money and start a small cooperative in order to pitch in and buy farm equipment and machinery for working their land. God, they have some of the best farm land in the world, but they use farming methods which haven't changed in thousands of years. No wonder they are so poor."

"So what has this got to do with a clergyman?"

"Well, agriculture to these people has a lot to do with religion. It's all tied up with all sorts of ancient pagan customs which they find hard to let go of. They need a lot of talking to. We have to gain their confidence in order to make them change their ways. I can give them technical advice, but someone like yourself can help with the human relations part."

The jeep had reached the outskirts of the city and began to climb the mountain road. Tom shifted into low gear as they scaled the hairpin curves. A breathtaking view unfolded below. The city lay in a long plateau surrounded on all sides by mountains. Tom pointed out the volcanoes in the area. Over there, a huge bare-ribbed perfect cone, the now extinct Agua volcano. Behind it, the dark majestic Fuego, spewing smoke from its crater. To the south of it, the less spectacular yet more active Pacaya, which erupted last month with fiery rivers of lava, causing nearby villagers to flee their homes.

Santa Teresa de Avila was a small village a short distance from the highway. It started on a small plain and continued on the side of the mountain. Small stucco houses, some with red tiled roofs and others with thatched roofs. A small village square with an old whitewashed stone church in a state of disrepair, a one story municipality, a police station and a few stores. As they parked the jeep and got out they were followed by a swarm of children.

"I once made the mistake of giving them candy," Tom explained, "They've been following me ever since."

He took Kaye to his new home. It was a small wood and plaster shack with two bedrooms, a small kitchen and an outhouse, situated on the edge of the village. Tom's partner's belongings were still there, packed in a trunk.

"Well, no great luxury," Tom smiled apologetically, "but it does make you feel like you belong."

He helped Tom load the trunk on the jeep. The trunk had to be taken down to the airport to be sent back to the States.

"It won't take long," said Tom, "In the meantime you go ahead and get settled."

His room consisted of a cot, a simple cupboard, a small table and a chair. The cot was made up with clean bedsheets and an army blanket. He opened his travelling bag and took out his clothes and put them in the cupboard. He then took out the few books he had brought along and stacked them on top of the cupboard.

After he finished putting away his things he went outside and took a walk around the village. In two hours by plane he could be back in the States. And here he was, in a country which seemed to date back to the dawn of time. It looked like an earthly paradise, and yet most of its people lacked food and had no health services or schools. Farther north in the mountains, he was told, there were villages which had no electricity or running water. They hardly used currency, and had to barter in order to obtain the things they did not make with their own hands. They still kept many of their pagan customs and beliefs alongside their official Catholic faith.

Time here seemed to have stopped, but it was not because these people wished it to stop. Those who ruled this land had imposed this lethargy on the people they ruled in order to exploit them and keep all the wealth to themselves. This is what had to be changed. The question was how.

He walked up to the village square and stopped at the church door. The church was empty. He wanted to introduce himself to the village priest, but could not find anyone in or around the church. He went inside and looked at the altar. Above the altar he saw a large wooden crucifix looking down at him. He recalled his dream at the hospital back in Quincy. A suffering Jew, he thought. The whole world worshipping a suffering Jew. But why? Was it because we Jews are expert sufferers? For a moment he felt Eve's presence next to him. This suffering Jew was Eve's beloved. He had once come between them. Was he going to come between them again?

As he turned to leave the church he saw an old woman standing outside looking at him. She wore a plain long dress and an old sweater. Her tanned face and hands were full of wrinkles, recording a life of hard work, but her dark shiny eyes were full of vitality.

"*Buenos días*," he greeted the old woman.

"*Muy buenos días*."

"I'm looking for the *padre*."

"You are the new Peace Corps volunteer."

"Yes, I am. How did you know?"

"I saw you arrive with Tom."

"And you are?"

"Everyone calls me Doña Maria. I help Sister Caridad take care of the church."

"And where is the priest?"

"We don't have our own priest at the moment. Father Romero comes here from the city twice a month."

"What happened to your own priest?"

"He left a month ago."

"Did he retire?"

"No, not exactly. He tried to make some changes which the people here objected to. He started celebrating mass in Spanish instead of Latin and the people ran him out of the village."

"How do you mean?"

"They actually began to attack him physically and he had to run for his life."

"I guess people here don't like to try new things."

Doña Maria studied the new gringo with a sly smile.

"You have to be very patient with our people. You *norte-americanos* always seem to be in a hurry to get things done. It is different here. I hope you get used to it."

He could not wait till Sunday. He lay awake at night thinking of Eve. He had arrived in Guatemala only three days ago, but there was so much he wanted to talk to her about. He had told Aguilar he was not concerned about the culture shock, and yet he had to admit it to himself he was not at all sure what to make of this place. The night before Tom had taken him to a meeting in which the Texan went over the savings project. The villagers hardly said a word when Tom asked them for their comments. They were quiet, inscrutable people. Kaye noticed that they seemed to like Tom. They were friendly to him and after the meeting they offered him food and drink. But when he raised the question of their putting aside a few *centavos* each day so they could save enough money in a year or two to buy some farm machinery, their response was dead silence. Later on the two of them tried to figure out why it was so hard to sell those people on a perfectly sensible idea. Clearly, the concept of saving money was foreign to them. They barely made enough money to put food on their table. Whatever few pennies they could spare were used by the women for buying candles for the Virgin and by the men for gambling and buying cheap liquor.

"Obviously, we cannot change in one day what they have been doing for generations," said Tom. "It is going to be a slow process."

On Sunday morning the villagers were getting ready to celebrate some religious holiday. Kaye tried to find out what the occasion was, but was not able to get a clear answer. From what he gathered it had to do with the patron saint of the region, but that was only one part of it. It also commemorated the Spanish Conquest of the place, and, in addition, it was a feast in honor of a great Mayan King who ruled the region long before the Conquest, and whose spirit was believed to reside in the mountain overlooking the village (someone told Kaye that whenever the earth trembled or the nearby Pacaya volcano erupted, it was the spirit of the Mayan king angered by the misdeeds of his descendants).

Around noon the festivities started. A young boy climbed the belfry and started ringing the church bell. People gathered around the village square, and suddenly out of nowhere a group of soot-faced youngsters in colorful rags led by an adult dressed like a Mayan priest came dancing into the center of the square, doing a slow, stylized dance, stepping sideways and going around in a

circle, when two horsemen came trotting from the opposite end of
the square and entered the circle of dancers, dressed in Conquis-
tador costumes, and flailed cardboard swords over the heads of the
dancers. Small children watched with wide open eyes. Women
looked on impassively, almost without expression. Men stood off to
a side and passed around a bottle of *aguardiente*.

Kaye walked away from the square in the direction of the highway. There was hardly a cloud in the sky. The sun stood high overhead as he walked away from the austere drabness of the village
and came upon the road, overlooking the lush green mountains
rising against the clear blue sky.

A bus came chugging up the road. It shifted into lower gear as it
came up the steep grade, and seemed to be running out of gears as
it made a final effort to reach the top of the hill where Kaye stood.
It screeched and gasped as it coasted and came to a stop off the
road. Some passengers were getting off. Two squat women carrying
baskets, trailed by a few children. Behind them he saw a tall
woman in a long dress, dark sunglasses, a white kerchief over her
hair and a small embroidered canvas bag slung over her shoulder.
The women and the children walked across the field toward the village, and the tall women remained standing by the side of the road
as the bus departed. His heart skipped. She saw him and rushed
toward him, taking off her sunglasses, and the next thing he knew
he was holding her in his arms, and as she drew back they stood
there looking at each other without saying a word, as if unable to
sort out their emotions, each waiting for the other to say what had
to be said, do the right thing, as if their meeting here in this
secluded corner of the world had been preordained and the next
step had been long foretold, and it was up to them now to find out
what it was.

He walked Eve to the village where the festivities were still in
progress. There were drunks milling around at nearly every corner
of the village. Two women were lifting a man—the husband of the
older one—who was wallowing in the mud trying to catch a dog by
its tail, and started carrying him back home.

He showed Eve to his own living quarters on the edge of the village.

She walked in, took off her kerchief and looked around.

"This is the kind of place I pictured myself living in before I came
to Guatemala," Eve said, looking around. She sat down on the edge of
the bed and clutched her hands in her lap, smiling at him. He took a
chair and turned it with the back facing her, and sat down astride the
chair, folding his arms over the backrest. She shook her head.

"Guess what," she said, "that project I told you about, of opening schools in Indian villages? We were told yesterday it was cancelled. I was furious when I heard it. You didn't know I had a temper, did you? You never saw me blow my stack? Well, this time I did. I told the mother superior at the Maryknoll Center they had brought me to Guatemala on false pretexts. I didn't come here to work at a rich girls' school. Those two Maryknoll sisters who came with me from the States to work on the same project sided with me. They were just as angry as I was."

"So what do you plan to do?"

"I'm not sure yet. I'll have to see."

They remained silent for a long time.

"There is so much to be done," Kaye finally said. "I'm finding out this country's problems are much more complex that I had ever imagined. I thought the Chicanos back home in Southern California had problems, but compared to most Guatemalans they were well-off. One hardly knows where to begin. Well, perhaps that's where the real challenge lies. If we can do something here then we can really turn the world around."

She stood up and turned to the window and crossed her arms as she looked outside. He got up and stood next to her and put his arm around her shoulders. She leaned her head against him.

"I don't know, Josh. I really thought the Church had the answer. But I'm not so sure any more."

✧ 21 ✧

He saw Eve several times during the month of June. She came to visit on weekends and he went to see her in the evenings once or twice during the week. They talked at length about his work at Santa Teresa and about her frustrations. She was becoming more and more disenchanted with the Church. Here in Guatemala, she said, the Church was still living in the Middle Ages, supporting a feudal system of overlords and vassals, practicing a variety of Catholicism that went out of style in Spain 300 years ago. Instead of educating the people and showing them how to better themselves, the Church was helping the government keep them ignorant, superstitious, backward, and poor. Here and there one of the local priests defied the hierarchy and tried to preach new ideas, but would invariably be "set straight" by his superiors.

On one of her visits to Santa Teresa, Eve asked Kaye to introduce her to that wise old lady he kept talking about, the one who helped take care of the local church. They found Doña Maria sitting in front of her house behind the church cracking pumpkin seeds and reading a *novela.*

"Doña Maria, I would like you to meet Sister Eve."

The old lady looked up, shading her lively black eyes with her hand, and studied Eve for a moment.

"*No puede ser,*" she said. "*It is not possible.*"

"Why not?" Kaye asked.

"A nun? What about her habit?"

"Some nuns in the United States no longer wear a habit. They feel that the habit separates them from their people."

Doña Maria thought for a moment.

"*Muy bien,*" she said, "I can see your point. But may I offer a word of advice? Don't tell the people here your friend is a nun. Not unless she wears a habit. They are not ready for this."

She asked Eve what she did. Eve told her she taught at the Maryknoll Center.

"*Ah, si?*" said the old lady, "I know the place. A school for rich girls. Why don't you come here and work with us? We need your help more than they do."

Eve said it was not a bad idea.

"Any time you're ready to come here you let me know," said Doña Maria. "I've plenty of room in my house and there's a lot to do at the church and at the school."

At the end of the week he got a call from Eve. She had something urgent to discuss with him. She was coming to see him that evening.

She arrived after dark on the last bus from the city. She seemed greatly agitated. He took her into the house and asked her to sit down while he made coffee. After he poured the coffee she clutched his hands and looked at him with deep pain in her eyes.

"What's the matter?" he asked.

"Oh, Josh!" she pulled him against herself. He pressed her head against his chest and stroked her hair.

"What's the matter? What happened?"

"Oh, Josh, please hold me. Please."

"Are you okay?"

"Yes, I'm okay. But I'm scared."

"What are you scared of?"

"Of what I'm about to do."

He let go of her and sat on the bed next to her.

"Well?"

"I'm going to quit the Maryknoll Center."

"Why?"

"You know the two Maryknoll sisters I've told you about, the ones who came with me from the States? I told you they were very upset when they found out they were going to stay at the center because the school project was cancelled. Well, last week they took their belongings—their clothes, kitchen utensils, bedsheets, blankets, even electric appliances—and distributed them among the workers of the center. They decided they couldn't live in the lap of luxury while those people didn't have the bare essentials. I guess it was an act of protest. They were trying to make a statement. Well, the bishop and the mother superior did not take to it too kindly. Yesterday they told them to pack up—they are being sent back to the States."

"You seem quite upset."

"Yes, I am. I tried to talk the mother superior out of sending them back, but she was adamant. I told her they were wrong in doing what they did, since those things did not really belong to them but were the property of the center. But I wanted her to see it from their standpoint as well. They came here to work for the poor and they were told they couldn't. She reminded me of the vow of obedience. God, I can't stand that woman! How can she be so callous? How can the bishop be so heartless?"

He took her hand and stroked it.

"So you're going to quit?"

"I'm not a member of their order, so I have a choice: either go back to my own order in the States or look for something else to do here. The question is what."

"What about Doña Maria's offer to help her at the church?"

She stopped to think and remained silent for a long moment. He could see a new look in her eyes, as if she were beginning to see things in a new light, come to terms with something she had been struggling with for a long time. She took his hand in hers and looked into his eyes.

"You want me to?"

Instead of answering he put his lips against hers. She responded, letting down her guards. She slipped her arms around his neck and moaned as he kissed her neck, her hair, her eyes. She clung to him and held his face in her hands and kissed him, then drew back.

"I love you, Josh. I'm so glad you came here. Without you right now I would be lost. You're my rescuer, my redeemer. I shouldn't have run away from you that time after Christmas Eve. You were right, except it took me a little longer to find out. Organized religion, yours, mine, it makes no difference which, is out of touch with the world. We have to make our own way if we are going to do anything to change things. We'll start right here, in this village, you and I. Man-made labels no longer matter to me. Not when they are used to oppress millions of people on this earth."

She was visibly happy. She stayed that night with Doña Maria, and when he walked her to the bus in the morning she kept talking about what the two of them could do for the villagers. She had discussed her plans with Doña Maria, and was going to move in with her in a day or two.

Later that afternoon Tom returned to the village from a meeting with Jorge Aguilar and informed Kaye the director of the Bank of America in Guatemala City had decided to loan the cooperative of the village of Santa Teresa 10,000 dollars to buy farm equipment. It was a major step toward making the cooperative a reality. It would give the villagers an incentive to save, and would help them make the transition from ancient to modern farming.

Tom added he was going to Miami for a week and would look around for some used equipment in good condition that would suit the needs and the budget of the villagers.

Kaye was swept by Tom's enthusiasm. In his mind he began to see visions of the future. Eve and he will spend a year at Santa Teresa and help turn the place into a model village. They will then go back to the States and recruit young Jewish and Catholic and other volunteers to work on similar projects in underdeveloped countries. Rather than a Jewish Peace Corps, it will be an alliance of Jews, Christians and others who will be committed to the proposition of doing away with the ills of humanity. They will not be bound by any state or religious authority or by the plutocracy. They will be free to act not out of any self-interest but out of a genuine care for all people. Once the idea caught on, no power in the world—political, ideological, economical—will be able to stop it. The words of the Hebrew prophet will be fulfilled. "The wolf shall live with the lamb, and the panther shall lie down with the kid. . . and all shall dwell under their vine and under their figtree and none shall make them afraid."

Eve arrived that Saturday and took up quarters with Doña

Maria. The two of them took to each other almost instantly. Doña Maria shared Eve's views on the hierarchy of the Church. She was a devout Catholic, but her long experience with the Church convinced her that the majority of the clergy were selfish and self-seeking and did not care about the poor. She agreed with Eve that some change had to take place if the Church were to become a force for good in Guatemala. She was fully prepared to help Eve and anyone else who was going to work for that change.

A few days after Eve's arrival they decided to go out for a hike in the mountains. It was the rainy season, and each afternoon it rained for about two hours. The mornings, however, were clear and sunny. They packed a picnic lunch and set out up the goat path leading directly from the village to the nearest mountain. Soon the village was left down below. The white church, the red tiled roofs and the thatched roofs looked like a toy model in the sea of verdure. The sun was high in the sky, warming the juices of the earth and the sap of the trees and drying the morning dew left on the blades of grass. Good mother earth, Kaye thought, so blessed and so fertile in this part of the world, and yet all this poverty, malnutrition, deprivation. What would it take to change all of this? Can these people lift themselves by their bootstraps, or are they so submerged in their oppression that nothing is going to change their lot?

They had reached a small plateau and stopped to rest. Eve's pale skin was flushed. She massaged her eyes with long distended fingers and looked at the view.

"Breathtaking, isn't it?"

"Yes, it is."

"What a beautiful village."

"Are you glad you came?"

She turned around and bussed him on his cheek.

"I've never been happier."

"I think it's going to work."

"Yes, it will. I'm sure it will."

"Some day they'll write about this little village."

"And about us."

"Yes."

"Well, we better get going."

They continued across the high plain and reached the foot of a majestic slope covered with a dense forest of pine and oak. A narrow trail led into the forest. It was a steep climb, and they had to stop from time to time to catch their breath. Finally they came into a clearing and decided to stop for lunch.

"Remember the first time we went out on a picnic?" Kaye said as they started to eat. "Out on the edge of the football field at St. John's College, in that little grove?"

"Oh, yes I do. That's how it all started."

"That was the first time I knew I was falling in love with you."

"I knew it the moment you showed up in my English Lit class."

"What about you?"

"Well, I guess it was the time I came to see you at the hospital. I knew I liked you a lot when I went to see you, but I didn't realize I was actually in love with you until I got there and you kissed me in the visitors' lounge."

"Are you sorry?"

"No, not at all."

"What about your beliefs, your vows?"

"I feel there's something that binds the two of us together which doesn't violate my beliefs. As for my vows, that's something I'll have to work out."

Clouds began to gather over the treetops, and as they got up to leave it started to drizzle. They walked back toward the village through the forest as the rain intensified. Soon the mountain trail turned into a stream, and they had to get off the trail and walk across a forest bed of pine needles and rocks.

"I think we're lost," Kaye said after a while.

"I'm soaking wet," Eve said and stopped.

He turned back to look. Her hair was pasted to her forehead and neck, and the rain came trickling from her hair down her shoulders. Her skirt was clinging to her knees and her open sandals were filled with rain water.

"We better look for shelter," said Kaye.

He took her hand and led her through the forest to a huge volcanic boulder. They found an open space underneath the rock and crawled inside for shelter.

A thunder shook the forest. They saw the thunderbolt strike down a large limb of an oak tree only a few feet away. The limb came crushing down against the rock. Eve let out a scream and clung to him, trembling. Her wet blouse and skirt were glued to her body. He could feel her heart beat against him as he held her close and rocked her in his arms. He took off his jacket and his shirt and started to wipe her face and dry her hair with his shirt. She took off her sandals and poured out the rain water and began to unbutton her blouse, looking at him questioningly. She peeled off her blouse and proceeded to unzip her skirt. She looked at him mistily and her lips parted. She undid her bra and dropped it next to her. Her skin gleamed in the dark like a pearl. Her small breasts heaved as he helped her divest herself of the rest of her clothing and took off his own. The two of them, with nothing between them, rose to their knees underneath the rock and touched each other, caressing each other, exploring each other's secrets parts. There was more thundering and the rain intensified, cascading over the rock outside their refuge. She pulled him down against herself and lay down flat on her back and took him in her hand and guided him into her, moaning and crying as he thrust against her virginity, begging him to keep coming as she dug her nails into his flesh and writhed on the ground in quick, intermittent spasms.

They lay next to each other, spent, breathing and panting against each other, nestling in each other's arms. She looked at him and then she looked down at their nakedness and smiled.

"I love you, Josh."

"I love you, Eve."

It had stopped raining. They got dressed. He gave her his shirt to wear and wore his jacket over his undershirt. As they came within sight of the village the sun had begun to set. Eve leaned against a tree and he put his arms around her and they remained standing in each other's arms long after the sun went down.

The ensuing weeks were the happiest time of their life. They had finally found each other, and they had found a purpose. They gave their days to the village of Santa Teresa, to improve agriculture, education, health services, and they had the nights to themselves. Things were looking up for the village. Eve enlisted Doña Maria's help with the Peace Corps savings plan. Doña Maria began to visit the matrons of the village and explained to them the importance of saving as much as they could in order to buy equipment to improve the village farming methods. She told them they should buy less candles for the church and make less offerings, assuring them Christ would understand. They could make it up to him later on when things improved. The women began to respond, and were able to get through to their husbands, and by the end of July the incredible sun of 5000 dollars was raised by the villagers. Plans were being discussed to raise another 5000 dollars by the end of August to bring the total—including the 10,000 dollar loan—to 20,000 dollars. That was the amount needed for buying the used tractor, plow, sowing machine and spare parts Tom had negotiated for in Miami.

At night they would meet secretly outside the village and go out into the woods on the side of the mountain. Their desire for each other seemed to increase each time they made love. Eve's passion grew more full, more subtle each time. It seemed that the years of abstinence had stored up in her a fire she did not know was there, and now that it finally was let out she could barely contain it. The moment they were back together she would put her arms around him and cling to him, and when they made love she would ask him to teach her new ways, show her how to do the things that pleased him.

One night after they made love they sat curled up next to each other, wrapped in a blanket, and discussed the future.

"I wonder where we'll be next year at this time," Eve said, snapping a twig.

"Back in the States," said Kaye, "recruiting volunteers for the cause."

"You and me?"

"Yes, of course."

"What about our relationship and my vows and our differing beliefs?"

"Are you going to go back to your order?"

"I don't know. I don't want to lose you."

"Do you still consider yourself married to Him?"

"I guess at this point it's questionable. But I do believe in Him. And I believe the Church, with all its faults, represents him here on earth."

"Then where does that leave me?"

"I love you. You are the only man I ever had. I believe in you. I believe you and I are on the right track. But of course I can't go on like this. Obviously I'll have to choose between you and my vows. That is, if you still want me after we leave Santa Teresa."

He pressed her against himself and nuzzled her neck.

"I'll always want you, my love. Whether I'll always be able to have you is another question. I can't see that far into the future. I can see us a year from now, working together. But as for our relationship, that's too difficult to predict."

They seemed to be content to leave it at that. Theirs was not an ordinary relationship. They had both committed their lives to something greater than their own personal fulfillment. Their coming together enabled them to work for what they both believed in. As for the love they could give each other, they had to be grateful for what they had. They could not ask too many questions about the future.

In the middle of August Tom decided to send Pablo Sanchez, the secretary of the cooperative, to Miami, to buy the farm equipment. The night before Sanchez's departure Doña Maria gave a small farewell party at her house, to which all those who had helped organize and work for the cooperative were invited.

It was a humble party. Some of the women had made *tamales, guacamole* and *tortillas*. Tom had bought soft drinks and beer at the American Embassy commissary, and Doña Maria made her acclaimed dessert of fried bananas and brown sugar. The men were shown into the living room where they were seated in straight-back chairs around a long bare-top table. The women, including Eve, assisted Doña Maria is serving the food. Pablo Sanchez, a young man in his thirties with ruddy cheeks, a trimmed black mustache, and small eager eyes, came in dressed in his Sunday finery. He took off his straw hat and bowed before the hostess, and was asked to sit at the head of the table next to Tom. After he sat down he produced a bottle of *aguardiente* from the inside of his coat and took out small plastic cups from a hip pocket and placed the cups next to each person around the table. He then passed around the bottle and each person filled his cup. Tom got up and offered a toast.

"My dear friends, as I'm sure you know, I'm not much of a drinker, but tonight I feel we really have something to drink to. This is a historical moment for the village of Santa Teresa. We're about to bring this village into the twentieth century. Our friend Pablo is leaving tomorrow for Miami where he will sign the agreement and pay for the equipment which we should receive before the end of the year. I know it's only the beginning, and it will take a few years before we begin to get the kind of harvests we know we can and should be getting. But there's an old Chinese saying, 'Even a thousand mile journey begins with one step.' Here is to the success of our undertaking. Long live the cooperative! *Viva la cooperativa!*"

"*Viva!*" they all raised their cups.

Kaye, Tom and Eve stayed at Doña Maria's long after the rest of the guests had left. They were too excited to go to sleep. Something which only two months ago seemed impossible was actually happening. And they all had a share in it. Many skeptics in the American foreign service and in the Guatemalan bureaucracy had told them not to raise their hopes too high, since they were swimming against the current, trying to get the local farmers to do something they had never done before. And now they proved it could be done. All the weeks and months of hard work and long discussions, of living under primitive conditions in this remote village in a foreign country so resistant to change, were now beginning to bear fruit. A more incongruous group than the four of them had never worked together for a common cause. A nun, an old Guatemalan woman, a Southern Baptist, and a rabbi. Right now Kaye felt closer to this group than to anyone else in the world.

Pablo Sanchez left for Miami on AVIATECA the next morning.

Tom had bought him a round-trip ticket. The secretary of the cooperative was going to spend three days in Miami, sign the agreement, pay half of the balance, and return on Thursday at 11:00 p.m.

On Thursday evening Tom and Kaye drove to the airport to pick up Sanchez. His flight was being delayed and the plane did not land until half past midnight. They stood at the door of the customs hall and watched the passengers file in. Sanchez was nowhere to be seen. After all the passengers cleared through customs and began to leave the airport, Tom went into the AVIATECA office and asked whether a person by the name of Pablo Sanchez was on the passenger list. The airline official went over the list twice but did not find the name.

Tom looked at Kaye with a tense unspoken question. Kaye knew what Tom was thinking. Sanchez had taken with him 10,000 dollars. Did he make off with the money?

The next day they called Jorge Aguilar, the Peace Corps coordinator, and told him what had happened. Aguilar immediately contacted the farm equipment company in Miami to find out whether Sanchez had been there and paid the money. The answer was negative. The man never showed up. Aguilar proceeded to call the authorities in Miami and asked for the whereabouts of the disappeared Guatemalan. He was told that Sanchez had given the farm equipment company address to the airport authorities as the place where he was going to stay while in the States. The officials added that looking for a Hispanic visitor in Miami was like looking for a needle in a hay stack. They would do the best they could.

Tom was beside himself.

"We're wiped out. He took 10,000 dollars. We have about 9000 left in the account, all of which we'll have to give back to the bank to repay the loan."

"I'll see what I can do," said Aguilar. "We'll try to postpone the repayment of the loan."

For two weeks they waited every day for news from Miami but the answer was always the same—there was no sign of Sanchez. He had disappeared without leaving a trace.

"It was a mistake sending one of the villagers to the States with so much money," Eve told Kaye. "Of course we have to trust these people and they have to learn responsibility, but it's going to take a long time for them to learn it."

"Time," Kaye shook his head in sorrow. "How much time do we have?Look at Tom, he had put his heart and soul into this project. He says he is not going to quit, but I can tell he is dispirited. I won't be surprised if he decides to go back to the States tomorrow."

"What about you? Are you ready to quit?"

"No, I'm not. But I feel you and I ought to get away for a few days. Take a week off, do a little travelling and see more of Guatemala, and get a better perspective on this entire situation."

They decided to take off the first week of September and travel west to see the highlands, Lake Atitlan, the Indian town of Chichicastenango, the Mayan ruins of Utatlan and Zaculeu, and then travel south to Tapachula across the Mexican border and come back by way of the Guatemalan Pacific coast.

✧ 22 ✧

They left early on Monday morning for Guatemala City, where they boarded a bus to Atitlan. Eve was in high spirits. She obviously loved to travel, explore new places, see new things. She entwined her arm in his and leaned her head on his shoulder.

"I've been dreaming about this, Josh. You and I going on a trip together. It was a marvelous idea."

"It certainly was."

"What are you thinking about?"

"Santa Teresa. The cooperative. I wonder what's going to become of it."

"From a purely practical standpoint, perhaps we ought to give up and start doing something else. But you and I are not supposed to look at things strictly in terms of dollars and cents. We have to have faith in those people, in their potential to better themselves. Besides, we now have each other. So what if we have to stay in Santa Teresa another year? I don't mind. Do you?"

"I guess you are right, *mi amor*. As usual."

At noon they arrived at Lake Atitlan. The placid blue water of the lake, surrounded by green and smoky blue craters and ringed with red, orange and white tropical flowers captivated them the moment they got off the bus. They checked into a small whitewashed resort on the lake, and were given the key to a second floor room with a balcony overlooking the lake. Alone in the room, he took Eve in his arms and gazed into her eyes.

"Remember the time I came to see you at the convent on Christmas Eve, and I told you I wanted to take you to never never land?"

She laughed. "Yes, and I asked you where that never never land was, and you told me wherever the two of us were together."

"Yes. Now I really think this never never land I had in mind is right here."

She pressed against him and brushed his face with her lips.

"Oh, Josh, I just want to stay here with you forever."

And they made love in the haze of the afternoon sun.

In the morning they went down to the dining room for breakfast. At a nearby table they saw a young priest reading the *New York Times*. The priest nodded to them as they walked by.

"What's new in the world?" Kaye asked.

"The usual," The priest smiled. He had short cropped dark hair and sad dark eyes.

"Mind if we join you?"

"Please do."

"I'm Joshua Kaye. My friend, Eve Gruner."

"John Reed."

They sat down and ordered coffee.

"You two are visiting Guatemala?"

"No. I'm working for the Peace Corps at the village of Santa Teresa near Guatemala City. Eve has worked at the Maryknoll Center and has recently joined me."

"I heard two sisters from the Maryknoll Center were just sent back to the States because they shared their belongings with the local people," the young priest said.

"Yes," said Eve, "it's true, unfortunately."

"A priest friend of mine from Guatemala City told me about it last week. I think the Center overreacted."

"The Church in Guatemala is burying its head in the sand," said Eve.

"Yes, I'm afraid you are right."

"Where do you work?" Kaye inquired.

"I'm with Catholic Relief in Tapachula, on the Mexican side of the border."

"This is where we're going."

"You are? I just came from there. It's not a very safe place to go right now."

"What is happening there?"

The priest looked around to make sure no one was listening. He pulled his chair closer to the table and leaned forward, examining his two companions as if trying to decide whether he could share a confidence with them.

The Guatemalan government, he explained, has launched an all-out campaign against a guerrilla band which has been operating between Quezaltenango and the Mexican border, headed by one Yak Lopez. It appears that the Guatemalan troops have orders to shoot anyone on the slightest suspicion of cooperating with the terrorists. The government seems to be mortally afraid of this group which is alleged to be trained and supplied by Cuba. When Fidel Castro first came to power in Cuba he took all the top brass of Batista's army and executed them without any questions asked. The Guatemalan military are afraid of meeting the same fate if a similar takeover were to occur here, and so they have practically given their troops a free hand in going after the guerrillas.

The Lopez group, however, has proved to be extremely evasive, and so far none of its members has been captured. Recently the army was tipped off about some guerrillas hiding in two Indian villages north of Quezaltenango. The army went into those villages and searched every corner but could not find any guerrillas, not even after some of the elders of the village were severely tortured. So the army lined up all the men of those two villages and shot them, pronouncing them members of the terrorist group. The word got around to the neighboring villages that the government had started a campaign of extermination against the Indian population of the region, and hundreds of people have been leaving their homes and crossing the border to Mexico. Catholic Relief has set up a refugee camp for them outside of Tapachula. Last week the Guatemalan army sealed off the border. It created a free-fire zone along the border in order to prevent the refugees from reaching Mexico, and has been shooting anyone who was seen in that area."

Kaye shook his head and looked at Eve who pursed her lips.

"Well. Here we are, Peace Corps do-gooders, trying to help those people while their own government is massacring them."

"With the help of our government, I might add," said the young priest.

"It's awful," said Eve.

"What can we do about it?" Kaye asked.

"This is why I'm here," said Father Reed. "I want to get to the bottom of what is happening here. I'm going to write a report about it and send it to some human rights organizations in the States. I want them to put pressure on our government to stop all military aid to Guatemala until the Guatemalan government stops its genocidal activities."

Kaye recalled the day he arrived in Guatemala City and saw the army patrols in the streets. It was obviously a foreshadowing of things to come. There was much more going on in this inscrutable country than he had been let in on. Were people like him and Eve and Tom mere pawns in the hands of the American and the Guatemalan governments? Were they being used as a cover-up for the covert activities of those governments? Was it Suburban Temple all over again, religion being used as a tool by those in power?

"Where do we go from here?" Kaye asked.

"I'm going tomorrow to Quezaltenango, where I will stay for a day or two, and from there I'll go back to Tapachula. You two are welcome to join me. I've plenty of room in my old van."

Kaye looked at Eve.

"What do you say?"

"Sure, I'm game."

The next morning they drove up the highlands to Quezaltenango. Father Reed had been given the name of a local merchant in that town who travelled regularly to the Indian villages in the region and was active in the Catholic Relief organization. Don Pascual, said Reed, was a good source of information on what was going on in that part of the country. Reed was going to talk to him and try to get a first hand report of how true the rumors about the extermination of the Indian population in that mountain region were.

On the outskirts of Quezaltenango the van was stopped at a road block by a military patrol. As happened the night he arrived in Guatemala City, the van was surrounded by soldiers wearing helmets and bullet-proof vests, carrying M-16 rifles and submachine guns. They were ordered out of the van and frisked by the soldiers, while the inside of the vehicle was being thoroughly searched. The commander of the group checked their papers and asked them for the purpose of their visit to Quezaltenango. They told him they had a week off from work and wanted to tour the Mayan ruins in the area. The commander cautioned them against travelling west toward the Mexican border. "Because of the bandidos," he explained, and told them they could not travel after dark because of the martial law.

Back in the van, Kaye asked Eve if she preferred to go back to Santa Teresa. No, she wanted to go on. It was important for them to find out what was actually happening there.

They drove through the narrow streets of Quezaltenango. Don Pascual had a small hardware store in the center of town. There were silhouette drawings of work tools on his show window, no doubt for illiterate customers.

It was dark inside the store after the bright sunlight in the street. When his eyes got used to the dark, Kaye saw stacks of tools which were common in Santa Teresa—curved machetes, long saws, hoes and spades, and burlap sacks full of nails of all sizes. The priest asked for the owner. After a short wait they were ushered into a back room in the bowels of the store where, surrounded by boxes of merchandise and ledger books, a corpulent man with a walrus mustache, prominent jowls, eager eyes and thinning black hair got up to greet them. Father Reed explained the purpose of their visit. Don Pascual listened intently and chewed on his mustache, remaining silent for a long time.

"Are you sure you want to pursue this, father?" he finally said.

"I'm aware of the risk," said the priest.

"What about your friends?"

"I've explained it to them."

"Very well," said Don Pascual. I'm going tomorrow to Huehuetenango. We can all go together. On the way we can take a side trip to that village you mentioned, La Merced, where they say the army has shot all the men. We'll see what we can find out."

"Why would the government do a thing like that?" Eve asked Don Pascual, "slaughter all those innocent people?"

"Because, *Señorita*," the merchant replied, "The government does not consider the Indians human beings. Their lives are worth less than sheep or cattle, or even chicken. To the government they are not people. They are *micos*, you know, little monkeys." He looked up and crossed himself. "Forgive them, Oh Father, for they know no what they are doing."

They left Quezaltenango early in the morning. Don Pascual's old Chevrolet was packed to the hilt. Father Reed rode in the front with Don Pascual, while Kaye and Eve squeezed in the back with all the merchandise. She took his hand and pressed it, letting him know without words she felt apprehensive. Perhaps they shouldn't have gotten themselves involved in this whole affair. There was an ominous presentiment in the air. They were about to come face to face with the kind of human evil they had heard and read about, but had never seen with their own eyes. How does one go into a village where innocent people have just been massacred? What does one say or do? It was a grim mission, but the young priest was doing the right thing, and one had to admire his courage.

They rode across a wide plateau in the mountains and began to climb the foothills of the mountain range going north. After a while

Don Pascual slowed down and turned off on a dirt road. The terrain
became increasingly rough, and the car bounced and lunged on the
rocks and on the deep furrows made by rain and erosion. There was
not a soul in sight. They reached the outskirts of the village. The
unpaved road leading into the village was blocked with large
boulders, preventing vehicles from going in. Don Pascual stopped in
front of the barrier and they all got out. There was a fetid smell in
the air. They walked slowly into the center of the village and looked
around. No sign of life. An eerie silence everywhere. As they approached the first house they saw soot stains on the wall. The inside of the house was completely burned out. They walked across
the village square to the church. All of them, except Kaye, crossed
themselves before they went in. The inside of the church was in
total disarray. The aisle was full of debris. The crucifix above the
altar was missing. The pews were broken and piled along the side
wall. Don Pascual called them to come over and look at the opposite
wall. They came closer and looked. There were blood stains on the
wall.

"What happened here?" Father Reed asked somberly.

"Worse than we thought," said Don Pascual.

"How do we find out?"

"I know one of the elders in Tayasal, which is the next village,
about two miles up the road. We can go there and see what we can
find out."

They drove back to the highway and took the next turn to
Tayasal. As soon as they made the turn they saw some villagers,
men and women, walking on the side of the road, carrying firewood.
They slowed down and greeted them. The group stopped and looked
at them with fear in their eyes, then resumed its march. Don Pascual accelerated and took a shortcut to a small finca on the other
side of the village. He drove through the gate and stopped in front
of a small house with a red tile roof.

The door opened and a lean, dignified looking man in a loose
shirt and sandals came out. When he recognized Don Pascual he
dashed forward and gave him a welcome hug. He invited the entire
party to his house and showed special respect to Father Reed. He
asked his guests to make themselves comfortable in the living room
and ordered his wife to make coffee.

Don Pascual started the conversation by asking his host about
his children, his crops, and the affairs of the village. After the usual
round of inquiry Don Pascual cleared his throat and told the host
he had just stopped at La Merced and did not find a living soul. The
host's face turned ashen. He covered his face with him hands and

his chest heaved. Don Pascual, who sat next to him, put his arms around him and comforted him. The elder wiped his eyes with the back of his hands and shook his head.

They remained silent for a long time, mourning the dead.

Yes, it was true. The army did go into La Merced and after they failed to find any guerrillas they took out all the men, age fifteen to sixty-five, and shot them.

The elder told Don Pascual not to tell anyone he was telling him those things. If the army found out they would put a bullet through his head.

The army, he explained, had organized a civil patrol here in Tayasal, to help look for guerrillas. In order to prove the loyalty of the civil patrol, the army has been taking patrol members along on its missions, in the course of which patrol members, including the elder's own son, were ordered to execute innocent civilians. This is what happened in La Merced as well. Members of the civil patrol from Tayasal were ordered to join the army unit that went to La Merced to look for guerrillas. When none were found, the men of the village who were around that night were taken out into a field outside the village. Patrol members were given guns while the soldiers stood behind them, pointing their own weapons at them. They were ordered by the commander to show their masculinity by shooting all the men of the village, among whom were some cousins of patrol members.

The elder stopped to compose himself.

This was only the half of it. The next day the army showed up again in Tayasal and rounded up the members of the civil patrol and took them by truck back to La Merced. The patrol members found out that the women and children of the village (except for a few children who managed to escape the night before and were hiding in the mountains) had been locked up the night before inside the church, some 200 women and an equal number of children. The soldiers proceeded to separate the women from the children. Next they divided the women into two groups—the old and the young. The older women were trucked to the place of execution, where the previous night's scene was repeated. Again the civil patrol was forced at gun point to kill the hapless victims, except this time they were told there were not enough bullets for the women, and they were given machetes instead and were told to do what had to be done. Meanwhile, the children were taken into the school house where they were murdered with machetes, bayonets, or by being picked up by their feet and having their heads smashed against the wall. Some soldiers remained in the church with the younger

women and spent the night raping them. In the morning the civil
patrol was ordered to kill the surviving young women, except for
two who were particularly attractive. One was taken away at the
commander's instructions, while the other was shot by the commander after she asked him to take pity on her and use one of his
bullets to end her life.

After the massacre was over, the army loaded everything they
could get their hands on on the trucks, set fire to the houses and to
the cultivated fields, erected a road block on the approach to the
village, and left.

"Has anyone spoken to the authorities?" Father Reed asked.

"The authorities?" the elder echoed, as if repeating an evil incan-
tation.

"Yes, people have tried to do this on previous occasions. They
were accused of being sympathetic to the guerrillas and were arrested and have never been heard from again. I'm told there is a
large concentration camp outside the capital city where thousands
of people are being tortured daily until they die. People travelling
on a nearby road at night have heard their screams. The government calls it 'pacification.' It tells us it is doing it for the good of the
country and for the glory of God. We are told that if the communists
take over they will turn the whole country into a graveyard and
whoever remains alive will become a slave. As if we Indians have
not been slaves all these years."

As they drove back to Quezaltenango that afternoon the young
priest kept shaking his head. When the car came down the moun-
tainside he pointed at the vast plateau stretching against the
horizon to the south. It was here, he told his two compatriots, 400
years ago, that a Spaniard named Pedro de Alvarado was sent by
his commander, Hernando Cortes, to claim Guatemala for the
Spanish Crown and for Christianity. Here on this plateau he fought
the battle against the Mayan hero, Tecum Uman, grandson of the
Mayan king, in whom the Mayans had put their hope to stop the
foreign invader. Tecum Uman fought his way through the Spanish
cavalry and reached Alvarado. He was able to kill Alvarado's horse
before he was pierced through with Spanish steel. According to
some Mayan accounts of that period and according to Fray Bar-
tolome de las Casas, a Spanish priest known as friend of the Indians, Alvarado killed and destroyed everything in his path. He
systematically massacred the Indians, burned their towns, and
took the able bodied men to fight the next tribe. Padre de las Casas
adds that Alvarado would give his Indian soldiers nothing to eat,
allowing them instead to eat the Indians they captured, and so a

solemn butchery of human flesh would take place in his presence, during which children were killed and roasted.

"Nothing has changed in 400 years," Reed concluded. "The same atrocities first introduced here by Western civilization are still the order of the day. As a Christian, I am ashamed of the legacy that had been handed down to us in this part of the world by people who call themselves Christians."

"So what is the solution?" Kaye asked.

He was sitting across the table from Eve on the porch of a small cafe in the Guatemalan town of Champerico, on the Pacific coast, not far from the Mexican border. Father Reed had to stay in Quezaltenango to work on his report, and they decided to resume their trip by themselves. Instead of continuing to Tapachula across the border, they had picked the safer route going down to the Guatemalan coast. They boarded a bus in the morning, and for the first time since they arrived in Guatemala they found out they were actually in a tropical country. As soon as the bus left Quezaltenango and rounded the curves going down the mountain road, the vegetation changed within minutes from pine and oak to palm and mango and broad leaf banana plants. As they kept going down the temperature went up, and by the time they reached the coastal plain people on the bus began to remove sweaters and coats and the women began to fan themselves with whatever was handy.

They were looking forward to two or three days of rest on a tropical beach (Eve had never seen a tropical beach before, having spent her entire life in the Midwest), but when they arrived in Champerico they discovered a black sand beach—a mixture of sea sand and volcanic ash—and a seething, stormy sea with a strong undertow. The town itself had seen better days, they were told, back in the twenties and thirties, when it was a thriving coffee port. They checked into a ramshackle *pension* and decided to return home the next day.

"I don't know what the solution is," said Eve, mixing a teaspoonful of sugar in her iced coffee. "I think John Reed is right. We have to pressure our own government to do something about this situation."

"Yes, I agree with you there. The first thing we must do is put a stop to the slaughter, and certainly our own government can do something about it. But what about all this terrible poverty, malnutrition, illiteracy, child mortality?"

"It'll obviously take more than you and I, or the Peace Corps, or any other organization of foreign volunteers to solve these problems."

"Yes, I agree. This is a far more complex situation than I have ever imagined."

"What a troubled land," Eve said, smiling wistfully. "When I first started working with you and Tom at Santa Teresa I thought we had finally found our own little Eden. We all thought the cooperative was going to be the turning point. And then this thing happens with Sanchez running away with the money. Well, I guess we have to keep trying. We must have faith."

"Yes," he smiled back at her. "And we do have each other."

✧ 23 ✧

Tom did not quit. When they returned to Santa Teresa they found out the bank had agreed to give the cooperative an extension on repaying the loan, and the villagers were able to buy the equipment and began to make plans for modernizing their farming methods. The Texan told Aguilar he would stay until June, when his two year term was up, and then go back to the States to complete his graduate studies. What had become clear, however, to him and to Kaye and Eve was that the change they had hoped for would take many years, if indeed it were to come about altogether. Kaye could tell Tom's heart was already back in the States, in his future plans.

As for Eve and himself, they had reached a crossroads in their feelings about the undertaking, and were not quite sure what long-range plans to make. Was Eve to go back to her order or give up her vocation? Would he go back to his rabbinical work, to the *havurah*, to help reshape the Jewish religious experience, or devote his life to general causes?

The two of them discussed those things at length for several days, but did not seem to come to any conclusions. Their lives had reached a period of indecision, which Kaye found unsettling. He was anxious to come up with a solution. He told Eve he did not feel the Peace Corps was on the right track. The two of them could spend a lifetime here in Santa Teresa but Guatemala would still be the same Guatemala, a handful of rich families owning the country, keeping the rest of the people poor and oppressed with the blessing of the Church and the military backing of the United States.

Something far-reaching had to be done. The two of them alone were only two grains of sand on the beach. They had to organize a movement of people of all faiths and nationalities who would be able to put pressure on their governments to change things. Someone had to awaken that moral power inherent in all religions and harness it for the common good.

Eve agreed with everything he said. The question, however, was how to go about doing it. She felt that while they looked for an answer they had to continue working at Santa Teresa in order to set a personal example. The cooperative project, in spite of the setback, was a sound idea, and her own work with the local school was an opportunity to develop a model school which would help upgrade education not only in Santa Teresa but in other villages where most children at present did not attend beyond the second or third grade.

And then what?

Well, that remained to be seen.

A week after their return to Santa Teresa they went out early one evening for a stroll. It was a warm, balmy night. Instead of taking the goat path up the mountain, they continued along the plain near the highway and crossed the road. After a short walk they entered a small pine grove. They sat down next to each other on a flat rock and remained silent for a long time when suddenly they saw a dark silhouette moving across the field in their direction. As soon as the shadowy figure reached the edge of the woods it stumbled and fell on the ground where it lay motionless. No doubt it was one of the village drunks who had lost his way and wandered in the wrong direction.

They got up and went over to help the man get back on his feet and head back for the village.

"Hello, there!" Kaye called out as they came within a few yards of the lying man. They saw him stir and rise, propping himself up on his elbow.

"Don't move!" they heard a strained young voice order. It did not sound like one of the villagers. Instead of the local tone of self-effacement, this person's voice was assertive and self-assured, which made it clear he was a stranger, probably from Guatemala City.

"Are you okay?" Kaye inquired.

"I said, don't move!" the stranger repeated his order. Eve grasped Kaye by his sleeve and pointed at a glinting object in the stranger's hand. Kaye now realized the man was holding a gun. No doubt he was a fugitive from the law, an escaped criminal.

"What can I do for you?" Kaye asked in a calm voice. The man, still aiming his gun at them, got up on his feet. He stood only a few feet away, but they could not make out his features in the dark. They remained standing there, frozen, as the man seemed to be deciding what to do next. Kaye felt a dryness in his mouth. He wanted to say something to persuade the man to put away his gun, but did not know what to say.

"We would like to help you," Eve tried to assure him.

"You are gringos, aren't you?" the stranger said.

"Yes, we are."

"Then you must have a car."

"Yes, we do."

"I want you to take me to the city. I'll show you the way. You do exactly what I tell you to do and nothing will happen to you. Understood?"

"Yes, sir," Kaye replied.

"*Bien*. Now turn around and start walking."

They began to walk back toward the village when they heard a groan and a thud. When he looked back over his shoulder Kaye saw the stranger writhing on the ground. He was still pointing his gun at them.

They stopped and looked at him, waiting for an explanation.

"I'm wounded," the man finally said in a hoarse voice.

"Let me help you," Eve said. "You don't have to be afraid. I'm a nun, and my friend is a Peace Corps worker. We won't turn you in. You can trust us."

"Don't move!" he ordered in a fading voice. His hand began to shake and he collapsed on the ground, face down. Kaye rushed to his side and took the gun out of his hand and put it in his pocket. Eve kneeled down and began to examine the lying man.

"Here," she pointed at his thigh. "He is bleeding from a wound right here. His pants are soaked with blood."

"What do we do now?" Kaye wondered.

"We'll take him back and have Doña Maria look at him," said Eve. "She has some medical experience. She told me she used to be a nurse. We won't turn him in. We'll see if we can get him back in shape to send him on his way."

They slowly lifted the inert body and began to carry it back to the village. He was small and frail, and they had no difficulty carrying him across the field. As they reached the village they ran into two men who were passing by, taking in the evening air.

"Whom have you got there?" one villager inquired.

"*Un borracho*," Kaye explained, "just a drunk."

They nodded with a perfunctory wave of the hand and resumed their walk.

They reached Doña Maria's house and took the man inside and put him into bed in the guest bedroom. Eve went out to look for Doña Maria and the two of them came back moments later and looked at the man who lay in bed perfectly still.

"*Ay, Dios!*" Doña Maria shook her head, "such a young man."

He looked more like a boy than a man. His face was pale and thin with long dark eyelashes, a shock of black hair and the virginal growth of a beard. He wore old faded jeans and a plaid woolen shirt too large for his size, and old worn out high heel pointed boots. He lay motionless with limp hands spread out, his face turned to the wall, and his wounded knee twisted inwardly from pain. Kaye could swear he had seen him somewhere, some time ago, before he came to Guatemala, under altogether different circumstances. But he could not for the life of him remember where.

"I wonder how he was wounded and how he got here," Eve was saying. "He looks like a student, not a criminal. Perhaps he got into a fight over something personal. But what was he doing in this neck of the woods?"

"He might be involved in some political activity," Kaye suggested.

"I certainly hope not," Doña Maria interjected as she began to apply a wet cloth to the wounded man's forehead. "That would be a very serious matter indeed."

The young man began to stir. His normal breathing seemed to be restored. He opened his eyes and stared at the ceiling.

"Where am I?" he asked in a faint voice.

"Among friends," Kaye reassured him.

"What's your name?" Doña Maria asked.

Instead of replying he closed his eyes again, seemingly too weak to talk.

Doña Maria examined the wound.

"He lost a great deal of blood," she explained. She showed Kaye and Eve two holes in his pants. One was in the middle of his under-thigh and the other one about three inches higher, on the other side of the thigh, under his side pocket.

"He is lucky," the old woman said. "The bullet went in the first hole and came out the second. It did not touch the bone. I'll clean him up and bandage him and after a few days of rest he should be on his way."

Eve heaved a sigh of relief. Kaye could tell she had become emotionally involved with the wounded youth and was relieved to find out his condition was not so serious as it appeared at first.

Things seemed to be under control. It was past midnight. Kaye handed Eve the gun for safekeeping and went back to his place. He was too tired to read. He turned off the light and went to sleep. He was fast asleep when he was awakened by a knock on his door. He put on his robe and went to open the door. It was Eve. She was wearing a coat against the night's chill. He looked at his watch. It was three o'clock in the morning. She told him she had something urgent to discuss with him. Could he get dressed quickly and come over to Doña Maria's house?

He found Doña Maria sitting in her living room, her elbows pressing on the bare table and her hands clasped tight in front of her. She looked at him with steady taut eyes as he walked in.

"*Que pasa?*" he asked.

"Please sit down," she motioned at the chair across the table. He sat down facing her. Eve took the chair on his right and pulled up closer, looking intently at Doña Maria.

The first thought that crossed Kaye's mind was the young man had taken a turn for the worse.

"How is he doing?" he asked.

"He is doing fine," Doña Maria said with unchanged expression. "He is sleeping now. But, about an hour ago, I heard him scream in his sleep and I went into his room. He must have been having a bad dream. He kept talking in his sleep. You will never in a million years guess who he is."

He looked at Eve. He could tell she knew. He could further tell he was about to hear something extraordinary.

"He must be someone important."

"He is Yak Lopez."

"Yak Lopez? The guerrilla leader?"

"*Si, señor.*"

"He is probably the most sought after person in Guatemala."

The old woman confirmed with a slow nod.

"Are you sure?"

"I went into his room after I heard him scream, and I heard him say, 'They are not going to get me. No one is going to get Yak Lopez.' And then he said, '*Viva la revolucion, abajo la tirania.*' And then he repeated, 'You are not going to get me. You are not going to get Yak Lopez!'"

"So you are certain it is him."

"Yes, I am. Besides, I once heard a description of him. Looks like a boy, short, slender, with light skin and dark hair, well educated, speaks in a strong commanding voice."

"What do we do now?"

"For all we know, the police are on their way right now. They may be here any minute." He could hear the fear in her voice. "If we don't turn him in right away we are doomed."

"We cannot turn him in," said Eve.

"We have no choice, my dear girl."

"If we turn him in they will torture him and kill him."

"If we don't, we will all die."

Eve got up and went over to Doña Maria and put her hand on the old woman's shoulder.

"Let me take him over to my place," she said. "I'll keep him there until he is well enough to leave. I'll take full responsibility for this. They'll have to think twice before they touch an American nun."

"*Muy bien*," Doña Maria agreed. "May God watch over you. But please be very careful and don't say a word about it to anyone."

"Are you sure you want to do this?" Kaye said as he got up. "He must be a very dangerous person."

She looked at him and put her hand in her coat pocket and took out Yak Lopez's gun.

"Here, take it."

Kaye examined the gun. In his teens his father had taken him target shooting. He studied the weapon. It was a .38 caliber revolver, short barrel, fully loaded. He put it in his pants pocket.

"Okay," he said. "Let's go in and take him over to your place."

Yak Lopez was asleep when they walked in. With Doña Maria's help they carried him to Eve's house which had one empty bedroom. They laid him down on the bed and covered him with an old blanket.

"I'll keep the door to his room locked," said Eve. "I don't think he'll get too far in his condition."

"Are you sure you don't mind staying here alone?" Kaye asked.

"I'll be okay."

He kissed her goodnight and went back to his place. He was not able to fall asleep as he lay in bed trying to decide whether they were doing the right thing. He was not able to come to any conclusions. He saw the dawn light up the sky outside and he got out of bed and got dressed and went over to Eve's house. He knocked lightly on the door, not sure whether she was up at this early hour. She opened the door immediately and let him in.

"Did you sleep?" he asked.

"No, I didn't. Did you?"

"Not really."

"I wish I knew how to get him out of here."

"Do you think we are doing the right thing not turning him in?"

"No, I'm not. I've been thinking about it since you left. I've been trying to put aside my own personal feelings and look at it objectively. This man is a terrorist. It is people like him who have started the cycle of violence in Guatemala, which is causing the death of so many innocent people. If we help him escape there will be more violence. I'm not a political expert. I don't know who is worse, the government or the guerrillas. All I know is that we are better off not getting ourselves involved in all of this."

"Then you think we should turn him in?"

"I don't know. I don't think we have the moral right to do it. After all, this is his country and these are his people, not ours. We may not agree with his methods, but, on the other hand, he is putting his life on the line for his people, and who are we to play judge and jury by deciding to turn him over to his executioners?"

She made two cups of instant coffee and put them on the table and sat down next to him. She put her hand on his and gazed into his eyes. He leaned his head against hers.

"Yes, *mi amor*, I agree. I don't want to play God."

"The question is, how do we get him out of here."

"We have to talk to him, let him know we know who he is, and find out from him how we can get in touch with his people and arrange for someone to come here and take him away."

"You better do it," she said.

He put his hand in his pocket and felt the gun. He kept his hand inside the pocket with his finger on the trigger and got up and tiptoed down the hall to the bedroom. He quietly unlocked the door and peaked in. Yak Lopez lay on his back, covered up to his chin with the blanket, his head resting on the pillow, his face lit up with the morning light. As he kept looking at the still face Kaye remembered where he had seen him before. He looked like the man he had seen in his dream at the hospital in Quincy, the small frail man with the sad Jewish eyes who came down from the cross that was hanging outside his hospital room in the hallway. He stood at the door, transfixed by the resemblance, when the lying man opened his eyes. He edged his way into the room without taking his eyes off him, and kept looking at him as he locked the door and put the key in his pocket.

"Good morning," he greeted the wounded guerrilla. He kept his hand in his pocket as he spoke.

"Good morning." The young man's reply was pleasant yet cautious.

"How do you feel?"

"Much better, thank you."

"How is your leg?"

He slowly pulled the blanket off his leg. Doña Maria had bandaged his entire thigh from the crook of the knee to his groin. He tried to move his leg but was not able to.

"It's numb," he said, visibly disappointed.

"You are lucky," said Kaye, "apparently you didn't suffer a major injury."

He decided to come right to the point.

"I've told you I work for the Peace Corps here at Santa Teresa. I do not mix in the local politics. But I've heard you talk in your sleep last night. You must've been delirious. You revealed your identity. Now it so happens that I've just come back from Quezaltenango, where I've visited the countryside, and I know the government is after you and will not stop at anything to get its hands on you. If they find out I've been taking care of you they won't ask any questions. They will take both of us and put us before the firing squad."

He stopped and waited for Lopez's reaction. The young man looked at him with distant indifference and did not say a word.

Kaye sat down on a chair in the corner.

"Do you have any suggestions, Señor Lopez?"

"Yak."

"Excuse me?"

"You can call me Yak."

Kaye smiled.

"Joshua." The tension he felt until now was suddenly relieved.

"I can give you a telephone number in the city. I'll give you a coded message, and my friends will come here and get me."

"It'll be safer, of course, for me to just turn you in."

"But you won't do it. You Peace Corps people are not like those other gringos who come here to help our decadent government. You work with the poor and you know what Guatemala is really all about."

"Yes, I do. I also agree with you that the right wing government is decadent. It's brutal and inhumane. I've been to La Merced and I saw what the army did to the Indians. Obviously, Guatemala needs a different kind of regime. What have you got to offer the poor masses of Guatemala in place of this government?"

"Land, bread, dignity."

"How?"

"Through equal distribution of the national wealth."

"You mean, communism."

"Yes, communism."

"You're going to trade one form of tyranny for another. You'll think nothing of massacring thousands of innocent people in order to force collectivization, or whatever you call it, on the masses. You may teach them how to read and write, but you won't teach them how to think. They won't be allowed to think. You'll take away from them the most precious gift God have given them—free will, individual freedom, the right to be a person, to disagree, to challenge human authority, the way you yourself are challenging it right now. How can you give them dignity by taking away their freedom?"

Yak Lopez pulled himself up with great difficulty and sat up in bed, leaning his head against the wall behind him. Despite his young age it was obvious he was a leader of men. His voice remained calm and controlled as he spoke. This kind of discussion seemed to be something he was well schooled in. His beliefs were being challenged by this gringo, and he was not about to be browbeaten. There was a new vitality in his face, a heightened determination. He is a true believer, Kaye thought. He is willing to die for his beliefs, and nothing I am going to say is going to make any difference. Obviously, he and I see the world from a totally different perspective.

"Freedom?" Yak Lopez chuckled. "What freedom? These people are free to starve, free to die in their thirties of old age, free to be exploited by the *latifundistas*, by the Church, by your own government, free, in other words, to be slaves. I know your President Kennedy meant well when he organized the Peace Corps. And I'm sure your personal intentions were good when you came to Guatemala to help my people. But the lot of our people will not change unless and until they take their fate into their own hands and build their own future."

"You mean, choose their own form of government?"

"Our people are not politically mature to choose their own form of government. The great majority cannot even read or write. Most of the Indians, as you know, still live in the stone age. The only form of government that can change their lot is communism. This whole country has to be reorganized. People have to be put to work, no questions asked. Those who don't work don't eat. Guatemala can be one of the richest countries in the world. It has many natural resources, and yet right not it is one of the poorest. Yes, my friend, you are right. Communism can be harsh. But a doctor can also be harsh when he treats a patient. He may have to amputate a limb in order to save one's life. Guatemala cannot be saved without radical surgery. It has been oppressed for too long. Lives may be lost, but it will be for the common good. The right wing government, on the other hand, is slaughtering thousands of innocent people for no other reason except to keep a handful of wealthy families in power and keep the masses poor and backward."

"You and I obviously disagree," said Kaye. "But when all is said and done, this is your country, not mine. I don't wish to tell you how to go about helping your own people. I'd certainly hate to see Guatemala exchange one form of tyranny for another. I know there has got to be a better way, and when I came here to work for the Peace Corps I had hoped I could help your people find that better way. But after I've been here for a few months and tried to work here at Santa Teresa and saw what was going on in other parts of the country, I'm no longer sure I can do it. So obviously Guatemala is either going to continue unchanged, as it has for so many years, or something radical is going to happen. Obviously, you are proposing a radical, violent change. I can understand where you come from. You may have no other choice but to do what you're doing. As an outsider, I don't have the moral right to stop you. So you can give me your friends' number and the coded message and I'll see to it that you get back to your people."

✧ 24 ✧

Kaye called the number Yak Lopez had given him and delivered the message. It simply stated: "Special prayer tonight at eight o'clock at the church in Santa Teresa." Lopez told Kaye his friends would know they had to come at eight o'clock to the church to pick him up. He should be transferred to the church a few minutes before eight and await their arrival.

After dinner Kaye went to see Eve. He could tell she was as tense as he was. They sat in her room with the door to Lopez's room locked and watched the minutes tick away on Eve's alarm clock. They tried to make small talk and get their minds off the anticipated departure of the guerrilla leader, but were unable to do it. Time seemed to have stopped. What if his friends did not show up? What happens then? Well, they better show up, Eve said. Or we may all be in deep trouble.

At a quarter to eight they went into Yak Lopez's room. The wounded youth appeared perfectly calm.

"It's time," said Kaye, "we're going to take you to the church."

Lopez looked up at them with a strained smile and propped himself up, turning his wounded leg across the bed and easying it down to the floor.

"Well, I want to thank you two for all you've done for me. I was thinking, we all use labels, religious labels, political labels. But there is something which goes deeper than all the labels. Oh, well, perhaps we can discuss it some other time."

Kaye took out Lopez's gun and handed it to him. Lopez took it without saying a word and put it in his pocket. Next Eve and Kaye lifted him by his arms and wrapped his arms around their shoulders and carried him limping on one foot out of the house. As they reached the outside they stopped to make sure no one was watching. The street was deserted. They proceeded across the street to the church. Without turning on any lights, they walked into the church and closed the door behind them and sat down in the back pew with Lopez between them. Kaye peered at his watch. It was almost eight o'clock. He stood up and walked to the door and looked outside through the peephole. He saw a red Volkswagen come up the street. The VW stopped in front of the church and two men got out and came over with their hands in their pockets. They reached the door and looked around before they knocked. Kaye cracked the door. They slipped in and he locked the door behind him. All three seemed to be overcome with emotion. Eve helped Lopez stand up. The two men thanked her and carried their leader to the car without looking back. Lopez was put in the back of the car and the two men squeezed into the front seats and slammed the doors and the car tore away with a shriek of tires on cobblestones.

Kaye turned to Eve. She leaned against him and he put his arm around her. She heaved a deep sigh of relief.

"Thank God he's on his way."

They went outside and looked down the dark street where the car had just disappeared on its way to the highway.

"It's done," said Kaye. "We've kept our word. Now we have to go back to our own affairs."

They heard an explosion. It seemed only a few yards away, but they could not tell exactly in what direction. Next they heard a short burst of automatic fire. For a moment there was total silence. Eve took Kaye's hand and pressed it.

"I'm scared," she said.

He felt numb. The scene of total annihilation at La Merced flashed before his eyes. The army must have found out Lopez had been hiding at Santa Teresa and had come to retaliate against the village.

Another explosion followed. This time they saw a swirl of orange flames shoot up into the night sky across the field near the highway, quickly rising and disappearing. It grew quiet again. They waited. There were no more explosions. The village was waking up. People began to come out of their homes and asked one another what was happening. Soon there was a small crowd in the street. Some people turned around and went back to their homes to stay our of harm's way. A few decided to go over and find out what went on. Kaye told Eve to go back home while he went out to see what had happened. She insisted on coming along with him.

When they reached the highway they saw several army jeeps with mounted machine guns and helmeted soldiers setting up road blocks. They walked down the side of the highway at a discreet distance from the soldiers. In a ditch near the road they saw a smoldering skeleton of a car. An army van stood nearby. As they came closer they were assailed by an acrid smell and had to hold their breath.

The van's headlights were switched on, revealing a mangled body lying on the side of the road, drenched in blood. It lay outside the burned out car which Kaye could now tell was once a red Volkswagen. Two soldiers picked up the body, not bothering to check and see whether the person was dead or alive, and hauled it by the hands and legs onto the van. Next they went over to the burned out car and looked inside. They began to pull out another body. It was burned beyond recognition. They laid it down on the ground next to the car. They looked inside again, and started to rummage through the debris in the back of the car. They brought out a third charred body. It was black from the neck down. The face was intact. One soldier pulled up the head by the hair and turned the face against the headlights of the van.

"*Es el*," Kaye heard the soldier tell his comrade excitedly. "It's him."

Lopez's eyes were wide open. His mouth hung loose with a frozen scream. Kaye knew he would see that face for the rest of his life. He felt a bitter taste in his mouth and a tightness in his chest. He turned to Eve. He saw her averting her eyes. He now realized there was a cluster of villagers standing behind them.

Some villagers crossed themselves.

"*Ay, Dios*," a woman standing next to Eve lamented. "*Santo Cristo, ten piedad de nosotros*."

The cindered bodies of Lopez and his friends were thrown into the van. An army officer turned to the group of onlookers and ordered them to return to their homes. He assured them everything was under control.

As they turned to leave Kaye saw Tom coming toward them. The Texan had spent the day in Guatemala City and must have just come back.

"What's going on?" he asked them.

"A shootout between the army and some guerrillas," Kaye explained. "It's over now. The soldiers are getting ready to leave."

"This country is becoming a very dangerous place," the Texan observed.

Kaye walked Eve back to her place. They went into the house and sat down at the kitchen table without saying a word. She sat erect next to the table and stared at the window and the dark street outside, clasping her hands in her lap. Her eyes seemed empty and lifeless. He went over to her and put his arms around her and pressed her against his chest, burying his face in her hair. Suddenly she heaved a sob. A loud cry followed, and then she cried quietly, bitterly, as he kept stroking her hair and rocking her in his arms.

"It's over and done," he tried to console her. "We did everything we could. Now we have to think of the future."

He handed her his handkerchief and she wiped her eyes and blew her nose.

"Oh Josh," she shook her head in sorrow, "how can people be so cruel? How can they do this to each other, to their own kind? I'm trying to believe as you do that religion has the moral power to change the world. And here we are, in a country which became Christian four centuries ago, and people are still killing each other like savages. Is there any hope, or are we all going to destroy one another?"

He was about to answer her question when they heard a knock on the door.

"Who is it?" Eve asked.

"Police. Open up."

She opened the door. Two men in leather jackets and pulled down hats stood at the door. One of them stepped forward and flashed a police badge.

"Sister Eve Gruner?" he asked politely.

"What can I do for you?"

He turned to Kaye.

"Rabbi Joshua Kaye?"

"I'm he."

"You're both under arrest."

"For what?"

"We're not free to discuss it with you. We have our orders. Please come with us and everything will be explained to you by the appropriate authorities."

The appropriate authorities, Kaye thought. He felt a shiver run through his spine. The same authorities that massacred the people of La Merced. The same authorities that have just blown up a wounded man and his two companions without any questions asked. What orders did these two men have? Are they going to take us for a ride and then order us out of the car and make us take a walk in the woods and shoot us through the head? Naturally, they will blame it on the guerrillas. They will tell the world Lopez and his men had killed us, and subsequently they, the defenders of freedom and democracy, pursued the three guerrillas and engaged them in a short battle in which all three were killed.

"We are U.S. citizens," Kaye said. "We want to let the American Embassy know you are arresting us."

"By all means," one plainclothes agent said. "As soon as we bring you in we'll let you notify the Embassy."

Kaye put on his jacket and helped Eve put on her coat. Outside they were told to step into the back of a Ford van. They climbed in and sat next to each other and heard the door being locked behind them with a key. They were in an enclosed compartment, separated from the front of the van by a metal partition with a small barred window. They heard the front doors slam shut as the engine started and the van jerked and began to speed into the night.

Eve bumped against him. He held her tight in his arms and felt a total calm come over him. He thought of the time his secretary, Ruth Levy, drove him to the hospital after he had started hemorrhaging. He recalled thinking he was going to die, and his only wish was to see Eve one more time before he died. Well, perhaps it was all fated. The two of them were bound by the things they believed in, which they refused to compromise. They could both be in Quincy now, living a comfortable secure life, he as a rabbi of Suburban Temple and Eve as a teacher in a middle class suburb. They could be spending the rest of their lives going through the motions of organized religion, playing the part of rabbi and nun and taking their cues from the higher ups and the rich. Yet they had both been driven by the same force, and now they had to face the consequences.

He had no regrets. He knew Eve had no regrets. He felt at one with her. He did not let her in on his thoughts. There was no need to. All that mattered was having each other.

"I love you, Josh," he heard Eve say, "I always will. I'm not sorry we did what we did. And I'm not afraid. You are the only man I've ever loved, and having you I have everything. I know we have not done anything wrong. We have nothing to be ashamed of. Those who torture and kill people in the name of the law and in the name of God are the guilty ones and are accountable for their actions. They may sit in judgment of us, but I know there is a higher law that will judge them. The evil they do will not go unpunished, and they won't stop us from doing what we know is right."

He stroked her long tapered soft yet firm fingers.

"No, they won't, *mi amor*."

They were taken into the police headquarters in Guatemala City. When they entered the building there were two policewomen in the lobby waiting for Eve. They escorted her down the hall as Kaye was taken in the opposite direction. He was shown into a room without windows. There was a desk with a black telephone in the middle of the room and two chairs. After waiting alone for a moment, Kaye was greeted by a young officer. The officer was clean shaven and sported a neatly trimmed black mustache. He tried to appear casual and relaxed, but his hand was resting on his belt next to his gun holster. He told Kaye to sit down and went around the desk and sat down facing him.

"You are Rabbi Joshua Kaye," he said in good English. "I am Lieutenant Ramirez."

"Before we begin I have one request," said Kaye.

"Certainly."

"I would like to call the U.S. Embassy to let them know I'm here."

The officer turned the phone around and pushed it across the table. Kaye dialed the Embassy number. The Embassy night receptionist answered the phone.

"I would like to speak to Jorge Aguilar. It's urgent."

"I'm sorry. Mr. Aguilar has already left for the day."

"This is Rabbi Kaye. I work for the Peace Corps. I need to speak to him immediately."

She gave him Aguilar's home number. He thanked her and dialed the number.

"Jorge, it's me, Joshua Kaye. I'm here in the city at police headquarters. There was a shootout at Santa Teresa earlier this evening and both Sister Eve and I were arrested and brought down here. I need your help."

There was a pause on the other end.

"Is there anyone there with you I can speak to?" Aguilar finally said.

He asked the officer to take the receiver.

"Hello, Lieutenant Ramirez here—yes, of course, don't worry about it, they are in good hands—yes, you can see them first thing in the morning. Good night."

The officer put the receiver back in its cradle.

"He will be here in the morning to see you. And now, may I ask you to tell me in your own words about your connection to Yak Lopez."

"What would you like to know?"

"How long have you known Lopez?"

"I ran into him the other night near the highway right outside Santa Teresa. He was wounded in his knee. He wanted me to take him to the city."

"Was the sister with you at the time?"

"Yes, she was."

"So you took him to the city."

"No, we didn't. He was ordering us at gun point, but he was too weak to stand up, he must've lost a great deal of blood, so he fainted. We took him back with us to the village and we accidently discovered who he was. He asked us to call his friends to come and pick him up, and we did. They came to pick him up. I'm sure you know the rest of the story."

"Why didn't you notify the authorities?"

"Because, as a clergyman, I don't mix in politics. I don't choose sides in this conflict between the government and the guerrillas. All I saw before me was a wounded young man who needed help."

"But you know he and his friends have committed many crimes. They've killed more than a few people, including some of your own people."

Kaye strained to remain calm.

"As I said, officer, I don't take sides in this conflict. I came to Guatemala to help your people find a way to improve their lot. I don't believe in violence. I said it to Lopez and I'm saying it to you. I don't think violence is the answer. you didn't gain anything by killing him. You have made a martyr out of him, and now there will be others who will take his place. But, as I said, I don't wish to tell you how to run your country."

"What else can you tell me about Lopez? What do you know about the whereabouts of his people?"

"Not a thing. I've told you all I know. You don't really think Yak Lopez took me into his confidence, do you?"

The officer did not respond. He picked up the receiver and called the guards, who came in and told Kaye to come along. he was taken into a small room on the lower level of the police building and was told he would be spending the night there. There was nothing in the room except a low cot and a chair. He lay down on the cot in his clothes and drifted into sleep.

In the morning he had a visitor. There was a clanging of keys in the door. He sat up on the cot as Jorge Aguilar, the Peace Corps coordinator, was let in. The two of them were left alone. Aguilar sat down on the chair in the corner and took off his glasses and wiped them on his sleeve.

"That's some business you and Sister Eve have gotten yourselves involved in," the Peace Corps coordinator came right to the point. "It appears that the night the two of you ran into Yak Lopez he was driving on the highway near Santa Teresa and he ran into a road block. He drove through the block and wounded two soldiers and was fired on by a third soldier. His car overturned but he managed to escape. The police were keeping close watch on the area, and picked up your telephone call to Lopez's friends. I found out all of this last night. I had to wake up the Ambassador and tell him what had happened. He agreed with me that our government does not want the publicity of a rabbi and a nun getting themselves involved with a leftist guerrilla leader. Our Ambassador immediately got in touch with the authorities and argued that you, as a rabbi, and Eve, as a nun, were bound by your religious beliefs and vows not to turn Lopez in after he revealed his identify to you. He assured them you two had no ties with the guerrillas and insisted that they let you go free. They have agreed to release Eve today, but they want to keep you for another day or two in case their investigation brings out any new evidence of complicity."

"I'm sorry to put you through all this trouble," said Kaye. "I hope all of this can be quickly resolved."

"Quite all right," Aguilar replied. "I'm glad things didn't turn out a lot worse than they did. you two have put your lives in grave danger. Now it's over. I suppose the Guatemalan authorities are overjoyed they got Lopez, which is why they choose to be lenient with you. But I don't believe they solved anything by killing him. I'm sure by now you've found out that the problems of Latin America are far from simple. Living conditions in most of these countries are such that others will soon come in his place. The Peace Corps, as you see, is only a drop in the bucket. We'll have to start doing something far more concrete than this Peace Corps operation, and we'll have to start soon, before it's too late."

He was kept in that cell for three days without seeing anyone, with nothing to read, nothing to do. Those were three interminable days. Each day seemed an eternity. There was nothing in the cell to tell time by. Neither day nor night. The light bulb in the steel cage embedded in the wall burned all the time. he began to fear the Guatemalan authorities had changed their mind. They had decided Eve and he had been working for the guerrillas. They might have found out about their visit to La Merced and concluded that they had tried to make contact with the guerrillas. Aguilar had mentioned that the American Government did not want the publicity of a rabbi and a nun getting themselves involved with leftist guerrillas. The Embassy might have received orders from Washington to tell the Guatemalan authorities to keep the two of them in jail indefinitely.

On the third day he began to think about taking some drastic measures, possibly a hunger strike. He began to pace the cell trying to decide what to do, when he heard footsteps outside. A guard opened the door. Behind him stood Jorge Aguilar. The Peace Corps coordinator was all smiles.

"Well, sorry it took so long, but you've no idea how much red tape I had to cut through in order to get the release papers. I guess anyone who gets arrested in this country does not see the light of day for at least a year, guilty or not guilty. The legal assumption seems to be that one is guilty until proven innocent. Anyway, I have to take you now to the Embassy for an important briefing."

He followed Aguilar and a guard to a central office where he was made to sign the release papers. As soon as he stepped out of the police headquarters he was nearly blinded by the bright morning sun. His heart beat fast, and he nearly burst out crying. Suddenly he knew what it meant to be free. For the first time since his arrest he realized he was back among the living. He had been prepared for the worst, and now he was given back his freedom. He was free to go as he pleased and do what he wanted.

Someone touched his shoulder. He turned around. It was Eve. She looked pale, but her eyes brimmed with joy. he pressed her against himself. Aguilar stood by, smiling benignly at both of them.

"Let's go," he said. "We have to be at the Embassy by twelve."

They rode through the teeming downtown streets. He could only think of one thing—to take a hot shower. Let the hot water run over him for hours.

At the Embassy they were shown into an upstairs office with a large mahogany desk and the American flag in the corner. A tall blond man in a business suit came in and introduced himself as a special assistant to the Ambassador.

"I've spoken to Sister Eve two days ago," he told Kaye, "but I wanted to speak to both of you together. As I'm sure you know, political conditions in Guatemala right now are far from stable. This affair you have gotten yourselves involved in is quite delicate. I'm glad we were able to get you two released, but in order to do it, as I've told Eve, we had to make a deal with the Guatemalan Government. We had to agree to have you two leave for the States by tomorrow night. Your flight back to the States will be paid by our government. Jorge is taking care of it. Do you have any questions?"

He looked at Eve. No, they did not have any questions.

"Please see me for a moment in my office," Aguilar told Kaye.

"I'll wait for you in the lobby downstairs," said Eve.

He went into Aguilar's office.

"Well, I guess it's goodbye," Aguilar said. "I really enjoyed meeting you. You have done good work at Santa Teresa. Here," he handed Kaye a sealed envelope. "Two tickets to Miami for you and Eve, and a check made out to you for 2000 dollars, your Peace Corps honorarium. My best personal wishes to you in all your future endeavors."

He took the envelope and thanked Aguilar and gave him a strong handshake. He joined Eve in the lobby downstairs and they went out and boarded the bus to Santa Teresa.

On the bus he learned Eve had gone to see the bishop after she was first told by the Embassy official about the deportation order, and she asked him to intercede on their behalf, since she did not feel they had done anything wrong by helping a wounded man. The bishop told her she should have stayed at the Maryknoll Center and none of this would have happened. He refused to do anything, and suggested that the Guatemalan authorities were being quite reasonable.

"It's just as well, " said Kaye. "We need to get away. We'll be able to get a better perspective on things."

"That may be true," said Eve. "But we should be free to go on our own terms. At this point I feel no allegiance to the Church. I think I may seriously consider leaving the order."

✧ 25 ✧

"And you shall not eat from the tree of the knowledge of good and evil," Kaye thought as the Pan Am aircraft soared into the Guatemalan sky. "For on the day you eat from it you will surely die."

They arrived in Miami at midnight. It was a hot humid Florida night. They were back home in the States, but they felt like refugees in their own country. On the plane Kaye had suggested they call the local papers and TV stations as soon as they landed and arrange a press conference at the airport, where Rabbi Kaye and Sister Eve would tell the world about the atrocities committed in Guatemala with the knowledge and backing of the U.S. Government. Eve did not like the idea. Clearly, if they called the media and presented their ecclesiastic credentials and mentioned that they had been deported from Guatemala, the media would be at the airport in no time. But it did not seem to be the right time for it. First they had to decide what their own plans were once they arrived in the States. The decision whether or not to stay in Guatemala had been made for them by the Guatemalan authorities. They had been banished from that country, and now the question was where did they go from there.

"We better rest up for a couple of days before we make any decisions," Eve had remarked. "We're in no physical or emotional shape right now to think clearly."

It felt strange to be back in the States. It seemed as if they had been overtaken by events. They had lost control and were being manipulated by an invisible force. It felt as if they had been shipwrecked at high sea and were drifting, tossed about by the waves, with no land in sight. The village of Santa Teresa was now a distant memory, a dream. The only reality was the two of them at this moment in time on a sweltering night in Miami. The huge airport, the people running in every direction, the sound of jets warming up for takeoff, seemed even less real than the events they had just been through. They decided to check in for the night at the airport hotel.

On the hotel registration card Kaye wrote "Mr. and Mrs. Joshua Kaye." They took the elevator to the top floor. They went into the room, and dropped their suitcases in the corner.

He put his arms around her and looked into her eyes.

"Well, Mrs. Kaye, alone at last."

"In never never land?"

"In our make-believe world."

"Pretending we are husband and wife?"

"Pretending we are newlyweds on our honeymoon."

"I have a feeling someone is watching us right now."

"Who?"

"Probably the FBI."

"You're probably right. We are like the characters in George Orwell's *1984.* Big Brother is watching us."

"Let'm."

He went into the bathroom and turned on the hot water. He took off his clothes and dropped them on the floor and stepped into the shower. The water kept running over him, scalding hot. Something inside of him was being cleansed, burned out, purified. He was not sure what it was. Oh, Lord, he heard himself pray, create in me a new spirit. Teach me Your ways, instruct me and enlighten me, and make Your will known to me.

Through the clouds of steam he saw a tall slender pink figure approaching him. A naked leg appeared, testing the water. Then the figure was next to him, sharing the hot spray, clinging to him, and they were washing each other with soap and washcloth, thoroughly scrubbing each other from head to toe. They stepped out of the shower and dried each other with large white towels. They dropped the towels on the floor and got into bed between the cool sheets.

"Heaven," Eve sighed.

She never seemed happier. Or more beautiful. He gathered her in his arms and kissed her eyes. He thought of the card he had filled out at the registration desk—"Mr. and Mrs. Joshua Kaye." Was he going to share the rest of his life with her? She might give up her vows, but somehow it was clear to him she was not his. She had another lover, an intangible one, whom she would have to renounce if she were to become his. She could not go on pretending. In order for them to share their lives she would have to start a new life, give up her present identity.

"Do you still love him?" Kaye asked.

She looked at him in surprise. She was not prepared for such a question.

"Yes, I do," she said hesitantly.

"Are you still married to him?"

She looked up at the ceiling. There was quiet sadness in her eyes.

"No, I don't think so. I love him, but I'm not married to him. Not since that time at Santa Teresa, under that rock, in the rainstorm."

"But he is your Lord?"

"Yes, he's my Lord."

"And you still want me."

"Yes, I want you more than anything else in the world. I guess you're telling me I have to choose."

"We both have to choose. We both want to eat our cake and have it. We'll have to choose eventually."

"Not tonight, please. Tonight let it be just the two of us. We'll have enough time to talk about it later."

They made love and she fell asleep in his arms.

He woke up at dawn. Eve was fast asleep. It took him a few minutes to grasp the fact that they were back in the States. He put on his pants and went outside and sat on the balcony. The airport down below was waking up in the first light of dawn. We are in transit, he thought, but in transit to where?

The events of recent weeks began to run through his mind. The trip to La Merced after the place was turned into a ghost town by the Guatemalan army. The night they ran into Yak Lopez. The police trap and the killing of the guerrilla leader. The arrest and the investigation and his three days in jail, and the subsequent deportation.

One thing was clear: Central America was a time bomb. It had to explode. It was only a question of time. The corrupt regimes could not go on forever. Their days, in fact, were numbered. What's more, what was happening in Central America was indicative of what was going on in other parts of the world, particularly in the so-called Third World countries. Poverty, illiteracy, hunger, disease, those were the ills that were pushing the world to the brink of disaster. The choice was clear: either turn one's back on the ills of the world and settle down to a comfortable middle class existence here in America, or find a way to do something about those ills.

He tiptoed back into the room and opened the desk drawer and took out stationery and envelopes and a pen. He went back to the balcony and started to write a letter to his father in Israel. He was letting the old man know he was in Miami on his way back from Guatemala, where he had spent several months working for the U.S. Peace Corps. He had learned a great deal from the experience. He had found out what life was really like in the Third World. Underdeveloped societies were on the brink of a major upheaval. Unless the more advanced countries of the world, working through government agencies and volunteer organizations started to do something about it, the future of the world was in jeopardy. The role of Judaism and, indeed, the role of all religion, was to awaken the conscience of the world and start acting before it was too late. As a rabbi, he was considering organizing a network of volunteers of all faiths to begin joint action in the world's most troubled areas.

He then wrote to his father-in-law, apologizing for not writing sooner. He inquired about Felicia and about his son, and proceeded to repeat what he had written in the first letter. He also wrote along the same lines to Rabbi Joe at his campus address. Finally he wrote to his mother, letting her know he was back in the States. He did not go in his letter to her into any of his ideas and plans, since he did not feel she would find if of particular interest. Instead he told her he was well and hoped all was well with her.

When he finished writing his letters, Eve came out on the balcony in her house robe and gave him a good morning kiss. She asked him what he was writing.

"Letters to relatives and friends. But I just realized we don't have a return address."

"We don't, do we?" she said. "Mr. and Mrs. Joshua Kaye, address unknown."

She sat down at the opposite side of the small round table. They remained quiet for a long time.

"So where do we go from here?" Eve finally said.

"Well, I was thinking of going to L.A. I think L.A. would be a good place to start an organization of volunteers for Latin America. First, because people in California are not afraid of new ideas. Second, because it's geographically close to Latin America. And third, because I've already started working there with the local clergy."

Eve looked down and knit her brow.

"Well. what do you say?" he prompted her.

"I'm not quite sure California is the place I had in mind," she said. "But then again, the only place I really know is Quincy, and I don't think that's the right place for what we are trying to do. Well, I'm willing to give L.A. a try if that's what you want to do."

"I think you'll like it," he said. "Besides, the only way to find out is to go there and see for ourselves."

The sun was out now. They could feel the heat rise. Another hot and muggy Miami day. The airport down below was bursting with activity.

"I was thinking," Eve suddenly said, "we never did get to go to Mexico. Perhaps we can do some travelling in Mexico first. We can fly to Mexico city and then rent a car and drive from there to L.A."

"I'd like to do that," he said. "I'd love to see Mexico again."

"I just remembered something," she said excitedly, "I'm sure you've heard of Leo Kahn."

"Of course. He is one of the world's leading psychoanalysts. What does he call his system, Ideotherapy?"

"That's right. He lives in Cuernavaca, Mexico, where he runs the Ideotherapy Institute. I have this friend, Joan Ritter, an ex-nun, who works with Kahn and with this ex-priest on some project having to do with psychology and religion. They were studying the psychological roots of the human need for religious faith. Perhaps we could go to Cuernavaca and spend some time with them."

"It sounds like a marvelous idea," said Kaye. "Why don't you try to call your friend and see if we can stay there for a few days?"

They went down to the hotel cafeteria for breakfast. Eve went over to the desk to place a call to Cuernavaca. She came back after a while with the good news.

"I spoke to Joan. She said she would love to have us come for a visit. She thought it would be great to have the input of a rabbi in the project. I'll be staying with her and she will make reservations for you at a very reasonable *pension* nearby. Here's the address."

Kaye took the slip of paper with the *pension*'s address. He added a P.S. to the letters he had just written, letting everyone know about his new address.

"I've read all of Kahn's books," he told Eve. "It'll be a real treat to meet him and talk to him."

Eve smiled.

"Things are looking up," she said. "Guatemala was certainly a harrowing experience, but it's over now, and thank God we came out of it unharmed. I'm sure we can look forward now to better things."

They booked a flight to Mexico City which departed that same afternoon. Eve was in high spirits. She had bought a wide brimmed straw hat, a white cotton skirt and a Mexican blouse which left her shoulders bare. He picked a light silk flower print shirt and light blue slacks and leather boots. They put on their new clothes and looked at each other through their sunglasses and laughed.

"Now we really look like American tourists," she said. "We're ready for Mexico."

They arrived in Mexico City later that evening. They checked into an old stately hotel in the heart of the city. They did not feel like going to sleep, and went out for a night stroll. Unlike Guatemala City, the Mexican capital was alive at night. Restaurants, bars, theaters were bustling with people. The creative genius of the Mexican people was evident at every corner. Great architecture, sculpture, art. Kaye recognized a Diego Rivera mural on the front of a public building. Squat, dark, wide sombreroed Mexican peasants rising up against a horseman armed to the teeth, wearing a death mask, a giant figure of oppression. In the background a new day was dawning, a bright sun pierced the clouds and new life was sprouting across green fields of wheat and corn, while on the other side a new city of small white houses and large factories rose out of the dark ruins and the heaps of corpses. Under the mural was the inscription, HOMAGE TO THE MEXICAN REVOLUTION.

They crossed a wide tree-lined street and stopped in front of an open air garden restaurant. A *mariachi* band was playing inside. They could hear the people inside singing along with the band. Eve suggested they go inside and listen. They went inside and sat at a small table and ordered a bottle of wine. Eve listened to the Mexican bolero, enraptured. It was a love song called *Sin un Amor*, Without Love:

> Without love, life is not worth living
> Without love, one's heart falters,
> Without love, the soul languishes and dies,
> Without a purpose, without passion,
> Without love there is no salvation.

"I'll drink to that," she said, raising her cup.

Some couples were dancing. He invited her to dance.

"I don't know how," she said. "I've never danced with a man."

"Well, it's time you learned."

Disregarding her objection, he took her by the hand and led her to the dance floor.

"What do I do now?"

"Just put your arms around me and sway to the time of the music."

She followed his step, tripping on his foot.

"Oh, I'm sorry," she said, looking embarrassed, "I'm so clumsy."

"Don't be sorry," he laughed, "just be yourself. You're doing fine."

He held her against himself and she became relaxed, falling in step with the music. They danced late into the night and got back to their hotel before daybreak. They slept until mid-afternoon, and went out in the evening to see some more of the city.

They decided to spend one more day in Mexico City before heading south to Cuernavaca. They got up early in the morning and hired a cab and toured the city. Around noon they stopped at the church of the Virgin of Guadalupe, patron and protector of Mexico. Eve covered her naked shoulders with a scarf and they got out of the cab. They walked over to some stone arches and looked at the old church across a vast yard paved with large smooth stones. Kaye now realized there were people walking on their knees at different points of yard, heading for the church. An old Mexican peasant, perhaps eighty years old or even older, got down on his knees next to them and began to wade towards the church. His entire body shook with every movement, and his face contorted with pain. Kaye turned to Eve. She was clasping her hands against herself and there were tears in her eyes. He asked her if she wanted to go into the church.

She shook her head. "I'd rather not," she said.

He wanted to know why, but decided not to ask. Something seemed to bother her, but she was not ready to talk about it.

She remained quiet and subdued for the rest of the day. They had dinner at the hotel and went up to their room. She took off her shoes and curled on the bed with a book. He sat down on the round armchair in the corner of the room and stretched out his legs on the coffee table.

"Are you looking forward to going to Cuernavaca?" he asked.

"Yes, I am." She tried to sound cheerful, but he could hear a tense note in her voice.

"I was thinking about the two of us, Eve. We're going to meet all those people at the Institute in Cuernavaca. And we'll continue to pretend we are just good friends. I'm wondering if we are really going to be comfortable with this arrangement."

He seemed to have read her mind.

"Yes," she agreed, "you are right. I was thinking the same thing. I feel we've been doing this sort of thing long enough. No, Josh, we won't be comfortable with it. And if we do go to L.A. later on we'll be even less comfortable. I feel we're finally coming down to reality. To be very honest, the reason why I wanted to go to Mexico first was because I was thinking of a place where we could both be away from our own kind, on neutral ground, so to speak, where, once I gave up my vows, we could live together without pretending and do the things we believe in. I don't think we could do it in the States. Here I feel we have a chance."

After breakfast the next day they took the bus to Cuernavaca. Eve was in high spirits. It was a bright sunny day. She leaned her head on his shoulder and he put his arm around her.

"I like Mexico," she said. "There's a certain openness and vitality about the people here. You feel a certain sense of optimism. Mexico may have the answer to the problems of Latin America."

"Let's hope it has the answer for the two of us," said Kaye.

They arrived in Cuernavaca at noon. The Institute was housed in a colonial mansion on the side of a hill in a quiet neighborhood of white stucco houses with red tiled roofs, overlooking the town. When they walked through the wrought iron gate they found themselves inside a breathtaking garden. A profusion of tropical flowers everywhere. A shaded pond with waterlilies. At the far end of the garden there were peacocks and flamingos freely roaming about. They walked up to the front of the mansion and rang the bell. The door opened and out came a young woman in blue jeans and a short sleeved blouse, her hair pulled back and tied in a red bandana.

"Eve! Hello! You must be Josh! Hi! I'm Joan. Welcome to Mexico!"

She embraced Eve and gave Josh a strong handshake.

"You look good, Joan," said Eve.

"You look terrific."

"Beautiful place you have here."

"It is, isn't it?"

"Leo Kahn must have good taste."

"Oh, yes, he does. Why don't we go inside and cool off with a glass of lemonade."

They walked through a long corridor and entered a large hall with deep carpets, a brick fireplace, large carved wooden chairs and deep cushioned sofas, and an iron chandelier hanging from a chain in the ceiling in the middle of the room. They sat in the corner around a low table with a pitcher of lemonade and tall glasses.

"So how was Guatemala?" the ex-nun asked as she poured the lemonade.

"Quite a harrowing experience," said Eve.

"I hear there's been a great deal of violence there lately."

"There sure has," said Kaye.

"You two have worked there together?"

He could tell she was wondering about the nature of their relationship. How long would they continue to play this game? Was this the place and the time to come out in the open and make their relationship known to the world? Well, it was too soon for that.

First Eve would have to make her decision about her vows. Then the two of them would have to come to an understanding about their respective beliefs. Eve must realize by now that she had to choose between him and the one she had been taught to believe in. There was no room in their relationship for both. She had once told him there was a common ground which transcended religious labels, a common belief in the One God of all humanity where she hoped to meet him. Was she ready for that common ground, or was she still bound by her own avowed doctrine?

"Yes," said Eve, "we worked together on that Peace Corps project. We've known each other back home in Quincy, where we became good friends. I went to Guatemala to help organize schools for the Mayan Indians, but after I got there I was told the project was dropped, so I worked instead on that farming project."

"So what are your plans now?"

"Josh and I would like to start an interfaith volunteer organization for Latin America."

"Sounds like an ambitious plan," said Joan. "Do you have the backing of any institution or any particular individuals?"

"Not yet," said Kaye. "The idea is still in the planning stage."

Joan showed Eve to her room upstairs and then took Kaye to his *pension* across the street. She had told them they were both invited to dinner that evening so they could meet Professor Kahn.

Kaye got settled in his small *pension* room and lay down to rest, and later in the afternoon Eve came over and they went down to the center of town and wandered through the narrow streets and browsed through the local shops.

At sundown they returned to the Institute for dinner. There were several dinner guests in the lounge, all sipping tequila and rum cocktails. Joan explained they were students of Professor Kahn. Most of them came all the way from Mexico City twice a month for a seminar on religion and psychology. Finally the eminent psychoanalyst walked in. He was a small man with thick lensed glasses riding on his prominent nose. His features were undistinguished, but he had a commanding presence. Joan introduced Eve and Kaye to the professor.

"Joshua Kaye," Dr. Kahn said in a thick German accent. "Which seminary did you attend?"

"Quincy."

"Oh, Quincy! A fine school! Do you know my friend, Professor Zamenhoff?"

"He is my father-in-law."

"Your father-in-law? Indeed! What a small world! I had dinner at the Zamenhoffs a few years ago. I recall they had a bright young daughter."

"Felicia."

"Oh, yes. How is she?"

"We are separated."

"I'm sorry to hear that. Come, let's sit down for a moment before they call us to dinner. I would like to hear about your work in Guatemala."

He briefly told the professor about his work at Santa Teresa and about the experience at La Merced, the subsequent incident with Yak Lopez and the deportation. Dr. Kahn listened without interrupting.

"Under the skin people are still savages," the professor said after Kaye finished.

"Sister Eve and I would like to start an interfaith volunteer organization for Latin America," said Kaye. "We feel that if all religions joined forces they could motivate people to work on solving the key problems of the underdeveloped countries."

Professor Kahn nodded slowly, peering at Kaye through his thick lenses. He puckered his lips as he kept nodding, formulating his thoughts.

"Yes," he said pensively, furrowing his brow, "I certainly applaud your efforts. But there are things to consider. First, the problem of ecumenism, and second, the problem of the Third World. Religion is the strongest force in organized human life. I mean religion in the broadest sense, which includes all social ideologies, such as communism, for example. It deals with individual and with group beliefs, on which people are ready to stake their life, go to war over, and die for. There are too many conflicting human interests among the various religions, which prevent them from putting aside their differences and working for the common good of humanity. Now, as far as the Third World is concerned, you can establish welfare programs for those countries, as the U.S. Government, the United Nations and other international bodies have done. But this does not solve the problem. The problem runs much deeper than that. It has to do with the work ethic of each society. Third World countries do not have the same work ethic as the more advanced, industrialized societies. Perhaps a hundred years from now some of them will. But they will have to do it themselves."

He paused and looked at Kaye with a ripple of a smile curling his thin lips.

"I understand where you are coming from, Joshua," he said in a soft paternal voice. "Liberal Judaism and the prophetic tradition.

Alvin Blumenfeld going south to help blacks register to vote and getting his head bashed by the bigots. Kennedy's dream and the upheaval of the sixties. Ah, well. This is 1970. Things are changing. You know that line in your Liberal Judaism prayer book about the fatherhood of God and the brotherhood of man? Unfortunately, the world today is not moving in the direction of brotherhood. Rather it seems that each society, ethnic group and religion is looking after its own interests. So perhaps Sister Eve and you ought to reconsider your plan."

They were being called to the table for dinner. Professor Kahn rose and put his hand on Kaye's shoulder.

"*Im ayn kemah ayn Torah*," he told Kaye in Hebrew. "Without bread there is no knowledge, so let's go and partake. By the way, be sure to give your father-in-law my best."

The next day he discussed Kahn's remarks with Eve. They were both impressed with the celebrated professor's keen mind and understanding of social and religious organizations. But they disagreed with his analysis. Kahn was looking at the world as it was, not as it should be. The function of religion was not to accept the world as it was, but to change it in God's image. If indeed the world was now becoming more and more polarized, so much more the reason to work against the polarization and seek unity among nations and religions.

The question was how. Could they do it here in Mexico? Where would they start? They were all alone in this country with their ideas and plans. Whom would they organize? Who in Mexico would listen to the grandiose ideas of a rabbi and a nun? Eve was reluctant to go back to the States. She felt that here in Mexico it would be easier for them to live and work together. Yet back in L.A. he had already laid the groundwork for a clergy organization and had his *havurah*, a group of like-minded people who were willing to work on the ills of the world. Clearly, he had to choose. He had to tell himself what he had told Eve in their hotel room at the airport in Miami—they could not have it all. No one in this world can. Everyone must choose.

On Sunday he went with Eve to church to hear the mariachi mass. The folk music mass attracted hundreds of Mexicans from Cuernavaca and the surrounding countryside, as well as many tourists. Mariachi bands came from far and wide to play at the mass. It was a blend of traditional Catholic liturgy and popular tunes from the various regions of Mexico. He listened to the simple words of the songs and observed the Mexicans around him. Some were singing along with the performers. Others were moving their lips. Some leaned forward with hands clasped and eyes shut and prayed:

> *Señor ten piedad de nosotros. . .*
> Oh Lord, have mercy on us. . .

He looked at Eve from the corner of his eye. She was deep in prayer. He felt shut out of her world. He could not join her in praying to her Lord. It was the man from Nazareth she was praying to. Her beloved. How could she pray to a person? It didn't make any sense. How could an intelligent woman like Eve believe that a person who once lived and died in the land of Israel was God? What was he, Joshua Kaye, a Jew, a rabbi, doing here in this church, in Mexico, coming between a nun and her Lord?

He did not let her in on his thoughts. After the mass they discussed the experience. They talked about the simple yet strong faith of the Mexicans, the beauty of their religious melodies, the blending of religion and art and folkways. But the only thing he could think of was Eve looking up at the large wooden crucifix above the altar, deep in prayer.

A week later he received a letter from his father. The old man was not much of a letter writer, and receiving a letter from him was always a special event. He wrote:

Dear Josh,

You sure get around. Last I heard from you you were back in the L.A., and then I get a letter from Miami letting me know you've just spent a few months in Guatemala and are on your way to Cuernavaca, Mexico. I'm inclined to believe you are looking for something. Then again, you have always been looking for something. This is what prompted you to go to Quincy and become a rabbi.

I read your letter with interest. You say you want to work on the problems of the Third World. Well, history repeats itself. When you were a kid I took you to Mexico for a year where I went to work on that irrigation project for the Mexican government. I have fond memories of Mexico. In many ways it reminds me of Israel. They only difference, of course, is that Israel is home.

Things are going well here. Since the Six Day War three years ago new frontiers have opened up for Israel. There is much talk now in the government about settling the Rafah salient in the Sinai. I went there the other day and fell in love with the place. The most beautiful beach you have ever seen—pure white sand, miles of palm groves, sapphire blue water. They talk about starting a new resort town here, called Yamit, the town by the sea. You can buy a house there now for a song. Some day it will be a city of one million people, a new Tel Aviv. Since you are looking for something to do, and since you are concerned about the future of the Jewish people, I thought you might want to come and take a look at the place and perhaps you will get some ideas.

Well, I hope to hear from you soon. Just because I am such a lousy letter writer it doesn't means that you have to emulate me. Take care,

Your loving father,
Abba

He envied his father. The old man had found his place in the sun. He was a man of action. He always seemed to have a project, and whenever he finished one project he would move on to the next. And here he was, about to turn thirty-one, still at loose-ends, having no idea where to go or what to do.

It was Friday afternoon. Eve had arranged to visit Joan that evening and meet some people who have arrived from the States. He sat in the lobby of the *pension* and waited for Eve. It was six o'clock. She was not due to arrive for another half an hour. He sat in the lobby and read a magazine. The *pension* owner, a woman in her sixties who most of the time sat behind the reception desk and knit, came in and took her seat behind the desk. She spoke English with a European accent, probably Hungarian. After she sat down an old man dressed in a new dark suit came in and greeted her. They exchanged some pleasantries. His accent was similar to hers, which led Kaye to believe they were related.

"We are short one person for a *minyan*," he heard the old man say.

"Excuse me," said Kaye, "did you say you were short one person for a *minyan?*"

"Yes, I did," the old man looked at him in surprise. "Are you. . ."

"Yes, I am," said Kaye, "I'll be glad to join your *minyan*."

He followed the old man to the guest lounge on the second floor. There were eight other old Jews in the room. None seemed younger than seventy. He found out they were all refugees from Austria, who came to Mexico when Nazi Germany annexed Austria in 1938. They all lived in Mexico City and spent weekends in Cuernavaca, which they chose because of its mild climate. They met regularly at the *pension* on Fridays for the Sabbath eve prayers, but one of their number had taken ill that morning and could not attend.

"You must be Elijah the Prophet," one of them told Kaye with a wink. "You came to help us make a *minyan* just in the nick of time."

Kaye was touched by his remark.

They started to pray, each in his own corner, each at his own pace, mumbling the prayers, each alone with his Maker, yet each bound to the rest by the ancient words.

They sang the medieval Kabbalistic hymn, welcoming the Sabbath queen:

> *Lecha dodi likrat kallah. . .*
> Come, my beloved, to greet your bride. . .

Old Jews, in Cuernavaca, Mexico, greeting the Sabbath. He joined them in the refrain:

> *Pney Shabbat nekabelah.*
> Together let us welcome the Sabbath.

He was transfixed by the words. Suddenly he began to cry. He shook like a leaf. Tears welled in his eyes and streamed down his face. Hot burning tears straight from the heart. He sat down in the corner and covered his face with his hands. No one noticed him. They were all deep in prayer, facing east, to Jerusalem. He wiped his eyes and joined them in the *Kaddish*. As soon as the prayer was over he went downstairs where Eve was waiting for him. He was quiet and subdued all evening. Later that night as he walked her up to her room at the Institute she asked him if anything was wrong.

He told her about the *minyan*.

"We have both been holding back our feelings from each other," he said. "I was watching you at the church last Sunday. There was deep yearning in your eyes. It occurred to me that it doesn't really matter whether or not you give up your vows. It is only a formality. Deep down you're a nun, no matter what you say or do. Deep down, I'm a rabbi. One does not choose a religious vocation. It chooses you. This is the one thing I've learned here in Cuernavaca. You cannot run away from yourself. I love you, Eve, I always will. But I've finally come to realize that I have to let you be who you are."

Her eyes were brimming with tears.

"I love you, Josh. Don't leave me."

He was sitting on the edge of her bed. She stretched out her arms to him and he took her hands and put them against his lips. She went down on her knees and buried her face in his lap. He stroked her hair and saw her chest heave and fall. He longed to take her in his arms and make love to her. No, it would only make things worse. Love does not conquer all. He had to let her be who she was.

He gently lifted her up by her arms and she sat on the bed next to him and smoothed down her dress.

"You're right," she said. "We have been denying our feelings. And because of who we are, we hear God's voice in a different way. My place is here, among the poor of Latin America. They are the people I must help. I'm not choosing to do it. They are choosing me, as you say. Josh, why don't you call your wife and find out how she is?

He called Felicia the next day. She asked him if he had received her letter. No, not yet. She had written to let him know her father died two weeks ago. He had received the letter his son-in-law had written him from Miami and was happy to hear from him. Two days later he had a heart attack—his third, and he died on the way to the hospital. There was a long pause on the phone.

"I want to come and see you," he finally said. "I want to see Danny."

"Sure," she said, "Danny would love to see you."

"How are *you* doing?"

"I'm fine. How about you?"

"I'm trying to decide about the future. I would like to discuss it with you."

"I'll be here."

On Sunday morning he packed his suitcase and went down to the lobby. Eve was waiting for him at the reception desk. She was pale, so pale he could see the blue vein on her forehead. But there was a certain calm about her, a certain peacefulness. When he saw her he knew he had done the right thing. He put his arm around her and they walked down the quiet street to the bus depot without saying a word. A clear blue sky stretched overhead, as far as the distant mountains. As he looked up he felt a watchful presence. He found himself uttering a silent prayer. He was entrusting her to His hands. Be with her, Oh Lord, now and always, watch her and keep her and make Your countenance shine upon her and give her now and forevermore peace.